COLD
WELCOME

"Landing imminent, less than ten seconds." The recorded voice again. Outside, the waves looked much bigger—bigger than she would have sailed in, in the small boat her family owned. She counted down silently. Eight, seven, six, five . . . a jolt; the shuttle tilted sharply nose-down as the aft cushions caught a wave crest, and again as the other cushions hit and splashed high enough to spatter on the windows, obscuring her view. She could feel the cabin roll as the crest of the wave passed under them, the forward end now tilting up. Through the blurry wet window she could see another wave bearing down on them.

She heard a scream from the middle compartment, then the hatch between them flew open and Jen staggered in, grabbing at the back of the Commandant's seat for balance. "Admiral—the Commandant's aide! He's dead!" She lost her grip on the seatback as the module lurched again and fell, her head banging the edge of the table.

By Elizabeth Moon

The Serrano Legacy
Hunting Party
Sporting Chance
Winning Colors
Once a Hero
Rules of Engagement
Change of Command
Against the Odds

The Serrano Legacy: Omnibus One
The Serrano Connection: Omnibus Two
The Serrano Succession: Omnibus Three

The Legacy of Gird
Surrender None
Liar's Oath

A Legacy of Honour: The Legacy of Gird Omnibus

The Deed of Paksenarrion
Sheepfarmer's Daughter
Divided Allegiance
Oath of Gold

The Deed of Paksenarrion Omnibus

Paladin's Legacy
Oath of Fealty
Kings of the North
Echoes of Betrayal
Limits of Power
Crown of Renewal

Remnant Population

Speed of Dark

The Vatta's War series
Trading in Danger
Moving Target
Engaging the Enemy
Command Decision
Victory Conditions

Vatta's Peace
Cold Welcome

with Anne McCaffrey
Sassinak (The Planet Pirataes Volume 2)
Generation Warriors (The Planet Pirataes Volume 3)

COLD
WELCOME

ELIZABETH MOON

www.orbitbooks.net

ORBIT

First published in Great Britain in 2017 by Orbit

1 3 5 7 9 10 8 6 4 2

A CIP catalogue record for this book
is available from the British Library.

ISBN 978-0-356-50628-9

Printed and bound in Great Britain by Clays Ltd, St Ives plc

Papers used by Orbit are from well-managed forests
and other responsible sources.

Orbit
An imprint of
Little, Brown Book Group
Carmelite House
50 Victoria Embankment
London EC4Y 0DZ

An Hachette UK Company
www.hachette.co.uk

www.orbitbooks.net

For Anne Groell and Joshua Bilmes, Editor and Agent, for their constant care and assistance.

And for Karen Shull, High School Librarian, whose background added perspective both professional and private.

COLD
WELCOME

CHAPTER ONE

SLOTTER KEY NEARSPACE
DAY 1

Ky Vatta stared down at her home planet as her pinnace took her from *Vanguard II,* her flagship, to the lower-orbit space station where she would take a shuttle down to the surface. Once there, she would have to assume the role of Grand Admiral Vatta, homecoming hero of the recent war. But here, between the place she had made for herself—as founder and commander of Space Defense Force—and the welcome that awaited her, she had a short time to deal with her own feelings.

She did not want to be here. She did not want to be anywhere near Slotter Key. She felt nothing warm or sentimental about her home planet, the city she knew so well, or the lost home in which she had grown up. She did not want the good memories to rise, because with them would come the immediacy and certainty of loss.

No, she wanted to be very far away, on a completely different planet, where the only person who knew all her secrets was equally eager to leave his old memories behind. Rafael Dunbarger, now CEO of the vast InterStellar Communications, had also survived family loss and treachery. Ky knew her darker side would not shock Rafe, as his did not shock her.

Rafe was born into wealth and privilege, son of a rising ISC executive; his accidental killing of a would-be kidnapper had consigned him to a vicious reform school. After that, his family had paid him an allowance to leave the planet, and he'd supplemented that remittance in various shady ways. Eventually, his father began using him as a company spy. When his father, mother, and sister were taken hostage, Rafe had organized their rescue. Finally, he'd succeeded to his father's job, as CEO of ISC.

Despite a difference in age and background, Ky thought, they matched well: both had killed, and both had enjoyed it. Both liked—needed—excitement. Both admitted to being bored with the routine of a desk job. They had planned a getaway several times, had been within a day of leaving for it, when *this* had come up.

This being Great-Aunt Grace Lane Vatta, eldest surviving member of the Vatta family and Ky's childhood nemesis, always critical and nosy. While Ky was far away, Grace had been appointed the head of Slotter Key's Department of Defense: the Rector. But Grace Lane Vatta had not used that as a reason to demand Ky's return to Slotter Key. No, this was a family crisis, some legal complication involving Vatta's commercial empire in which Ky still owned a large block of shares.

So Grace insisted, as she always had, and Ky obeyed, as she always had, resentfully. And that—her inability to just say no, politely but firmly—infuriated Ky. She was an admiral now. She had commanded fleets, won battles against high odds. And to cave because an old . . . even in thought, she dared not say anything but *old woman* . . . had said "Come" was intolerable. The words she might have said, should have said, ran through her mind again.

Then her implant dropped a microgram of neuroactive into her brain's circulation and she felt her breathing and heart rate slow again. She turned in her seat, looking across at Jen Bentik, her aide. Commander Bentik, since Jen was so very Cascadian, so very committed to that particular and demanding level of correct behavior. Fifteen years older than Ky, and a head taller, she had been Ky's aide for almost a standard year—another problem Ky needed to deal with.

Jen had been watching her, a line between her perfectly shaped brows indicating concern. "Does it look familiar, Admiral?"

Ky nodded. "A lot of water, a lot of islands. Very different from Cascadia, for sure."

"I still think it would have been more appropriate for you to take *Vanguard*'s shuttle down to the surface," Jen said, changing the topic. In her mind, Ky's status in the Space Defense Force gave her the right to land an SDF shuttle anywhere she pleased.

"It doesn't bother me," Ky said. "They see sending up a Spaceforce shuttle as a military honor."

"I suppose. I don't mean to be critical of your home planet, Admiral—" Really? Jen had so far been critical about Slotter Key's every detail, as Ky shared them. "But it seems to me that they're not quite—" Jen paused.

"Up to Cascadian standards?" Ky asked. Jen flushed; her lips thinned. Ky sighed inwardly. She had needed an aide: an admiral's life in peacetime was far more complicated than she had imagined, and Jen was efficient, organized, and capable of handling many situations Ky found difficult. But Jen didn't stop there. She assumed her own sober middle age and Cascadian background gave her license to treat Ky like the child of uncouth barbarians when they were alone. "I did tell you," Ky said, keeping her voice light and pleasant, "Slotter Key's a lot more casual. You will find it difficult, I expect, at least at first."

Up came Jen's hackles, so easily raised. "I will be perfectly polite." In a tone that meant she was still angry.

"Yes, of course. You always are." Impossible to explain to someone who had never been outside her own culture that another set of rules might be legitimate. The last visit to Moray had been marred by Jen's complaints that it was not like Cascadia. This was the core reason she'd planned to change aides soon. "If someone's being rude—rude in Slotter Key terms—I'll make it clear."

"They don't have etiquette books? To warn strangers about the rules?" Cascadia handed every arriving passenger a thick book of rules, and no one could leave the ship until they had agreed to abide by them or face a court. Ky had never found another system so obsessed with etiquette.

"We do—did—but they're mostly for children. For adults, it's a matter of mutual negotiation. There's no legal standard. In my religion"—the one she didn't follow anymore—"it's important not to take offense unless offense is meant."

"I will do my best, Admiral," Jen said, as if picking up a burden almost too heavy to carry.

"I'm certain you will," Ky said. "You always do." Ky's skullphone pinged. Her flagship's captain, Pordre, reported that a Slotter Key Spaceforce shuttle had arrived at the main space station. "Thank you, Captain," she said. "Shouldn't be any time wasted, then." She looked out the viewport, now in a better mood, though whether from her implant's chemicals or Pordre's report she did not know. She could see ships docked at the space station clearly; several Vatta ships clustered together in Vatta's dedicated section. Back to normal, then—another sign of Stella's fitness to run the family business.

When she'd left Slotter Key, she'd been a disgraced former cadet, a political embarrassment to be whisked away out of reach of the media as quickly as possible. How naïve she'd been, how easily fooled by a first-year cadet asking for help, how blind to the political implications. She wouldn't make that mistake again, though she should probably expect someone to bring up that mess. Most wouldn't. Aunt Grace had told her she was billed as a hero returning in triumph. A trickle of humor rose. Maybe it wouldn't be that bad to come home for a few days; it surely couldn't be worse than her departure had been.

Below the viewport, the familiar shapes of continents and island chains passed in review. Port Major, the oldest city and planetary capital, was obscured by thick clouds, but north of it on Voruksland's east coast, she picked out Grinock Bay, center of an extinct volcano. She'd never been there. Corleigh, the island her family had lived on, Port Major on the mainland, and her uncle's country home south-west of Port Major: that was the extent of her onplanet experience.

She turned from the viewport again; Jen handed her the latest memtip. Ky uploaded it to her implant. The schedule for the rest of the day; the draft of the speech she would give at dinner that evening; the faces and names of notables who would greet her after landing onplanet or be seated at the same table at dinner. For one of them, she needed no memtip: the Commandant of Slotter Key's military academy.

She could have done without that. The last time she'd seen him, he'd told her she must resign. Now she was an admiral at only twenty-nine, and from a political point of view—something she had learned to recognize—she represented one of the Academy's triumphs. It was bound to be awkward.

"Thank you, Jen," she said. "Your usual excellent briefing." Jen nodded.

The pinnace docked smoothly. Ky stood when the light came on, and the pinnace pilot came into the cabin. "Good flight, Morey," she said to him.

"We'll be back to pick you up anytime, Admiral," he said. "Just let us know."

That was another thing about this visit. Open-ended, Aunt Grace had said. It might take longer than planned. *No longer than necessary,* she told herself. Her life was elsewhere. "I'll let you know the moment I know," she said. "I don't plan to take a vacation down there."

"You want us to wait until you've boarded the shuttle?"

"No need. It's already docked. I'll be fine. Captain Pordre has all my contact codes." All but one, the very secret one she shared only with Rafe Dunbarger.

Jen Bentik stood aside as Ky walked to the hatch. All lights green.

A perfect match, and thus no reason to worry. She worried anyway. The past few years had given her every reason for caution and few for complacency. She still wore her personal armor under her clothes; she still carried a loaded weapon in all circumstances.

The hatch opened into a standard air lock. Beyond was the ramp down into the station itself, where the Commandant—erect as ever but showing his age now—awaited her. Professionally impassive, of course, the telltale eyelid not drooping today, and his gaze boring into her like an industrial laser. To either side, behind him, rows of media reps were held back by station security.

"Admiral Vatta," he said. Nothing in his tone but courtesy; the sawtooth edge to his voice that had greeted her at their last meeting was undetectable. She had no doubt he could still deploy it. "Welcome to Slotter Key. The Rector of Defense and the President both asked me to convey their sincere regrets that they could not meet you here."

She had wondered if he would call her by her rank—the rank she had assumed of necessity, not through the usual process of regular promotions overseen by a Board. But of course he did in front of the media. The snakelike tendrils of media feeds hovered over them both. People onplanet would be watching it live. It made her skin itch, but she had the experience now to handle it as blandly as he did.

"Thank you, Commandant." He had a last name, but no one ever used it. "I am delighted to meet you again."

His smile held a glimmer of warmth. "And I you, Admiral." He glanced aside, and two of the enlisted personnel with him moved past her toward the hatch to fetch her luggage and Jen's—just one regular case each, and their survival suits, packed by her own trusted crew. That last had necessitated a brief tussle with someone on the Spaceforce end, who had only grudgingly agreed that she could bring it if she wanted. The Commandant's aide, she saw, had turned slightly aside, clearly listening to something in his earbug.

"This is my aide, Commander Bentik," Ky said. "She is from Cascadia, in the Moscoe Confederation."

"Glad to meet you, Commander," the Commandant said. "Forgive me that I am not fully acquainted with Cascadian protocol."

"It is my honor, sir," Bentik said. "I assure you I will not take offense. Cascadian protocol is not an issue here; I must hope that I have mastered that of Slotter Key."

"Let there be no strain between us," the Commandant said, the proper Cascadian mode for senior to junior, and turned to Ky. "As the shuttle is ready, Admiral, we might defer further courtesies to the shuttle lounge, if that suits you."

"Of course."

"The Rector asked me to tell you that her new arm is in good shape, but she had a minor accident two days ago—nothing to worry about, she insists. Her physicians recommended she not come up, or she would have met you herself."

Ky's wariness went up a notch—accident? Or attack?—but she kept her face and voice smooth. "I was wondering about her arm. We don't comment on her age, but a complete biograft—"

"Could be a difficulty, but has not been for her." The Commandant's aide, head still cocked a little in the manner of someone receiving more information, led the way down the ramp to the arrival lounge, and the six-person security squad closed around them. The media presence melted away as they left the lounge for the first station corridor.

They moved through corridors Ky recognized from what now seemed a distant earlier life, bypassing Customs & Immigration, where a knot of uniformed officers smiled and nodded. Then into the commercial section, with its storefronts, eateries, and people lined up, not quite casually, to see her. More media clustered there, holding up recorders and calling out to her. She ignored them.

"The trip down will be somewhat longer than usual," the Commandant went on. "I presume you received the weather bulletin?"

"That front moving in?"

"Yes. You know what the early-spring storms are like. Right now it's blowing snow downside in the capital, but they say we'll be delayed only a couple of hours. Should be clear by 1400 or so." He gave her a sideways glance. "We could have delayed the shuttle but the media have been very pushy. Rumor has it that you've come back with a warship to take revenge for the attacks on your family. That you're in cahoots with the Rector, planning to seek and destroy the guilty. I thought it best to get you aboard quickly rather than give them a chance at you right away. A few extra orbits should see us safely past the storm; security's better downside anyway."

Ky shook her head as they reached the Spaceforce section. "It's true Aunt Grace told me to come, but—"

"But rumors are rumors," he said. "We still haven't found out who started that one."

He led the way to the shuttle departure area, where a group of Spaceforce personnel waited. They all stood; Ky found she remembered the insignia and marks of rank and grade, though she recognized none of the people. They looked at her with interest; she wondered how many knew about her past. Most, probably. Two were obviously flight crew, in the uniform of AirDefense rather than Spaceforce.

"Luggage just cleared Customs," the Commandant's aide said, finger to his earbug. "Perhaps four minutes; the crowd's thickened. Admiral, I have the passenger list with notations, if you'd like to see it."

"Thank you," Ky said. She added his memtip to Jen's and her implant began matching faces in the room to names, rank or rating, home region. Several were Miznarii, the most numerous and stringent anti-humod group on Slotter Key. No matter; they were not her concern, not in her chain of command.

"With your permission," one of the pilots said, "we'll start preflight." As he spoke, Ky's implant gave her his name: Commander Tarik Hansen. She glanced at the other pilot: Major Sunyavarta.

"Go right ahead," the Commandant said to Hansen. "Our steward—there he is. Staff Sergeant Vispersen—"

"Yes, Commandant." Vispersen, a slender dark man with graying hair and gray eyes, gave Ky a quick glance. "Did you want to board now or wait for the luggage?"

"Now, thank you."

As she remembered, the shuttle boarding hatch was in the aft compartment; she and the Commandant boarded first. Vispersen led them forward through the aft compartment, with seats three abreast on one side, and two on the other. He directed their aides to the second compartment of four seats only, then waved them into the forward one. Here one side held pairs of seats with a fold-down table between them; across the wider aisle were six rows of two seats each. A far cry from the shuttle Ky had ridden as a cadet, with fold-up seats along the bulkheads and grabons with tethers down the middle.

Only one table was extended, laid with a white cloth and Spaceforce china. Ky was reminded of the Vatta china she had bought at . . . where was it? . . . that had been blown to bits with the old *Vanguard*. She and the Commandant sat down facing each other.

Vispersen went to the rear compartment. When he returned, he held the case with her survival suit. "Admiral, do you want this stowed with the rest of your luggage? We do have a suit sized for you."

"Stow it up here," Ky said. He nodded and moved forward past their table, then came back to stand beside it.

"Commandant, Admiral: regulations require me to remind you of emergency procedures—"

The Commandant waved his hand. "I paid attention on the way up, Simon."

"Yes, Commandant, but the Admiral also needs to know—"

"Very well." The Commandant gave a slight shrug. "I suppose something might have changed since she was last on a Spaceforce shuttle."

"Admiral, this peep has all the audio and visual, and will sync to your implant if you'd rather."

Ky took the sliver of black and silver but said, "I'll hear it from you, if you don't mind."

"Of course." He rattled off an obviously memorized speech listing the safety features, the kinds of emergencies most commonly encountered, the emergency supplies carried on board the passenger compartment—"which in extreme emergencies can be jettisoned and parachuted down safely, although this feature has been needed only twice in the past twenty-seven years." Holograms formed in the air to illustrate what he was saying; Ky let her implant record it all for playback if she needed it, as she sealed the peep into one of her uniform pockets.

After that, Vispersen offered refreshments, and then retreated to a niche, closing a thick sound-baffling curtain behind him. She glanced at the platter of sandwiches and fought back the urge to laugh: the sandwiches were exactly the same kind she had been offered the day she'd been expelled from the Academy. She suspected the tea was, too.

The Commandant's smile broadened. "It must feel very strange," he said. "Here we are again, in a situation neither of us, I'm sure, anticipated. I had no idea what you would do, after that unfortunate day, though after having watched your excellent performance in the Academy, I trusted you would not be destroyed by it." He paused; Ky said nothing. He gave a slight nod and went on. "But I did not imagine that within so few years—and after the devastating loss of your family—you would have raised a fleet larger than ours and saved so many worlds. Including ours. In hindsight, forcing you to resign was the best thing I could have done for everyone, not just Slotter Key. But tell me, did you really learn how to do all that in your Academy classes? Or did Rector Vatta give you private instruction?"

"Aunt Grace?" Ky laughed. "No, Commandant. Aunt Grace's lectures were all about etiquette. I had no idea that she'd been in the Unification War, or run Vatta's security and intelligence. We kids thought she was just a fussy old lady with a passion for manners."

"Well, then, I'm even more impressed. We do our best, but we don't usually have new-hatched cadets who can command ships, let alone a fleet in battle. I've seen the vids our ships made of that battle at Nexus Two. Our analysis said it should have been impossible for you to win."

"I had a lot of help," Ky said. "And I wasn't that confident." Just that desperate. Turek's armada had defeated one system after another, and his agents had destroyed or sabotaged vital communications and financial ansibles, gaining wealth and ships with every conquest. By the time Turek attacked Nexus II, it was obvious that only Ky's fleet and the allies she'd made had a chance of defeating him. A slim chance.

"Yes, of course. But by all accounts, you were the one who analyzed Turek's tactics, grasped the potential of shipboard ansibles, gained the trust of multiple system governments to supply ships and personnel—and commanded in the battle itself. Your Space Defense Force has created a new paradigm for both military actions and political alliances. I hope you'll consider giving some lectures to the instructors and senior cadets while you're downside. We've cleared space in the schedule if you would."

Return in triumph to the Academy, wipe out the former humiliation? Visiting scholars had plaques on the wall in the library; she imagined one with her name on it. Despite her desire to stay only as long as necessary, she felt the first temptation to linger and enjoy her fame.

"I can't answer that immediately, Commandant," she said. "I have nothing prepared; I was thinking only about the family business." And since part of the reason for the victory at Nexus II was a secret she shared with Rafe—and had promised to keep—it would be hard to explain how she'd done it.

Vispersen returned. "Commandant, the pilot reports disengage imminent." As he spoke, safety harnesses emerged from their seats.

"Very well," the Commandant said, fastening his harness almost as fast as Ky fastened hers. "Any more on the route?"

"An extra orbit or two, sir; the new forecast puts the storm clearing Port Major an hour later than we were told before."

"Keep me informed," the Commandant said. He cocked an eye at Ky. "We shall try to keep it as smooth as deep space once we descend, but this *is* Slotter Key."

She grinned and shook her head. "I haven't forgotten that about Slotter Key. A thunderstorm or two isn't going to bother me, Commandant."

"Good." He nodded at Vispersen, who retreated again behind the curtain.

Ky watched the other Spaceforce ship's gleaming flank as they slid past it. "Most places I've been use tugs, even for shuttles. When we broke loose from a station without one, they were upset." The shuttle cleared the station's crowded docking space, angling away so that her view was again the planet's surface, as if the planet, and not the shuttle, had moved.

He chuckled. "I imagine so. But clearly you didn't hit anything. And here, Spaceforce has clearance to dock and undock smaller vessels without a tug." He took a few sips of tea. "I'm delighted you turned out as you did, and yet sorry I can't claim to have had much to do with it."

Ky couldn't think of an answer to that; she smiled, instead, and picked up a sandwich They ate in silence for a time. Ky wasn't really hungry, and wondered whether the invitation to lecture at the Academy had really been his main point. Outside, the view below changed moment by moment as they slotted into a slow descent, several orbits shifting from Main Station's to more polar. Sunlight on clouds and sea, darkness with flickers from lightning storms and lights outlining shores near the larger cities. She had a better view than she'd had before, even in the pinnace. Finally, the Commandant put down a last sandwich.

"About the lectures, if you choose to do them. Visiting lecturers have the assistance of staff—someone to help with library research, someone to run any visual displays you might want to use. There's the speakers' fee, too, and we can put you up in guest quarters—you and your aide both, if you wish."

"How long were you thinking?" Ky asked. "I do have some issues back at headquarters—I shouldn't be gone too long."

"Whatever time you can spare." He started to say something more and then shook his head. "It's entirely your decision, of course. One thing I'd like to ask about is your organization—you mixed ships and commanders from several different worlds. Did you use Slotter Key's tables, or come up with something new?"

"Even though I had another Slotter Key privateer, I thought it would be better to come up with something that fit what we actually had—the ship types, the command and combat experience. I gathered all the seniors around a table and held them there until we had something everyone thought they could work with."

"That makes good sense." He nodded. "I wondered how you melded different militaries into one force. We have enough trouble with all of us in one place working under the same organization. Were any mercenaries in on that?"

"Not then. Moscoe Confederation, Moray, Bissonet, a few others including the ships Spaceforce sent, and"—she grinned suddenly—"a group of gentlemen adventurers from somewhere—you would not believe—"

"Gentlemen adventurers?"

"Brave, rash, romance-of-adventure types, rich enough to own their own ships. Storybook characters." Cannon fodder, though it would be rude to say so, especially since all but one had died with their ships.

"But now you have an organized fleet, and—any action?"

"Since Nexus, only a few minor actions against pirates. Probably some we didn't get at Nexus, hoping to set up in between systems. That's one of the reasons we have some issues."

He opened his mouth as if to speak, then shut it again and sipped his tea.

Ky wondered if he'd been about to ask what the issues were. Probably someone with his experience could guess, but he'd never had to deal with more than one government. "It's political," she said. "And since it involves the politics of other governments, I probably shouldn't gossip about it."

He nodded. "Money and power. We have that, too, though I'm sure it's much harder to juggle with multiple governments. I wish you good luck with it. As for the lectures, if not this visit, another time perhaps. I'm sure you'll be back to visit family."

Not if she could help it. But she shouldn't say that. She nibbled one of the lemon-flavored cookies instead.

He changed topics. "Will you stay with the Rector on this visit?"

"No, with my aunt Helen and cousin Stella. That's why I'm here—the legalities of transferring corporate roles from Helen to Stella, since I'm a major stockholder."

"Were you close to your cousins?"

"Fairly. We all spent time together every long vacation," Ky said. It was easier to talk about than she'd expected. "They'd come over to Corleigh for a tenday or so to fish and sail, then we'd go over to the mainland with them—sometimes in the city and sometimes at the country place. Stella was the closest to me in age, just three years older; we were both the youngest of our families."

"I've heard rumors that your cousin Stella was actually adopted . . ."

"It's true. Neither of us knew until it all came out in a court in Cascadia. A shock to all of us—except Aunt Helen, of course." She did not want to talk about Stella's parentage. She especially did not want to talk about Stella's birth-father, Osman Vatta, whom she had killed. Whom she suspected had been Gammis Turek's associate, if not his father, and a reason Vatta had been attacked early in Turek's campaign. The Commandant did not need to know—or have cause to notice—that she had discovered herself to be a natural killer, and killing Osman in close hand-to-hand had given her a solid jolt of glee. She looked out the viewport again.

They were on the other side of the planet from Port Major, somewhere over the Oklandan, the largest open ocean, with the southernmost continent, Miksland, just coming into view, dawn lightening its eastern end. A shelf of cloud overlaid much of the western end of it, but she could see a bit of the poleward coast, sharp red-brown against the dark-blue ocean, stark white of snow on what must be mountains. No one lived there; its description in Slotter Key geography books was "Terraforming Failure."

"I've never seen Miksland before," Ky said.

"There's a weather station and Air-Sea Rescue base on a chain of islands west of it," the Commandant said. "Too bad it's under the clouds. Nothing on the continent itself, of course."

"Why a base near it?" Ky asked. "I thought shipping stayed to the north."

"It does, but there's a very long gap between the next base to the east and the next one to the west, pushing the limit for Search and Rescue aircraft when they're needed. This gives much better coverage for shipping. It's harsh, though. And something about the continent interferes with communication."

Vispersen reappeared, offering more tea and removing the plates. "We should start descent into atmosphere on the next orbit, about fifty minutes," he said. "If you need the toilet, Admiral, that's forward, across from the galley."

"Already?" the Commandant said, then nodded. "Pleasant intervals pass quickly," he said to Ky. "I had no idea we'd been chatting so long."

"Nor I," Ky said.

"If you wouldn't mind—the flight crew were hoping to meet you—actually all the passengers were—"

"Of course, if we have time."

"Estimating arrival in Port Major at 1530," Vispersen said. He disappeared once more into the forward galley area, sealing the curtain behind him.

"Please," the Commandant said, nodding toward the front.

Ky went forward and found herself in a more spacious area than she'd expected—a seat for the steward to starboard, along with luggage storage and a cubby with three orange bundles she recognized as personal survival suits. Her survival suit, in its blue case, lay on top of the luggage. Forward of that was the toilet, and across from it a galley; Vispersen was washing out the teapot. The hatch to the piloting compartment was open; she glanced in, seeing only the backs of the pilots' heads and banks of half-familiar instruments. They wore full survival gear but for the helmets secured just above and behind them.

When she came out of the toilet, Vispersen wasn't in the galley, or in his seat. She tapped on the rim of the cockpit hatch. Commander Hansen turned and smiled at her.

"Admiral, thanks for looking in."

"Glad to meet you—Commander Hansen, isn't it?"

"Yes. It's an honor to meet you."

Ky turned to the copilot, who grinned cheerfully. "I'm Yoshi Sunyavarta, Admiral. Delighted to meet you. My daughter saw you on the newsvids and told me she wants to grow up to be you." His grin widened. "Though I must admit, last year she wanted to be a mountaineer, and the year before it was a racing jockey."

"How old is she?"

"Nine."

"Sounds like me at that age," Ky said. "Tell her I said good luck."

"Thank you, Admiral."

"The Commandant asked me to say something to the troops in back—do we have time?"

The two pilots looked at each other. "Just barely," Hansen said finally. "We really like passengers to be seated once we start descent."

"I'll tell him we're short on time," Ky said. "Thank you both for a lovely flight."

"Thank us again if we don't have a rough patch coming in behind that front," Sunyavarta said, grinning.

Ky laughed and turned away. When she went back through the curtain, Vispersen was speaking with the Commandant, who was stretching his back.

"The pilots said we're short of time for a full introduction," Ky said. "Unless you would like me to just say a few words to them as a group."

"I let time slip up on me," the Commandant said. "I was thinking mostly of Tech Betange—he's on compassionate leave after his parents died, and he's got younger siblings to arrange care for. I'll make sure everyone has a chance to meet you once we're down; it never does to upset the pilots."

Ky slid into her seat and fastened the safety harness as Vispersen and the Commandant moved forward.

Out the port she saw darkness again, flickers of lightning below, then an arrangement of lights that must be a city. She couldn't tell which by the pattern the lights made. She thought again of the Commandant's suggestion that she give a lecture—or was it more than one?—at the Academy, and that reminded her again of the ansible in her implant. The Commandant came back to his seat and fastened his own harness. "Won't be long," he said.

"I noticed the pilots were in survival suits," Ky said. "I remember they made us get into them on the way down, on our cadet trips."

"That was more to be certain you knew how to put them on," the Commandant said. "If something does happen, the flight crew shouldn't need to change, but passengers will have time."

Ky nodded and looked out the port again. She enjoyed this view of Slotter Key as they passed through the night to dawn, then day.

A soft chime rang. "Commencing reentry in three minutes," said a recorded voice. "Secure all loose items, ensure safety toggles are engaged in case of any situation. Final warning at one minute. All personnel should be seated and in safety webbing at that time, with all loose items secured."

Vispersen reappeared, glanced at their safety harnesses, and then went behind the curtain. At the one-minute warning, a louder chime, and reentry shields slid closed across the viewports. Ky felt nothing at the moment the shuttle should have been braking for reentry, which meant the artificial gravity was functioning normally. She wished she had the flight plan and knew this shuttle's rate of descent, but she was a guest here, not a commander. It felt strange, after all the years in which she had always known exactly what was happening.

"There are some political complications you should be aware of," the Commandant said.

Ky dragged her mind back to here and now. "Yes?"

"I don't know if MacRobert briefed you on the situation on Slotter Key when you met him after the Nexus battle—"

"Not entirely, no."

"Your great-aunt, now Rector, gathered most of the information about the origin of the attack on Vatta. She and MacRobert—whom I assigned to liaise with her—concluded that cover had come from the highest levels of government. She would have acted, if she had not been shot when assassins tried to kill the children she was guarding. And that is why I was the person to assist the former President to make a decision regarding his future."

Ky blinked, trying to parse that statement. Did he mean he'd talked to the man or—something else? MacRobert had told her little, really, about the change of government on Slotter Key, except that Aunt Grace had provided key information and the former President had committed suicide. Had it been suicide? And why would the Space-force Academy Commandant be involved?

He continued before she could think what—and how—to ask.

"What you do not know—what only a few other people now living know—is that your great-aunt and I became acquainted during that civil war when we were both young. I was just a boy, in fact."

That was not just a surprise; that was an immediate flare of curiosity. She didn't know much about that war except that it had had something to do with the formation of the planetary government. It had been over long before she was born, and was barely mentioned in her school history class.

"I don't think you need to know much about that," the Commandant went on. "But there are still political repercussions from that nasty little war, and she and I both feel that the attack on Vatta may have been motivated by more than Osman Vatta's personal malice."

Ky could not think what to say; she was still struggling to imagine the Commandant and her great-aunt involved in a civil war.

"Recent intelligence suggests that there may still be some conspirators we haven't identified. Rector Vatta has had difficulties with elements of the military, though it may not be related. She rubs some people the wrong way." Ky could easily imagine that. He shrugged and went on. "The current President, though amenable to reasonable suggestions when he succeeded to the role, has been less so after the elections that followed. There's a faction that strongly opposed sending ships to support your force. We think they—"

A loud chime interrupted him. The flight crew announcement light came on.

"Commandant, we have a situation." Ky could not tell which of the pilots it was, but the voice sounded tense.

Ky forced herself not to ask questions. She looked at the port, still covered. She stared at it anyway. She hated being cut off from ship's systems. She tried to imagine what would be below now, but without the course data the pilots had, it was only a wild guess.

"We're going to need to make an emergency landing, possibly wet." That same tense, over-controlled voice.

This was not her shuttle, not her command. The best thing to do was keep quiet and out of the way. She thought of her aide. This would only convince Jen that Slotter Key was a chaotic, undisciplined, dangerous place.

"Why?" The Commandant's voice rose a fraction. She glanced at him, then back at the blank gray of the shield just outside the port.

"Threats, Commandant. Station Traffic Control reported credible threats during the previous orbit, and now there are anomalies in the instrument readings that were nominal before. We'll be descending faster, and hoping to make it to Pingat Islands, the nearest field, but we're getting more anomalies—some systems may fail. You will need to take steps—"

"Sirs—with respect—" Vispersen came into their compartment. He carried two bulging packages in his arms and set them down on the table. "You need to change into survival suits. Commandant, this is yours. Admiral—"

Ky looked at the packages, then back at him. Her suit, transported from her flagship, was in a blue duffel; both these were orange. "I need my own suit," she said. "I can get it—" She started to release the safety harness.

"Ours has our own codes loaded in its transponder," Vispersen said. "We got your measurements from your ship. I understand you brought your own—insisted on it—but it's not compatible with our emergency communications channels."

The Commandant was already pulling the tabs on the larger package. Spaceforce should be reliable, but—in light of the recent conversation and this emergency—she could not be certain. Survival suits could be sabotaged in any of a hundred ways, with fatal results to the user; she knew who had packed hers, back on *Vanguard II*. She glanced at the Commandant, and saw the same surmise in his eyes. Yet if they were going down they had to have the suits on. She stood up.

"I'll use my own suit," she said, allowing a little edge to her voice. "It's in the front locker; I can find it."

"No need, Admiral; I'll bring it." Vispersen snatched up the package she'd rejected and hurried forward, returning in a moment with her sealed blue duffel.

She peeled back the closure. "There are enough suits for everyone?" she asked the steward, lifting the suit out.

"Yes, Admiral," Vispersen said. "Nobody left out." He grinned. "Even me, when I've seen you safely suited. The aft stewards will be taking care of the other compartments." He paused, then asked, "Will your aide be in her own suit?"

The Commandant gave him a sharp look but said nothing; he had his suit unfolded now, and was unsnapping the front closure. Tiny alarm bells rang in Ky's mind.

"I'm certain she will," Ky said, unfolding her own. "I know she brought it."

"You can leave your shoes on if you want, Commandant," Vispersen said. "These new models accept any footgear that doesn't have an aggressive sole. Admiral, yours—"

"Is the same," Ky said.

Ky's stomach lurched a little as the anti-gravity failed to compensate completely for the increase in deceleration. She struggled for a moment with the tabs on the suit; one was stiffer than the others. Then she put her legs into the suit legs and stood up, one hand automatically on the nearest grabon, the other pulling the suit up over her uniform. The shuttle jerked and rolled to starboard; the Commandant, who had both hands busy fastening the torso toggles on his, fell sideways, but Vispersen caught him.

"AG compromised," said a mechanical voice from above. "Expect unpredictable vector accelerations."

Ky worked her free arm into the suit arm, changed hands on the grabon without letting go, and worked her other arm into the suit before another lurch came. She saved herself a knock on the head by stiff-arming the bulkhead. Vispersen was helping the Commander attach the helmet and its connections. Ky maneuvered back into her seat, slid one arm under the emergency seat restraint webbing, and fastened her own torso closure. Then she dug into the suit bag for her helmet.

"Secure for shuttle rotation. Expect zero G first, then hard Gs."

The artificial gravity cut out completely during rotation. Sandwiches and tea tried to wiggle up her throat, but Ky kept them down. To her surprise, the viewport screens retracted, letting daylight into the cabin. Shouldn't they stay covered in an emergency? Vispersen, legs swinging above the deck briefly, moved from the Commandant to her.

"Let me get that helmet hooked up and sealed for you."

"Thank you," Ky said. The Commandant, now webbed into his seat across from her, helmet face-shield open, had the inwardly focused look of someone in serious discussion with his innards. Vispersen closed the tabs she hadn't yet managed, then attached the helmet and its connectors. "I've got the display now," she said. Her own familiar display, with all the readouts in the right places, including readouts Spaceforce would not have and a seamless integration with her implants.

Vispersen opened an overhead locker and pulled out another suit, easing into it with practiced efficiency. Like Ky, he slid an arm through the seat webbing of the remaining seat before putting on his helmet.

She felt pressure against her back as the shuttle braked hard. More, and then more. Something popped in her suit, and she felt a protective cushion expand. Her mind seemed to split into separate tracks: questions (who, why, what, when, how?), a stream of possible outcomes (if the shuttle blew up, if it made it to land, if it crashed in the ocean), and an inchoate swirl of animal emotion, frantic. She locked that into a mental cupboard. That was panic. *This* was real: here, inside the shuttle. She set aside the things she could not predict or control (would the shuttle explode? Would they crash?) and reviewed what resources she had. A functioning survival suit, her bulletproof armor under her uniform, her 10mm pistol, her implant stuffed with her father's Vatta data and her own for both Vatta and her own organization. The ansible implant, and the cable for it she wore as a hidden necklace.

If she survived to landing, she was not without resources, not even counting what might be on the shuttle or in others' kits. "I don't think this is aimed at you, Admiral Vatta," the Commandant said. "I have annoyed many people in my time, some of them quite dangerous."

"Two fish with one hook," Ky said.

He grinned; she could tell it took effort. "Possibly. But sabotaging this shuttle almost had to be internal, in Spaceforce, where you're more popular than not. We've got good crew—and there's a master sergeant in back. You got the full list in from my aide, right?"

"Yes, Commandant."

"If anything—well, if you need to, take care of them." If she survived and he didn't, that meant. His trust in her gave her an instant's warmth.

Ky's implant pinged her: Pordre, her flag captain. "Admiral—the course changes—are you in trouble?"

"Sabotage," she said. "Shuttle problems—"

"We've launched one of our shuttles. Any chance of matching orbits? Doing a transfer?"

"No, we're already too far down," Ky said. "Where's ours?"

"High and behind, but we've got an eye on you. Looks like you're headed for a cluster of islands west of that line of cliffs—what is that, anyway?"

"Small continent, terraforming failure," Ky said. "Patch me through to the shuttle crew."

"Right away, Admiral. That's Lieutenant Sonducco."

"*Vanguard Two* shuttle—this is Lieutenant Sonducco—Admiral?"

"Vatta here," Ky said. "You still have us visually?"

"Yes, but you're going into that cloudbank before we can get down to your altitude. It's several layers deep—top's at seventeen thousand meters. We'll lose you to visual, and to scan until we lose some vee. *Vanguard* should be able to track you, and we've got a good probable trajectory."

"There should be islands ahead of us—how far?"

"Not going to make it on that course, Admiral. You'll be east of them, approx—"

The transmission ended as if someone had flicked a switch: no hiss, no crackle, nothing. They were in cloud now, but cloud should not have interfered. Ky assumed another form of sabotage though she could not think what would have that effect, then remembered the Commandant had said something about Miksland itself affecting communications. She wished she'd told Pordre about that. They dropped through the first layer; beneath were more clouds, these showing more structure. Ky hadn't paid much attention to planetary meteorology for years, not since she'd lived on Slotter Key; she could not read the clouds for clues to the weather. At least they were down in atmosphere, descending fast into breathable air, the first requirement for survival.

She forced her attention back onto what she could do, assuming they landed safely and ignoring the possibility that the Commandant might not survive. The Commandant would take command; everyone knew him. The pilots and stewards, as the shuttle's crew, would direct passengers; the shuttle had life rafts, and they would know how to deploy them. Once down, they would get into the rafts . . . she reviewed what she remembered about the raft drills her father had insisted on, those times he'd taken her and her brothers sailing.

Her job would be to follow crew instructions, and then offer whatever assistance she could. How many of these people had sailing experience? Many of them, probably; most people on Slotter Key lived near enough to open water, and all the early colonists had built sailing craft. Some would have had cold-water experience she didn't have. She ran through the contents of a typical life raft in her mind, wondering if Spaceforce rafts had additional supplies. An initial supply of fresh water, and then a desalinization pump to produce more from the ocean water. Another pump to remove water from the raft. Rescue rings, lines for various purposes, sea anchors, nonperishable food, warming blankets, transponders, signaling devices of several kinds, fishing tackle, paddles, first-aid kit—it was a long list, and she couldn't remember some items, but trying kept her mind occupied as the descent continued.

CHAPTER TWO

SLOTTER KEY NEARSPACE, SPACE DEFENSE FORCE FLAGSHIP *VANGUARD II*

"Signal cut out, sir." Lieutenant Sonducco's voice was steady but a half pitch higher. "Nothing from the transponder, either. They're in the cloud, steep descent. We could follow them—"

"Stay clear of the cloud," Captain Pordre said. "We don't want to lose contact with you. Scan what you can."

"Signal loss confirmed." The com officer on the bridge worked on their com controls. "No response from the ansible relay satellites in that sector."

It had to be sabotage. It had to be more than just sabotage of the shuttle, if it affected ISC relay satellites. "See what you can scan of that landmass, anything to identify a probable landing zone." He turned to his com officer. "Contact their Defense Department; I want to talk to Rector Vatta and offer our support."

SPACEFORCE SHUTTLE

Down through layer after layer of cloud, until they finally dropped below it, into a dimmer world of dark water below with the distant cliffs of Miksland well off to port. Ky could not see much detail in the water surface. The Commandant, peering out the viewport in the direction they were going, shook his head. "I don't see anything to land on. They should've tried for Miksland."

"Does it have a landing—?"

"Attention-attention-attention." A recorded voice, not one of the pilots, interrupted her. "Emergency—" A click, then another voice came over the com.

"This is the pilot." His voice sounded strained, as if he were in pain. Certainly he was busy. "We are about to jettison the passenger survival capsule; the shuttle controls are inoperable and we have reached low enough altitude. Take emergency positions immediately. On my count of ten, we will disengage—"

Ky slapped her faceplate closed and locked it, as did the Commandant. Passenger survival capsule . . . that meant coming down without any controls at all, with only parachutes. If those had not been sabotaged as well. The thought of death intruded; she pushed it away. Nothing she could do now but follow procedures—as in the battle at Moray, when she'd survived something as dangerous as this, but without gravity. Or atmosphere. The shuttle would have all the standard tracking devices; the net of navigation, weather, and scan satellites around the planet would be receiving data, sending it on to multiple facilities. Someone was watching; someone would know exactly where they landed.

". . . four . . . three . . . two . . . disengage . . ." A loud bang, a jolt as if the shuttle had been hit by something—explosive bolts, Ky thought—and the passenger module slewed sideways then fell, tipping down and sideways. The dark water, flecked with foam, came nearer. Ky could not guess their height at first, but they were certainly not the ripples of the bay at Corleigh on a quiet day. This was not how she'd planned to die, but then she'd never planned to die. She realized the absurdity of those thoughts, then the module jerked again—once, twice, three times—and returned to level. Their fall slowed. Ky could not see the parachutes out the viewport, but could think of nothing else that might have caused the change.

"Chutes deployed," said the recorded voice. "Do not leave your seats. Do not unfasten safety restraints. Do not unseal helmets until after landing, on crew instruction. Landing may be rough; module may tip or even roll. Items may fall or fly about the cabins. Landing cushions will deploy at three hundred meters above the surface."

The module swung beneath the chutes. Out the viewport, Ky could see water below and the coast of Miksland again; she could tell they were lower, but not how much lower. As they came down, she could see more of the water—that there were waves, large ones, the kind she associated with open ocean from her sailing experience as a teenager. Wind direction—she had no reference, but surely the wind would be acting on the parachutes, moving them downwind. Was that likely to be helpful or not? Something popped below the deck; out the port, Ky could now see an expanding curved shape—the landing cushions? She hoped they were flotation devices as well.

Across the table from her, the Commandant's expression—what she could see of it through his faceplate—was fixed, the same steady, emotionless look she had seen so often in her Academy years. She said nothing; if he wanted a conversation, surely he would speak first. The pilots, she supposed, were too busy to talk to the passengers; she heard nothing from the rear compartments.

"Landing imminent, less than ten seconds." The recorded voice again. Outside, the waves looked much bigger—bigger than she would have sailed in, in the small boat her family owned. She counted down silently. Eight, seven, six, five . . . a jolt; the shuttle tilted sharply nose-down as the aft cushions caught a wave crest, and again as the other cushions hit and splashed high enough to spatter on the windows, obscuring her view. She could feel the cabin roll as the crest of the wave passed under them, the forward end now tilting up. Through the blurry wet window she could see another wave bearing down on them.

She heard a scream from the middle compartment, then the hatch between them flew open and Jen staggered in, grabbing at the back of the Commandant's seat for balance. "Admiral—the Commandant's aide! He's dead!" She lost her grip on the seatback as the module lurched again and fell, her head banging the edge of the table.

CHAPTER THREE

SLOTTER KEY, PORT MAJOR, MINISTRY OF DEFENSE
DAY 1

Grace Lane Vatta, Rector of Defense, would rather have brought her niece Ky down from the station in a Vatta shuttle, but politics made that impossible. The returning hero must have a proper military escort. It was her department, after all, and she was bound—however unwillingly—by its traditions. Her job was hard enough already, as a civilian whose last military position had been as a clandestine fighter in what she thought of as a civil war but history books preferred to call an insurrection.

At least she'd spoken to Ky when the Space Defense Force ship arrived insystem, and was reassured by her state of health. Clear-eyed, bronze skin glowing, black hair snugged tight in a short braid—she'd never seen Ky with that hairdo, and it showed off the sharp planes of her face. Not a girl anymore, but a woman to reckon with, a woman whose command presence Grace could feel through the screen.

She was delighted. Both her great-nieces, Ky and her cousin Stella, had matured into women she could respect, women capable of restoring and protecting the family. They weren't much alike, but that didn't matter. She'd watched Stella rebuild a large part of Vatta's trade network from a separate headquarters in the Moscoe Confederation or Confederacy or whatever they called it. Ky's military genius had already thwarted the greatest threat to interstellar trade in Grace's lifetime, and Ky would, Grace was sure, make space safe for tradeships into the future. Her own responsibility as Rector of Defense, the space within Slotter Key's home system, would be easier with an interstellar fleet operating between systems.

Ky would arrive in a few hours. Grace looked at the action items on her desk screens—scarcely time enough to clear everything before then. She checked briefly when Ky's pinnace reached the station and when the Spaceforce shuttle undocked, and then settled to work again. The weather had turned foul before dawn; hailstones battered the reinforced windows of her office in between spurts of snow, and if she looked, she knew she'd see the mix whitening the lawn below. The shuttle would be delayed some hours to avoid the rough weather, but the forecast said a clear night would follow as the front pushed offshore and the storms went with it.

She was deep in the intricacies of the proposed biennial budget request when her implant pinged. "Yes?"

"MacRobert," he said. "The shuttle's had a problem."

Ice ran down her spine. "It's . . . gone?" Always expect the worst, then anything else would be good news; she'd learned that early.

"No. Emergency landing, a long way out in the Oklandan. They were trying to make the Pingat, but didn't—"

"Sabotage?"

"Almost certainly, and internal at that. I've opened a case; I need your sign-off."

"You have it." She punched a sequence of buttons on her desktop and pressed her thumb to the reader. MacRobert was the one person in the Defense Department she trusted absolutely, as he trusted her. *Two old spooks,* she thought as her door opened; she touched her tongue to the correct molar, signaling MacRobert to wait a moment. Olwen, her personal assistant, looked in, her face pale.

"Rector, they've just reported a problem of some kind—a course change."

"Malfunction?"

"Yes, Sera, but no details. They're planning to land somewhere in the Pingat chain. I've notified Meteorology and the satellites, but . . . but the transponder went off."

A line of curses crackled through Grace's mind; she used none of them. "We'll have to change the schedule," she said, her voice steady. "I'll need the President's staff first, then Port's militia, Spaceforce Academy, finally Vatta headquarters. Set up the calls, please."

"Does this mean someone attacked us? Is it a war?" Olwen's eyes were wide.

"No, it's not war. I expect the shuttle had engine trouble," Grace said. The war rumor had started as soon as Ky's flagship showed up in the system. "Get me that line to the President's staff, please." Olwen nodded and shut the door. Grace's heart was racing. She wanted to charge out of her office, do something, but she must not. One thing at a time. She spoke to MacRobert. "I'm shutting down the airfield reception here; ping me when you know anything definite. I'll be back with you when I can."

"Got it," he said, and the connection blanked.

The President's staff received the news that the welcoming ceremonies would be delayed due to a shuttle problem with their usual mix of whiny complaint ("but it was arranged . . .") and demands for information she didn't have ("Well, when *will* the shuttle arrive, then?"). She declined to talk to the President on the grounds of other urgent duties, and made the next call to the special events coordinator already waiting at the shuttle landing field near the city.

"I heard something," he said. "But is there no ETA?"

"Not yet," Grace said. "They're not landing here in any case, so the ceremony should be postponed indefinitely."

Next, Spaceforce Academy. She did not want to imagine losing the

Commandant, who had been such a stalwart ally in the difficult time after the attack on Vatta, who had lent her MacRobert as a liaison and seen, himself, to the treasonous President. Since she had become Rector, they had become almost friends—as much as the Commandant admitted having friends. She knew this attack might have been aimed at him as much as at Ky or Vatta.

His second in command, whose appointment they had both approved, answered the call at once. "You've heard," Iskin Kvannis said.

"I've heard they had trouble and went down. Do you have the location yet?"

"They didn't reach the Pingat airfield and they were below its sensor net. Ditched, is what we assume. No contact so far, but the survival gear could have been sabotaged as well as the shuttle."

Kvannis was younger, blunter, than the Commandant; Grace appreciated the bluntness. "Survivable?" she asked.

"Depends," he said. "It should have separated the passenger module, free-fallen to eighty-five hundred meters with a streamer chute, then come down more slowly with parachutes. I don't know if you saw the demonstration video—"

"Yes, I did, before we approved the modification of more shuttles."

"Well, this one should have had the full load of survival equipment: survival suits, rafts, supplies including advanced communications gear. But given the logical supposition that the shuttle drive and/or controls were sabotaged, so might the supplies have been. No way to know until we find ... whatever we find. I've spoken to the safety officer here in Port Major; he says someone ticked the right boxes that everything had been inspected, but there would not have been another full inspection at the Station. Both survival suits and the rafts are fitted with transponders; we'll hope Admiral Vatta used the one we customized for her."

"Why didn't she bring her own?"

"It didn't have our transponder codes loaded. Her security people didn't want our codes in her suit, and we wanted her to carry our codes in case of any mishap. Of course, she might have brought her own anyway, but her people approved the specs for ours and gave us her measurements."

"Location codes. So you should be able to locate them?"

"If the suits weren't compromised. Rector, the fact that we've had no contact—and it's now over two hours since the transponder went off—we must assume that either the crash was fatal, or the communications capability of any rafts and suits was compromised, either by the crash—which would likely mean it was fatal—or by sabotage."

Grace's skullphone pinged before she had a chance to say what she thought about not being informed for over two hours. "Just a moment," she said to Kvannis. "I'm getting info. Stay online."

"Rector Vatta, this is Captain Pordre, Admiral Vatta's flag captain. Are you aware—?"

"That the shuttle carrying Ky has gone down? Yes, Captain. Do you have new data?"

"We put a shuttle down as soon as hers made a radical course change and descent from the flight plan we'd been given. Our crew had eyes on it and we had contact with the admiral shortly before it descended into a heavy cloudbank, then we lost it. Our shuttle then circled just above that cloud layer; I wouldn't let them go lower, since we were starting to have communications breakups as well."

"You have a location?"

"Not precisely, though closer than you have probably. But Slotter Key's air defense forces are hassling us now about having dropped a shuttle without a proper flight plan and pre-authorization. We tried to tell them where we think the shuttle went in, but I don't think they're listening."

"I'll take care of that. Send me all the data you've got; I'll forward it to our Search and Rescue Service—" Grace went back to Kvannis. "I've got a location from Admiral Vatta's flagship; they dropped a shuttle to keep an eye on ours when it went off-plan. Now I need to get AirDefense off their case and give SAR the location data. Talk to you later."

"Yes, Rector. I'll leave any new word with your staff."

As Rector of Defense, Grace had oversight of all planetary defenses, but AirDefense and its emergency Armed Interdiction Unit had, until now, occupied the least of her time. It had shrunk, after the civil war in her youth, and had narrowly escaped elimination as unnecessary and expensive during budget cycles since. Slotter Key's criminals preferred to use the sea-lanes and the complicated island geography for whatever they were up to. AirDefense had absorbed and expanded the Search and Rescue Service from the old Coastal Patrol, mostly in an effort to stay on the budget at all. Grace called Ilya Ramos, subrector for AirDefense, and asked for the name of the Region VII commander of AIU.

"You'd better talk to Admiral Hicks first," Ramos said when she told him what had happened.

"No time," Grace said. "If they take potshots at the SDF shuttle, we'll have even more problems. Besides, we need to find our shuttle and any survivors now, not hours from now."

"Commander Orniakos, then. Basil Orniakos; this is his direct line."

The link came through. Grace said, "Thank you, Ilya," and hit the link. "This is Rector Vatta, Commander," she said, when she heard Orniakos answer with his name. "I need an immediate cease-and-desist order on that pursuit of the SDF shuttle."

"You're who? The Rector?" He sounded both grumpy and half asleep. She hadn't thought to look up the time at his location; could it have been night there? "Why would the Rector contact me directly and not through my chain of command? Who are you, her secretary?"

"I am Rector Vatta and I'm contacting you directly because the matter is too urgent—"

"Prove it." His tone was truculent, even defiant, rousing a responsive flare of white-hot anger. Not only had she not been told immediately about the shuttle's problem, but now some boob less than half her age who had probably never seen combat was defying her.

"I assure you," Grace said, as she sent her official seal, image, and right-hand fingerprints to him, "you do not want to wait for your senior to be involved in this. It will not benefit his career or yours." She knew this was not the right approach, but Ky was down, and if she was alive—

"This is not the right way to contact me; I don't take operational orders from you," he said. "I don't care what you—"

"If you fire upon a Space Defense Force craft of any kind," Grace said as rage whited out her vision for a moment, "I will see that you lose your commission, if *they* don't simply blow you to pieces." She pressed the button that ended that call and called MacRobert.

"What d'you have?" he asked.

"A likely location where they went down. And a base commander who needs to be relieved of command when I have a spare moment, which I don't. A guy named Basil Orniakos—"

"*Regional* commander, not base commander. Son and grandson of Academy graduates, ranked thirteenth in his class, switched from space duty to planetary due to his father becoming disabled . . . *that* Basil Orniakos?"

"I suppose. I asked Ilya Ramos who was in charge of AirDefense in that sector—"

"That would be Orniakos. And you contacted him yourself? You didn't call Admiral Hicks first?"

"Yes. He threatened Ky's ship. It had launched a shuttle to shadow the one she was on when it seemed to be in trouble, and it had eyes on her until the shuttle went into thick clouds. They have the best location on the crash site. He wouldn't listen to me."

"Grace—Rector—I've tried to explain before—"

"That I shouldn't try to break into the chain of command. I know. I *know* that, Mac. But we don't have a lot of time."

He said nothing. She could almost see the words forming in his mind: *Time you've already wasted by alienating Orniakos.* Then a sigh. "You need to give Air-Sea Rescue the location data you've got. It would be best to contact Admiral Sumia."

"Pingat Base is closer to the location—"

"Admiral Sumia. Or I can do it for you. I know someone on that side."

"Fine. You do it. I'm just a mere civilian Rector." She hated the edge frustration gave her voice; Mac didn't deserve it. But she was full of rage, old and new rage both.

"Just a moment until I'm at a secure desk," Mac said. Then he said, "Ready now. My usual code."

"Here goes," Grace said. "Straight from *Vanguard*."

"Got it," Mac said, a moment later. "I'll get hold of my contact right away. And Grace, be careful. If this is another deliberate attack on Vatta, you're a major target. If it was aimed at the Commandant, or the Defense Department as a whole, you're the Rector. Either way, take all precautions."

"I'm always careful."

"I'm always concerned."

Grace sat back in her chair for a moment, not quite slumping. Ky gone. She had to think of it that way, face the likelihood that Ky had died in the crash, after all she had survived before, and that meant not only a great loss to the family but the frustration of the very plan that had brought Ky back to Slotter Key at all.

Unless she hadn't died. Ky—who had come through so many perilous adventures—would not die easily if only she made it to the sea in one piece. Mostly one piece. With the experience of age, Grace tested the near-certainty of death against the splinter of hope that Ky lived. Which would she rather live with?

Hope, of course. She looked down at her left arm, now the same size as her right one but completely different to look at, with the skin she remembered from her distant youth—smooth, unmarked, so different from the uneven color and wrinkles of her right. She had been willing to lose that arm to save a child; she had fought to have a biological replacement grown in situ; she'd been told there was only a small chance it would live. And there it was—full-size, fully functional. She would believe Ky was alive.

* * *

Stella Vatta, acting head of Vatta Transport's branch office in Cascadia, and soon to be CEO of the entire corporation, sat quietly in the car beside her mother, Helen Stamarkos Vatta, current CEO of Vatta Enterprises, as they drove to Vatta's rebuilt headquarters in Port Major. Breakfast had been surprisingly pleasant, she thought, and with a little luck the rest of her visit would pass with no familial drama. Her mother looked older, to be sure, as expected in a woman who had lost three of her four children and her husband in the attack on Vatta several years before, but Stella sensed that her mother wanted a peaceful reunion as much as Stella did.

They had touched lightly on the family business during breakfast, each congratulating the other on what had been accomplished since that great upheaval. Now, as the car moved along familiar streets and neared the new headquarters building, Stella felt her skin tighten.

"Do you drive yourself every day?"

"Yes, but not the same route. Or the same car." Her mother turned right for two blocks, then left. "We'll go past the front, circle around. The entrance is in back, as before."

Vatta's new headquarters building, on the same site as the bombed-out former one, had a similar façade on State Street but a different footprint on the block as a whole. Stella eyed the new building, recognizing subtle differences from the old headquarters where she had been so often. As they entered the private access, she looked around the large open court.

"What's this? The building's not nearly as big."

"Couldn't afford it," Helen said. "We'd lost too much, and the banks balked. Over on State, as you saw, it looks much the same. Here on Trade, it's not as tall and only half as deep. Also, having had the basements mined, we've handled the underground portions differently."

The car shuddered to a halt; Stella's expression stiffened. "What—"

"It's all right." Helen touched the control panel, entering the codes.

The car rolled forward a short distance and stopped. "We're going to the belowground entrance," Helen said. The car sank without any vibration. Stella stared as they passed through what looked like solid pavement, coming to rest in a well-lit space with uniformed guards.

"It's an application of tractor beam technology," Helen said. "Illegal onplanet, but it has many advantages. An intruder driving into that courtyard will fall into one of several holes." She opened her door. "Don't worry; this vehicle's programmed to stop safely short of the entrance. We do have plans to fill in that space; the foundations are poured, but that can wait."

Stella watched her mother's progress through the building with a mixture of grief and trepidation. Most of her time in the old headquarters had been with her father—a few times with both her parents—and what she remembered overlaid the present building like a transparency. Only the wall-stripe in the passages, the familiar red and blue against cream walls, was the same.

"The public entrance—almost as large as before—and the executive offices need to look prosperous," her mother said as they rode the lift up from one floor to the next. "So those offices are up high and they seem to have windows to the outside. But the apparent windows on the outside aren't, and on the inside the blast-shielded rooms have viewscreens."

When the lift door opened, Helen nodded to the security station across from it—another change from the old days—and led the way to the CEO's office down the hall. Stella followed, into an office smaller than her father's had been, though still impressive. The viewscreens, framed as windows, gave the same view of State Street, the financial centers, and, at a little distance, the pink stone of the Presidential Palace.

Helen moved to a black-and-gold desk positioned diagonally and sat down, touching the active surface. Stella looked around; the room had changed in more than size. Her father's oversize tikwood desk, its bold red-and-black grain gleaming above the two slabs of green marble that held it up: gone. Gone also the handsome hand-knotted carpets on the floor, the colorful tapestries and paintings from a dozen or more worlds, souvenirs he'd brought home when he still captained a Vatta ship. Everything bold, intense, colorful … like him. Gone, like him, in the explosion that destroyed the building and so many lives.

Now pastel prints of sailboats, seaside cottages, and flowery gardens with small children or furry, big-eyed pets hung on bland pale walls. Helen's desk, half the size of Stavros', looked delicate enough to be in a lady's boudoir. Stella remembered it from their country house, as well as the two chairs that sat near it. The carpet, matching the walls, reinforced the bland, almost colorless effect.

Helen spoke without looking up. "I couldn't match it, Stella. To have it like Stavros' but not quite … I couldn't stand that. I had to make it completely different. And this cost less."

"I understand," Stella said.

"Ky should be boarding the shuttle about now," Helen said. "Grace was going to give us a signal—there it is—" She pointed to one light on the desk display. "She's made it safely from her ship to the Spaceforce shuttle. It'll be hours yet before she's down. Might as well give you the grand tour."

The rooms, the arrangement of departments, all different from her memory. All the new division heads were strangers, as were all the people sitting at desks working, entering or retrieving data. All equipment was new, and the rooms could have belonged to any business. Stella's offices on Cascadia looked much the same, she realized.

They were in the small executive lunchroom when Stella saw her mother stiffen and set down her glass of white wine. She waited, dread rising up her chest like a tide. Her mother's face had paled.

"The shuttle went down," Helen said, her voice not quite steady.

"Ky?"

"They don't know. It was in the ocean. They don't have any location other than that."

"So she could still be alive."

"She could. But they—we—don't know—"

"Was that Grace calling, or someone else?"

"Grace. She's canceled all the ceremonies and said we should leave here. Go home, was her suggestion, before the news crews start stalking us."

"Do we have a secure connection to the local ansible?" Stella asked. She put down her fork and pushed back her chair.

"Whom do you want to call?" *And why,* Helen's expression said.

"My people on Cascadia need to know, and I want to let Toby's parents know. If someone did this to kill Ky, they might be after Vatta as a whole again. All our ships and facilities need to be warned."

Her mother stared. "Stella, wait! I wasn't going to tell you yet, but you need to know now—"

"What?" Stella had already stood up; she paused. Her mother still sat, looking as if she might faint. "What is it?"

"I didn't want to upset you—" Her mother shook her head. "Sorry. It's about Osman. I can't—we don't know—"

"What?" Stella sat back down. "Just tell me!"

Her mother's voice was low, choked with tears. "Osman. His sons. We mostly found girls. We were sure he had sons, but they weren't in orphanages. Maxim—he's one. There must be more; he may have had them nearby—"

Stella closed her eyes a moment as the information sank in. Boys—of course he would have kept them where he could influence them—the most promising ones anyway—and aim them like invisible weapons at the family.

"You've no idea how many? Or where?"

"No. Don't be angry with me, Stella; I was going to tell you on this visit, but—"

"Never mind." Stella opened her eyes; her mother's face had crumpled as if made of wet paper, tears running down her face. Across the room one of the waiters hovered in the doorway, looking worried. "I'm not angry," Stella went on, pitching her voice low. "But you need to dab some cold water on your eyes, and we need to get up and walk out together. Staff are noticing."

That worked, as it had in other emergencies when her father had said it. Her mother took a long breath, touched her napkin to her eyes, and then took another long breath.

Stella went on. "I need to notify my office and have all Vatta facilities put on alert. I'm sure this will affect the legal procedures as well, so we'll need to consult on that. Can you stand now?"

"Y-yes. Of course." Her mother's voice firmed; she moved to push back her chair.

Stella stood again and came around the table. Her own eyes were dry, burning dry, and her hands were steady as she helped her mother up. She caught the waiter's eye. "Mother's not feeling well; don't worry."

"A glass of something, Sera?"

"No thank you."

As they cleared the door, Stella said, "The secured combooth?"

"That way." Her mother nodded to the right.

"Please contact Legal and tell them we'll need an immediate conference when I'm through here," Stella said.

The combooth bore the familiar ISC logo, and Stella's implant gave her the list of codes to use and the local time at the destination for each. Her own office now had round-the-clock coverage; she recognized the second-shift operator's voice when he answered and identified herself.

"Yes, Sera Vatta?"

"We've had an incident here; I want you to raise the security status in the office and our docksides, and warn any Vatta ships insystem. Take all precautions."

"Are you all right?"

"Yes. The shuttle with Admiral Vatta aboard has gone down; that's all we know so far. But I have received information that makes tighter security essential. We must start checking DNA on all employees, and all applicants for employment, as of today. Priority emergency."

"What are we looking for?"

"Osman Vatta's other children," Stella said. "I'll explain when I get back."

"Got that," he said. "You do realize, Sera, that under Cascadian laws, you will have to do this openly, or get a judicial order to review existing employee medical records?"

She hadn't. "Is anyone from Legal still in the office?"

"No, Sera. But I can give you Ser Brogan's number; it's not that late."

"Please do," Stella said. She read it into her implant. That would be another call. "Please do transmit to all the ships based from Cascadia that we now require a gene match against Osman Vatta's DNA for all new hires; it will trigger a deeper background investigation."

"Yes, Sera."

"And thank you for your service this shift, Aldon. You have been most helpful."

"My pleasure, Sera. May you be safe in your travels."

Stella closed that link and opened another to Toby's parents' home. It was after midnight there, but she did not want to risk the boy's safety by waiting; Toby's genius was one of Vatta's most precious resources. To her surprise, Toby himself answered and she heard the sounds of people talking in the background.

"Toby, it's Stella Vatta. Are you all right?"

"Cousin Stella!" He turned from the com and she heard him speak to his parents. "It's Cousin Stella! She didn't forget!"

Didn't forget? What was she supposed to have remembered? Then she did. The invitation to Toby's graduation and after-party. It was on her calendar back on Cascadia—office and house both—but she hadn't put it in her implant, and events had driven it from her mind.

"I'm glad the party's still going on," she said. "Congratulations, Toby."

"Can I have that job now?"

The job she'd promised him when he finished his basic schooling, a lab of his own to tinker in. "Toby, right now I can't. I'm on Slotter

Key, and there's a situation. Let me talk to your parents, either of them."

"Oh. Sure."

The next voice was Toby's father. "Cousin Stella."

"Cousin Ted. I'm sorry not to have called earlier, but we've had an emergency here on Slotter Key, and I'm raising the security level of all Vatta facilities."

"Not another bomb—"

"No." Not yet. She hoped not ever. "But you remember I was coming here to firm up some company legal stuff—"

"Yes."

"My cousin Ky, as you know, is a major shareholder. She was to meet me here and formally agree to the rearrangements in person as required by Slotter Key law. Unfortunately, the shuttle she was on went down somewhere in the ocean. We must suspect sabotage until we know better, and I will not be able to leave here until we know whether she survived the crash."

"Do we still—do you really think we still have enemies?"

"Yes," Stella said. "And you need to take care, individually and in your department. From now on, all new hires must be tested for genetic linkage to Osman Vatta. And if your world permits, run the existing employees' gene scans as well. If not, when I can, I'll start dealing with the legality of that—"

"It's not a problem here. Our laws take into account the frequent use of short-lived DNA reboots. Everyone, or everyone of a certain age, or—?"

"Anyone young enough to be Osman's get," Stella said. "To be safe, anyone under fifty."

"I'll see to that locally," he said. "Do you want to talk to Toby again? He's pretty excited. He tied for first in his class. Guess who with."

"Zori," Stella said. "Except perhaps in a tech class." Zori, Toby's girlfriend, was every bit as smart, but hadn't had the same early education.

"Yes. He tutored her in that one and she tutored him in law."

"Are they still so close, then?"

"Indeed. Sera Louarri seems resigned to it now, though we parents all think they should wait longer. Not that young love can't succeed, but they're still *so* young."

Stella, remembering herself at that age, agreed. "Is Rascal still alive?"

"That dog! I know how important he is to Toby, but how did you stand him in an apartment? We have space and he's still a menace." A pause, then, "And still bringing in an income, so I shouldn't complain."

Stella laughed, surprising herself. "He's a handful, true. Listen, I'm not going to tell Toby that Ky's missing," she said. "But I would like to talk to him."

Toby came back on the line with Zori beside him, as she could hear. She heard about their academic triumphs, about Zori's decision to go on to university, and Toby's wish to go straight back to the lab. "We can do both," he said, his voice dropping a tone. "We can live near the university—a lab can be anywhere, can't it?"

"Just about," she said. "But I'm afraid it'll have to wait until I get back to Cascadia, Toby. It shouldn't be too long; you can work in the local Vatta lab until then, but I can't set up a new one until the legal complications here are worked out."

"That's all right," Toby said. "It's just—I have some new ideas. Dad says not to talk about them, even on a secure line."

"Good," said Stella. "I'm sorry, Toby, but I must go—I have appointments waiting. When I get back to Cascadia we'll talk again about a lab for you. Be well."

"Be well, Cousin Stella."

Despite the gravity of the shuttle crash, Stella realized she was smiling as she closed that link. It was almost impossible to be gloomy around Toby and Zori. Who to call next? Ser Brogan, certainly, though that could wait until she got to the house, since it was late on Cascadia Station and he was probably in bed. Grace, though she would be busy; certainly they needed to talk. She didn't need the combooth for that. Rafe. Her breath came short. She had to call Rafael Dunbarger, current CEO of InterStellar Communications. Once he heard that Ky was in danger, he would do something—something that might be disastrous.

She should ask Grace first. No, she should most definitely *not* ask Aunt Grace. She didn't have time for that; she had to contact Rafe, convince him not to intervene, before he heard about this via one of his clandestine communications networks and intervened on his own. She placed the call, after checking the time in his zone on Nexus II. Text, not voice: she did not want to talk to him; she had no answers for the questions he would ask. She tapped out the message, stark and plain. Before she was done, a knock on the combooth door distracted her. A screen came up, her mother on the typepad, fingers busy.

ARE YOU ALL RIGHT? COME OUT NOW. I NEED YOU.

She ended the call quickly and unsealed the booth.

Her mother stood nearby, talking to a tall, dark, distinguished-looking man with graying hair. Helen turned to her.

"This is Ser Targanyan, head of our Legal Department. He's briefing me on the legal and tax problems we'll face if Ky—or her body—can't be found."

The last thing Stella wanted to think about. But she recognized the need. "In a secure office," she said. Targanyan nodded and led them to Legal, and his office within it.

"We're shielded here," he said. "I'm very sorry, Sera Vatta, Madam Chair, to bring this up when a search cannot even have been mounted, but we've already filed the preliminary papers for Sera Stella Vatta to become the CEO of Vatta Enterprises, Ltd., and whichever division is subordinate to have a subordinate executive. Here is the schematic Madam Chair and I had worked up—it will have to be approved, Sera Stella, when you take over." A holo appeared between them. With a flick of his finger, he rotated it so that Stella could read the labels.

"It looks like a reasonable organization," Stella said.

"Thank you, Sera. The difficulty is not in this so much—you can change it, of course, as you think best—but in the fact that we have this as part of the filing. And we set the date for a court appearance, based on your and your cousin Admiral Vatta's presence here over the next several days. If she is not quickly found and transported here, I'll have to change the court date, and we may need to re-file. That will delay things across your fiscal year boundary, with tax consequences. It might be better to let the court know now that we won't make the hearing because of the accident."

"We'll need to talk to the Rector," Stella said. As he started to speak, she shook her head. "I know, she's not holding Ky's proxy, and she hasn't the shares to overturn any decisions my mother and I make, but she should be in the loop. This is a political and military matter now: Ky was coming down on a Spaceforce shuttle. Releasing information about the crash should at least have her permission." And the sooner Grace knew that Rafe knew, the better, painful as that interview might be.

He frowned. "I see—yes, Sera, that is quite correct. But unfortunate."

"The crash is unfortunate," Helen said. "This is merely inconvenient." Her gaze was steady, her eyes dry.

"Exactly," Stella said. "And it may be that Grace can give us an answer immediately." She hated using a skullphone, but in this instance its security features tipped the scale—no one could tap into Grace's end of the conversation. She entered Grace's office number, and argued her way through two layers of underlings before Grace came on.

"Yes, Stella, what?"

Stella ignored the tone. "Ser Targanyan at Vatta HQ Legal says we need to inform the court if Ky isn't going to be there for the filing on the new organization. Ideally, today or tomorrow, because the judge is an idiot—"

"I did *not* say that," Targanyan said, eyes wide.

"No, I did," Stella said. "So, Aunt Grace, can we do that, or do you have the shuttle crash under some kind of security wrap?"

"It just came unwrapped," Grace said. If she was as angry as she sounded, Stella was very glad not to be in the same building, let alone the same office. "I got a call from a media outlet wanting confirmation that the shuttle had gone down. And I have a strong suspicion who the leak came from, and he is—" A pause. Grace's voice, now mellow as cream, finished with, "So, I think it's perfectly reasonable to inform the court of a possible—no, call it a probable—delay in the filing of that paperwork. Now if you'll excuse me, I have visitors." The contact ended.

Stella smiled at Targanyan, who was still glaring at her. "See how quick that was?" she said. "Aunt Grace said go ahead and inform the court of a probable delay. You can do that right away. Mother and I need to return to the house for now; it's a security matter."

"Just a moment," her mother said. "Stella, Ser Targanyan—please, I simply cannot go on as before. Stella, please take over. I'm—I'm done." Her eyes filled with tears again. She stood up, wavering a little. Stella moved quickly to offer her arm.

"Come, Mother; I'll help you downstairs." She looked back to see Ser Targanyan openmouthed behind them.

"You enjoyed that," Helen said when they were in the lift.

"Yes," Stella said. "Yes, I did. Didn't you tell me once to find something enjoyable in any situation?"

"No," Helen said. "That was your aunt Grace." And after a pause, "But I meant what I said. This is too much for me. I need you to take over. Now."

"Of course I will. It's understandable you'd want to recover from another shock."

Stella opened the passenger door for her mother and took the driver's side herself. Her mother entered the exit codes, but Stella drove them home.

She said nothing on the way back to the house, her imagination presenting a series of vivid horrific pictures: the shuttle exploding, flaming shards falling into the sea, Ky's dismembered body among them. The shuttle, whole, slamming into the sea, fragmenting, sinking, never to be found. She tried to force her imagination to something better, but had no idea how that could happen ... *could* a shuttle settle quietly onto the surface of a calm sea? Was that sea calm? The only pictures she'd ever seen of the Oklandan had been storm images, news stories of ships battered and limping into port somewhere to the north of Miksland.

"I really miss Onslow Seffater," her mother said, into that silence. "Targanyan is such a difficult man."

Stella struggled with the name for a moment then remembered her father's legal adviser, whom she'd met on the embarrassing occasion of the family silver disappearing from the country house vault. Ser Seffater had been gentler than her father as he coaxed her to admit she'd given the gardener's son the combination. The silver had been recovered, the gardener's son having been as feckless in his theft as she had been in her trust in him, but no one ever forgot that lapse. She had become "that idiot Stella" to the family just as Ky had been "Ky ... well, at least she's not like that idiot Stella."

"He was killed in the explosion, wasn't he?"

"He was just coming into the building," her mother said. "Blown to pieces. At least they could find the pieces. Your father—"

She knew about that, too. The upper floors had collapsed onto the lower floors and her father's remains, all anyone found, were smears of blood and tissue identified as his by a gene scan.

"I hope we can at least find Ky's ..." Her mother let that trail off.

"She could be alive," Stella said, over her own certainty that Ky must be dead. "She's tough. I've seen her in emergencies."

"Gravity has no pity," her mother said. "Nor physics. Relentless ..."

Stella glanced at her. Her mother's gaze was straight ahead.

SPACE DEFENSE FORCE HEADQUARTERS, GREENTOO

With the news that the Grand Admiral had arrived safely in Slotter Key nearspace, tension in SDF headquarters had relaxed somewhat. She was safe; the Slotter Key ansible was working; they had real-time communication with her if they wanted. When eight of the admirals then at HQ met in the Senior Officers' Club and settled around the big table in the meeting room with their favorite evening drinks after dinner, they were ready for a pleasant few hours of chat and discussion. Issues of some weight were set aside while the Grand Admiral was away; they could relax. Padhjan, the admiral who had retired from Slotter Key Spaceforce to serve under Ky Vatta, answered questions about Slotter Key protocol.

"We're not nearly as formal as Cascadians," he said. "Fairly casual, in fact. I expect there might be a parade, and some politicians will shake her hand, but—"

"Sir! *Sir!*" The pale-faced young officer who flung open the door to the Senior Officers' Club meeting room had a printout in his hand. Dan Pettygrew, facing the door, scowled at him.

"What is it?"

"It's—it's a message for Admiral Driskill, sir. It's really urgent—it's bad—I mean—"

"Spit it out, Hopkins," Driskill said with a quick glance at Pettygrew. "Everyone in here has all the clearance they need."

"It's the admiral—Grand Admiral Vatta, I mean. She's—she's gone, sir."

Pettygrew felt as if he'd been flash-frozen; for a moment he could not move or speak. The pleasant dinner he'd eaten earlier congealed in his stomach. Down the table, Admiral Hetherson of Moray System shifted in his seat; no one else moved. Pettygrew struggled and finally said, "What happened?" His own voice sounded strange to him.

"The shuttle crashed on Slotter Key. Into the ocean. They don't think anyone survived."

"No!" Argelos, seated on Pettygrew's left, slapped a hand onto the table. "She can't—it's a mistake!" Then, before anyone else could answer, he went on. "What kind of shuttle? When? What kind of search have they done?"

"This is all we've got," Hopkins said. Now the first was out, he seemed to realize he'd burst in on the senior admirals without the slightest courtesy. "It's from Captain Pordre on *Vanguard Two*." He handed the hardcopy to Admiral Burrage, the Cascadian.

Instead of reading it aloud, Burrage read it through silently, lips pursed, then handed it to Hetherson. As each admiral read it in silence, and passed it on up the table, Pettygrew felt his stomach knotting ever tighter. Ky Vatta could not be gone. Dead. She was the reason the Space Defense Force existed; she was the reason he was an admiral, and not just the captain of a single warship fleeing disaster. She had made them, willed SDF into being, commanded them in one after another engagement, against odds that no one else, he was sure, could have beaten. His own planet, Bissonet, though it had suffered badly under Turek's domination, was free again, and though his immediate family had not survived, many people he'd known were alive because of her.

The transcript, when he saw it for himself, made it clear Pordre did not know whether anyone had survived or not, and that he was annoyed with Slotter Key's official response. "I have been in contact with their Rector of Defense, also named Vatta, and she has assured me of her full support, but confirmed my suspicions of sabotage in the shuttle failure. We are parked in a more distant orbit; from here we can do nothing but wait for permission to land one of our own shuttles. I intend to remain in Slotter Key space until search and rescue operations have finished."

Pettygrew handed the transcript on to Argelos and waited until it reached the far end of the table. When Driskill had read it, he spoke. "Hopkins, you will not speak of this to anyone else. Were you the one who decoded it?"

"Yes, sir. The comtech called for an admiral's aide with the relevant security key; I was already in the area."

"Good. Do you know where the others are?"

"Outside this door, sir, I expect."

"This information will be shared in due time, but we need to communicate with Captain Pordre and with Slotter Key's government to make more sense of it. Go tell the other aides to hold themselves in readiness—if any are not in the club, call them in. Do not reveal any of this message. Is that clear?"

"Yes, sir. I won't, sir."

"You may go."

When the door shut behind him, Hetherson said, "I told her not to go back there. We needed her here. This is where she should be."

Pettygrew fought down a surge of temper. Hetherson was a former senior admiral of Moray's space navy and still considered himself senior to them all, purely by time in grade, though he had not been part of the fleet that fought at Nexus.

"She went, and now she's been in a shuttle crash," Pettygrew said, more harshly than he intended. "Until we know if she's dead or alive, it's our job to hold SDF together, in readiness for whatever comes, until she's back."

"Or she's dead and one of us takes over." Burrage looked at each of them in turn.

Trust Burrage to bring that up. The succession through the admirals had been a touchy issue ever since the end of the war. Each senior admiral had come from one of the contributing systems except Mackensee's, since the mercenaries did not want to commit ships and personnel permanently to SDF. They had, however, recommended a couple of other systems from which SDF had acquired supplies, systems willing to host SDF bases, though they had not actually been in the war against Turek. Ky had agreed, citing the strategic benefit of having more allies in more places. But the original member systems wanted to be sure their admirals took precedence, and within those, Moray and the Moscoe Confederation pushed hardest to be named first in succession should anything happen to Ky Vatta.

Ky herself had chosen Pettygrew, when Argelos refused, on the basis of his lack of military background. And though most of the other admirals agreed he had been with her longest and knew her best, their system governments were less cooperative.

"Right now," he said, before anyone else could start more argument, "we need to ensure that SDF continues to function at high efficiency. In Admiral Vatta's absence, she named me the senior admiral. Admiral Padhjan, you know more about Slotter Key than the rest of us. You will be our liaison with Captain Pordre and with the Slotter Key government. Admiral Driskill, make discreet contact with InterStellar Communications and find out what they're planning to do about this. I can't imagine their CEO will be twiddling his thumbs." Someone coughed; someone else twitched. They all knew Rafe Dunbarger and Ky Vatta had some kind of relationship. Pettygrew finished giving out assignments. He could almost feel the currents of curiosity, sorrow, ambition, resentment, flowing back and forth around the room, but he didn't comment on that. "It's 2300 now. It'll take time to get more information, and I would imagine Slotter Key news agencies will be saying something soon. We'll meet in Briefing One at 0830. Call me if you need me; we all need some sleep."

By the time he reached his quarters, the brandy fumes had left him to a familiar cold, hollow feeling, now colder and more hollow than before. He did not want to believe she was dead. She had survived her ship being blown apart around her; surely she would survive a shuttle crash. But how many near misses could someone survive?

And most of all, what if she was dead and he had to take over the SDF and hold it together until the next major attack? Could he do it? He was older; he had assumed he'd die first, that his appointment as her successor was a courtesy, a recognition of their long cooperation. But if he did not, who would? Hetherson, who had never actually been in combat, who was a senior admiral because he had run the shipbuilding program on Moray? Hot-tempered Driskill, a competent combat commander under Ky, but only in one battle, the defense of Nexus II, often at odds with both civilians and military? Padhjan, older, military-trained, perhaps the obvious choice? But he knew that Moray, Cascadia, Nexus, and Bissonet would not consent to another ruling admiral from Slotter Key, not right away. And he knew that with no obvious enemy like Turek, governments were beginning to question whether SDF needed to be so big and expensive . . . if it was still needed at all.

And what should he do about Ky's flagship, still in Slotter Key nearspace? Recall Pordre? Leave him there? He left his quarters and headed for the headquarters communications center. "Get me Captain Pordre on *Vanguard Two*," he said.

CHAPTER FOUR

SLOTTER KEY, OKLANDAN SOUTH OF MIKSLAND
DAY 1

"Passengers may open faceplates and breathe cabin air." That impersonal recorded voice, after Jen's hysterical scream, made the landing seem unreal for a moment. Ky opened her faceplate; Jen clambered up from the deck, both hands clutching the table, lurching with every pitch and roll of the shuttle. Her gaze was unfocused and her mouth still open.

"Commander Bentik!" That got Jen's gaze back to Ky. "Sit down there, behind Sergeant Vispersen." Ky pointed to the seat behind the steward, who now had his faceplate open. Jen made it to the seat and pulled herself into it. "Right arm-pocket, sick-pill, under your tongue, now." Jen followed these instructions. Ky looked across at the Commandant, who had left his faceplate closed. Perhaps he also felt seasick and was accessing an implant drug.

The module pitched steeply again, slid down the back of one wave, wallowed in the trough, and then rolled to port riding up the next. Ky's stomach roiled in spite of the dose her implant had given her. But she was alive, with air to breathe, and the ship wasn't immediately disintegrating. Better than a hull breach in space. She turned to Vispersen.

"Do the parachutes release on landing, or are they dragging us around?"

"I don't know, Admiral. I've never been—done it—only read about it—" His face glistened with perspiration and his lips were pale.

She needed him alert and thinking. "Seasick meds," Ky said. "You have them?"

"Yes, Admiral. Let me get you—"

"For you; I'm fine. *You* need 'em."

Lips tight, he opened a pouch on his sleeve and pulled out a packet, but could not open it. Ky unfastened her safety webbing and carefully—dealing with the pitch and roll of the module—made it across the aisle to open the packet and put one of the chewables in his mouth. He nodded his thanks. In seconds, his face was a better color and he unfastened his safety harness. She looked at Jen, who looked less green.

"Commander, are you better now?"

"Yes, but you didn't listen to me! He's dead!"

"I heard you. How do you know?"

"He didn't answer me when I spoke; I reached over and shook him and he—his head—it just flopped. I thought he needed air; I opened his faceplate and he's—he's dead." Her voice rose.

"Commander Bentik, stay where you are." Dread added to the cold lump in her belly. What if the Commandant— She turned to look at him again.

"The Commandant?" Vispersen unhooked his safety restraints.

"Hasn't said anything." Ky lurched back across the aisle. "Commandant? Sir? Are you all right?"

The Commandant didn't reply, didn't move. She could not see his color through the faceplate; Vispersen slid it back. The Commandant's face was gray, his expression fixed. His lips were bluish, with a little white foam at the corners of his mouth.

"No!" the steward said. "Did he—it must have been a heart attack—" He felt for a pulse and found none. "He's so cold—"

"He's dead, then?" Ky felt a chill too deep for her suit to compensate. The Commandant *and* his aide? What about the flight crew? The rest of the passengers? What would have happened to Jen and her if they'd worn the Spaceforce survival suits? And who, now, was in command?

"It's just like his aide." Jen was up out of her seat again, crowding in next to the steward to look. "That foam at his lips."

Ky agreed on dead. She'd seen it before. "Let me check his pulse. Get his helmet off and his survival suit open." The steward gave her a startled look, then unlocked the neck ring, pulled off the helmet, and peeled open the upper third of the suit.

Ky stared at the Commandant's neck, where a steel needle was embedded; when she leaned to look, another needle had penetrated the other side of his neck. "Poison," she said. "It's murder." She glanced at the steward. He looked stunned, confused. She turned to Jen. "Did you see a needle like this in his aide's neck?"

"N-no. I didn't open his suit, just the faceplate. What if—what if the suit they wanted me to wear had poisoned *me*?"

"You'd have been dead," Ky said. "And so would I. But we don't know that those suits were rigged to kill." She was sure they had been; she was sure whoever had done this had intended to kill at least all the officers aboard. She pulled a stylus from her sleeve pocket and poked into the neck of the suit. "Quick-acting, didn't let him thrash— didn't activate just from putting the suit on, because we were talking after that. When he closed the faceplate maybe . . ." She looked inside the helmet and prodded the inside, near the faceplate.

"Admiral, we need to exit the module—" Vispersen touched her arm. He still had that stunned expression, the words coming out of his mouth in a monotone, as if read from an instruction card. Perhaps they were—one he had seen many times.

"We need to find out who else is alive," Ky said. "The flight crew; the other passengers." Jen, with a bruise rising visibly on her forehead, would be best sitting down for now. "Commander, sit back down over there. Sergeant—Vispersen, isn't it? Check the aft compartment and get a count of survivors and any injuries. I'll check the flight crew."

Ky made her way forward and opened the hatch to the cockpit. Both pilots were immobile and unresponsive in their protective gear. One was dead—no vital signs readout on his helmet nor, when she opened the faceplate and unlocked the helmet, any pulse in his neck. Like the Commandant, his face was gray, his lips blue with a line of foam. The copilot's face was the now-familiar gray, but she could hear his staccato grunts. Not dead yet.

She looked back and saw the steward, whose expression now was more alert, and, she thought, appropriate. Except that he wasn't where she'd told him to go.

"Same as the Commandant. Poison," she said.

He nodded. "The suit was sabotaged?"

"Yes. Go check the aft compartment, Sergeant." She put more bite in her voice. He stared at her.

"What are you going to do?"

"Retrieve the flight recorder and the crew's IDs. Gather evidence. Go on now. We need to get the life rafts ready to deploy and I'll need a medtech up here if there's one aboard."

Vispersen headed back down the aisle; Ky turned her attention to the copilot again. She unlocked his helmet, opened the neck ring, and saw that only one needle had penetrated his neck. Would he live?

She lacked the training to do anything; she hoped they had a medtech aboard who could. Meanwhile, that flight recorder . . . there, a compartment with the familiar orange stripes. She opened the latch and unhooked the connections, then pulled the flight recorder out of its hole, slightly reassured by the blinking light on its top surface. It might have been sabotaged as well, but unless it contained no data at all, it should have something useful. It just fit into the external chest pocket of her protective suit. She put the pilot's ID tags and the shuttle's command wand into one of the leg pockets.

She heard voices from the other end of the module; when she looked, Vispersen was making his way forward, followed by several others in orange survival suits. The suits had no name tags or rank insignia, but they introduced themselves briefly: Sergeant Cosper, Corporal Inyatta, Corporal Riyahn, Tech Lundin.

"Master Sergeant Marek has taken charge in the rear compartment," Sergeant Cosper said. "He's the only one of us who's ever been through a passenger module landing. It was just in training, though."

"Much better than nothing," Ky said. "Pilot's dead. The copilot's been badly injured—I think poisoned like the other, but he's still breathing, and I think his leg's broken. Anyone here trained in trauma?"

"Me, sir. Uh, Admiral." Tech Lundin was a strongly built woman with a steady gaze out of gray eyes. "I'm certified fourth-level trauma life support."

"Excellent," Ky said. "You're in charge, then."

"Yes, sir . . . Admiral."

"Just sir," Ky said. "Be sure to collect the copilot's tags; I have the pilot's, and the flight recorder."

Lundin pointed to a bulkhead compartment. "Should be a basket in there, Corporal, and an IV setup in number four. I'll need both. Sergeant, if you'll follow me." She moved forward past Ky.

Ky looked at Vispersen. "I'll go back and talk to Staff Sergeant Marek."

"Yes, sir."

"Is there survival equipment in this compartment that we'll need?"

"Yes, sir." He pointed to the overhead. "Life raft there—three more in the rear compartment. Contents of some of these lockers—"

"If Tech Lundin doesn't need these two, start getting supplies together."

"Deploy the raft, sir?"

"Not yet—just get supplies we'll need from bulkhead compartments; put them on the seats. I'll talk to Marek first."

She made her way down the aisle; when she came abreast of Jen, who looked both scared and offended, she hoped a touch of humor would help. "This is not the homecoming I planned."

"I thought not," Jen said. "It is certainly not what I expected. This doesn't happen back—"

Ky held up her hand. Jen said no more. "We must focus on the here and now. I need your report—did you check the aft compartment before you came forward?"

"I told you about the Commandant's aide being dead. And Senior Lieutenant Ghomerti, in the compartment with us. I didn't go back—I came to find you," Jen said, her voice uneven. "All poisoned. If we'd worn those suits—"

"But we didn't," Ky said. "And we're not the only survivors." Her thoughts raced; most of them would not help Jen stay calm. Whoever sabotaged the suits had chosen the most critical targets first. With the pilots dead or incapacitated, the shuttle would crash at sea, maybe without separating the passenger module, and the others would die in the crash.

"I've got the Commandant's aide's ID packet," Jen said. "Anything else I should collect?"

"Did he have an external com device? It'll be loaded with Slotter Key access codes."

Jen opened a locker beside the aide's seat. "This is all he was carrying." She pulled out the case Ky had seen back at the station.

"Hang on to that," Ky said. "Have any background in planetary survival, Jen?"

"No, Admiral. I was born and raised on the Cascadia Station. Only visits downside."

Ky led the way into the aft compartment. Master Sergeant Marek—a tall, brown, fit-looking man with some gray in his short-cropped brown hair and a deep heavy scar from the left side of his forehead up over his head—had the personnel in the rear compartment divided into teams. She could tell he had no implant; the scar suggested why, a serious head injury.

"Admiral," he said when he saw her. "What about those up front?"

"The pilot, the Commandant, and the Commandant's aide are all dead—poisoned—their suits were rigged to kill them. The copilot might make it, but I doubt it."

His face tightened. "Yours, too?"

"I haven't looked yet at mine; my aide examined the one designated for her and it was also rigged. Everyone accounted for back here?"

"Yes, Admiral. One fatality, Corporal Gassar. Needle in the neck." He grimaced. "That means you and your aide are the only officers aboard . . . unless the copilot lives." She could read the look he gave her as if his thoughts were displayed on a screen. Was this high-ranking officer from a different military going to be a problem? Or could the admiral who'd led an outnumbered force to victory be an asset?

"Come with me a moment," Ky said. She led him into the middle compartment, where the Commandant's aide was still strapped into a seat, his dead face a gray mask. "Yes, Commander Bentik and I are the only live officers aboard. And yes, we're not in your chain of command. Nonetheless, it is my duty both as an officer, and as a native of Slotter Key, to offer my services. We both know the relevant citations in the Code." Ky kept her eyes on his and her voice steady. "Do we have a problem, Master Sergeant?"

He scowled at her for a moment. "It depends, Admiral. Do you have any idea what to do in this situation?"

"Some. It has distinct advantages over a space emergency," Ky said. "We have air to breathe, food, and an abundance of water. Our mission is survival until we get back to a safe base. This module hasn't sunk yet; we have modern life rafts and supplies. We're rich, in survival terms. So our first task is to get into the rafts before this module goes down, then stay alive in the rafts until we reach land. I understand you've had training in the module."

"Yes—I know how to deploy the rafts, and what supplies are in them. But the training was a long way from here, in warmer waters."

"But you can do it." It was not a question; she saw from his expression that he took it as she meant it, that his resistance to her taking command was weakening.

"Yes, Admiral. I'm certain I can get a raft deployed. We'll be crowded in it; they're rated for twenty, but—"

"We'll need two rafts deployed," Ky said. "We don't know if we can reach Miksland, or how long it will be until we're found and rescued—we need the supplies in both. At least."

"So you're—you're really taking command?"

She had not expected such indecisiveness from him, but it was a circumstance he'd never faced. "Yes. I ask you again: is that going to be a problem, Master Sergeant?"

His expression firmed, this time to a tight grin. "No, Admiral. I accept your command, on behalf of the Slotter Key personnel aboard. And your orders?"

"That you prepare to evacuate this thing. How long will the passenger module float?"

"As long as one of the cushions doesn't deflate," Marek said. "The range was up to ten hours in calm water." He shook his head. "All this rocking around puts more stress on the cushions—the manual said even one deflation could make it unstable enough to tip over. We should launch the life rafts as soon as we can."

"It doesn't feel"—Ky grabbed for a seatback again—"like the parachutes are very efficient sea anchors."

"No, Admiral, they're not; they were supposed to detach. These seas are too big. And we're too big and sit too high. Wind's shoving us around."

"How do we transit from the module to the rafts? As you said, we're sitting high."

"There's a slide installed into the hatch itself; deploy that first, attach the raft's tether to the hull, then inflate the raft and let it slide down to the water. Then personnel can go down. Anything else we take can slide down to the rafts and be pulled in." Once focused on the task, he seemed more confident.

"Vispersen told me there are four life rafts; every one will have supplies—"

"Four, yes. Far more than we need. I was about to pull one and check it. With the shuttle sabotage, maybe the rafts were sabotaged as well."

Ky had been trying not to think about that possibility. She kept her voice level. "Go ahead. We should bring all the rafts, one spare to each inflated one."

His brow wrinkled. "Why the others?"

"Sabotage, again. We don't know if there's another saboteur among us. This is a big cold ocean and I'd rather increase our chances of staying afloat, not treading water."

He nodded. "That makes sense. I'll get a raft down and do the exterior inspection, then pop a hatch. If we can open just one, it'll be better."

"Carry on, then. I'm going to collect some forensic data forward," Ky said. "I'll leave you to assign personnel to each raft. If you need me, tell Commander Bentik."

"Yes, Admiral."

When she went back forward, Tech Lundin had the copilot on the rescue basket, but shook her head when she saw Ky. "We've lost him, sir. I got IVs in, intubated him, but there's a mark on his neck—like the needle only went in partway. It wasn't the injuries—the poison killed him. I'm sorry."

"You tried your best," Ky said, looking down at Major Sunyavarta, father of a nine-year-old daughter who wanted to be like Ky—at least this year. "We shouldn't leave him to the fish. We'll bring his body home to his family—all of them, in fact, if we can."

"Yes, sir. I'll suit him back up, shall I?"

"Good. I'm going into the cockpit to see if there's any other evidence investigators might want later," Ky said. "When I've done that, you can retrieve the pilot's body, too. Anyone know something else that might be useful in establishing the cause of the problem?"

"Sir, if you can pull the flight recorder—"

"I have that already," Ky said, patting the pocket it was in. "Anything else?"

"If we're taking the bodies, why not leave his ID on him?"

"I want the IDs separately. If we're not found fairly soon, we may have to bury them at sea."

In the cockpit, she noticed a notepad clipped to one side of the pilot's control panel and shoved that in the same pocket as the flight recorder. In the same locker where the flight recorder had been, she found a stack of plastic envelopes and used her stylus to take a little of the foam from the pilot's lips and smear it inside one of them. She folded that and put it in another pocket, then wiped the stylus on her survival suit's leg. She looked again at the control panels. Surely the passenger module would have a transponder, some form of communication. But all the lights were off. She flicked switches; nothing happened. The module's communication was as dead as her skullphone.

When she came back into the cabin this time, Tech Lundin had the copilot once more concealed in his survival suit, helmet fastened on. "Here's his ID, Admiral," she said, handing it over.

"He mentioned his daughter when we were introduced. I will do my best to see that they learn what happened to him," Ky said. A nine-year-old child had just lost her father. Ky had been—she thought back—twenty-three when her father was killed. She had been too shocked, too horrified, by the needles in the Commandant's neck to feel the anger she felt now. Six men—good, competent, productive men—dead by treachery. No time for that now; she had these men and women to care for.

"Pack up any medical supplies you find," she said. "We may need them. We're going to be evacuating this module, getting into life rafts, as soon as possible."

Only then did she remember that she had not collected the Commandant's identification packet. She did that and started back down the aisle. Tech Lundin called to her.

"We can put the pilot on the same basket as the copilot, sir, and drag it, but we can't fit any more in it."

She could see that, and she could see the outline of the forward emergency hatch. Lifting dead bodies up and over that, to slide down and then be hauled into the rafts like so much dead—like the dead men they were—would be very difficult.

"Staff Sergeant Marek will be opening a hatch and letting the slide down, then a raft," she said. "There should be time to move them one by one. If we're found quickly—" And if not, they could not keep corpses in the same rafts with the living. In a separate raft? No. And the other injured man, whom she hadn't checked on yet. "Tech Lundin, there are other injured back here. Let others move these."

"Yes, sir." Lundin moved quickly past her with the case of supplies.

Vispersen, she saw, was sitting down again, looking uncertain. "Staff Sergeant Vispersen," she said. "Need something to do?"

"But I—but you're—"

"Take another seasick pill if you need to. There's plenty to do before we move to the life rafts." She realized after a moment that he was either confused or scared. "Get that life raft down," she said, pointing to the bulge in the overhead. "Move it to the aft compartment." He got up, then, and moved to unlatch the raft hard-case.

Ky followed Lundin into the aft cabin. Marek had made his assignments; the other personnel were in two groups, with Commander Bentik off to one side. Her first impression was that all the survivors looked like good troops—not surprising, considering the selection, but they were all alert, attentive, and at least outwardly calm. Three life raft hard-cases had been propped on seats. Marek nodded to her.

"Ready to open the escape hatch, Admiral."

"Go ahead."

When the hatch opened, a wash of cold, wet air came in, along with the sucking and splashing of water against the inflated cushions.

Despite the cold, it smelled like home to Ky. She was surprised to recognize the smell here, in a place she'd never been.

The weighted evacuation slide rolled out, inflating as it went, smacking the water hard as the module rolled toward it. Spray flew up; a little came into the shuttle; it stung like ice. Marek had already made a line fast to the raft bundle and now shoved it out the door, yanking a second, short line as he did so then letting go. With a whoosh, the raft inflated and the canopy popped up, its entrance hatch open.

"Go Team One!" Marek said. Ten orange-suited figures hurried through the hatch, one after another, skidding down the slide. They had just reached the bottom when Ky felt the module shift again as the wave passed beneath it, lifting the slide now, and the raft at the end of it. "Grab on!" Marek yelled. "Stay with the raft!"

Six were able to hang on to the raft; four rolled away, back down the slide, but managed to grab on to loops set on the inside of the slide tubes. They made it into the raft when the next wave lifted the module higher again. Marek sent a raft package after them, and they hauled it in as well. "Team One's supposed to be checking all the equipment in the inflated raft to see what's missing and what doesn't work."

"Good," Ky said. "We've got six dead bodies to get aboard the second raft. The copilot died. Who checked the crash gear at the station?" Ky said.

"Bai Gassar," Marek said. "Our dead steward. So at least we can be certain he didn't have anything to do with the sabotage."

"He had some kind of fit just before we landed," someone else said. "I saw him kind of twitching in his seat, so I checked him out first when we got up."

"Did you open his suit?"

"No, Admiral. He was dead." Ky's implant reminded her that this was Corporal Riyahn. "Master Sergeant opened it."

"And found a needle." Ky nodded.

"Is that what killed the Commandant?" Riyahn's eyes widened.

"We think so. And the pilot and copilot."

"Does that mean Bai was the one who sabotaged the suits?" Riyahn's voice rose; two others looked at him.

"Unlikely." Unless it had been suicide, but if the saboteurs had committed suicide then the pilot and copilot might have been in on the plot as well. She could not believe that, not after Sunyavarta's mention of his daughter. "No way to be sure yet, and we can worry about that later. For now, we need to get everyone off this thing and into a raft." She turned to Tech Lundin, who was applying a splint to Corporal Barash's arm.

"How many injured?"

"This is the worst, sir. The rest are contusions, some abrasions. They'll heal on their own. And the arm may not be broken; I'm splinting it as a precaution against further injury."

"Good work," Ky said. She started to say more but was interrupted.

"Do you want Corporal Gassar's ID packet, sir?" That, her implant informed her, was Sergeant Chok.

"Thank you, Sergeant," Ky said. "Stick it in a pocket and keep it safe; I have the others."

"Yes, sir."

"The *correct* address is *Yes, Admiral*," Jen said, her voice harsh with disapproval.

Chok looked confused. "Sorry, sir—Admiral—I mean, Commander—"

"No problem, Corporal," Ky said. "Commander Bentik is more familiar with the protocol of the Cascadian forces."

"And in the Space Defense Force," Jen said, her voice still edged with disapproval.

Now they were all watching her and her aide, even Marek. This was exactly the way Jen had caused tension on that visit to Moray, criticizing Moray military usages as not being Cascadian. Ky kept her voice even.

"In an emergency such as this, *sir* is perfectly appropriate," Ky said to Chok. Then, to Jen, "But, Commander, I appreciate your care for the courtesies when under such stress." She meant it as a softening compliment, but from Jen's expression she felt it as an insult. Jen would have to deal with it; she had no time to placate her aide.

She looked at Marek. "Time to launch the second raft?"

"Not yet, Admiral," Marek said. "We need a report from the team in the raft on what's missing—see if it can be replaced anywhere in this module. Then we need to arrange everything that will go into it for quick unloading. The remains, for instance, can't be lifted into the raft with the rescue basket; it could snag the life raft fabric. They'll have to come in by hand." *Or not,* his tone said.

"I'm sure someone will be looking for us," Ky said. "My crew tracked us into the cloud cover. If they find us in time, these bodies can be brought home to their families." And perhaps yield clues to the saboteurs' identities.

"And if not?" he asked, under his breath.

"Then a sea road for their souls," Ky said, words she was surprised to remember. "We'll speak the words and sing them home."

He nodded. "That we will, Admiral. And it's cold, that's one good thing."

"Master Sergeant!" That was a yell from the raft. "There's no com equipment aboard! No navigation beacons, nothing! No optics, either."

"Not anything? Sure you're looking in the right pocket?"

"Yessir! Just where you said, and we looked in the others, too."

"Where would that have been stowed?" Ky asked.

"Sidewall, number seven pocket," Marek said. "Should be a transponder, a two-way com for surface, a satellite phone, a GPS." He looked around. "If they were taken out at the station—there wasn't much time to unpack and repack—some of that stuff could be in other lockers here." Without waiting for Ky to say anything, he turned to the others. "Lanca, Hazarika, check every starboard compartment for any com or nav gear, anything electronic—it's not in that raft, probably not in any of them. Droshinski, Riyahn, same for portside. The rest of you—when I launch the second raft, you'll go into that one. I'll send down the spare raft; get it lashed down on the opposite side from the entrance, to weight that side. Then we'll send down the medic, the wounded, and the deaders."

"Master Sergeant, either my aide or I should be in that raft—" Ky pointed out the hatch. "I think she should go next." A little separation would do neither of them any harm.

"We'll want Tech Lundin in with the injured." Marek's brow furrowed. "With respect, Admiral, I think it would be best if you went on in the first raft, and Commander Bentik went in the next. I'll be last out, so I can loose the mooring lines—if we cut 'em from the rafts, we lose that rope and we might want it."

Ky nodded. "I agree with the assignment, but I'd prefer to stay until we've got the wounded out."

"I understand, Admiral, but with respect, I want you aboard that raft to ensure that when I'm in the water hanging on to that line, someone'll pull me in and not cut it."

"You think we have a saboteur here—?"

"Don't you?" He gave her a long look.

"It's a possibility and no time to sort it out here. Right." She liked the obvious competence of this man, so similar to other good senior NCOs she'd known. She signaled and Jen came closer. "I'm going down now, to board this raft. You'll be the officer in charge of the next."

"I don't know what to do! You can't leave me with these—" Jen's voice rose. Ky took her arm and moved her aside.

"Jen, you're the only other officer aboard. We need an officer in each raft so if one goes down there's still an officer in the group. I know this isn't what you were trained for, but you do know procedures."

Jen took a deep breath, pressing her lips together. "They're strangers," she said finally. "I don't know any of them."

"I don't know them, either. But I do know you, and you can do this," Ky said. "They're just people; you're good at managing people."

"What—what do I need to do, then? I don't—I don't know what orders to give."

"You'll have Sergeant Chok—" Ky consulted her implant. "He's from Hylan Reef; he'll have more knowledge of seamanship than you, and I imagine—" She turned to look. "Sergeant Chok—"

"Yes, sir." He came over, easily balancing on the lurching module, a stocky man Ky guessed to be about her own age. Dark hair, brown eyes, skin a shade or so lighter than hers.

"Do you have small-boat or raft experience?"

"Yes, sir; my family has a fish farm. We use inflatables quite a bit."

"Commander Bentik will be in the raft with you. Her background is different."

Chok smiled and nodded to Jen. "Commander, these rafts are very sturdy. Bigger than the ones I learned in, but I have had training with this type. Anything I can do, be sure I will do to keep the raft and you safe."

"Very well, Sergeant," Jen said. Stiff, but no longer sounding panicky.

"We'll want the two rafts connected by a line," Ky said. "Getting separated would worse than halve our chances of survival."

"Where can we go?" Jen asked.

"Right now, where the wind and water take us. That land to the north, Miksland, is uninhabited and inhospitable but if we can't get into a northward current that will carry us past it, we'll have to make for it and stop there—at least for a while."

Jen shivered. Ky couldn't afford more time trying to help her aide. She had everyone to think of. She said nothing, and after a moment Jen said, "Yes, Admiral. I hope—I hope you believe I will do my best."

"Of course you will," Ky said, despite the conviction that Jen's best in the matter of organizing receptions and office staff was not going to be meaningful in this crisis. She watched as Jen moved carefully away from her and over to Marek. His nod to Jen was cordial, but he was watching Ky.

"Ready?" he asked. "I'll give you *Go* when we're at the best part of the wave. Grab on hard when you get to the raft."

Ky moved to the hatch. The weather had not improved; wind blew harder, and the distant land had disappeared in rain and windblown spume.

"Go!" Marek said. Ky threw herself onto the slide, startled at the feel of the water shifting and heaving underneath as she slid down. The wet wind felt icy cold; her face stiffened under it. But she smacked safely into the raft, grabbing the ropes just below the entrance, and struggled to get her feet on the rope ladder. Hands from above grabbed her p-suit, pulling her up and finally over the inflated side into the raft. She rolled over, pushed herself back to the side, and looked around. The canopy was up, the struts firm, holding even when spray landed on it. The raft floor was already wet, from the water people had brought in with them, and someone had thrown up; she could smell it from here.

Across from her, one of the spare rafts in its container was lashed firmly to that side, holding it down, but the people in this raft were clustered too near the entrance along with the extra supplies. They stared at her, some pale, clearly nauseated. Her implant provided names, ratings, and a home location, but no more. "Spread out," she said. They'd been told that, while still in the module, several times. "Take some of these supplies with you. Weigh down the perimeter." After a moment, they did so.

She remembered her own first time in a life raft, on a day out sailing with her father. It had been warm, the sun pouring down making the raft fabric hot enough to burn. Still, she'd thought it was fun, that first time, something new, an adventure. Nothing like this; she lurched to the side as a wave heaved them up, higher than the shuttle hatch, and their tether dragged them back down.

Out the canopy opening she got her first good look at the passenger module. It was three-quarters the length of the whole shuttle and half as tall, riding on six long bright-orange, sausage-like inflated tubes, each larger than one of the rafts. She couldn't tell if all were equally inflated, because the module leaned one way and another as the waves passed underneath. She could see Marek in the hatch, Jen beside him, and others moving around.

Even with one raft already in the water, it seemed to take a very long time before the next raft launched. Ky watched what she could see through the hatch for a short time, then turned back to those in her own raft. Her implant provided the names: Staff Sergeant Kurin, Sergeants Cosper and McLenard, Corporals Lakhani, Yamini, and Inyatta. Tech Betange, who was going on compassionate leave, Gurton and Kamat, both Specialists, and Ennisay, Private. Frightened faces looked back at her, uncertain.

They needed something to do. So did she; what was next? *Always have a rescue ring ready to throw, and a spare handy.* Another of her father's rules. Kurin and Cosper were each in easy reach of a rescue ring. "Staff Sergeant Kurin, pass me that ring to your left. And Sergeant Cosper, pass me that one to your left," she said. She tucked the first one into the rim pocket directly behind the canopy opening, and made its line fast to the grabon just left of the ladder outside, ignoring the cold water splashing her face as the raft bobbed and tugged on its line.

Next task? *Have a line made fast, ready to throw to another vessel.* Where was a line? Fatter than the rim pocket, a storage compartment bulged out. She felt for an opening, then pulled it free. Inside were several coiled lines, labeled with lengths from ten to thirty meters. She chose a ten-meter and lashed one end to the grabon to the right of the ladder. She could use that to connect the two rafts together.

Next? *Attach a sea anchor to one rescue ring, in case of drift; it gives the person in the water more time to get to it.*

"We need a spare sea anchor," she said, and explained what she wanted to do.

Kurin nodded at once. "Yes, sir. Everyone look in the storage spaces nearest you. It may look like a canvas bucket—" She looked back at Ky.

"We can use a canvas bucket if there's not a spare," Ky said. Sergeant Cosper was already rummaging in the storage bag next to him, and urging those nearest him to hurry.

Corporal Lakhani found one first and said, "Here's a sea anchor, sir." He handed it to Gurton, sitting next to him, and the others handed it around to Ky. It already had a line attached to the handle and a thinner line to the bottom; she gave thanks for the raft's supplier. She lashed the sea anchor's line to a third rescue ring.

"Admiral!" Marek yelled from the hatch.

She turned around and peered out from the canopy entrance.

"Ready to launch number two," he said. "Letting out your tether to make room for it."

Ky raised her hand. He loosened their mooring line, bracing himself, as the raft drifted downwind, opening a gap of water between the module's flotation and itself. Then he made it fast again. Another raft's container moved into position in the hatch, tipped over the edge, and started down; Marek yanked the line attached to it, and it popped free, inflating almost instantly, floating when it hit the water. The canopy came up a moment later.

"Now!" he yelled, and one by one those waiting in line at the hatch slid down, bumped into it, grabbed hold, and clambered aboard. Next came the spare raft container, wrestled aboard with difficulty, then the wounded Corporal Barash with her splinted arm, then the bodies, and finally Jen. That raft steadied in the water as weight came into it and the passengers spread around its perimeter.

"Admiral!" Marek called again. "We need a line from one raft to the other." He was letting the line to the other raft out slowly; the wind pushed that raft closer to Ky's. Ky threw the line she had prepared downwind into the canopy opening of the other raft, where Sergeant Chok caught it and hauled it in. The two rafts swung together.

"Make it fast," Ky said into the other raft. She kept an eye on Marek, in the hatch. "Don't let it slip—we need to stay together." Chok signaled when he'd done so. Then she signaled Marek.

He let loose the second raft's tether and slowly reeled in the first raft's line until both rafts reached the bottom of the slide. Ky wrapped the end of the mooring line around her hand. Marek had unclipped the single mooring line from the bracket just inside the module hatch, wrapping it around a cleat for a little help in reeling in the raft. Now, as the raft bumped into the bottom of the slide, he made a loop in the end of that line, then lifted it to put it over his head.

Just as he did, one of the forward flotation sausages burst with a loud bang and whoosh. The module lurched, leaning toward them. Then a second one blew, on the other side. The module nose slammed into a wave, sending a large splash downwind, toward the slide and raft. Marek stumbled, fell out the hatch onto the slide, and tumbled down it. Through a faceful of water Ky saw the loop of rope flying through the air, blown by the wind away from Marek.

Instantly, the rafts drifted away from the slide, rotating in the swirl of water from the splash. Ky had just time to see Marek hit the water meters short of the raft, when the raft rotated so she could not see him. "Hold on to my legs!" she said and leaned out, trying to keep an eye on him. Someone grabbed her ankles; the raft swung back and she could just see him, now swimming determinedly toward the raft, but the two rafts, their canopies acting like sails, moved faster than he could. Behind him, the passenger module dipped lower and lower, lifting its aft flotation bags out of the water.

Only one thing to do—connect line to line, hoping to leave enough trailing behind for Marek to grab. As it was, the mooring line did him no good; she'd have to make it longer, and make it move slower than the rafts with the slack in it. Ky reeled in the mooring line as fast as she could, coiling as it came, then took the end of the spare rescue ring's line and threw a fisherman's knot to join them, tugging it into place, mentally thanking her father for all those boring knot drills he'd insisted on.

She tossed the rescue ring into the face of the next wave. The bucket of the sea anchor she'd attached to it earlier filled instantly, pulling the ring under briefly, but she saw it rise to the surface again as the line uncoiled between it and the raft. The wave lifted the raft;

Ky spotted Marek and yelled into the wind, though she knew he might not hear.

"Ring. Swim to it!"

He lifted his head, got a faceful of water, then came up and looked again as a wave lifted him. Ky pointed. He swam on, now aiming more for the ring. The raft moved faster, but hadn't yet used up the extra line. Wind and waves were pushing Marek the right direction, if only he could get to the ring before the rafts pulled it away. Coil after coil of line slid out. Ky leaned out farther, as the wind turned the linked rafts again, to keep an eye on him.

He was gaining on the ring, still losing on the rafts—would he make it in time? Not without still more line. She could leave the other rescue ring still attached to the grabon, but she would have to risk untying the mooring line so she could tie that line to the ring. Her hands were stiffening with cold; she took extra care, wrapping the mooring line elbow-to-hand several times before untying it from the raft, and struggling to make the right connection to the ring. Risky. Her father would not have approved, but she had no choice. She used her teeth to pull the line snug; her hands were too cold. And tossed the second ring out the canopy. She rubbed her hands hard and ducked her head back inside for a moment, blinking the stinging ocean water out of her eyes.

"Don't let go," she said to those still holding her ankles. "There's more to do."

"Would this help, Admiral?" Kurin asked, holding up a carabiner.

"Yes, thanks," Ky said. She took it, hooked it into one of the attachments on her suit, then clipped into the nearest grabon. If she fell, she'd get wet but be dragged along with the raft. The wind blew cold spray in her face, but she could see well enough to spot Marek only a meter from the first ring, though the spare line she'd thrown was almost extended and his swimming less coordinated.

Then he caught the ring, got an arm through it. A wave came down on him; she held her breath until she saw him come up through it, still clinging to the ring, now with both arms through. He started trying to swim, kicking his legs, but sluggishly. Ky took a firm grip on the line and slid back into the raft. The canopy entrance was reinforced but she laid a coil of rope on it before she started hauling in, as steadily as she could, given the waves and wind. The line dripped as it came into the life raft. She glanced back; the puddle of seawater and vomit in the middle was growing.

"Staff Sergeant, there should be a hand-pump in one of the sidewall pockets; we need to get that water out of here."

"Yes, sir," Kurin said. "All of you—check the pockets nearest you. When you find it, pass it around to me. Admiral, is it safe for me to come assist in pulling him nearer?"

"Yes, Staff. Good idea. Done this before?"

"No, sir."

"We want a steady, even pull, no jerks that might break his grip on the ring." Ky looked outside again. The line was still attached to the first ring—she couldn't quite see—no, there was the second ring, with Marek's orange p-suit sticking out of it. His arms moved, but not very effectively. If his suit had leaked, he'd be wet and chilling rapidly. Even if it hadn't, he looked exhausted. She nodded to Kurin, who took hold and adjusted to Ky's movement. That was easier. Meter after meter of wet line added to the water inside the raft, though she could hear the *whish-grunt, whish-grunt* of the pump, and water spurted out the slender hose beside her. She looked to see who was working it. Sergeant Cosper. "Good work, Sergeant," she said over her shoulder.

She and Kurin had a rhythm now. Ten meters, twenty, thirty. In came the nearest rescue ring. Ten meters more and twenty and thirty and more of the mooring line. The knot she had thrown came under her hand; she could see Marek's orange suit clearly now, even in the blowing spray and cold rain. His face looked grayish in the dimming light; had he been poisoned, too? He hadn't looked sick at all in the shuttle. They kept pulling, hand over hand, and finally he was bobbing in the water only a meter away, his lips purple-gray. Toxin? Or cold? No way to tell until they got him into the raft.

Ky pulled him right up to the raft. "Master Sergeant, how are you?"

"C-cold." His voice was barely audible over the noise of the sea and the rafts. "C-ca-can't—swim—any—"

He wouldn't be able to get himself into the raft, either, she could tell. She looked back into it, chose the two tallest of its occupants, and pointed to them. "Cosper and McLenard: need you to help pull Master Sergeant Marek inside. He's too cold to climb the ladder. The rest of you, space yourselves around the far side of the raft to keep it weighted evenly."

Ky's hands, even in gloves, were so stiff with cold that she could do nothing but hold on to the line. When the two men came up beside her, she explained what they would have to do: lift Marek's full weight out of the water and into the raft.

"We're in the way, Admiral," Kurin said. "Let me help you get your suit free."

"Thanks. I should have thought of that."

When she was free, she and Kurin moved away from the entrance. At first Ky couldn't unclench her hands from the line she held, and watched Cosper and McLenard struggling with Marek and the raft's erratic movements. Finally they pulled Marek in, along with enough water to more than refill the puddle in the raft's center. "Close it up," she said; one of the men yanked on the zipper string of the canopy hatch and it closed; the relief from wind-blown spray made it seem warm. Ky struggled with her hands, blowing on them, and finally pried them off the line. She looked at Marek—his suit had a long gash on the sleeve nearest her, and another on the leg. He must have caught it on something as he fell out of the module hatch. Water ran out of his suit.

"Keep that pump going," Kurin said. "We need to get this place as dry as possible." Ky saw her point to one of the others—Corporal Lakhani, her implant informed her.

Marek lay, eyes closed, his head up on Sergeant Cosper's knees as the sergeant wrestled the rescue ring off him. Across the raft Corporal Lakhani vomited again, and immediately two more gasped and did the same. Ky ignored the stench, struggling to make her stiff fingers work. "We need to get Marek out of that." Staff Sergeant Kurin took over, unfastening the clasps down Marek's chest. Underneath, his uniform was soaked; Ky laid a hand on his chest; his heart thudded against her hand.

"We should strip him down and dry him," Cosper said. He pulled the tab on Marek's uniform, and laid his fingers against Marek's neck as if he knew what he was doing. "Got a pulse. Regular enough."

"Sir, we found these blankets—" Specialist Gurton handed Ky two, blue on one side, green on the other. "Directions say the blue side goes on a wet person."

"Good," Ky said. "Thank you; that should help." Kurin and Cosper stripped off Marek's wet clothes and wrapped him in the blankets.

Now that all the survivors were aboard one of the rafts, Ky leaned back against the sidewall and tried to think what to do next, but her mind moved as sluggishly as her cold fingers. It had happened so fast: they had been dry, warm, in comfortable seats, expecting to land. And now they were being thrown around by mountainous waves, in cold that sapped strength and energy. In the dim light, the faces of most of the others looked dazed, confused, frightened.

Although sheltered from the direct blast of the wind, spray, and rain, she felt every movement of the raft under her as it rose and fell with the waves passing under it, jerking a little side-to-side as its tether to the other raft, and its own sea anchors, shifted the two rafts' positions. The wind howled; rain hammered the canopy, and occasionally the raft smacked loudly onto a wave.

Through the canopy windows, smeared with water, she saw blurred glimpses of waves and sky, sky and waves. *What can you do right now to make things better?* Her father's voice, in memory. What was the order her father had taught her in case of capsizing at sea? Raft—they'd accomplished that. Seal the canopy—they'd done that. Stop, take stock, think. She was doing that. Except she hadn't gotten past *stop*.

Take stock: she knew they had no communications devices or

transponders, but what did they have, besides the life rings, lines, and blankets they'd found so far? *You can't use it if you don't know you've got it,* her father had said. Which in his boat had meant every child knowing everything in the life raft and where it was stored.

Ky raised her voice over the noise of the storm. "We need to inventory our supplies," she said. Cosper, Kurin, and Yamini looked up at once. "We found the pump and the survival blankets, and I know you didn't find any nav gear or comunits—what else do we have?"

"There's the standard survival manual," Kurin said. "It's right— here." She pulled it from its pocket. "It's got a list of supplies; there's a stylus for checking them off."

"Good," Ky said. "Does it have a diagram with locations, too?"

"Yes, sir. Starting dextral from its own pocket. R-1 to R-4 contain ration packs, then R-5 to R-10 contain drinking water." Kurin turned, opened the next pocket, and reported. "One unbroken pack, twenty individual rations, correct." The next two pockets also held rations. In a few minutes, as Kurin directed the others which pockets to examine, they had located all their supplies: food enough for twenty for thirty days, potable water for five days, a hand-pumped desalinator to convert seawater to potable water, eight more survival blankets, fishing lines and hooks, eight plastic paddles, and more items than Ky remembered from her father's equipment.

"We're in good shape, then, Staff Sergeant."

"Aside from not having any way to tell where we are or contact those who should be looking for us," Sergeant Cosper said. "Someone should be court-martialed for that."

"I'm sure they will be," Ky said, "assuming we can survive to complain, and the guilty party can be found. In the meantime, we're alive, the rafts are floating, and we have air, water, and food."

"It's not enough!" Corporal Lakhani said. "What if they never find us? Or not before the food runs out? We could starve—or freeze—"

"That's enough, Corporal," Kurin said. "The admiral's right: for now, we're in good shape, considering what happened. Keep pumping until the water's gone."

"Do all of you know one another already?" Ky asked.

"No, sir," Kurin said. "Corporal Inyatta and I served together on Myseni Reef, so I know her by sight, but we weren't in the same assignments." Others were shaking their heads as well.

"Time for more than handshakes and names, then," Ky said. "You know my name; I spent most of my childhood on Corleigh. Did some sailing with my father and brothers, including a few overnights, and practiced in a life raft a lot smaller than this one." She glanced at Marek, who seemed to be dozing; his color was better, but she didn't disturb him. "What about you, Staff Sergeant?"

"Jana Kurin, from Seelindi, the second largest island in the Mandan Reef chain. My family has a big farm; we grow rice and vegetables, about fifty hectares in fruit trees. We export produce out of Mandan Home over to the mainland. But like all the island kids, I learned to sail, paddle a cane raft, fish. My other uncle is a fisher, and so are my cousins." Kurin sounded calm and confident now, and Ky was sure she'd be an asset.

"I'm from Arland," Sergeant Cosper said. "Hautvidor, very modern city, where everyone has a good work ethic. The mountains make us healthy, that and a healthy lifestyle. Everyone spends time outdoors, year-round. If we want to survive, we must all commit to a rigorous exercise program, starting today. I have training as a physical fitness instructor, as well as a secondary tag as first responder."

Arland, Ky knew, had been one of the original nation-states, and a major factor in the war Grace Vatta fought. Cosper was tall, clearly very fit, and as clearly proud of it. Though he had been polite so far, his glances at her made it clear he thought of her as a small woman in need of toughening up.

One by one, the others offered bits of personal history— background that might be useful in this situation, or lack of it; what their military specialties had been. Sergeant McLenard, one of the stewards in the aft cabin, had spent the past seven years assigned to shuttle duty. Married, with three children, he had no deep-space or combat experience. Corporal Lakhani quit pumping long enough to say his father ran a hardware store in a small town three hundred kilometers from Port Major. Corporal Yamini confirmed Ky's guess that he was related somehow to Commander Yamini ("He's my second cousin") who had served with Ky in the recent war.

All of them seemed alert now, listening to one another—better than the initial blankness. Master Sergeant Marek pulled himself up to sitting before all the others had finished.

"I'm from the west coast of Arland, Sogrun," he said. "Twenty-five years in, communications specialist. Just in from duty on one of the big satellites."

"Glad you're feeling better, Master Sergeant," Ky said.

"I'm fine now. Don't worry—I'm not that old."

She hadn't meant to imply he had been hypothermic because he was old. "Your suit had rips in both arm and leg. We can't fully repair it, but we did find rolls of repair tape that should hold for a while."

"Thank you, Admiral," he said. "I think—" He was interrupted by someone yelling from outside.

CHAPTER FIVE

SLOTTER KEY
DAY 1

Ky slithered over to the canopy opening, unfastened it, and looked out; cold rain stung her face. Her aide was staring out a narrow opening in the other raft's canopy. "Admiral! What am I supposed to *do*? I don't know any of these people and—and I don't have the right training for this! They're just—just sitting there, staring at me and there's water in the bottom of the raft, and—"

"You've got some good people there, Commander Bentik. Tech Lundin—is she caring for the injured?" Best to be formal when a Cascadian was upset. Jen did not look any less upset.

"*I don't know what to do*," she said again, her voice rising to a wail. Behind her, Ky caught a glimpse of another face, looking worried. With Bentik acting and sounding terrified, no wonder.

"Maybe I can calm things," Marek said from behind her. "Would you like me to switch to that raft and help her out? She is a stranger to Slotter Key, after all."

Ky managed not to snap *I know that* at him; it was a good idea if he could manage it, but she didn't want to risk his falling into the water again. "Thank you, Master Sergeant, that's a good idea. Get someone to tape up your suit, and we'll hook in a safety line for you." To her aide she said, "I'll send you Master Sergeant Marek; he's been through the training and will help you out. I still think it's important to have an officer in each raft."

"Of course it is," Jen said, scowling now. "It would be even better if I were in their chain of command. Tell me when he's coming over and I'll open the canopy for him." She jerked it closed before Ky could answer. Ky sighed and looked around. Marek was taping up the rip in the arm, and Kurin was taping the one in the leg. In a few minutes, as Marek wrung out his wet uniform and put it back on, wincing at the damp chill, Kurin finished taping all the gashes. Marek kept one of the blankets, folding it around him as he worked his way into the survival suit and fastened it. Then he scooted over to the hatch and unfastened it. Ky clipped him in to the safety line she'd left attached to the outer cleat, and he called across to the other raft.

"Commander Bentik—I'm ready to board now."

The other hatch opened, this time with Staff Sergeant Vispersen's face visible. Vispersen reached out; he and Marek clasped arms and Marek slid from raft to raft with only one foot hitting the water as another wave passed beneath them. Marek turned around and looked at Ky as he unclipped the safety line and tossed it back to her. "Don't worry, Admiral; I can handle the situation over here. Call if you need me." He gave her a brief, tight smile then fastened the canopy hatch again; Ky did the same on her side.

Everyone in her raft was watching her now. Kurin put the mending tape back in its case, sealed the case, and put it away.

"Orders, sir?" Kurin said.

"For now," Ky said, "all we have to do is keep the rafts afloat." Tentative grins from some; others—Kurin, Cosper, McLenard, Yamini, Inyatta—nodded, clearly focused on what she was saying. "Let's finish the introductions while it's still light enough to see faces. Then

Staff Sergeant Kurin and I will set up a schedule for meals, raft maintenance and hygiene, and a regular on–off watch rotation. I'm sure Master Sergeant Marek and Commander Bentik will do the same in the other raft."

"Yes, sir."

Tech Betange spoke next, in a monotone, looking down. "Space drive technician. I'm—my parents were killed—I'm going home to arrange something for my brothers and sisters. I'm the oldest. I—I need to be there!" He looked up for a moment. "If I—if we die, they'll have nobody."

"We will survive," Ky said. "You will get back to them. We just have to be smart and careful."

"You're sure?"

"We're breathing air and not water, we have supplies, and nobody's shooting at us. To me, that says survival is possible. I intend *all* of us to make it home."

He relaxed a little, sagging back against the side of the raft.

"Specialist Gurton?"

Gurton looked older than most of them, a broad-faced woman with a slightly crooked smile. "Twelve years, started in shuttle maintenance but switched to food service. If you can find us a stove, Admiral, I'll cook anything we can eat."

"Fish?"

"Yes, sir. But I do need a stove."

"When we get to land," Ky said. "Specialist Kamat?"

Kamat had green eyes, startling against her dark face. "Six years in, Admiral, space drive maintenance, rated for every class of deepspace ship Spaceforce has. I have an engineering degree from Arland University, too. Family's been in some tech field for several generations, so it comes naturally, but they're nearly all civilians. My aunties kept saying, *What's a pretty girl like you doing going into the military?*"

"I had an aunt like that," Ky said. "But she didn't call me pretty. I have a cousin who is the family beauty."

"My family does that," Corporal Inyatta said. She had seemed quiet, almost withdrawn, but now looked interested. "Everyone's got a role: the smart one, the quick one, the athletic one. We're farmers; we grow rice, vegetables, fruit trees, and we have chickens and pigs. By the time I was seven, they'd decided my gift was with chickens. I didn't want to spend my life with chickens."

Private Ennisay was the last to speak. Just out of recruit training, only eighteen years old, he was the youngest and least experienced, but the most eager to talk. And talk. Finally, as he was extending his family tree in all directions, Ky broke in.

"Save some stories for later, Private. We've got a long way to go and there will be time." She looked over at Kurin. "Staff Sergeant, issue a ration pack and water to everyone. If you're hungry, eat a few bites now. Then—did the first-aid kit have seasick patches or pills?"

"I'll check," Yamini said.

"Fit people with a good mental attitude do not become seasick," Sergeant Cosper said. He was sitting as bolt-upright as anyone could in a raft in high seas.

"If Medical agreed with you, they wouldn't issue meds to prevent it," Ky said. His attitude was not going to help.

"Here they are, sir," Yamini said, holding up a packet. "Twelve patches in this one, and there are more packets."

"Everyone who hasn't had a patch since we undocked, apply one now," Ky said. "Whether you think you need it or not—what if we get worse weather?"

Cosper opened his mouth, but shut it again and applied a patch when the packet came around to him.

In another hour, by her implant, her raft's occupants were all looking more comfortable, and each had a day's ration of food and water in hand or tucked in one of the side pockets. Kurin had set up a rotation for pumping out the puddle, and the raft was as dry as it could be in the circumstances. All the gear had been either returned to the storage pockets or lashed down safely. Ky wished they had a way to communicate with the other raft that didn't require opening the canopy hatches and letting in more spray and rain, but with both Lundin the medical tech and Master Sergeant Marek over there, they should do as well as her raft was.

"Do you know where we are?" Tech Betange asked.

"Generally, yes. But not an exact location. I'd need to be able to tag a satellite for that, and my skullphone's as dead as anyone else's. I had a message on it during descent, but it cut off suddenly."

"Message from Spaceforce?"

"No, from my flagship. When they saw a severe course deviation, they launched a shuttle to come to our aid. But since they probably lost the signal as we went into the cloud cover and neared the surface, they wouldn't have had eyes on us when we landed."

He nodded, eyes downcast.

"But knowing Captain Pordre—my flag captain—he won't quit." She looked around at the others. They were all watching her. "Spaceforce will be looking for us. Space Defense Force—my flagship—will be looking for us. But we'll improve the odds by getting ourselves to land, feeding ourselves from the sea, making shelter. We won't be lounging around like drunken sailors on holiday until they find us." A few grinned; most did not.

"But there's nothing nearby but Miksland and it's nothing but rock and ice," Ennisay said. "It's a—"

"Terraforming failure. I know. That's what I was taught in school. Barren and worthless. On the other hand, it's not as barren as deep space. Land has advantages over ocean."

Someone laughed. "The raft can't sink?"

"Among other things." Ky realized she could not see faces clearly now; it was getting dark already. "Staff Sergeant, it's been a long day already. You had me first on the watch-list, didn't you?"

"Yes, sir. My implant has it ten ticks to the hour. Start then?"

"Right." Ky waited until her implant hit the mark then formally took on the watch. The others settled down to rest as best they could.

Twelve minutes into her watch, she heard a roar from outside. Her first panicked thought was a ship bearing down on them, but then the squall hit, the wind shoving the two rafts into a sickening whirl.

It was almost night-dark inside the canopy; Ky could not see the others, or hear them for the noise outside. Rain and spray both pounded on the canopy, a tattoo almost as loud as the wind. Someone let out a yelp.

Then she heard Kurin yelling: "Lie beside the sidewall—*beside*! Hold it down!"

Ky twisted, stretching herself along the sidewall as best she could. The raft tilted on a steeper wave, and her legs slid downslope. At the bottom of the trough, it tilted up again, pushing her back against the sidewall. The raft pinwheeled when it came into the wind again; she wondered how the other raft fared, but it would have been stupid to open the canopy hatch and look.

After a few minutes that squall passed, but the seas were higher, steeper. In the relative silence, Ky shouted across to the other raft. "All right?"

"All right!" came back in Marek's deep voice.

Then the main storm hit. Howling wind, spray battering the canopy, steep irregular seas. Ky hung on to the grabons, trying to convince herself that these rafts had been rated for such situations, trying not to imagine what the seas really looked like. When her watch ended, and Betange took over, she could not rest, and was sure no one else could. Through the dark hours, each one feeling longer than the one before, the watch changed as Kurin kept them to the original schedule. Ky was thankful for Kurin's initiative and steadiness; she was sure to need that help in the days to come.

CHAPTER SIX

NEXUS II, INTERSTELLAR COMMUNICATIONS HEADQUARTERS
DAY 2

Rafael Dunbarger, CEO of InterStellar Communications, ignored the first ping of his implant, the header ADMIRAL VATTA LATEST. That would be confirmation of Ky's safe arrival at Slotter Key, no doubt, and he had to finish his analysis for the next day's Board meeting. A second ping followed the first, the same sound, and then a third, plus a ping to pick up a private message.

What could Ky be up to now? Rafe flicked on the first news bulletin in the stack.

GRAND ADMIRAL VATTA PRESUMED DEAD IN SHUTTLE CRASH.

What? Rafe flicked the next, from Slotter Key's Central News Bureau.

SLOTTER KEY TRAGEDY: COMMANDANT SPACEFORCE ACADEMY PRESUMED LOST IN SHUTTLE CRASH; GRAND ADMIRAL VATTA ALSO ABOARD.

Rafe felt light-headed. This had to be a mistake, some kind of joke. He called up the private message. Stella Vatta, from Slotter Key.

Rafe. The shuttle Ky was on went down in the ocean. We think it was sabotaged. We don't know if she survived. There's nothing you can do; don't come—there's nothing you could do here, either. I'll send word as soon as I know anything. It will be on the news soon; I wanted you to know first.

He forced a deep breath, then another. It was real then. Stella would not lie to him, not about this. It felt . . . strange. *He* felt strange. He'd convinced himself before that Ky was dead, but—no. Not this time. He got up, feeling shaky, and went to his office door to speak to his assistant. "Emil. No interruptions until I say."

"Ser, I just saw a news bulletin—"

"I know. I will be extremely busy for a little while. Hold all calls and visitors, even Penny."

"Yes, Ser."

Rafe locked the door, unplugged his desk communications, and set the room security as high as it would go. Then he took off the wristband he carried all the time, pulled out the cable to his implanted ansible, plugged it into the desk power supply, and checked the voltage. Exactly what it should be. He plugged the other end into his implant's recharge socket.

The unpleasant smell that accompanied the implant ansible connection made him wrinkle his nose, even though the smell's source wasn't outside, but inside. Relief flooded him; she was alive. She had to be alive, because her implant ansible was there, functional. The reports had been wrong. But why?

The connection existed, but could not be used unless she plugged into an external power source. She might be aware of the smell and do so, though she might be where that was not possible. Or she might not smell anything, especially not if some other strong smell existed in her environment. He had no idea what Slotter Key smelled like. He tried to send the contact code they'd established, informing her that he was powered up, but in fifteen minutes nothing about the signal changed.

She was alive. A shuttle crash into the ocean—that would have killed her, so the reports must be wrong. With some reluctance, he unplugged from his implant, removed the cable from the desk power, and wrapped it back into the wristband, sealing it in. He opened the most recent of the news reports (there were nine in the queue now) and read it all. Shuttle loss of power and control. Shuttle observed descending, off course, by a Space Defense Force shuttle from the Space Defense Force cruiser—Admiral Vatta's flagship. Presumed impact location in the southern ocean, poleward of an uninhabited continent. Weather conditions foul. Chance of survival minimal. Twenty-four passengers and four crew, names withheld pending notification of families on Slotter Key. Brief bios of the Commandant and Ky, both more public figures, with the comment that Ky was visiting her home planet for the first time since leaving the Academy. No details on the reasons for that, or even that she wasn't a graduate. His attention went back to the critical detail: chance of survival minimal.

But not zero. And Ky had survived one disaster after another; she would, he knew, fight hard to survive in this, given that she was alive. And she was; he knew it.

But for how long? He shook that away. He had work to do here; he could not be there—not today anyway—and Stella was right that he could not do anything to help from here. He unlocked his door and went out to speak to Emil. "I'm working on the report to the Board for tomorrow. Screen calls as usual, please."

"Do you know any more?"

"No. Just that she was in a shuttle that went down. Was observed going down by her flagship. Bad weather, no chance of quick rescue. Her family messaged me; they don't think I can be of any assistance."

"I'm sorry, Ser."

"She's a very resourceful person, Emil. If anyone can survive it, she will." Unless. Unless any or all of the many things he could think of all too easily. He shoved that aside. "I'd best get back to work," he said, and went into his office again, closing the door. He left the desk communications unplugged—no one was going to get in without Emil's filtering—and forced himself back to the job he didn't like anyway.

He was down to the last page when Emil knocked on the door. "Ser, it's the government."

In that tone of voice it could be only the Premier. Rafe allowed himself a gusty sigh before fixing his face and voice into an acceptable neutrality. "Here, or on the com?"

"He wants you to come to his office. Soonest possible. And Ambassador Veniers has called, wants to speak to you. I have him on right now."

"I'll speak to him; if the Premier calls, tell him I'm talking with the ambassador and will call him when I can."

Abram Veniers, Moscoe Confederation, knew both Ky and Stella Vatta, and might have heard something more. Rafe picked up his own earpiece. "Yes, Ser Ambassador?"

"You have heard about the tragedy, of course," Veniers said.

"Yes, but few details yet. May I ask if you have any more than the newsvids?"

"No, Ser Dunbarger, I do not, alas, know more than the newsvids at this time. Since Sera Vatta is on Slotter Key and I do not have her private code, I was hoping, perhaps you—you have known the Vattas longer than I—it is a very great setback for the Space Defense Force, of course, and also I think to Vatta interests."

"All I know is what I've heard, that the shuttle went down in an ocean, near an uninhabited continent in bad weather."

"Ah, yes. Well. If you permit, Ser, I make a formal request that ISC supply my office with the latest information you may receive, whatever that may be, concerning this matter. I have received questions from my government, which as you know presently has about half of Space Defense Force's ships in its territory. I presume those questions, or some of them, came from SDF, because if an issue should come up and the Grand Admiral be delayed past the time she specified, someone must—there must be a clear order of command, you see." A pause, then, "Not that anyone is blaming the Grand Admiral, of course. It was not, if I understand correctly, an SDF shuttle that went down."

"No, it was a Slotter Key Spaceforce shuttle," Rafe said. "I assure you, Ser, that I do not know any more than I have told you. The ansibles at Slotter Key are functional; I would think you—or any captain in SDF's fleet, at least—could contact the Admiral's flagship for more information."

"You have not done so?"

"No, Ser, I have not. I do not want to interrupt whatever emergency procedures they're using, distract them."

"But you—and the admiral—"

"Ser, with all due respect, in an emergency these personal matters are inappropriate. I quite understand why your government—and mine: the Premier will be my next call—have an interest in this—" He would not call it a tragedy. Not yet, while she lived. "This event," he said. "And Space Defense Force, of course, which has done so much for all of us. If there is assistance that ISC can give, be assured that we will give it."

Veniers bowed and the screen blanked. Rafe looked at the time display on his desk, the numbers moving tenth of a second by a tenth of a second, and in every one of those . . . Ky and the others were in the water. Cold water. He could not escape the memory of his father's captivity, the blurred image on the infrared, the false color showing by its changes his deepening hypothermia. His right hand moved to his left wrist, to unfasten the power cable for the cranial ansible yet again, but he made himself stop. He could do nothing now. He had other calls to make, demands only he could meet. He signaled Emil. "Get me the Premier," he said. "I'm ready to talk to him."

Two hours later, Rafe was back in his office, fuming. He had kept his temper, with great difficulty, but really—why did every older man with power on Nexus continue to go on about Vatta influence and distrust the woman who had saved the planet from destruction? Yes, Ky's great-aunt was Rector of Defense on Slotter Key, and yes, Stella Vatta ran both Vatta Transport and the new Vatta Industries from Cascadia, and yes, her mother ran Vatta affairs on Slotter Key, but that did not mean they—or any of the Vattas—wanted to conquer the Moscoe Confederation or Nexus, let alone the whole universe. The man who had spread those rumors first had been a sociopath, a clever criminal—why, now that everyone knew about him, did they still believe his lies?

The Board meeting an hour later ruffled him all over again. Like the Premier, the Board members as a whole still thought of Vattas as dangerous. It was unreasonable how fast Stella had managed to get Vatta Transport on its feet. Toby's technical brilliance was uncanny, unbelievable: no boy could really have done what he did without some other adult geniuses guiding him. "At least now," Vaclav Box said, tapping Rafe's shoulder on his way out of the room after the meeting closed, "we shan't have to worry about you marrying into that family."

"Because you're sure she's dead," Rafe said. He could feel his face stiffening in a rush of anger, and tried to force a smile. What right had they to worry about, let alone consider governing, his choice of a wife—if he and Ky ever got that far, which they had not.

"You're not? Be reasonable, Rafael. A shuttle crash into an icy ocean? Nobody survives that. Only if they'd had rescue immediately, maybe then—" He shook his head. "Accept it, grieve, and get over it. You need a wife, and heirs. Your lovely sister needs to marry again, have some babies. Admiral Vatta saved us all in the war, but she's not the sort of woman to settle down and make anyone a good wife." Box turned away. "You'll get over this, Rafael. You're a good son."

He was not a good son. He had been labeled a bad son, a renegade, and he had lived into that label with gusto for years. He watched Box and the others chat on their way down the hall to the elevators, the weight of ISC heavy on his shoulders. It was one thing to come in at a crisis and take over. Crises were, in some way, fun. But this . . . he foresaw year after year of nursing ISC back to health, always less powerful than it had been, always condescended to by men who had worked with his father.

He should be on his way to Slotter Key now, despite what Stella said. He should be spending his time and his wits finding Ky, rescuing Ky, and then . . . that vacation they'd both wanted? He wondered if that would ever happen, and if it did . . . what would it mean?

CHAPTER SEVEN

SLOTTER KEY, OKLANDAN
DAY 2

When the first dim light seeped through the canopy, the storm still raged. Ky felt bruised all over, and what little she could see of the others looked as bad as she felt. Her mouth was dry and tasted foul; she took a sip of water that did not help much, and watched the puddle slide back and forth and around—then wished she hadn't. Her seasick meds must be wearing off. Staff Sergeant Kurin appeared to be asleep, curled on her side. Sergeant Cosper, who had the watch that hour, had fastened an elastic cord to one of the grabons and was exercising. Ky blinked; that would not have occurred to her.

He opened his mouth, said something she couldn't hear for the howl of another gust of wind, then shrugged and went on with his exercises. Ky gave him points for initiative. Her implant dinged; it was her turn to take the watch again. Kurin moved, opened her eyes, and caught Ky's gaze. Ky gave her a thumbs-up with one hand, the other still firmly holding the grabon. Sergeant Cosper, still exercising his free arm, looked at her and when she nodded at him, closed his eyes and went right on.

Ky thought of checking with the other raft, but Marek would call if he had a problem and needed her. She wondered how Jen was getting along with Marek. Surely he had had experience with difficult officers before. Her hour wore on, the light only slightly brighter and the violence of the storm unabated. She imagined the rafts being blown right past Miksland, around and around the empty ocean, stuck in the same storm until they froze or starved. Storms passed over ships drifting at sea; if they didn't sink, they would live out the storm and be somewhere else.

Late in the day, the light already dimming, the wind's roar eased, and though rain or spray still fell on the canopy, the seas were not as violent. Ky tried to speak; her mouth and throat were dry. She sipped more water from her suit tube and tried again. "Roll call." Eyes opened, faces turned to look at her. "Report any injuries. Betange?"

"Present, no injuries, sir."

One after another they answered, all present, no injuries to report.

"Good. I'm going to check with the other raft." When she had unfastened the hatch and eased it open, they were in a trough, with what looked like great hills of dark water all around. The air felt colder but smelled fresh compared to the interior. The other raft was still there. She called out to Marek.

"Sir, just a moment—"

She could see the movement of the hatch as someone tried to unseal it, and then it opened a slit and Marek's face looked out. "What's your situation, Master Sergeant?"

"All present, Admiral."

"Good. Same here. Maybe tonight we can get some sleep."

"I wanted to ask you—about the deceased—"

"Yes?"

"They're—one came loose of the lashings and was rolling around bumping into people in the storm. And hitting the spare life raft—there's damage, and it bothers people. Very bad for morale, Admiral. Unless there's a chance of rescue today—at least by tomorrow—wouldn't it be better to give them burial at sea?"

"Who was it, Master Sergeant?"

"The pilot, Admiral."

"Do you have him lashed down safely now?"

"We think so, but we thought so before. It's that there's too many of them. Six . . . it's too many."

"It's almost dark; we can't just throw them out like trash. Wait until tomorrow, Master Sergeant. If the storm's past, maybe the sky will clear and someone will get a satellite image—or even a search plane. If not, we'll have daylight to send them on."

"Yes, Admiral." He gave a crisp salute; Ky returned it, then refastened the canopy hatch.

"We still need to set a watch tonight," she said to her raft. Her crew. "But I expect we'll manage to sleep. First, though: congratulations."

"For what?" asked Corporal Lakhani. "All we did was get seasick and scared . . ."

"You did more than that." Ky shook her head at him. "You stayed alive. All of you—" She looked around. "You all did everything necessary to get through the emergency so far, and if you keep doing that, solving one problem at a time, doing the next necessary thing . . . we will make it."

"You really think so?"

"I really think so."

"What's the next necessary thing?" asked Ennisay.

"Suits have limited waste-handling capacity," Ky said. "We need to arrange a better solution."

"In a *raft*?"

"In a raft. Do you want to perch on the sidewall half naked in the cold and fertilize the ocean?" She paused; no one said anything, and she went on. "In the meantime, how many people finished the rations handed out yesterday?" Five hands went up, including her own. "Dehydration and hunger will dull your wits; we should all drink and eat—slowly, with pauses—before sleeping tonight, and we'll assess conditions tomorrow, when it's light."

DAY 3

Ky woke to the sound of voices.

"We could use the survival blankets for a kind of hood around it—"

"I don't see why—"

"Because some of us have to get out of our survival suits and the clothes inside them to use it, that's why."

"It shouldn't matter—"

"It matters to me!"

"And everyone has to strip for some functions."

The raft's motion up and down had eased even more; light inside the canopy was bright enough to recognize the speakers. Sergeant Cosper, Corporal Yamini, Corporal Inyatta. Others were still asleep. Ky sat up, felt water on her face, and looked up. Condensation had beaded on the inside of the canopy, and a small puddle had re-formed in the center of the raft, sliding around as the raft tilted on the waves.

"Good morning," Ky said. "I see you're working that first problem."

"Morning, Admiral. We've got a can, a liner, a seal for the liner—"

"Good work. I see we're also developing internal weather." Ky pointed to the canopy overhead. "Fresh water, if we captured it before it puddled on the floor."

"We have water in the raft supplies," Cosper said.

"Yes, and if we get to land or are picked up in the next thirty days, that's enough. But if we aren't? At the least we should get busy with the desalinators."

"You think it might be more than thirty days?"

"I don't know. We should know more today—if it's clear enough, we can tell how far we are from Miksland and try again to make contact with someone—a satellite, anyway."

Ky slid over and unfastened the hatch, opening it far enough to put her head out. The two rafts were in a trough; on either side was a hill of water at least twice the height of the rafts, dark and smooth as glass. The raft and canopy immediately across from her limited her view to a sideways slice in either direction. When they rose on the next wave Ky could see beyond the crests of the nearest: endless rows of waves under high clouds like a flat pale-gray roof. Far off she saw a darker area, but could not distinguish anything; it looked more like a rain shower than land.

She heard voices inside the other raft, though she could not distinguish what they were saying. "Commander Bentik, what's your situation?"

After a short wait, the other raft's hatch opened and Jen peered out. "Admiral, you're awake."

"Yes, of course," Ky said. "How's your crew?"

"As well as can be expected after that horrible storm, when we don't even know where we are, or if anyone is looking—"

"I'm certain they are," Ky said. "Are there any new injuries?"

"No, Admiral, there are not. But one of the, uh, bodies came loose again and rolled right down on top of me—a *dead* man!—and—" Her eyes filled with tears and her voice shook. "I have never had to—to touch a—a dead person in my entire life, Admiral. It's not—it's not *decent*. Combat troops—they're trained for things like that."

"I'm certain it was a very hard shock for you," Ky said, in what she hoped was a soothing voice. "You have done very well, Commander—"

"Don't patronize me!" Jen went from what had seemed like panic to anger in an instant. "Just because you're used to combat and death—" She stopped as suddenly as she'd started. "Admiral. That was unseemly. My apologies."

"Accepted," Ky said. She couldn't think of anything else to say. What was Jen's problem with dead bodies? These were not, after all, gory. They were just dead. Neatly, tidily dead, at that, enclosed in their survival suits. Was this something else about Cascadian habits that she didn't know?

"But we really cannot keep them. Soon they will . . . you know . . . begin to . . . to become really offensive. And we have all of them in *this* raft. *You* don't have to put up with it."

There was no tactful way to ask if anyone else was as bothered by the bodies as Jen herself. And driving her only other officer to the edge of sanity—if that's what was happening—by forcing her into proximity with the dead bodies endangered them all. She needed Jen to regain stability, to be an asset. The evidence the bodies contained would be lost, but the trade-off was worth it.

"I will need to speak with Master Sergeant Marek," Ky said.

"But you're in command—"

"Yes, but there is an appropriate ceremony," Ky said. "And for that I need information from him."

Jen disappeared from the gap in the hatch, and Marek replaced her. "Yes, Admiral."

"I will be conducting a service when we consign the remains of those killed to the sea. It will be later today. The weather's moderated; it is not an emergency, and we must honor those who died."

"Yes, Admiral. Thank you; some individuals here were becoming upset. How may I assist?"

One by one, the bodies slipped into the cold dark water. Both raft canopies had been partly retracted, and the tether between the rafts lengthened, so everyone could see and hear. Ky spoke the words chosen to be inoffensive to any of the religions on Slotter Key, then named each person as Master Sergeant Marek made sure each descent over the edge of the raft was slow, entering the water with no unseemly splashing.

They had had nothing to weigh the bodies down with. The orange survival suits kept them just afloat, disturbingly like survivors who needed to be hauled in and revived. Ky was sure others had the same urge. It was hard to watch them bob in the waves as the wind caught the rafts' partly open canopies and pushed them on faster than before. Her vision blurred—with the cold wind, she told herself, as the bodies were left behind in death, as they had left life behind.

With the canopies partly open, and the weather less violent, Ky could see Miksland clearly every time they came up from a trough. From the raft, it appeared a solid block of dark red rock rising straight from the sea. No place to land. Surely the whole coast wasn't like that.

"We should paddle while the weather's better," Master Sergeant Marek said. "Get closer. There's bound to be someplace—"

"If we get too close we could end up on the rocks," Ky said. "These rafts wouldn't stand dragging on rock. We need a wide enough gap that the inside's likely to have a safe landing place. For now, we need to close up the canopies again, get out of this wind. And we need to start regular raft maintenance and inventory. Does your desalinator work?"

"We haven't tried it yet. We still have plenty of water in the raft."

"We need to know if it works," Ky said. "And how's your raft for weight distribution without the—"

"We're light, but we were heavier than yours before."

"I'm setting regular watches at night, and we'll have a chore schedule starting today—"

"You'll tell me what it is?"

"You and Commander Bentik can set up your own, as long as you keep track of resources and see how much fresh water you can produce with your desalinator. I'll want a daily report."

"Yes, Admiral. Should I lash the rafts together again?"

"Closer than they are now, but leave a meter of open water; we'll be able to see better."

A short time later, Marek reported that they could not find any desalinators in their raft.

"We have two," Ky said. "Both are working." She turned back to the others. "Staff Sergeant, pass me one of the desalinators; the other raft needs it." As she handed it across to Marek, she said, "This is faster than the one my father had—produces about a liter in fifteen minutes. We should be able to provide all our own potable water with it, as long as the seas are this calm. The top of the spare raft packing case makes a good base."

By evening, the wind was light, the swells even lower. Ky tried her skullphone's satellite connection again, with no luck; nor did her separate comunit pick up any signal. So it could not have been the storm that interfered. She could not think of anything to do that would fix the unknown problem. So . . . what was something she *could* fix?

Supplies: with four rafts and only twenty-two people, they had rations enough left for 109 days, assuming the two unused rafts carried full rations. But if they couldn't get out of the Oklandan's southern gyre, 109 days didn't really help. At least the two desalinators gave them plenty of capacity for making drinking water out of seawater.

What they didn't have was any real cold-weather gear but the survival suits. The shipsuits the others wore under their survival suits were, she knew, meant for comfort in the even, pleasant temperature of a spaceship; her uniform was warmer, but not designed for severe cold. And the survival suits—though they were windproof and waterproof—had limited battery life for warming. They couldn't even huddle together in anything but the lightest breeze, or the raft might blow over.

CHAPTER EIGHT

PINGAT ISLANDS SEARCH AND RESCUE
DAY 3

Pingat Islands Base had gone on alert as soon as they received word the shuttle was in trouble. SAR-One, the active rescue crew, waited for the order to go, and then—when the weather in the suspected landing zone was downgraded—waited for better information and orders. They didn't have another briefing until the third day after the shuttle went down.

"They'll still be in that storm, most likely," the base exec said. "But you might find something—from the rest of the shuttle. The passenger module would have been blown east of where the shuttle body went down."

"And been moving east ever since, assuming they made it out of the raft. When is that long-range aircraft coming in?" Arvi McCoy, pilot of SAR-One, looked at the chart display with a sinking feeling. Everything was at the limit of his craft's range.

"Not until tomorrow or the day after. So go as far as you can safely, but don't push your luck unless you see something definite."

The crew of SAR-One moved out to their aircraft, not saying much. McCoy and his copilot Jamie Sonder went through their preflight while data recorder Seth Lockhart and hoist techs Benji and Caleb Reston checked their own equipment. All were well aware of the difficulties inherent in finding anyone south of Miksland. Impossible in the frequent storms, improbable at the best of times, which autumn-shading-to-winter was not.

Four hours out, Lockhart spotted something—white lumps floating in the water.

McCoy circled over the debris; Lockhart zoomed in on it. A line of numbers . . . a few letters. "Could be part of the shuttle itself. If it disintegrated before it hit—"

"There's another," Cal Reston said. "Bigger piece."

"Got it." Lockhart increased magnification. "E-code for Spaceforce. We can run it in the system when we get back."

"Ten minutes more, then we have to go back," McCoy said. "I'll fly an arc."

They saw nothing more but dark sea with dark land rising out of it. On the way back, no one spoke. Their instruments told them water temperature was one degree Celsius, with survival in the water measured in minutes.

"Code's right," Tech Larson said, in the forensic laboratory at Pingat Base. "Spaceforce shuttle, the one that went down. You found its debris, not something else."

"So . . ."

"So that's all. This is coded for the starboard aileron. Your scan gives the right density, the right shape—here's the overlay. It's not the whole thing, just a part, but it fits."

"Shuttle, not passenger module."

"Yes. Nothing from the passenger module."

"We went as far as we could—how far could the module be from the shuttle?"

"You need somebody else for that," Larson said. "Those things come down with parachutes, don't they?"

"They're supposed to."

Grace Lane Vatta glared at the man shown on the screen. "We already knew the shuttle went down there."

"We didn't know for sure exactly where."

"But the debris tells us nothing about the passengers."

"It gives us a westernmost point to search, Rector. The shuttle was ballistic at the time: engines had failed, and the pilots were ejected with the passenger module. The module, descending more slowly under parachutes, would have been more affected by the prevailing wind; it must have come down farther east. Survivors in rafts would also be affected by the wind and the currents, carrying them still farther east—beyond range of the SAR craft usually based at Pingats."

"What craft do you have that can search farther?"

"The Long Range Recon and Search squadrons; the nearest operational is up on the northwest coast."

"There's nothing closer?"

"Closer, yes, but there's a typhoon at Gerrault; all aircraft are grounded. They expect at least a three-day delay before they can get out again; storm surge made it over the seawall and they won't know the damage to the runways until they get the water off."

"I see. So another three to four days?"

"That's our best estimate. It would be better to get the northern squadron down to Pingats, in case the Gerrault runway needs major repair. The LRRCs aren't the fastest aircraft we've got, but nothing else has their range at low altitude."

"Do it then, Admiral. All those people deserve our best efforts."

"I'll see that you're kept informed of progress, Rector."

Grace called Helen and explained the status of the search. "I'm concerned that the eastward drift will take them out of even that aircraft's range, but there's nothing else we can get, this time of year."

"I don't know what to do about the legal situation," Helen said. "Should Stella just move into the CEO's office here, for the duration? She's met all the department heads, now."

"How critical is it that Ky appear in person?"

"Unless she's been declared dead, or been missing without communication for two planetary years, very. That's what the law says."

"See if there's any leeway for cases like this. Yes, there's a chance she might show up later, but she wasn't contending with Stella. She had signed over her proxy before. This just makes it permanent."

"I'll see what we can do," Helen said.

Grace looked at her status list. Yet more people wanted to talk to her about the shuttle, its disappearance, the personnel who'd been on it. She knew the questions already: who had done it, had she known, why hadn't she known, when would she know, what was she doing . . . she read through that list and then the list of the passengers once again. Betange, compassionate leave. Parents killed, siblings . . . She called in her assistant.

"Find out who is taking care of Tech Betange's siblings, and when it's a decent time in their zone, put a call through for me. I need to know what their situation is."

Waiting for an answer gave her an excuse to ignore the other demands for a time. Finding out what the caregivers needed—besides Betange himself—would give her something she could accomplish.

CHAPTER NINE

SOUTHERN OKLANDAN
DAY 4

"We ought to name these things," Corporal Yamini said the next morning. Only a thin skim of cloud covered the sky, though darker ones edged the west.

"What?" asked Cosper.

"These rafts. They saved our lives, and clearly we're going to be in them for a long time. They should have names, just like boats."

Ky grinned. "That's a good idea, Corporal. We should have a contest. Everyone think up a name—I'll tell the other raft." Cold as it was, the increased light and calmer sea had made a change in everyone's mood—everyone but Betange, maybe. She called over to the other raft and suggested the name contest to Master Sergeant Marek.

"How long have we got? And who decides?"

"Two hours, two names: one for your raft and one for the spare." Ky said. "And make it a vote."

By the deadline, each raft had a name, including the two spares. Several variations on "Duck" had been offered, with *Lucky Ducky* as the winner, for Ky's raft; the spare was *Stitch in Time.* The other raft's crew combined two suggested names, "Gratitude" and "Goose," to become *Grateful Goose,* and its spare had another combined name: *Bouncing Ounce* from "Ounce of Prevention."

Ky declared a feast to celebrate the naming, and the rest of that day was spent checking all the equipment and cleaning out rafts, including the honey buckets. So far, they were all healthy—tired, cold, and worried, to be sure, but recovered from the violent seasickness during the storm. Despite the cold and uncertainty, she lay down that night and did not wake until her turn at watch.

A faint, strange sound came from outside. When she looked out the hatch, she could see snowflakes falling, one after another, into the dark water, and lightly frosting the upper sidewall of the raft. She shivered, sealed the hatch opening again, and tried to think how they could improvise another desalinator. She knew they had some kind of filter or membrane or something. Surely it was related to the recyclers on spaceships that took in human waste and turned it into potable water and fertilizer for the 'ponics.

DAY 5

She lay down to sleep still thinking about their water supply and woke in the morning to find that it was lighter, the sky almost clear. Sunlight hit the canopy and the interior warmed up. Outside, it seemed warmer as well. No snow remained on the canopy or sidewalls; the seas were still gentle compared with those earlier. And the view of Miksland was much clearer, the red rocks rising straight up from the sea with a fringe of surf below.

Roll call, the morning chores, a pause for rations. Everyone ate quickly; Ky suspected they felt hungry, as she did. The daily rations—

in four separate packets—were supposed to supply ample nutrition, so perhaps it was just recovery from seasickness and return of appetite that made them seem meager.

Ennisay looked up from his ration bar. "They're not going to find us, are they? We haven't seen or heard any searchers at all."

"Ennisay!" Kurin glared at him. "Don't talk like that."

"We need to think about what we can do," Ky said. "We don't know how long to plan for, but we can plan. The rations we have in the rafts won't last us the whole winter, for instance, so we'll need to find other food."

"You think we'll be out here that long?" Kamat widened her eyes. "Even if we catch enough fish, can we even survive in the cold?"

"We can," Ky said. "If we work together and make good decisions. And with that in mind—do any of you know exactly how desalinators work, how to make one?"

"Isn't ours working?" Kurin asked.

"Yes, but I'm trying to think ahead. We will be careful not to drop it overboard, I know that, but I don't know what conditions might make it quit. If someone knows how to fix it—"

"I know the theory," Betange said. It was the first time he'd spoken, except to answer to roll call. "They're pretty sturdy, but the membranes they use do wear out, and we can't make the kind of membrane needed for the hand-powered ones. If they stocked spare membranes, though, we could maybe make something—probably slower—"

"So we should start by looking for spare membranes. So can the other raft." She called across and explained what they were looking for.

"What about fishing?" Marek said. "This is as good weather as we're likely to see."

"Open both canopies halfway, so we can see what we're doing. And we don't want to catch any hooks in the flotation."

With the canopies partway up, the light breeze moved them just faster than the current. Everyone seemed to cheer up with the fresh air and sunlight; those who had fished before unpacked the lines, hooks, and packets of bait, and then—two at a time—let their lines out into the water.

Ky took the opportunity to get an even better look at the coast. Behind, to the west, the long line of cliffs faded into the distance. Ahead, the cliffs marched on, high, forbidding, with no welcoming bays. She squinted east, her back to the wind. Were the cliffs a little lower that direction, or was it just the way things looked smaller in the distance?

She looked over at the other raft. Two designated fishers were braced on what was now the trailing edge of the *Goose,* just as on *Lucky Ducky,* watching their lines in the water. Corporal Lanca, to one side, pumped slowly at the desalinator, just as Corporal Inyatta was doing in her raft. The others were farther under the canopy, with Commander Bentik almost out of sight, and Master Sergeant Marek beside her. She looked pinched and pale. Marek caught Ky's glance and spoke to Bentik. She looked over at Ky.

"When can we close the canopies again, Admiral? It's so cold."

"I hope we can catch some fish," Ky said. "To extend our rations."

"Rations? You mean to *eat*? Animals out of the ocean?"

"You eat fish, Commander."

"Raised in clean circumstances. Not like this. And how will we cook them?"

They would eat fish raw, of course. And they had the little SafStov cans, for heating rations if they had to. She was spared having to explain this to Jen by a shout from one of *Goose*'s fishers. "Got one I think. See over there?"

A blur under the water, surprisingly large. And behind it, on the next swell, another rose to the surface, a fin slicing the water's surface. The fisher's line went slack. "Lost him. Drat."

But the blur came on, faster than they were moving, as if seeking refuge under the rafts. Over a meter long, spotted on the upper surface. Behind it the fin came faster, and soon Ky recognized the familiar steel-blue back of a very large shark. The fleeing fish vanished under *Goose,* then bumped against the bottom as the shark followed.

The raft's floor bulged up; the fishers and Lanca, who had stopped pumping to watch, lost their balance. To Ky's horror, something below poked up the raft floor as if the tines of a giant fork were trying to spear it. Dozens of them. Another fish—the shark?—shoved against the raft; the tail thrashed between the two rafts. "What is that?" someone yelled. Corporal Lanca grabbed the desalinator and started beating on the points as the raft fabric stretched, thinning enough that they could see the outline of spines.

"Lanca! *Stop!*" Ky and Marek both yelled at him; Sergeant Chok dropped his fishing gear and tackled Lanca, rolling him away from the spike. But one had already poked through the rubbery floor—a dark spine. Memory hit Ky. Aside from being much larger, it looked like the spine of a puffer—a reef fish a little longer than her hand that could swell into a mass of toxic spines the length of her thumb to repel predators.

Over a meter long and with spines that could pierce the raft's floor? Even as she thought of it, two more poked through. The raft floor sagged over the fish as water entered the space between the layers, and more spikes outlined its size. It wasn't maneuverable in its bloated form, but it didn't have to be, to do damage. "Get patches," Ky said. "Don't touch the spines; they're toxic. When the fish swims away you'll need to mend it when the spikes come out. All fishers, get your lines back in; we need to get the rafts snug again."

Could they patch the raft before it sank? If it did—"Master Sergeant!" He looked over at her. "Start transferring essentials over here and prepare your spare raft." In her mind the sequence unfolded; Marek spoke to Jen, then turned to the others, telling them to transfer rations and water to Ky's raft beforehand, just in case—

Ky saw the spines withdraw a little; water welled up beside each, and then the shark struck at the puffer, pushing it up into the raft floor as the spines erected again. Everyone in *Goose* was down now, struggling to the sidewalls, away from the violent struggle below and the growing leaks in the middle of the floor. Vispersen grabbed Jen's briefcase and slung it wildly in the direction of Ky's raft; it bounced off the canopy and into the ocean. Lanca, with a howl, grabbed the sidewall and wallowed over it into the raft with Ky. Some of the others were yanking open the storage bags along the sides. Suddenly the spines vanished, only to reappear a meter away.

In the chaos that ensued, Ky called out "Marek! Inflate the spare raft! Throw all the rations and water you can into it! The desalinator—"

"Admiral! What can I do?" Jen's call ended in a shriek as the shark's snout broke through the weakened center of the raft and its razor teeth ripped a bigger hole. Marek, struggling with the spare raft's case latches, was instantly up to his waist in water; others had a good hold on the grabons of the wall, but everything that had been on the raft floor slid inexorably toward the center and down into the gap.

Ky threw the rescue rings she'd left stored near the canopy opening. Sergeant Chok caught one and handed it to Jen. The cover of the raft pack finally snapped back, and Marek pulled the inflation cord. The raft whooshed open, tilted up on one end by the sidewall of the *Goose,* and the canopy popped up automatically, blocking most of the *Goose*'s passengers from access to its interior.

Sergeant Chok caught one of the grab-lines and worked his way to the hatch opening, got in, and lowered the canopy so others could throw things over the sides. "Get the rations from the side pockets, throw them in here!"

Kurin, now beside Ky, had hold of the lines connecting the two rafts and pulled them snugly together. Marek made it to the entrance ladder of the spare raft. It tilted more. "We'll have to puncture flotation on this side," Ky said. "So it can float out." She looked around; Corporal Lanca was crouched on the other side of their raft. "Get back over there, Lanca; they need the weight in *Ounce.*"

"But I'll get wet—"

"GO! Now!"

Lanca scrambled back across to the entrance and heaved himself into *Ounce*, muttering.

In the scramble to free the *Ounce* from the *Goose* and get everyone aboard, only some of the supplies made it.

"Get a line on your raft!" Ky yelled. "We're linked to *Goose*, not to you."

Chok threw a line, and finally *Ounce* was linked to *Ducky* and free of the *Goose*. Ky and Kurin worked together, hands stiffening in the cold water, to free the line to the *Goose*.

By the time they had everything that could be salvaged from *Goose* in *Ounce*, the wind had picked up, ruffling the swells with miniature waves. Another shelf of dark cloud neared. Looking toward the wind, Ky could see a blur of fog or rain in the distance. "Close canopies," she said. "Might be more squalls."

When the squall hit, a mix of rain and sleet soon turned to wind-driven snow. The foul weather lasted all night.

DAY 7

Ky woke to the sound of the storm and in dim light saw Kurin bracing herself on their spare raft's case and poking at the canopy with the desalinator.

"What's wrong?"

"Ventilation flap frozen down. I got the other one open this way—it's—a matter of—timing."

Ky could see that, with the raft pitching and rolling on the heavy seas. With a last jab at it, the flap popped up and a few chunks of ice fell in. Kurin sank down on the raft case, breathing hard, then slid the desalinator into one of the storage pockets, leaving enough sticking out to identify.

"Good thing it was your watch," Ky said. "We'll have to check regularly."

"I hope this storm doesn't last as long as the last one," Kurin said.

CHAPTER TEN

SLOTTER KEY SEARCH AND RESCUE, PINGAT BASE

DAY 7

The Long Range Recovery Team's aircraft could stay up in the huge oval designated as the target area for hours. Long enough to make finding survivors possible, though not certain. SAR-One joined the crew that had brought the plane out. "The more eyes, the better," Commander Depeche said from the pilot's seat. "The Rector's got her undies in a wad over this. Says it's about the Commandant, but I figure it's more about her niece or whatever—a Vatta aboard."

"It's a hit to Slotter Key's reputation, too," McCoy said. "Especially sabotage. The inner worlds have been snooty about us out on the margins for a long time."

"There's that," Depeche said. "Ula, let McCoy have your seat for a while. Take a nap or something."

"Fine with me." Ula Maillor grabbed her hot-cup out of its stand on the way out of the cockpit. "I slept the last third of the way to

Pingats last night. But don't think I don't know you just want to talk politics with McCoy."

"I live for talking politics with McCoy," Depeche said.

"Gossip," McCoy said. "Not politics. You just like the down and dirty."

Depeche raised an eyebrow. "And you don't?"

"You know I do. So who's sleeping with whom that's new and interesting? Any tagged dirty money?"

"No sex, but there's a rumor that Vatta Transport is going to reorganize and move its headquarters to the Moscoe Confederation. Slotter Key will just be a regional hub for them."

"Already heard that. Blondie coming here was public."

"And the admiral. Between those two and the Rector, they hold the most shares." Depeche glanced over at McCoy. "And someone I know knows someone who claims the old lady is sure who bombed their headquarters back when."

"I thought it was the wicked cousin. Whatsisname . . . Osmar or Osmin or something—"

"Osman. No, not him. He was with that pirate bunch, all right, but he'd been banned from Slotter Key permanently decades ago. They're thinking the construction firm did it, put the bombs in place in one of the expansions."

"Paid to do it, or their idea?"

"Guy I know thinks someone hired 'em. Maybe just a foreman or something, maybe the head. But if the Rector thinks it was the head . . . then heads will likely roll."

"Can't blame her for that," McCoy said.

"No. But it makes life too interesting for the rest of us, her being head of Defense and all our lives in her hand. Made Orniakos furious when she called up and reamed him out for doing his job."

"I hadn't heard that."

"That Space Defense Force ship Admiral Vatta came with sent their shuttle after the one that went down, when it changed course. Came right down into our airspace without asking permission, live weapons and all, and Orniakos told them to get out and stay out. Rector wanted them left alone on her say-so."

"Sounds . . . like a mess."

"It was. Is. Admiral Hicks is mad at Orniakos for making the Rector mad, and mad at the Rector for not informing him first, and there are rumors all over Region V headquarters about it. At least she asked Hicks to send us, so here we are. I get flight hours, so I'm happy, if no one else is."

McCoy laughed. "In-law trouble again?"

"No. Kids. Kory's turning out too much like me, and the school's nagging at us about him and my so-called parenting style. I just need some time away."

"Lost prime signal," Jamie said from the station behind them. "Right on schedule."

"What's happened?" Depeche said. He twiddled some controls, scowling at the displays.

"It's all right," McCoy said. "We won't have satellite contact for the duration, but Jamie's a great navigator. Besides, in this weather it's dead simple. Miksland to port on the way out and Miksland to starboard on the way back. Just stay in sight of the coast."

"But what happened to the satellite?"

McCoy shrugged. "Something about Miksland, they told us. Sounded like a lot of hand waving to me, but after all—it is a terra-forming failure. For all I know it's made out of giant magnets or something, but unless you're way, way high, nothing works right. Jamie, are you running the nav string? What's the weather and fuel situation?"

"Yes, sir. Tailwind now, and headwind coming back," Jamie said. "You want sixty-three percent of the fuel for the return trip, or we have to cut overland, and we don't like that."

"Why not?" Depeche glanced back over his shoulder.

"Instruments don't just fail to connect to anything, they go crazy," Jamie said. "If there's ground fog or clouds, you can get mixed up easily. Some of the mountains are high."

"You'd think someone would put a landing strip on that place, even just an emergency one," Depeche said. "I'd feel a lot safer if they had."

"Floater!" Seth called from the starboard side. "Debris."

LRR's recorder, Van, brought it up on the screen. "Code matches what you found before. Different piece?"

"Looks like," Seth said.

"I'll do a circle," Depeche said. They spotted seventeen pieces of debris, none that looked like a body or a part of a raft, and recorded every marking on them.

"Back on original course," Jamie said finally. They flew on another hour. This time, Lili Vela saw something first.

"Floater. Orange. Could be a body."

When Van brought the image up on the screen they could see that it was, at least, an orange survival suit. Missing part of one arm.

"Floater Two," Seth said, from the other side of the plane. "Appears intact . . . no . . . foot missing." In the next half hour, they found two more bodies. All were clearly dead, all in survival suits, all damaged by either the shuttle crash or sea creatures, and without retrieval capability they could not tell which.

"I don't suppose there's much reason to keep going," Commander Depeche said.

"Do we have enough fuel?" McCoy peered out the cockpit window.

"Yeah, for another hour, about, but why? We're not going to find anyone alive."

"We don't know what happened yet. If there's more debris—a raft, even empty or damaged—it shows some might have made it down, deployed the rafts."

"Sure. Fine." They flew on in silence.

"Floater. Orange. Might be a raft." Seth pointed; Van zoomed in on it. Oval, the right shape for a raft as they came nearer. Flotation chambers mostly full. Canopy down, water sloshing—he felt cold to the bone suddenly. That water sloshing inside the raft wasn't a layer over the raft floor; the floor hung down in two ragged—partly ragged—pieces, as if someone had sliced through it.

"Debris got it," Lili said, peering at the screen. "Puncture marks—shrapnel from an explosion maybe—and then something sharp, some part of the shuttle or personnel module—some of that may be sea life, too—it's a wonder it's still afloat."

"If they had only one raft in the water, that would explain the bodies—whatever did this would've killed some, knocked others overboard. The cold would've done the rest."

As the plane circled, Van recorded every detail he could.

"Time to go," Depeche said. "Have you got what you need?"

"Got it," Van said. And under his breath, to those in the rear compartment, "I hate this kind of flight."

"Do you mostly get the bad ones?" Seth asked.

"We've had some saves. Found people in rafts, then could tell a ship where they were. But this—without the proper navigational aids—nobody takes a ship through here, do they?"

"Not in my lifetime," Seth said. He leaned back against the hard seat. "No nav help, no satellite contact, and the water's cold enough to kill you in less than an hour, even in summer. Ice on it in winter—solid off toward the pole, windblown chunks of it here. Shipping all stays north of Pingat Base, and mostly north of Miksland altogether."

"And you actually run SAR out here?"

"Practice runs," Seth said. "This is the first emergency—nobody's crashed while I've been stationed here. So our usual routes are north and west of Miksland. We come here to practice navigation without modern instruments in case we need it somewhere else."

"You found bodies? How many? Who?" Grace felt her heart skip a beat, start again.

"We don't know." Admiral Hicks sounded depressed. "They saw five, and the remains of one raft. This was the Long Range Recovery plane—it can't land on water and can't hover; there's no way to retrieve anything. The bodies had damage; they filmed everything but there are no facial features and we can't tell if injuries preceded the crash or not."

"And the total number on the shuttle when it left the station?" She had been told that, but she'd gone blank on it.

"Twenty-eight, Rector. If they were alive and able when the passenger module landed, I'm sure they'd have tried to launch two rafts. If they were all in one, it would be overloaded; the storm that hit the area shortly after they went down could have caused it to fail." He cleared his throat. "We must consider it likely that no one survived. The weather, the water temperature—no one could survive in it for more than an hour at most. Five bodies—others could have sunk, been taken by sea life—"

"Fish?"

"Most likely, yes. Or cetaceans. If the crew or passengers survived, if they made it into more than one life raft, we would still expect some communication, some transponder signal."

"And there's nothing."

"Nothing at all. I know your particular interest—"

"My primary interest is that Spaceforce personnel, from Private Ennisay to the Commandant of the Spaceforce Academy, were aboard a shuttle that crashed and we haven't found them," Grace said. "That my grandniece was on the same shuttle is unfortunate, and yes, of course, I am concerned about her as well. But my duty, as Rector, is to Spaceforce. Five dead we know about but that leaves twenty-three who might be alive. We must not abandon them."

"Rector, the winter storms are lined up now and we do not have any bases nearer than Pingats to fly from."

"One more search," Grace said. "One more, the next day they can. I take your point; I'm not going to insist on risking crews after that, but—"

"One more. We will do that."

It was over. Grace leaned back in her chair and stared through the solid wall into her imagination: giant seas, tiny rafts rising and falling on them, rain or snow or sleet, howling winds. If they were not all dead, what would they be doing? How long could they survive in that cold, with just the resources in the rafts? Even if they caught a lucky current, and it swept them north out of the polar circulation, that was still winter, still cold. Suppose all twenty-three were alive, and in two rafts—thirty days' rations for forty would feed twenty-three for . . . fifty-two days. That would not get them even to midwinter, let alone to spring.

"We have to find them in fifty days or less," Grace said to MacRobert.

"How?"

"I don't know. But in fifty-two days, if they're all alive, they'll run out of food. We can't let them starve to death, Mac. We can't."

"They can fish," Mac said. "The rafts have fishing gear." He grimaced. "If the weather lets them fish. If the fish are there."

"Water?"

"They have desalinators. Hand-pumped."

"We need to locate them. Hicks has authorized one more search. They could cut off some of the distance to the search area by flying over Miksland. High altitude, to avoid that communications problem." Grace cocked her head at him. "If we knew what it was, maybe we could fix it. ISC might have someone—"

"Government's not going to like involving them, and if crews think flying over part of Miksland is especially dangerous, Hicks isn't going to push them."

Grace glared; MacRobert's return look exuded patience. She sighed. "Mac, sometimes you are annoying."

"The truth sucks." His expression offered no hope.

"Yes. It does. Let's hope the next flight shows something."

SPACE DEFENSE FORCE HQ, GREENTOO

"You know they'll call off the search," Admiral Driskill said. "She's bound to be dead. We should inform our governments that you're taking over."

Dan Pettygrew, interim commander of SDF, felt the knot in his belly tighten. "I'm not ready to assume that," he said. "We've been told there'll be one more search mission, and that the reason for ending the search after that is distance and weather. They could well still be alive."

From their expressions, none of the other admirals agreed.

"Pordre thinks she may be. He thinks the communications problem is a deliberate event, and thus indicates someone may know they're alive and be frustrating attempts to find them."

"That's ridiculous," Admiral Hetherson said. "No one would do something like that."

"Oh, they would if they could, but I doubt it's possible." Admiral Driskill leaned back. "I wonder if they've contacted ISC to ask about it."

"Have you?"

"No. I'm sure someone at ISC is aware of the problem, given that Admiral Vatta is—was—somewhat involved—"

Pettygrew wanted to wipe the smirk off Driskill's face, and others, but held his temper. "I will inform the governments when I myself am satisfied that either she is dead, or her absence is impairing our ability to respond to threats. Neither is the case now."

Pursed lips, sideways glances—but they didn't argue. Good.

"And now for the quarterly budget review," Pettygrew said, tapping his stylus on the agenda.

CHAPTER ELEVEN

SOUTHERN OKLANDAN
DAYS 8-9

During the eighth day, the wind lessened again, but snow continued to fall. Frozen condensation frosted the inside of the canopy, and every watch had to poke open the ventilation flaps. Consultation with the other raft revealed that most of the rations from *Goose* had not been salvaged.

The ninth day brought a clear sky and good visibility. Ky ordered the canopy on her raft opened enough that she could see the coast again in both directions. The same barren wall extended behind them, but straight across it was already lower, obviously lower. Ahead, the cliff wall disappeared into the sea. The current pulled them on; soon they would be even with the rocks low enough to see over. She could not see what lay beyond, but if there was an eddy current heading north, this was the place to look.

"Wake up!" she said loudly. "Kurin, lower our canopy completely. Master Sergeant, lower the canopy in your raft. It's time to start paddling." In her own raft, those offwatch stirred, looked up sleepily. Those awake looked around. Kurin grinned and reached for a paddle.

"It's too cold!" Commander Bentik said from the other raft as its canopy retracted. "It's freezing."

"We don't want the wind's push now, and we'll be paddling," Ky said. She had already assigned the first teams of paddlers from those with experience in small boats. "We're heading across this current, hoping to find an eddy that will carry us around that point and on north. These rafts won't be easy to steer, but if we find the right current we should be able to do it."

At first, the paddlers seemed to make no difference in the rafts' movement, and as they passed the point of rocks, she could begin to see what lay on the other side: a bay, like a chunk bitten out of this end of Miksland, with a slope—steep, but not a cliff—up to the high plateau. Beyond it, another line of cliffs marked this end of the continent, with rising ground beyond.

After something over an hour of paddling, another current caught them, moving them north, though not nearly as fast as the main ocean current had moved them east.

"We could go all the way north," Marek said. "The current might carry us all the way past Miksland into the shipping lanes. Toward warmer water. I think we should try that."

"I'm worried about the food supply," Ky said. "And the cold. Doesn't the sea freeze down here in winter?"

"I don't know how much of it," McLenard said. "How far north, I mean, but I've heard it freezes as far as this."

"These rafts won't stand up to sea ice," Kurin said. "We could get stuck in it when it's too thin to walk on, but thick enough to crush them."

"Warmer to the north," Marek said again. "Probably more bays up there, less likely to freeze."

"I take your point, Master Sergeant," Ky said, "but as short as we are of food, and with these rafts—we're going into this bay while it's good weather and we can see what we're doing."

They came nearer, nearer, the paddlers switching out now for a fresh crew. Once out of the eddy current, it was easier paddling between the arms of the bay. Waves were smaller, mere ripples on the surface. Ky could see the shore on both sides and ahead clearly.

"It's just rock," Jen said, from the other raft. "No trees, no driftwood—nothing to build shelters with." Ky said nothing.

"We could build a hut with rocks," McLenard said. "Stuff mud in the cracks."

"We're closer to this side." Marek nodded to the north. "Head for that?"

"No," Ky said. "Keep going, all the way in. It should be shallower there, maybe enough to walk the rafts ashore. We need lookouts to watch for rocks beneath."

The rafts moved with agonizing slowness toward the shore. Gradually the bottom came into view, tumbled rocks and then seaweed, shellfish clinging to the rocks, several fish. Ky was heartened. With the loss of supplies, they needed every extra calorie they could find, and she saw no sign of plant life around the bay.

When the rafts finally touched bottom on shingle, everyone sat silent for a moment.

Marek started to climb over the side into the water. "Not you," Ky said. "Your suit's not sound. We want to preserve the rafts for shelter and future need, so we don't want to drag them loaded over the rocks. Only those with whole suits."

She rolled over the side herself, confident in her suit's integrity, into knee-deep icy water. Her first lurching steps on the slick, rounded cobble reminded her that days at sea made for shaky legs. She pulled on the lines between the two rafts, moving them only a few centimeters, but soon others were there to help. Finally, only Marek and Jen were still aboard a raft. He helped Jen over the side, and she splashed ashore, almost falling.

"We need some protection under the rafts," Ky said. "These rocks will wear through them. We'll use the uninflated spare raft for one, and its canopy for the other."

It took longer than she had hoped to get everything ashore, the improvised groundsheets laid down, and the rafts securely held down with piles of stones serving instead of stakes. But Marek and the two staff sergeants kept things moving, and before dark the makeshift camp was complete.

Everyone gathered into one raft-shelter out of the rising wind. Even sitting down, Ky felt that the land was moving like the sea, rising and falling. Underneath, the stones were unyielding lumps instead of smooth, resilient water. And the ration bar, last of the day's ration, did not satisfy her hunger. She looked around at those who'd been in the other raft, whose stories she didn't yet know, but she was too tired to ask for them now. And here, on land, they would have more time to get to know one another.

"At least I'm not seasick," Hazarika said. "And we're not going to drown." He patted the floor of the raft.

"Not sure I think freezing or starving is any improvement," Lanca said. Staff Sergeant Gossin glared at him and he subsided.

"Should be more things to eat in this bay," Kurin said.

"Did you recognize anything as we came in?" Ky asked.

"A few things, yes, Admiral. Some of the seaweed looks like an edible type, and the shellfish certainly should be."

"Then you'll teach the rest of us." If only they had a small boat, something other than the rafts, so they could use the rafts for shelter and have access to the bay's water for fishing. It was far too cold to dive into, even if they'd had the right gear for it.

But here, at least, they could have a real latrine, far enough away from the rafts they were to live in. Here, at least, someone flying over might see their bright-colored rafts. If anyone flew over. If the search hadn't been called off. In any case, everyone was still alive and they were on land, not adrift at sea.

SLOTTER KEY, OFFICE OF THE RECTOR OF DEFENSE
DAY 9

"Bad news." Grace looked at Helen's face on the vidscreen, Stella behind her. "The last flight we can make, they found nothing more. No more debris, no more bodies. We've notified surface shipping to the north to be on the lookout for anything, but the search has been called off. Given the weather conditions down there, the danger to their own crews, it was the only reasonable decision."

"You let them?" Helen said, a little breathlessly.

"Yes. Admiral Hicks is convinced they could not have survived this long even if they'd survived the crash. If there is anything found, it will be next spring, when—" She stopped, trying to find a way to edit what she'd been told. "If anything does come up, it might be found when the ice melts."

"I can't believe—" Helen's eyes glistened with fresh tears. Her shoulders shook. Stella put an arm around her.

"I still hope they're wrong," Grace said. "I believe Ky is a lot more capable than they think, but it's true she never had cold survival training or experience."

SLOTTER KEY, MIKSLAND COAST
DAY 10

The tide turned. The ebb was gentler, the waves lapping more quietly, slowly leaving behind rock pools. Staff Sergeant Gossin assigned work parties: one to forage for food in the rock pools, one to find a location for a latrine, one to locate fuel for a fire and any materials for building a better shelter. Two worked the desalinators, until all the containers they had were full, then joined the food foraging party. Ky moved from one to another; Jen said she would work on cleaning and organizing the shelters.

Despite the biting wind, Ky was glad to be out of the confines of the raft, eager to find better shelter, more food supplies. Inland, at the head of the shingle, a tumble of boulders looked at first like a natural fall of rocks from the cliffs on either side. She clambered up the slope to the first, a head-high block of rough rock, about a meter from the next to the right, and a half meter from the one to the left. Ky glanced down the line of them. Except for being different sizes and shapes, they looked like a row of bollards blocking traffic from a pedestrian-only square, closing off the beach from higher ground. One of them was low enough for her to climb; she was hauling herself up the side when she heard Marek calling her.

Sighing, she let herself down. He was toiling up the slope, brow furrowed. "Admiral, what were you doing? You could fall, break your leg or something."

"I thought if I could climb it, maybe I could find a way up."

"Up—where? And why?"

"Not much to live on down here, Master Sergeant. We've got a long cold winter ahead of us; we need better shelter, a source of heat, and more food."

"You won't find anything up there but rock and ice." He looked worried. She wondered if he might argue again for continuing north in the rafts, but he didn't. "Commander Bentik asked me to find you."

"Of course," Ky said.

She started back to the camp, but detoured to speak to the latrine detail when they waved her over. Neither the location nor the hole itself was really adequate, but it would do for a short time. When she got to camp, she found that Jen had done another inventory of supplies, a chore that had kept her in one or the other raft all day.

"And I really think, Admiral, that we should both be here, available to each other and anyone else. We could use one raft for a sort of office."

"I appreciate your work on the inventory," Ky said, "but I need to check on each working party while they're at their tasks. It's good for morale, besides ensuring that the work is going well."

"As you wish, Admiral," Jen said. "Though I should think you could leave that to their own NCOs." Ky reminded herself that Jen had always been staff, never in a command position.

The foraging party brought in some seaweed and shellfish scraped off the rocks at low tide. That night they had the first hot food since the crash, boiled in a pot from the raft over one of the SafStov cans. Everyone had a taste of the shellfish along with a regular ration bar; the seaweed, Ky thought, was a taste she hadn't acquired yet, but she chewed through a portion to encourage the others. Eventually it was all gone.

DAY 11

Cloud hung over them the next morning, ominous, the color promising more snow. Ky elected not to explore the trail to the top of the plateau, and when the snow began falling, she declared a holiday once morning chores were done. She designated one raft for resting quietly or sleeping and the other for conversation. Some started with a nap, and then came out to chat and eat. Others moved over to sleep after looking over the stores in the conversation raft. Snow fell steadily, covering the stones outside. The canopies began to sag; Ky told the staff sergeants to make sure they didn't sag too far. She took this opportunity to chat with those she hadn't met yet, starting with Staff Sergeant Gossin.

"My family's military back as far as the civil war, at least," Gossin said. "My second cousin was stationed at headquarters when you were in the Academy—" She gave Ky a wary look then went on. "But I don't tell people what he said about that situation you had." An invitation, or a test.

"I was a young idiot," Ky said. She had expected someone to bring up her expulsion from the Academy. Only one way to handle it, frankly and without excuses. "I didn't think it through."

Gossin didn't smile, but Ky saw a slight relaxation in her face.

Something had worried her, and now didn't. "He said right away it was a setup and they'd be sorry to lose you."

"I created a mess," Ky said. "They had no choice."

Gossin nodded, meeting Ky's gaze. "Well—I told my cousin I might get to meet you, and he asked me to give you his regards. Staff Sergeant Antak Birgirs, Joint Services Command at Ordnay."

Birgirs. Should she remember a Birgirs? Then she did. "Sergeant Birgirs, then—fitness instructor? He ran us off our legs." Ky grinned. He had taught her how to handle larger opponents. "Are you staying in?"

"Absolutely," Gossin said. "This is my life and what I want. Not going to complicate things with marriage or family; if I don't screw up I could make sergeant major. Maybe. At any rate, I'm in for the duration."

Ky liked her: sensible, direct, and utterly professional. She considered asking Gossin about the others in the second raft, but Gossin spoke first.

"Admiral, by your leave, I'll take a party outside to brush the snow off these canopies. I see a little sag over there."

"Go ahead," Ky said. They could talk again later. She watched as Gossin chose a crew, noting that she mixed personnel from both rafts. Then she went out herself to stretch and look at the bay, the snow melting quietly into dark water. Sergeant Chok was just coming out of the other raft, and Ky beckoned to him.

"You've got inflatable raft experience," Ky said. "How long do you think the ground cloths we made will protect the raft bottoms?"

"You mean to use them again as rafts?" he asked, brow furrowed. "The longer we're on land, the more abrasion they'll have, even with people trying not to scoot around inside and rub the fabric against these rocks. If we're here all winter, I doubt they'll be seaworthy when it warms up again." Ky nodded; he went on. "You think no one will come?"

"If we're out of communication long enough, they'll likely think we all died in the crash. And if whatever has kept people's skullphones from working affects aircraft communications, they may not fly over the continent."

"Yeah, I can see that. Well, if we take to the sea again, we'd better do it soon, and figure out a better way to steer. It's going to get colder—this bay may freeze over and then we're really stuck."

"Better here than out at sea."

"Yes, sir. Absolutely. Except there's nothing much to eat. How many days' food do we have now?"

"Not enough to get through the winter. We have to have another source, and right now the sea is it. You said your family farmed fish?"

"Yes, sir, but we can't do that here. We don't have any way to net off the bay, or make cages for them, so predators don't eat them. And unless we move everyone into one raft and use the other one, we'll have to fish from shore."

"Where would be the best place?"

"Out along one of the arms, toward the open sea. Should be deeper water close in there." He pointed into the snow. "Dangerous getting there and coming back, though, with tides and current and wind. Easy to get blown back out to sea." A pause. "I wouldn't advise it, sir, but I'll try if you want."

"Maybe when it's not snowing and the wind's still," Ky said. "We should go back inside now. Get some lunch." Meager as it was, she wanted that little lump of protein.

Chok followed her into the active raft. Kurin looked up. "Two more for lunch?"

"Such as it is." Ky identified the speaker as Corporal Lanca, dark like her but beak-nosed and round-shouldered. He had been in the other raft with Commander Bentik. "It's not enough."

"It's the same for everyone, Corporal," Kurin said. She handed the little packet to Ky and another to Chok.

"I'm going to take a nap," Lanca said. He unfastened the hatch, stepped over the sidewall, and made a sloppy job of fastening the hatch again.

"Typical," muttered Kurin.

"Got it," Chok said, and snugged the flap down.

"Problem there?" Ky asked.

"He has a certain reputation," Chok said. Kurin nodded. "I'd heard of him from time to time. Lazy Lanca, they call him."

"Should never have made corporal," Kurin said, lowering her voice. "Should have washed out in Basic."

Chok shrugged. "We need all the hands we have."

"But not all the mouths."

Ky gave her a sharp look. Kurin spread her hands.

"He tried to talk me out of more food—said he had a metabolic problem. I know—and I know you heard the same story, Gus—he's got a reputation for that, too, cadging extra rations and then trying to skip out on physicals."

"Any other problems I should know about? Or just background on the others in your raft, Sergeant Chok?"

Chok looked wary. "Well . . . we had Master Sergeant Marek with us; he was a big help. I think—I think Commander Bentik thought I was a bit young to take charge. And she's not from here."

Ky already knew Jen had been difficult at first. "The commander's culture is much more formal," Ky said. "But I was wondering how the other personnel were—any problems I should know about? Anyone you think deserves a commendation?"

Chok relaxed. "The rest—this is just my first impression, and they may be different now we're on land." He looked at her; Ky nodded again. "Barash is a stickler for regulations, likes to correct people. I think she's just scared and that's her way of coping. Riyahn's a motor-mouth, yammers on and on, and he can panic—you saw his reactions the day our first raft was holed. He's Miznarii, too, if that matters."

Ky shrugged. "Not to me, if he can do his job. Do you know his training?"

"Yes; electrical systems, what in a civilian would be installation and maintenance electrician."

"What about Tech Lundin?"

"Steady as stone. I guess most medics are. She said she worked for a field trauma team before she joined Spaceforce."

"Good person to have along," Ky said, and Chok nodded his agreement.

"Now Tech Hazarika, he's weapons maintenance with a secondary in communications. More an indoor type; he's had a rough time. Seasick a lot, and I don't think he's up to hard physical work. And . . ." Chok paused long enough that Ky gestured to him. "Well . . . he's crazy about Drosh—Tech Droshinski. Who if you ask me, and you did, is a drama queen right out of vid programs. Smart enough, but the kind of woman who makes trouble."

"Um. Sleeps around?"

"Not on this trip, so far. Just—everything is drama with her."

"Did she start trouble with Commander Bentik?" Ky could easily imagine that happening. Offense taken, reproofs resented. She would have to be on the lookout for trouble in that direction.

"Not that I saw, Admiral, but Master Sergeant Marek was keeping close watch on the commander." After a moment, Chok said, "I hope I didn't rattle on too much, Admiral."

"No, you didn't. That was fine. I'll be talking to everyone again myself, making my own assessments, but it helps to have something to start with."

Everyone gathered for the evening meal—a single ration bar—as it grew dark, and then returned to their usual raft for the night. Ky thought about scrambling the crew, but put it aside for another day. Snow fell all night; the night watches had to brush it off the canopies every hour or two.

DAY 12

In the morning the snow still fell, though more lightly. When it stopped, the temperature dropped; the wind picked up, rattling the canopy fabric. Nobody wanted to go outside, but Ky insisted.

"Master Sergeant, we need work parties to gather seaweed and shellfish; Staff Sergeant Gossin should take several along the margins of the bay to find the best place to fish. The waste buckets from inside go to the latrine. Someone needs to use the desalinator pump to refill all the water containers with fresh water. And we need some kind of windbreak to protect our shelter. I wonder if we could pile up rocks."

Marek looked at her as if she were crazy. "Build a rock shelter? Do you know how to do that? With round rocks?"

"No, but rock is what we've got." She picked up a rock, carried it over, set it down. Another two. Another. Another three. "I'd rather have lumber and tools, but I don't see any."

"Very well, Admiral. I'll get the work parties moving."

That day, twelve of the crew carried rocks and dropped them into a long curving pile along the outside of one raft. It didn't reach the top of the flotation walls, but it was a start, and it felt like doing something. They took turns, two by two, with those pumping the desalinators on the far side of the bay from the latrine. The others searched the rock pools and shallows for food. They came back with two small fish, sixteen of the black bivalves, and more seaweed.

Seaweed was more palatable, Ky decided, when people had worked hard all day. The daily ration, which had seemed just adequate on the rafts, left them hungry here; the seaweed and individual bites of fish with one or two scallops or pieces of clam stilled the hunger pangs for only a few hours. And the cold never let up.

CHAPTER TWELVE

NEXUS II, HEADQUARTERS OF ISC
DAYS 9-12

Rafe Dunbarger looked up when his office door opened. His sister Penny had dressed in the exact shade of blue that best suited her, a flowered scarf at her neck. She closed the door behind her, thumbed the lock, and walked across the carpet to stand on the other side of his desk, a challenging look on her face.

"I'm busy," Rafe said. He knew he had been scowling, glaring even, before she came in, and hoped he'd adjusted his expression quickly enough.

"Is it Ky?" Penny asked. Rafe looked at her, but staring his sister down did not work these days. "I saw the latest news reports," she went on. "They've ended all searches; they're saying survival is highly unlikely."

"Stella told me not to come," Rafe said. He unclenched his hands deliberately. "I could have gone—"

"And done what?" Penny shook her head. "You know what your old friend Gary said—"

Rafe snorted.

"He told you that you lacked the skills to rescue us. Why do you think you could do anything for Ky, on a planet you've never visited, a foreign state, where you have no connections—?"

"Stella's there," Rafe said.

"And do you think she and Ky's family are doing nothing? Her aunt or great-aunt or whoever she is, that's head of their military?"

Rafe took in a long breath and shoved all he wanted to say back down. Penny meant to be helpful. She was his little sister. She couldn't possibly understand.

Except she could, and he knew it, and the unfortunate effect of being Ky's—whatever he was—had been a contamination of his insouciant attitude toward truth with her absolute white-hot honesty. At least in some things. At least where it mattered.

"They are. I'm sure they are. But there's something they don't know, and you don't know, about Ky and me. And I can't tell you; it's too dangerous."

"If you mean the implant ansible, I do know."

"*What?*" Terror and outrage met. "You can't possibly—"

"I saw you use it, remember? You tried all sorts of ways to hide what you were doing, but that's all it could be—"

"Penny, *never* talk about that. Never." He felt cold sweat trickling down his backbone. "It could be fatal. For me, for Ky—"

"Of course I won't. You were the prototype, right? And somehow she got hold of one—"

"The less you know, the better." He scrubbed his face with one hand. "I shouldn't even—the thing is—*I* know she's alive. I can't communicate, but I can tell if the implant's still working. Which it wouldn't be if she were dead."

"Well, then?" She folded her arms.

"So—I need to be in range to get a heading from it. I can't do that from here. And the report says her skullphone's blocked—no signal they can detect—so either there's some solid jamming going on, or she's dead, but she can't be dead because the implant's still on." He looked up at her. "I check every day. I have to know, Penny."

Her expression this time was tender, more motherly than sisterly. "There's only one way you can go, you know."

"Go? What do you mean?"

She sat down in the chair across from him, leaning forward a little. "Arrange for someone to run ISC while you're gone. That would be me, the only one who *should* be running this monster, other than you. Just step down, name me as your successor—"

"You!"

"You're the one who told me once I had more head for the business than you."

"Yes, but—but you're—"

"Younger. Prettier. And have more friends on the Board than you do. They won't worry about *me* falling in love with Stella or Ky Vatta, for instance."

"But are you ready? After all that—"

"Shall we ask my therapist? Rafe, I know you started me working here as a kind of therapy—but you also know I'm long past that now. I haven't been to my therapist for over a year now; we sometimes run into each other socially, but that's all. You're not stuck here anymore, Rafe, if you don't want to be."

"And you think I should go."

Penny shrugged. "I think you should decide whether running ISC is the life you want. You've said before you hated it; you took it when no one else could have, and you saved both ISC—to the extent anyone could—and Nexus itself. But I don't see you inhabiting the big office with the big windows forever, and I've seen you looking more and more dour these last months. You enjoyed your freedom before. I expect you'd like it again."

"But Mother—"

"She's doing well enough in Port Bergson. She has her friends and we talk several times a week. She doesn't want to move back to the north, she says. So—if you want to go, *go*." She tilted her head. "I would never push you out—"

Rafe laughed in spite of himself, a bubble of unreasonable joy rising through his chest. "But you are, Pennyluck. That's exactly what you're doing. And—you're probably right. No, you *are* right. I never liked this job, even when I did it well—"

"Which you did, brother mine." She smiled at him, the smile he'd seen her use on others: approval of his cooperation.

"And just the thought of getting off this stuffy planet—but what about the house?" The house their parents had given them, when they moved.

"We sell it. *You* sell it and take the money—I've got plenty, and I like my apartment. We'll visit it one last time together, pick out anything we want. I'll send Mother that damned potted tree she was crazy about; in Port Bergson it can grow outside."

"Penny—it's none of my business, but will you ever marry again, do you think?"

She flushed a little. "Maybe. But not for another two years. Frieda said I should wait five years before marrying. I am, as I think you know, seeing someone, but casually."

Nothing would be casual with the heir to ISC's CEO, but Penny knew that already.

"So," she went on, "how about it? What's on your schedule the rest of the day? We could go out to the house now, after asking Emil to call a Board meeting for . . . let's see . . . two days from now? Three?"

Rafe raised his brows with intent. "You don't waste time, do you?"

"No. I learned not to wait," Penny said. For a moment memory darkened her gaze; then it lightened again. "Besides—I do want to be the boss. This office will suit me." Her glance around it was somewhere between predatory and proprietary.

And Ky was somewhere—surely still alive—and if not, if she died before he could find her, he would have the whole wide universe again, anywhere he wanted to go anytime he felt like going.

"All right," he said. "Let's do it. I've nothing on today that can't wait a day; I finished the quarterlies last night." He signaled Emil in the outer office and leaned back in his chair. He felt lighter already.

That lasted only until he was once more in his room at their house with all the things his parents had saved. Clothes. Books. That fateful sword with which his eleven-year-old self had killed a man. He came out of the room after a few minutes only to meet Penny coming out of hers, hands as empty as his.

"Maybe we should just—" she began.

"Burn the whole thing down?"

"No. Not the musical instruments. Not the library. But there's nothing of mine from up here that I want."

"Me neither, and yet I don't want strangers digging through it." He called up a business directory. "Documents destruction first."

Within a few days the house was empty, put up for sale; the real estate agent would have it professionally cleaned and prepped under Penny's supervision. The Board had agreed to let Penny take over for the time being, and granted Rafe a leave of absence with pay for six months. He didn't explain why, but "the strain of the past months" covered it. Penny agreed not to announce the change in her title until he reported from Slotter Key. "But must you go in disguise?" she asked, watching him prep for departure.

"It's safer," Rafe said. "You don't want ISC involved in whatever trouble has hit Vatta again; neither would the Board. And if I have to transfer through some of the places I've been, there might be legal complications."

"You were in trouble," Penny said.

"Let's just say I wasn't always a perfect citizen," Rafe said. "And not all the bodies stayed buried."

She laughed. "I'm not as tame as you think, Rafe. I think I'd have liked knowing you then."

"I'm glad you didn't." He kissed her forehead. "I hope you enjoy running ISC as much as I expect to enjoy being free of it."

CHAPTER THIRTEEN

SLOTTER KEY, MIKSLAND
DAYS 13-25

The camp settled into a routine: fishing, gathering seafood from the rocks they could reach, desalinating water from the bay, emptying the honey buckets, moving rocks to piles around the base of the raft-shelters. The piles grew slowly, but now reached the top of the flotation chambers of one raft, with a gap matched to the canopy hatch. They all slept in that one now, crammed in uncomfortably, but slightly warmer. Work on the next windbreak pile went on.

If shelter had been the only lack, Ky was sure they could overcome it in time. Thanks to the desalinators, they had ample water from the sea. Slotter Key's tides were not large, but Ky hoped the movement of water in and out of the bay would prevent dangerous contamination from their cesspit.

But day by day, hunger and deepening cold took their toll, sapped everyone's energy. Their initial inventory of rations, after landing, revealed that only thirty-six portions of the original six hundred in the lost raft remained. They still had 600 each from the *Ounce* and *Stitch,* and 479 left in *Ducky,* but it wasn't enough. Seventy-seven days from now, at one pack per person a day, it would all be gone. And winter would last longer than that.

She herself was hungry and cold all the time; she knew the others were as well, including the ones who never complained. It was harder to walk over the rocks to the water, harder to pile rocks up, harder even to think. Hardest on those who foraged in the water, their hands so stiff they could not unclench from the bucket handle. Rations calculated for warmer conditions and less exertion were not nearly enough in this cold. She looked at the total calories on the ration pack and asked Tech Lundin, as their resident medic, how many were really needed.

"Three and a half to four thousand, in this kind of cold, without heated shelter. Almost double what these packs contain. And before you ask, I'm having to guess what the bay can supply. If it was all fish and shellfish—plenty of it—it might be enough, but so far each person's getting only a few hundred calories more per day than the ration packet." Lundin leaned closer. "Admiral, I hate to ask this, but have you considered that some people may be stealing food already? Not everyone is losing condition as fast as the others."

"Surely not! We need each other."

"I would recommend a daily count, and some surveillance."

"Who do you suspect?"

Lundin shook her head. "I'm not going to accuse without proof. Two people should make the count, one from each raft, and it should change every day."

Ky nodded. "I'll do that. The situation's too critical to be careless."

The first count, that evening, showed the number was five short of what it should have been had everyone eaten a single pack every day. The next day's count was five short again. Nobody had seen anyone taking rations; no one admitted to suspecting anyone. The day after, the count was only two packs short. But at the supper call, two people were missing: Staff Sergeant Vispersen and Corporal Lanca.

"I saw them out near the point there," Staff Sergeant Kurin said. "They were on the foraging team today and it looked like they were fishing."

"I thought they caught something," Kamat said. "And then threw the line back in. But I was on desalinator duty and just thought we might have fish for supper."

"They're supposed to bring a fish in right away," Kurin said. "They were told that; everyone knows a fish is important."

"Maybe they thought they could catch enough for a feast."

"Not Lanca," Corporal Lakhani muttered.

"What *is* your problem with Corporal Lanca?" Ky asked. It was not the first time Lakhani had made a comment about his fellow corporal.

"Beyond he's lazy and selfish and I wouldn't be surprised if he and Sergeant Vispersen had themselves a fish supper just to hog it, nothing," Lakhani said, getting it all out in a rush. "At least this time I can't be blamed for what he did or didn't do."

"Have you any evidence that he's taken food before?" Ky asked. Before he could answer, she turned to Lundin. "And what about you?"

"I told you I had no proof." Lundin frowned. "I did see both of them—one at a time, I mean—enter a shelter when others were out working. It could have been to use the bucket instead of walking over to the cesspit. Or they'd forgotten something. But neither one looks as pinched as everyone else. So if they're having a private feast, it wouldn't surprise me."

"We were in the same recruit platoon," Lakhani said, less truculently. "The DI was always on him about being lazy and gossiping. Only, we're the same height, same coloring, and my name's next to his, alphabetically. So the DI would yell my name sometimes when it was Lanca shirking. A year later, we were both assigned to that base west of Port Major. Stuff went missing. They found out he took it, and he was punished, but the gossip paired me with him, mixed us up. I even heard an officer say, 'Lakhani, Lanca, it doesn't make any difference—they're both slugs.' When I was up for sergeant and didn't get it, I'm sure that was what happened."

"You haven't impressed *me* as sergeant material," Sergeant Chok said, scowling. "But not as a thief, either."

"I see." Ky nodded. "Before I assume that Lanca and Vispersen are thieves, I, too, would prefer some proof. Meanwhile they're missing, and we need to find them before dark. Four of us—me, Staff Sergeant Gossin, Sergeant Chok, and Master Sergeant Marek—will go out far enough to see if they're still where they were fishing. Commander Bentik, you have the camp until we return; Staff Sergeant Kurin is your second."

"Admiral, I think I should stay in camp," Marek said. "No offense to Staff Sergeant Kurin, but Commander Bentik should be backed up by the most senior NCO."

Ky glanced at her aide. "I would prefer that arrangement," Jen said. "No insult to Staff Sergeant Kurin, of course."

"Of course," Ky said. "Fine, then. Staff Sergeant, come along with us."

When they were well out of earshot, Ky said, "You have any problems with Commander Bentik, Staff?"

"No, sir—Admiral—I haven't. I think she just feels comfortable with Master Sergeant Marek. Maybe because he's older, more her age. And they were in the same raft."

"Possibly." It was something to think about, along with why she herself hadn't considered asking her aide along on this trek.

They found both men lying crumpled among the stones, stinking of vomit, with the carcass of a fish, mostly consumed, and a single SafStov can between them. A section of fishing rod with several chunks of fish still on it made it clear how they'd cooked the meat; the rest of the rod lay under Vispersen. The skin and spines to one side showed it was a puffer fish as long as Ky's arm, a smaller relative of the one that had speared the raft.

Tight-lipped, Ky bent over to check. Both were dead, their bodies cold. She looked in the pockets of Vispersen's suit and found two ration bars. Lanca's pockets had three of them. She handed them to Kurin for safekeeping and collected their ID tags.

"How fast does it kill?" Gossin asked.

"It varies with the dose," Kurin said. "And the particular species, and what it fed on. I don't know why the terraformers imported such a horrible fish."

Ky looked in the foraging bucket. Nothing. They had come out, caught their big fish, and then instead of eating their hoarded ration bars, decided to eat the fish. "I told people when the other one was being hauled in—they had to know it was poisonous."

"It's my fault," Kurin said. "I—I said we could eat them where I lived, and then you said it wasn't safe to trust these. But Lanca asked me later—after we got here—how to tell. I said I didn't know, but ours were blue-green on top, no spots. But that the location made a difference, too. If the water has the right bacteria in it, they're all toxic. He must not have paid attention to that."

"Would you have eaten one?" Ky asked.

"No! Only at home, because they're farmed and checked carefully."

"Their carelessness," Gossin said. "Their greed." She shook her head. "Unmilitary. Both of them."

"We need to get back," Ky said. "It's almost dark. They're well above the tide line, and it's cold; we'll tell the others and retrieve the bodies tomorrow; I should have brought rope but I didn't think they'd be dead. Nothing's out here to bother them."

Next morning a working party went to retrieve them, only to find nothing at all but the little red SafStov can. Even the puffer fish skin was gone.

They had nothing to bury, so McLenard picked up the SafStov can and they went back to camp. No more rations went missing, but everyone was hungrier as the cold deepened. Ky recalculated how long they could last: the loss of two extended their survival another seven days. She didn't tell the others. Soon a fringe of ice collared the shore, thickening as high tides left layers on it.

On the twentieth day since the crash, Ky woke to a strange sound outside, not the usual sounds of waves lapping. She left the shelter, peering into the dim predawn light. Something about the water looked strange, though she couldn't define it. As the light grew, she could see that the water looked thick, not clear as it had been. She could feel the wind at her back; she should have seen the familiar feather-look of ripples, but the water didn't show anything but heavy low swells, thick and sullen. She could hear that strange sound, as if the water were almost full of something—sand? Gravel?—and had as much as it could hold. Her mind groped for words to describe the sound, the sight.

In the distance, the waves that had broken in normal fashion the day before heaved up slowly, thick and gelid. They fell with a plop, like very wet mud, not like water.

"It's freeze-up."

Ky looked around. Others had come out to stare at the strange water. "Freeze-up?"

"Yeah. It's cold enough for ice crystals to form in it. Opposite of melting snow but the same kind of slush." Sergeant McLenard kicked a chunk of the ice on shore into the water. "It gets like this before it actually freezes, but from here on it can freeze really fast."

"What about gathering food?"

"Much harder. Until the ice is thick enough to walk on—and even then, all you can do is cut a hole and drop a line through."

"Do you think the sea will freeze?"

"Yes, certainly right here. See that patchy bit out there? At least the ice isn't as salty as seawater, which is good because the desalinators can't handle slushy water."

And they had no fuel for melting quantities of ice or snow for water. Just the few SafStovs.

"We have to move," Ky said. "We have to find someplace where there's better shelter and fuel for fires." And another food source.

"There isn't anyplace," Marek said. "I've seen reports on Miksland. Scans." *I told you so* seemed to be hanging over his head, but he didn't say it.

"Are we just going to starve? You have to do something!" Jen sounded on the edge of hysteria. The others looked away from her.

"I intend to," Ky said, trying for a confidence she did not feel. "But first, we eat breakfast."

"That's not what I meant!" Jen said. "You got us into this; you said to land here—"

Marek touched her shoulder and gave Ky a sympathetic glance. "It's not the admiral's fault," he said. "There's nothing she can do; once the shuttle was sabotaged, once we landed where we did . . . even if we'd stayed at sea, there's no guarantee we'd be found before the rafts sank or the food ran out."

"Breakfast," Ky said again. "Everybody back inside."

Inside was only a little warmer. Breakfast was a meager cube of biscuit and a small protein bar. Everyone was looking down, away from others. Ky finished hers and waited until everyone had eaten.

"Here's what I know," she said. "Our food will not last the winter, and we won't last without more food and better shelter. Our best chance is to look for more resources somewhere else."

"But we don't even have a map!" Corporal Riyahn said. "We can't just wander around without knowing where we are." He glanced at Marek, as if for support.

"Actually we can," Ky said. "And we do know, in a way, where we are. I'm going to take a small party up to the top and see what's there."

"It'll take a long time to get through all that tumbled rock—and it's dangerous; someone could fall . . ." Riyahn again.

"It's the chance we have," Ky said. "If we don't move, we'll freeze or starve, one or the other or both." Several flinched, as if she'd struck them. "If we explore we might find something we can use to live longer."

"I'll go with you," Betange said.

"Good," Ky said. "We won't leave today. We need good weather and there's clearly some bad on the way. Today, before the next weather hits, I'm going up to the rock tumble and see how bad it really is in there."

"Looks impassable," Marek said, though he smiled at her. "But I imagine you'll find a way."

"That's what admirals are for," Ky said, grinning. About half the group managed a laugh. "Sergeant Cosper, Corporal Yamini, I'd like you to come along as well. Anyone else who has mountain experience, you're welcome to join us."

They set off at once; the clouds were already thicker. "It looks to me," Ky said, "like there's a real gap in the cliffs beyond these boulders. They could be what's fallen off the cliffs, but there's a regularity—it could be intentional, to block the way."

"I'd agree," Yamini said. "A roadblock, not a complete barrier."

When they got in among the rocks, they found a mix of impossible unstable piles and narrow gaps that sometimes led to another narrow gap. In several hours, they'd worked out a path to the slope beyond, rising between walls of rock to either side, and marked the way with reflective stickers.

"I think we can get up to the plateau in—one day?"

"Easily," Sergeant Cosper said. As Ky had expected, he had proven both strong and untiring. "We could go up today, in fact."

"But not make it back to camp by dark," Ky said. "We'll need supplies for two days, and some of those survival blankets, because we'll need to overnight up there somewhere."

"I could go on just a little way," said Cosper. Even as he spoke, a wall of cloud lowered down the slope.

"It's going to snow," Yamini said. "We'd better start back."

By the time they reached the camp, it was hard to see more than ten meters. "We're not starting out in this snow. But the next clear spell, we leave at first light."

Later that evening, Marek asked to speak to her privately. "Sir, I'm not—well, I am, actually—questioning your decision. People are already losing weight on these short rations. The effort to climb up there, to explore—it's just going to cost them more. It won't help."

Ky held up her hand, and he stopped. "Master Sergeant, I believe we're on the same side here—we both want the best for everyone here. Tell me how staying here, with no more shelter than we have, and no more food than we have, will let everyone live through the winter, in shape to find a way to signal for help when the weather eases."

"Sir—Admiral—I can't. I don't think there is a way. But I think what you're doing is just giving them false hope."

"We won't know that if we don't try, Master Sergeant."

He nodded, looking down. "I understand, sir. I hope you're right."

"So do I," Ky said.

"I know you mean well," he said. "And good luck on the search."

It was an odd farewell, but Ky thought she understood. For all that she was from Slotter Key and had been to the Academy, she wasn't really part of his chain of command. It worried him—it would have to worry him—to have her making life-or-death decisions for Slotter Key personnel.

CHAPTER FOURTEEN

SLOTTER KEY, PORT MAJOR
DAY 21

"I have to get back to Cascadia," Stella said as soon as the door to Grace's inner office closed behind her. She had come to the government offices early, by cab, avoiding the media avid for her reaction to Ky's presumed death. "I can't wait until Ky is found or is officially declared dead—I have work to do there that cannot be done by ansible connection. I've already stayed longer than I planned. And the Cascadian government is probing my office about what happened, because of Ky's aide."

Grace nodded. "I don't like it, but I do understand. What does your mother say?"

"What does my mother *always* say but *Family comes first*? But Ky's not my only family; the entire Vatta family is my family. I can't shut down everything because she's missing. If I'd done that when she went off to fight, where would we be?"

"I know," Grace said. "And my sources suggest that the Commandant was the real target in this, though I haven't yet gathered proof enough for a court."

"Any idea who?"

"Oh, the Quindlans. The former President's family, especially his uncle Byron. They've made tries at me, too, but so far unsuccessfully, as you can tell."

"The *construction* Quindlans? The ones who built our old headquarters?"

"Exactly. Who claim to know nothing, absolutely nothing, about how terrorists got hold of the plans and knew where to plant the bombs for maximum effect. Thing is, it was mostly Alexander, the former President, who arranged it, and with operatives from outside. It's possible, though unlikely, that Byron didn't know. His son Egbert certainly did, but again—the proof isn't admissible in court."

"Any connection with Gammis Turek?"

"No, but a good one with Osman Vatta, with that branch of the family. I wish we had Turek's genome; I suspect he was one of Osman's by-blows." Grace leaned back, stretched. "So, when are you leaving, Stella? How will you travel?"

"Vatta ships only. We have three in dock right now, with three departures in the next four days. I might be on any one of them."

"You're not telling me?"

"No, Aunt Grace."

"Indeed. You're right. I'll have Olwen and Mac arrange your return to your mother's; we have enough visitors on official business that another anonymous black car won't be noticed."

"Thank you, Aunt Grace."

"Safe travels. Keep hope; she still might be alive."

DAY 23

Grace looked out the window, blinking back tears. Twenty-three days here had brought brighter weather, flowers, green leaves to the trees.

Twenty-three days on the other side of the planet could bring only shorter days, deeper cold, more storms. Sea ice would have formed all the way to Miksland's south coast now.

Twenty-three days—she had told Stella to keep up hope, but she herself had none. No one survived twenty days in that ocean at this time of year.

A tap at her door brought her back to her desk. "Yes?"

MacRobert eased into her office and shut the door behind him. "I found this in the archives." He handed over a roll of paper. "Really old map, with markings not on any of the newer ones. Apparently it's never been included in the digital map collection."

"Miksland?"

"Yes." He unrolled the map as he talked, weighting the corners with files. "It was stuffed in with 'unreliable, archaic, possibly fantasized' material in the old university library annex. They have an enthusiastic research librarian over there who's found odd things for me before. I said I wanted everything, no matter how ridiculous, on Miksland." He pointed at a mark near the eastern edge of the continent. "See that?"

Grace peered at it. "What is it?"

"Nobody knows, but it's not a natural feature. Natural features don't come with neat straight lines and ninety-degree corners. It's almost five kilometers long, this skinny bit—and down at this end there's what may be a shaft leading underground."

"But nothing's seen on flyovers?"

"Haven't been any sightings *reported*," MacRobert said, with a little emphasis on the last word. "The map's hand-drawn, you can see that. There's no proper legend, no real provenance. My source said she first saw it years ago, when she was an undergraduate volunteer and they were sorting very old materials into the newly built annex. She remembered a few handwritten pages as well, but those were separated from the map and she's looking for them in a different archive."

"But we know the age?"

"Not precisely, not without testing the paper and ink. Personally, I think it was one of the early explorers, three or four hundred years ago, someone unofficial. In a boat of some kind. I can't imagine an aviator marking the shoals and reefs—here, you see, and there. And these faint lines could be courses charted."

Grace sighed. "I don't see how whatever it is could be of use to Ky now, when nothing's shown up since, not even from space."

"Ah. Well. That's the other thing. I suspect whatever's there is from the first surveys five-hundred-something years ago . . . or earlier, from whoever terraformed the place. We had only one minimal space station, one weathersat, and one comsat at first—standard for a new colony—and only one shuttle. Colony was dropped off with a load of equipment, and the transport company's big ship went off somewhere else."

"I didn't know that," Grace said.

"First couple of hundred years were spent growing a population big enough to support technological development. We did have visits from traders but limited ability to get into space, even up to the station. Your family came later. By the time we put our own first satellites up, everyone knew Miksland was a barren waste, good for nothing, and satellite scans didn't bother with it."

Grace frowned. "But, Mac—that doesn't make sense. You wouldn't do that; I wouldn't. For one thing, it's a security risk—a platform someone could use—"

"Exactly." He nodded. "And I think someone *did* use it, and reinforced the belief that Miksland wasn't worth looking at. It's got nasty rough seas all around it, frozen—at least the poleward half—more than half the year."

"Is that where the attack on us came from?"

"I don't know. The evidence I've seen—and you've seen—is that the attack on Corleigh came from that island off to the east, the one with the dead volcano. Miksland—" He shrugged. "I think if Ky made it there in a raft with some others—and it's possible that she could have—then it's possible she could find and shelter in that thing that looks like it could be a mine shaft. If it's been used recently, there might even be supplies in it."

"If it's been used recently, whoever's been using it might come back and kill her," Grace said.

"Yes, but she's not easy to kill."

"I can order satellite surveys now, though, can't I?"

"You can, but if someone's still using it and wants their secret kept, they'll be watching for new surveillance. They'll interpret your interest as the possibility that she's there."

"What we need is a really good sneak," Grace said.

"With no connection to either of us—we're too well known—and no connection to the whole planet if possible."

"I can think of someone, but it would take too long to get him here. Rafe."

"Unless he's on the way," MacRobert said. "From what I saw of him on Cascadia, he will be." He gave Grace a sly look. "He's bound to know she's missing. News media have been all over the story."

Grace snorted. "He knows. Stella told him to stay away, from the first day."

"That won't stop him if he wants to come. It's not Stella he's interested in. If he goes commercial, it'll take him forty days or more; if he takes an ISC courier direct, half that."

"He's security-conscious—if he does come, he won't take an ISC ship. And he'll probably be in disguise."

"If he has the sense he should have, he'll get word to you," MacRobert said. "Maybe through Stella."

"She's left—or soon will. She didn't tell me which ship she was taking. She'll contact me when she's back on Cascadia. Depends on which ship, how long that will be."

"Then we wait and hope," MacRobert said. "Ky's near Miksland; she could be on it. She's smart, tough, and she won't give up. Neither should we."

CHAPTER FIFTEEN

CASCADIA STATION
DAY 28

Rafe Dunbarger arrived at Cascadia's main station from Nexus in one of his fake personas, using different temporary DNA mods. He had his tools, his weapons, and the skills that came to him as easily as ever. And he had Teague, one of Gary's men who—as Gary put it—could use a vacation for a good six months to a year, but was reliable in any situation Rafe might fall into.

Teague had traveled separately, in the character of a spacer hoping to sign on with Vatta, Ltd., and Rafe, in business class, did not see him during the voyage.

"'Scuse me, sir," he heard and turned from the tagger dispenser to see Teague's long, bony face arranged in an expression of slightly worried confusion.

"Yes?" Rafe said. His Cascadian accent made that word plummy and arrogant.

"Edvard Simeon Teague, sir, citizen of Nexus Two. I was wondering, sir, if you knew how to find a business address here?" Teague's accent was pure backcountry Nexus II.

"This machine," Rafe said. "It dispenses direction tags that will ensure you reach your proper destination. Do you require assistance in using it? It would be my pleasure. Hilarion Bancroft, of Mountain Home."

"I wanna get to those Vatta people, Ser Bancroft," Teague said. "Maybe getta ship? Gotta Class Two license."

"Vatta Transport, you mean?" Rafe asked. "As it happens, Ser Teague, that is where I am going. I want to book passage to Slotter Key, and I am informed that no other line has frequent service."

"They take passengers?"

"I am informed they do, but a limited number per trip as they primarily ship freight."

"May I come with you, then?"

"Certainly." Rafe inclined his head and gave the hand wave of a polite Cascadian, then led the way in obedience to the tagger directions.

Pertinent parts of this conversation had been prearranged as confirmation of identity. As they made their way through the curious architecture of Cascadia Station toward the branch where Vatta, Ltd., now had its Cascadian headquarters, Rafe wondered if he would have any trouble with whoever ran the office while Stella was on Slotter Key. Rumor in the business news had it that Vatta might well abandon the Cascadian base except as a local office to service Vatta ships on that route, once more headquartered at Slotter Key. And would Stella still be in charge here, or would another, more local, Vatta take her place?

In his last conversation with Stella, the year before, they had not discussed Vatta's future plans, only a new order for shipboard ansibles that Rafe wanted for ISC's remaining fleet. At that time she had expanded Vatta's offices on Cascadia Station, clearly not anticipating a move back to Slotter Key. And yet she had gone there, and stayed there long enough to spark rumors of a move. Rafe knew how unreliable those could be.

But at least her being there meant his appearing in the Vatta booking office in disguise should not cause any problems. Her subordinates would know him only by his use-name. And Stella would not have the opportunity to ask him what the hell he thought he was doing, running off to Slotter Key. He wasn't ready to answer that question for anyone, least of all himself.

The Vatta insignia, displayed boldly on the entrance to the correct branch, stood proud above the other two labels for that branch. VT Communications Technologies, he knew, was the name of a spin-off from Vatta proper, the outcome of young Toby Vatta's genius while he was Stella's ward. Stella had been adamant that Rafe not offer Toby a job. The near end of the branch had another firm, Brindisi Logistic Solutions, and a cluster of service outlets—cafés, a pharmacy, a grocery—and then the wall color changed to Vatta colors: blue below, cream above, with a red stripe between them.

Vatta Passenger Services was across the corridor from Vatta Freight Services. Beside each entrance, a schedule of arrivals and departures, with openings marked in red. The freight schedule, Rafe noted, had no red openings on either the Vatta ship in dock or the next to arrive. The passenger schedule, however, had several openings. One required a change of ship at Allray; the other, two changes of ship, at New Balestra and then at Variance.

"Allray's the quicker route," Teague commented.

"I would have to stay in persona," Rafe said after a quick look up and down the corridor, empty at the moment. Teague shot him a glance. "I left Allray in a bit of a hurry a few years back." Being shot at, in fact, with Stella and Toby. He had liked Allray and his quiet life there, easiest of his years as a remittance man.

"Will they question your preferring the longer route?" Teague lounged against the wall.

"A moment." Rafe accessed the station database. If he switched personas to a scholar doing research, if he could find relevant list-ings ... Ky had regaled him with more military history than he'd really wanted to know. Ah: if he'd had an interest in military history, a museum on New Balestra held the only remaining complete set of Paruts and Ghoneh's *Early Colonial Wars of the First-Millennium Expansion from Varkan*. A university library on Slotter Key had an almost-complete printing of a different edition (missing volumes 23 and 28). It would have to do.

"Scholarly research," he said to Teague. "Military history of first-millennium colonial wars."

"So you're a professor?"

"I'm a chameleon," Rafe said. "As Gary probably told you."

"That wasn't exactly the term he used," Teague said.

"That does not surprise me," Rafe said in his prissiest voice. "Was it *unprintable snake* or *unprintable idiot*?"

"Both," Teague said, with the first hint of humor Rafe had heard from him. Rafe led the way inside the Passenger Services office.

At the desk Rafe handed over his identification papers to a clerk, who called up the arrival data and nodded. "You've just arrived from Nexus Two—your final destination is Slotter Key—but, Ser Bancroft, I see you've chosen a route that is less direct."

"Ah, let me explain." Rafe put on the enthusiasm of an amateur scholar. "There is, as you see, a twenty-eight-hour delay in New Balestra, and so I will have time to visit the Decan Museum. Did you know they have the only known complete set of Paruts and Ghoneh's *Early Colonial Wars of the First-Millennium Expansion from Varkan*? Every single volume, complete—it's the fourth edition, too. On Nexus there is only half the volumes, and I shouldn't even say *volumes*, be-cause they're apparently printouts that a historian made for personal use at least a century ago. Now, Slotter Key has all but two volumes of the second edition, in the Arvene University library's special collection—"

"You're a historian, Ser Bancroft?"

"Oh, no," Rafe said. "Or only in a small way. I spend my vacations, though, pursuing my historical interests. If one visits these smaller museums and archives personally, one is often able to obtain access to materials by ansible later."

The clerk had lost interest, and was looking at the booking screen on his desk. "Well, Ser Bancroft, we have a single compartment, Class A, or a double, Class B. Vatta, as you may know, is primarily a merchant shipping company; our passenger accommodations are graded three-star by Travelers Express, but I will tell you frankly they are not the equal of luxury passenger liners. You can order in supplementary items, including food." The clerk nodded to the display facing Rafe; it filled with lists of add-on luxuries. He had just marked "Menu Upgrade 2" (all beverages included) and "Bedding Upgrade 1" (more pillows) when a stir by the entrance caught the clerk's attention.

"Sera Vatta! Welcome back!" The clerk jumped up and bowed.

Rafe turned his face a little away, like a polite customer who would not stare at everyone who came in. Sera Vatta wasn't supposed to be here. She was supposed to be still on Slotter Key. There was no way she could get from Slotter Key to Cascadia in the time it had taken him to come from Nexus—

She was now at Rafe's shoulder, speaking to the clerk. "Good day, Hani. I'm glad to be home, indeed. Staff meeting at 1430." Stella's voice, no doubt about it. She turned to Rafe; he thought he saw just the flicker of recognition in her eyes before she spoke. "Ser . . ." She glanced down at the information on the screen, "Ser Bancroft. I hope Hani is taking good care of your reservation. Perhaps you will take tea with me when it is complete."

"He is being most helpful," Rafe said, in his plummiest voice, hoping against hope that she had not seen through his disguise. She had, of course, seen the destination. "Very kind. I do not know if there would be time, Sera, to accept your kind invitation—"

"But Ser Bancroft," Hani said. "Allow me to introduce you. This is Sera Vatta, our CEO. And the ship on which you have reservations does not depart until tomorrow; there is ample time."

He was sunk. Cascadian manners demanded he accept her invitation. And there was no way he could sit and chat politely over tea with Stella, even if she had not yet recognized him, without that recognition coming.

"My pardons, Sera Vatta," he said, holding on to his persona with full attention. "It was not my intent to be discourteous, only—"

"No offense has been taken, Ser Bancroft," she said. The glint in her eye was now obvious, but no shadow of it touched her face or her voice. "I wished only to assure you that although passenger service is not our main mode of operation, we do care greatly about the comfort and safety of those who choose to travel with us. And is this your associate, Ser . . . um . . ."

"Teague," Teague said.

"My research assistant," Rafe said. "On my vacations, I do research in history—early colonial military history, to be precise."

"How interesting," Stella said, in a tone that conveyed nothing but polite concern for a guest's welfare. "Perhaps Ser Teague can complete your reservations while you and I have tea. Hani, should any difficulty arise, please just forward it to my desk." To Rafe she said, "Our passenger reservations, unlike our freight reservations, are fully refundable in case some circumstance requires your presence elsewhere."

"Thank you, Sera Vatta," Rafe said. He was doomed. He was not going to get on that ship without Stella knowing everything about his intent. "Ser Teague," he said, "do feel free to choose upgrades to menu and conveniences, if you wish."

"To what limit, Ser Bancroft?"

This was ridiculous, this was becoming a farce. Why couldn't Stella have shown up an hour later? For that matter, why hadn't Stella stayed on Slotter Key? "Don't go overboard, Ser Teague," he said, hoping his frustration at the whole situation sounded like the fussy, pedantic businessman-*cum*-scholar he was pretending to be. Teague's bland dip of the head in response was the last straw. He turned to Stella.

"Sera Vatta, I am at your service."

"Just this way," she said. All across the broad front office of Vatta, Ltd., her employees stood, bowed, spoke to her, and Stella greeted them all by name before she led him through an opening into an office occupied by three assistants at desks, and then through a closed door into her own. She waved him to a seat, sat down herself, touched her desk, and said "Tea and pastries, please, Gillian." Then she looked at Rafe, opened a drawer in the credenza behind her, took out a security cylinder, and placed it on the desk between them.

"Is this satisfactory, Ser Bancroft?"

He leaned a bit to see the blinking light on one end of the cylinder. "Yes, Sera Vatta, more than satisfactory. One is grateful for your kindness."

"I am curious," she said. "From the little I've seen of your route, on the screen display out there, you seem to consider . . . um . . . Slotter Key as your ultimate destination, but you are not taking a direct route there. Research at intermediate points?"

"Yes, Sera." He launched into the explanation he'd given the clerk until the tea and pastries arrived and the person pushing the cart had left the room.

Stella dropped her slightly bored expression. "Rafe, what do you think you can accomplish by going to Slotter Key?"

"Finding Ky and saving her life," he said.

"You can't," she said. "She's dead. Shuttle went down in the ocean—a very cold ocean—with winter coming on. It's twenty-eight days now. No communications at all. No transponders, no radio, no skullphone linkage, nothing." Tears glittered in her eyes. "You have to—we had to—accept it. I know you loved her—"

"Love. Present tense. And she's not dead. We have a—a link, a bond. I would know if she was dead."

"That's wishful thinking, Rafe. Emotional thinking. But it's no use."

"I will not believe that until I find her dead body myself," Rafe said. "I don't just hope she's alive. I *know* she's alive."

Stella's expression changed. "How?"

"I can't tell you."

"If you want me to believe you, you must tell me. Otherwise I'm going to find ways to delay you, keep you away from Slotter Key—the last thing Aunt Grace and my mother need right now is a lovesick loose cannon crashing into their lives."

"It's not illegal to travel to Slotter Key," Rafe said. "You can't really stop me, even if you keep me off Vatta ships. You can only delay me, and that delay, Stella, could mean Ky's death. Why didn't you want me to come as soon as you heard?"

She ticked off items on her fingers. "Lovesick. Loose cannon. Fully occupied in running ISC, which is what you should be doing right now. Rogue at a level above—no, below—loose cannon. Totally untrained for locating or rescuing someone adrift in a lifeboat on a cold ocean—"

"Not entirely," Rafe said. "I located and rescued my family, who had been abducted and were held on a cold plateau—"

"With considerable help," Stella said. "Are you claiming Teague is your help this time?"

"Yes. From the same source. The task is different and I am assuming your aunt, the Rector of Defense, can deploy assets equivalent to those I had hired before."

She sat back, frowning slightly. "You really are convinced she's still alive, from something other than your personal feelings?"

"Yes."

"But you won't tell me what . . . so I assume it has something to do with a communications link that you and Ky share, that no one is supposed to know about—"

Rafe said nothing, though she stared at him for over a minute. A very long minute. Finally, she nodded.

"Well, then. I think Ser Bancroft needs to change his itinerary. I think it would be wise to go straight to Slotter Key, and visit—what was it, some obscure museum?"

"Yes."

"On the way back, if it's still of interest. I suspect, Ser Bancroft, that your reluctance to take the more direct route has to do with something you did at Allray, am I right?"

"Possibly," Rafe said. She knew perfectly well what he'd done there. She'd been there.

"I have a Vatta courier onstation right now, refueling and resupplying for another mission. That's how I came here. It is fast, long-range, but not as comfortable as the passenger quarters on our freighters. It would be cramped for you and Ser Teague."

"How long?"

"How urgent is secrecy? If your disguise must remain undiscovered, then you need to miss that departure tomorrow for some plausible reason—no—let me think. A transfer—no, that won't work, either. We need to discover a family relationship, Ser Bancroft. Then I could discover you as a family member and offer you the use of a courier, to give you more time for research."

"You're now known to be Osman Vatta's daughter. What if I were one of his sons?"

Her brows went up. "You aren't, are you?"

"No," Rafe said. "I've seen my own gene scan many times, and that of my parents and Penny. I'm all theirs. But as Bancroft—"

"Fine. We'll do it that way. A bit shady but it could be taken that I just want you far away from me—even that I'm sending you to Aunt Grace to be checked out for, um, rogue behavior."

"Of which, in my checkered past, there's plenty. All right, beautiful lady, now that we're alone I reveal to you that I am the natural son of the evil Osman Vatta, reared in a foster home and discovering my real identity only by accident. Shocked and horrified, I became fascinated by Vatta family events, and now I am shivering in anticipation of what you might say in return."

"Shivering in anticipation—a bit over the top, Rafe, don't you think?"

"I'm not Rafe, I'm Hilarion Bancroft—"

"Hilarion? Also over the top. Oh, well. You are Osman's son after all, and *he* was over the top. I am naturally startled, and then appalled, to think that you might have been stalking me, so the best thing to do is stuff you into a courier—you might want to lose the fat suit before that—and send you to Aunt Grace, who will wrap you in deepest darkest secrecy and force you to give up whatever vile plans you had made."

"They aren't vile," Rafe said.

"Oh, I think they are," Stella said. "And meanwhile it has been strongly suggested to you that you and Ser Teague stay with me—Vatta Security feeling safer that way—in a friendly sort of house arrest. It will take the courier almost two days to be ready, but less than half the time of any other ship to get to Slotter Key."

"What do you use for couriers, fairy dust?"

"Couriers are always faster, Rafe, you know that. But Toby's come up with something."

"Which you won't tell me about."

"Trade secret," Stella said. "Just like yours."

For the first time since he'd heard about Ky's shuttle going down, Rafe laughed. "My God, you're a smart woman," he said.

Stella was laughing, too. "Yes. We're both smart. And that, if anything, might help Ky, if she's still alive, which is why I'm going along with this. My young cousin is a pain sometimes, but I love her anyway. So now, I think, we begin the next charade you and I are about to be involved in. I will call my security staff in, and you and Ser Teague will spend a pleasant night, maybe two, in my guest quarters. Will you need to visit anything else onstation?"

"I should visit Crown & Spears," Rafe said, "or—I was planning to. Set up a transfer to my next destination. But as it is—"

"We would prefer you not have a contact here besides Vatta," Stella said, making her face prim.

"Then I will be pleased to accept your hospitality," Rafe said. "Shall I pour us tea now?"

"I will," Stella said. She poured two cups of tea, handed him one, and put two pastries on a plate for him. "Eat fast."

She drank half her cup of tea while Rafe allowed crumbs to find their way down the front of his suit, and then touched a button on her desk. In moments, two serious-looking men in a uniform he hadn't seen before appeared at the door. They eyed him with disfavor.

"This is Ser Bancroft," Stella said. "I find that he is a relative of sorts—a natural son of my natural father from a different mother. He and his research assistant, Ser Teague, will be staying with me until *Morningstar* is ready for another trip, and then they'll be passengers to Slotter Key. He has reason to visit my aunt Grace."

"Yes, Sera." Their looks became colder.

"He is a guest; he has done nothing—" A tiny pause suggested an unspoken *yet*. "—to warrant anything but a pleasant visit in the guest suite. I believe, however, that the reservations he intended to make on *Allie Verger* may have progressed to the point of payment; those reservations should be canceled and a refund applied to the paying account. Perhaps one of you would ask his travel companion Ser Teague to step this way so the new arrangements can be explained to him."

"At once, Sera," said one of the men. The other moved to stand behind Rafe's chair. Rafe took another pastry.

Teague, when he entered the office, had the deliberately blank look that Rafe recognized as "criminal playing dumb." Rafe spoke up at once.

"I told Sera Vatta that I was related to her," he said. "You know, this is the first time I've told someone important that I'm also one of that criminal's children, but if a rich, beautiful woman can admit it in public, then why not? And I want people to know we're not *all* bad—we didn't inherit criminal tendencies or anything like that."

Teague's expression congealed further. He must be wondering what Rafe was up to. He said "Yes, Ser Bancroft."

"And Sera Vatta very kindly offered me the use of a Vatta courier that can get us to Slotter Key quickly, leaving plenty of time on the return trip to visit that other archive. She's even going to give me a letter of introduction to her aunt, in Slotter Key's Defense Department, so I'll be able to do research in their archives. We're staying with her until the courier's ready to leave."

"Yes, Ser Bancroft. Will you be visiting the bank, though? I thought you wanted to set up accounts at intermediate destinations and Slotter Key."

Rafe made a dismissive movement with one hand and grabbed another pastry with the other. "I'm sure Sera Vatta can arrange that for us—can't you, Sera Vatta?"

"Certainly," Stella said. "There's a terminal here in our office. We can have your luggage transferred, as well. And what would you like for dinner this evening? Just let my cook know, and I'm sure we can accommodate any dietary restrictions."

Rafe glanced down at the crumbs on his suit. "I'm not fussy, Sera. I like food."

"I can't eat melons," Teague said. "But that's all."

A key phrase Rafe had to answer. "Melons are fine with me," he said. "But I don't insist on them." That should keep Teague from doing whatever Teague was thinking of.

"The cook will bear that in mind." Stella glanced at her security. "I think these gentlemen would be more comfortable in the guest suite than in my office." She smiled at Rafe. "Don't you, Ser Bancroft?"

"Yes, Sera, whatever's convenient." To the security man now near Teague he said, "I can't believe I met my real sister—well, half sister— such a coincidence that she happened to come in while I was in the office. I hadn't even dared hope—"

"I will dine with you later," Stella said with a nod to the others. Rafe stood, brushing the crumbs off himself.

"Thank you very much, Sera," he said. "You've been most gracious. I wish—I wish we'd known each other sooner."

He went out when one of the men gestured for him to go first and then walked beside him as he started, still brushing at his suit, across the outer office. Teague followed; the second security man delayed long enough to ask Stella, "Leech, or really dangerous?"

He heard her laugh and say, "Harmless, I think, but Aunt Grace will sort him out if he's not."

The door closed. Rafe and Teague went peacefully along with their escort, out the entrance to Vatta, Ltd., back down the branch, and then along one passage after another until they arrived at Stella's residence.

Rafe approved of the level of security: their escorts were, he thought, properly alert and well armed, and the servant who opened the door of Stella's apartment was no mere butler. The guest suite, essentially another complete apartment, had no direct exit to the outside except an emergency hatch, heavily alarmed and marked with a big red sign: EMERGENCY EXIT ONLY.

"I'm Dosi Farbur," one of the men said. "I'll be outside if you need anything. Ron here will let the rest of the staff know you're here, and the cook will be contacting you shortly, if she doesn't come herself, to learn about your needs. Then he's going to arrange your luggage. All outgoing calls go through the house board; I believe Sera Vatta feels that you should avoid making your presence here known. Many of her guests have a need for discretion."

"Yes, Ser Farbur," Rafe said. "I understand. I'm sure we will be quite comfortable. Is there a vidscreen? There's a sports match I wanted to watch."

"Through there." Farbur nodded toward a door on the left. "Also a small library of both informational and entertainment cubes and a cube reader that displays on the large screen. All local news, sports, and entertainment channels are available."

"Thank you," Rafe said.

The study included a small bar at one end where a pitcher of ice water, a tray with glasses, and a plate of pastries had already been set out. When Rafe opened the little cooler below the counter, he found a selection of wines and spirits.

"This is—I've never been in a place like this," Teague said. He glanced around.

"Sera Vatta is, I believe, a very wealthy woman," Rafe said, for the sensors he knew would be observing them. "I have seen such luxury only on entertainment cubes, or in high-class hostels when at conventions. We will certainly be comfortable here."

"I wonder what the bedroom is like," Teague said. Rafe followed him out into the sitting room. There were three bedrooms, all with separate bathrooms. Teague stared for a moment at the plumbing fixtures, then shook his head. "You read about things like this," he said. "But seeing it . . . I suppose you know what it all does."

"Yes. On a station like this, where recycling every drop matters more, some of it's involved with that. This mysterious coil here, for instance. And this extra pipe. Don't worry about it; the actual function, from the user end, is standard."

"But this thing?" A nozzle on a long flexible pipe.

"Vacuum, for cleaning staff. We could use it, if we were being especially tidy guests. It sucks up every drop of water or condensation—on the bath compartment walls—and sends it to primary decontam before shipping it off to the station's own water treatment facility."

"They recycle *all* the water?" Teague looked pale.

"Every drop. Teague, is this your first extended period in space?"

"Yes—I was born, raised, and worked all my life on Nexus."

"Every space-based facility depends on complete recycling. So do spaceships. Don't think too much about it."

"Right." Teague's color returned to normal.

"Which bedroom do you want?"

"Uh—I don't know."

"I'm taking the green one, then. I'm going to lie down until our luggage arrives—or the cook—whichever comes first."

That evening, Teague elected to eat in the guest suite, ostensibly to repack their luggage but actually, Rafe suspected, to make sure none of whatever equipment he'd packed had disappeared. Rafe accepted Stella's invitation to dine with her. Stella had a table set in her tiny garden, made to look larger than it was with a combination of vid-screens around the margin and careful planting.

"Secure," Stella said. "We can talk."

But first, they ate her cook's excellent dinner while Rafe tried to think what he was going to tell her that he hadn't already.

"Your certainty," Stella said immediately after swallowing her last bite of the crème brûlée. "Rafe, I understand you don't want to tell me, but I need to know something."

He'd been afraid of this.

"Stella, it's a danger to anyone who knows that it exists. Worse than shipboard ansibles. It's a danger to anyone who has it. I must not say more; I don't want you in danger, too."

"Ky's in danger from knowing about it—or does she have it?"

"She has it. And yes, she's in danger from that, although she's in danger for so many other reasons it hardly adds to the total. But you, Stella, are the rock Vatta depends on now. And you are more secure than someone who goes out into space and attacks warships, like Ky."

"I certainly hope so," Stella said. "Are you and Ky the only ones who know?"

"Unfortunately not. My sister Penny found out by accident, during the late unpleasantness. Observed me with it. But she's not a blabber and no one else knows she knows."

"They might infer—"

"Yes, enemies might, if they knew about it. And someone else knew before all that, when I first got back to Nexus. No one should have known, but—"

"The inventor?"

"Maybe. Or someone who tortured the information out of the inventor. I have no clue; I'd been away too long. The thing is, there may still be people who know *I* have it. I have no idea where they might be. Penny's the only other person who knows Ky has one."

"I see. Aunt Grace is going to want to know. And she's a lot more persuasive than I am. With more power behind her."

"Perhaps. We'll see. Stella, I really appreciate what you're doing. I believe I'll know for certain what I'm reasonably sure of now, once I get to Slotter Key and can tune the local ansible . . ."

"You're going to do *what*?"

"News reports suggest to me that Slotter Key's ansible may still not be fully functional. I can fix that. You know I can."

"But how will that find Ky?"

Rafe just looked at her. Stella glared, but then shrugged. "All right. Don't tell me. Here's what I've arranged. You and Teague, whoever he really is—"

"You know what I know about Teague, except that Gary said they were working a criminal hostage situation and apparently the bad guys got into one of Gary's computer systems. A mole he hadn't spotted; the mole's dead, Teague killed him, so Teague's a marked man. They got his partner. I have a year of his services in return for giving him new biomarkers and ID; the stuff's already working, but will take another one to two years to complete."

"That's rather a lot under *except*. I suppose he's already looking less like his old self?"

"Yes, much less like his old self. Biomarkers on scans are quite different, but the rest is, as you may know, limited by the rate of cell replacement. He did have one surgery four months ago to change the shape of his jaw. I see a difference in skin tone—he will be distinctly less brown and more yellow when he's finished—but it's not nearly enough yet to make him safe on Nexus."

She blinked. "So—I could choose to become plain—even ugly—"

"Do you want to?"

"No. I don't think so. There's still a usefulness in what I have. But it's tempting to become someone completely other, at least for a while."

"The kind of treatment Teague's getting isn't for *a while*."

"I understand. But back to your travels. The courier crews have been completely checked out, gene scans and all. You will travel more comfortably without your add-ons, but it's up to you. The facilities are, as I said, cramped and not overly comfortable, especially for two.

This crew's been briefed, though not to your real identity. They won't ask; they don't want to know, even if they figure it out."

"Good. But I think I should arrive at Slotter Key in my persona."

"Yes. And you should leave here wearing it; Cascadia's tightened its exit protocols. They won't mind you leaving by Vatta courier, but you must check out with them or we'll all be in trouble."

"So—when, exactly, are we leaving?"

"Tomorrow evening, local time. The courier's on the schedule for a 2300 departure; you'll need to go through exit procedures by 2230. I'll provide an escort at 2130 to continue the cover story. The deposit money for the other reservation is already in your account on Slotter Key."

"My account . . . how did you do that?"

She gave him the look he'd given her years before, and the same answer. "I have connections. Now: no one but crew will know you're on our courier; when I hear from them that they've made the Slotter Key downjump, I'll call Grace."

Alone in the bedroom he'd chosen, Rafe took off the accoutrements that made him look fifty kilos heavier and ten years or more older. He cleaned and hung up the various pads and their attachments, then took out the cable for his cranial ansible. Should he? Probably not. But he plugged in the cable to the power outlet anyway. After that difficulty during the war, he had made an addition to it that could convert any standard line power to the ansible's power requirement and not burn out his brain.

As he had once a day since he found out about Ky's situation, he plugged in. And there it was: the peculiar smell that told him he had an ansible-to-ansible connection with another just like his . . . and that could only be hers. He could not communicate with her; the signal was too weak. But she was still alive. He closed his eyes, concentrating. Was it weaker than it had been? Was she dying, right then?

He disconnected, coiled the cable without looking at it, and returned it to the case. He snapped the lock and tried to put Ky and her problems out of his mind.

The next day was one long stretch of boredom, despite the books, the vids, the games. Stella was away in her office. The cook fixed them breakfast, lunch, afternoon tea. Teague slept a lot; Rafe knew the treatment was tiring for him. By the time Stella came back to the apartment, it was almost time to leave. He and Teague were both ready. After a quick supper, their guards led them back toward the main Vatta docks, where a departure desk staffed by two Cascadian officers waited. Stella stayed behind.

CHAPTER SIXTEEN

MIKSLAND
DAY 29

Not dead yet. Ky reminded herself of that every time her thoughts drifted on the long slog up to the plateau. They had started under starlight, well before local dawn; the clear, still weather was too good to waste; recent snowfall had drifted in between boulders, slowing progress. When they finally cleared the deepest drifts, the flimsy shelters they'd left were now hidden by the swell of ground. Like those with her, those left behind were hungry, cold, weakening day by day since the bay had frozen over and put an end to fishing. It was Ky's job to make them hang on, to ensure that they had the best possible chance to survive.

By the time daylight made visibility easy, they were past the tumble of boulders and onto the snow-covered slope above. Here the snow wasn't as deep; walking was easier. They were, Ky estimated, halfway up the gulch when a gust of wind blew all the snow off a smooth slanted surface in front of them.

"I could almost believe that was a road once," Betange said. "But if it was a road why would it stop—or start—here?"

Ky turned to look back down the slope. From here she could not see the shore at all, only the ocean end of the bay, dark water showing between slabs of ice. "So it couldn't be seen from below, I guess. But it could've been seen from the sea—if anyone had looked. Or satellite surveillance. If it is a road."

Soon it was clear that, if not a road, it was a much smoother path upward than they'd had before. Again and again gusts of wind blew the snow off it. Eventually the slope eased, then eased again. Now they could see ahead and to either side. Low hills with taller ones behind them rose to the right. Thirty meters away a group of large grayish animals she had no name for fled abruptly, kicking up snow. Ky had never seen anything like them—shaggy, heads high, strangely shaped antlers, slender legs, short tails sticking up like flags.

"I thought this was supposed to be barren," she said. Whatever the animals were, they slowed to a bouncy trot about a hundred meters away, then to a walk, and headed off in single file.

"Just rock and ice, they said in school," Betange said. "Terraforming failure, nothing grows there."

"I wish we had a gun," Sergeant Cosper said. "Real meat, and lots of it—"

"We'll find a way," Ky said. At the thought of meat, fresh meat, her stomach cramped. She looked away from the animals, now disappearing into a dip. There, ahead to the right, something looked odd. Straight lines, not natural. "There!" she said, pointing. "That's got to be a structure."

"How far away is it?"

"Do you think anyone's there?"

"What *is* it?"

Ky didn't wait to answer the questions. The road—she was sure it was one now—aimed that way, and she kept going. "We'll find out when we get to it," she said.

"But—"

"Let's go."

Another upward slope dragged at their feet, but the structure—clearly now a structure—loomed higher with every step, and they were clearly on some kind of intentional roadway, a surface smooth as pavement beneath the uneven covering of snow. When they reached the brow of the low hill, they saw a broad, shallow bowl with a tower rising from it.

"Bet it's a mine shaft," Betange said. "And buildings."

"And that looks like a landing strip," Ky said, looking beyond the tower and the buildings near its base to a long, straight, nearly flat stretch of snow at least three times wider than the road they'd been walking on. "And a hangar. Long enough for a shuttle landing, do you think?"

"Might be," Yamini said.

The way down was steeper and slippery with ice under the snow; as they neared the bottom of the bowl, the snow to either side lay deeper. They hurried as much as they could; Ky knew they craved the potential shelter of real walls and a roof.

"Slow down," she kept saying. "No broken ankles—we'll get there—"

The sun was long gone and green auroras danced overhead before they arrived in that cold unwelcoming light. Finally they reached the first building, a simple rectangle with a steeply pitched roof. Corrugated metal walls, metal shutters over what Ky hoped were windows. A metal door, locked, had a weathered stenciled label, A-2, and a keycard reader that looked newer than the buildings. They banged on the door and yanked, but the lock held. "Who's got a Spaceforce ID card?"

Yamini fished his out. "Try it," Ky said. She didn't think it would work, but she also couldn't think of anyone using this place but the military, and just possibly it would open to any current ID card.

"It wants a code number, too," Yamini said. "ID maybe?"

"Try yours," Ky said. Yamini keyed in a string of numbers, but the lock didn't release. The tiny illuminated screen read ERROR. ONE OF THREE ALLOWED ATTEMPTS.

"We're done," Yamini said, shoulders slumping. He leaned against the wall and slid down until he was sitting on the ground.

"I'll try," Ennisay said, reaching for the keypad.

Ky put out her hand. "No. If it won't take Yamini's, it won't take yours. We need to think it through. We can't afford guesswork. It must be working from either a list of those locally authorized, or some chain of command." The others looked at her blankly, exhausted, clearly beyond hope. She felt like falling on the ground herself, but that wouldn't accomplish any more than would her own command code from the Space Defense Force.

What might? An officer's code number? They had none . . . unless her original number from Spaceforce, back when she was a cadet, would work. Had they disabled that number? Were officers' numbers any more useful than enlisteds'? No way to know. But she had nothing else to offer, and they had—if she interpreted the screen aright—three tries. She knew her own number; she'd had to recite it many times as a cadet. She entered it.

The screen flashed twice. ERROR. TWO OF THREE ALLOWED ATTEMPTS.

"It's no use," Corporal Lakhani said. "Coming up here was just wasted energy and now we don't even have a canopy to break the wind."

As if to emphasize the importance of that, the wind strengthened, whistling under the eaves of the building.

"We'll break in some way," Ky said, though she had no idea how, without tools. Her mind felt stiff, unwilling to think. She needed numbers, the right numbers, numbers from Spaceforce, from some command position in Spaceforce . . . like Aunt Grace. But she was Rector of Defense, not *in* Spaceforce. She had no number . . . or did she? Even as she felt the wind sucking warmth from her suit, even as she struggled not to shiver visibly, a vague memory of Aunt Grace and numbers came to her.

That message granting Ky command of Slotter Key's privateers had strings of numbers—routing numbers, she'd assumed. She hadn't understood any of them, or needed to; the message had been clear enough. But one string, immediately under the Rector's seal—could that be a code identifying the Rector? Was it the same as on the other messages she'd received?

She couldn't remember—but her implant should have recorded every detail. Yes. Under the Rector's seal on every message from Grace had been a single numeric string. She retrieved messages from the other Slotter Key ships, from the admiral who had come to Nexus: different strings. If only she hadn't wasted that second try on her cadet number—stupid idea. Because now she had a choice of the Rector's number or an admiral's. The admiral was active duty; he was high on the chain of command. But this installation—on a continent declared uninhabited, a terraforming failure—this installation, combined with the sabotage of shuttle and officers, suggested a secret group within Spaceforce. The door code might be limited to such a secret group. Was that admiral in it?

She was certain Aunt Grace was not. But if she hadn't changed her authorization number from the previous Rector's—and the previous Rector, she'd been told, had been involved in the treason that killed her family and brought down the government . . .

Her hand was shaking, partly with cold and partly with anxiety, but she entered the numerals carefully, one after another. 4 1 1 9—"Are you sure, Admiral?" asked Kurin. "I mean, it's the last chance—"

"Not entirely," Ky said. Her voice was steadier than her hand as she entered the last digits: 7 6 0 1. Nothing happened for a moment, then the display blanked and the locking mechanism clunked. Ky tugged; the door resisted, then scraped a path through the snow as it opened. She glanced at the others. Most were still standing, hunched against the cold; Yamini still sat beside the door. "Let's get inside," she said. "Sergeant, use your pin-light. Staff, help Corporal Yamini up."

She turned on her own pin-light. She could just see a solid smooth floor as the others shuffled and staggered past her, disappearing into darkness that looked solid after the flickering auroral light outside.

As the last one passed her, she turned to go in, pulling the door almost closed and tugging off a glove to put in the gap to keep the lock from connecting.

In the darting shafts of Kurin's pin-light and her own, Ky saw two metal-framed double bunks, a table with four chairs, two desks each with its own chair, and a door to the right. On the desks were dimples that might have been made by equipment feet, and each one had an electrical outlet mounted flush to one end.

It wasn't actually warmer in here, but they were out of the pervasive wind, and the interior walls were smooth, not corrugated. Presumably, in this climate, the walls would be insulated. If they could heat up the interior, even a little—but as the cold bit into her ungloved hand, she turned her pin-light on the inside of the door. They needed it closed all the way, and they needed not to be locked in.

No emergency bar for exit, but also no card slot or numerical keys for a code number. It did have a lever. She focused her pin-light on the edge of the door, where a bolt—no, three of them—would come out when the door was locked. She moved the lever up and down. The bolts slid out; the bolts slid in. There was a push button on the door as well; she tried that, and found that it kept the lever from moving up and pushing the lock-bolts out. She set the button to prevent locking, picked up her glove, and closed the door.

The others had moved around the room; some were now sitting on the bunks, on the chairs.

Sergeant Cosper's pin-light was now off to her right. "There's a little kitchen on one side and a toilet and shower on the other." He sounded excited. "Maybe there's food. Supplies."

"And there must be power, with those outlets," Ky said. She looked on the wall near the door and found a touchplate. Nothing happened when she touched it, but her pin-light aimed at the ceiling revealed lighting panels. "But first—running water? Food in the kitchen?"

"There'll be some kind of powerplant," Cosper said.

"Of course. Thank you. One of the other buildings, maybe."

They were all tired, stumbling-tired, but unable to rest until they'd explored a little more. They found a generator in the smallest building, primed and ready to start. Yamini looked at Ky, brows lifted.

"Go ahead."

He pulled the lever and the generator came on. So did several lights, immediately blinding them to the darker night around, but showing up other details they'd missed.

"Power's standard," Kurin said, looking at the readouts on the generator. "Just like any other power source. And this thing's a Foster-Moray Model 3100-D. It can't be more than a few years old; there's one of these on my cousin's farm."

"So the failed terraformed continent's inhabited," Ky said. "Did you ever see anything about that on the news—in the last few years, maybe?"

"No. If we can find whoever it is, they can call for help, can't they?"

"If they're friendly," Ky said.

"Why wouldn't they be?"

She couldn't think. She was too tired, too hungry right now. "We'll go back to the first building, see if there's anything in the kitchen, any heat source, a furnace or something—"

"Right."

The kitchen was basic—a very small version of the big kitchens in the houses she had known. A stove across from the door, its top marked with the circles of heat sources. A counter running along the wall to the right, with a large deep sink halfway along it. No programmable drink dispenser. No automatic recycling cleaner unit. No speed oven. But the simple stove worked when Betange turned the knobs, heating the circles quickly.

They all crowded into the tiny kitchen as the room warmed. On the shelves they found rows of sealed containers, none of them labeled, and several sizes of cooking pot, as well as a stack of plates and another of bowls, and mugs hanging from hooks. But water did not flow from the kitchen faucet, nor was there water in the toilet.

"Someone drained the pipes for winter, so they're probably not coming back anytime soon," said Cosper. "I guess there's a well; we'll need to find the pump."

"In the meantime, we'll melt snow," Ky said. "Take the biggest pot and fill it with snow."

Drawers below the counter contained cooking utensils, openers for the containers, and—in one drawer—eight each of knives, forks, and spoons. What, Ky wondered, would they find in those containers? Her mouth watered at the possibilities: canned stew, canned fish, any of the foods carried on spaceships. But the first opened container turned out to be flat round crackers, just like the ones in the life raft kits. They looked delicious. The next container had more of the same; the next was full of bean paste. They all looked at her, eyes almost feral with hunger.

"We need to be careful," she said, remembering her earlier experience with hunger. She didn't want to be careful; she wanted to eat the whole thing herself, now. "We don't know how long this must last, and if we eat too fast we'll waste it by puking it back up." They looked sullen, but nodded.

"When Sergeant Cosper comes back with snow, we'll melt that, boil it, make a sort of soup with the paste and the crackers and the protein strip from our rations."

Though it took longer than any of them wanted to wait, the snow finally melted and then warmed to a simmer. Betange put some of the water into a smaller pot, stirred in some bean paste, two handfuls of crackers, and the protein strips from everyone's ration pack. Ky handed out mugs, and Betange served out the mixture precisely.

"Drink it slowly," Ky warned. "We don't want to waste any." She took a spoon from the drawer and tasted hers. It wasn't raw fish. It wasn't raw shellfish. It was hot, thick, bland with the bean paste. She could have wolfed down the whole mug in one go. She made herself use the spoon, methodically, spoonful by spoonful.

"More," said Cosper.

"Wait a little," Ky said. "We've been hungry a long time; we've all lost weight."

In an hour she let Betange heat more; everyone had another half mug. She herself felt more alert, though still hungry. She began automatically making lists: what they would need here for the next few days. If they couldn't get the water working again they would need some kind of latrine and a better water source than snow. They needed heat in the building, not just the kitchen. They would need to move everyone up here—even with just this one building, and crowded as it would be, this was better than the canopies of the life rafts down by the shore. Someone would have to go back. Tomorrow. Two, not one—one might be injured, and anyone who lay out alone at night would die. Did they dare delay one day to check out the other buildings? No—the situation below was too critical. In another day or so, some of those would not be able to walk up the slope. She could send a canister or so of food down to them; that would help.

Once it started, her mind buzzed on, busy as usual. She authorized another half mug of the warm mix, this time diluted with hot water. As she sipped her own serving, she considered how those who stayed could ready this place for the others and who should go. Some had struggled to make it here; they couldn't possibly make a return trip so soon. But Sergeant Cosper could, and so could Sergeant McLenard. "You four"—she pointed them out—"get some rest now; we'll be hot-bunking later. Double up on the lower bunks; if you find bedding storage in the next five minutes, wonderful—otherwise, in your suits, under the survival blankets. Betange, we need a complete inventory of food supplies here. A team will take a couple of canisters down to the bay tomorrow, share that food, and bring everybody up the next day."

CHAPTER SEVENTEEN

CASCADIA TO SLOTTER KEY
DAYS 30-36

Exit clearance went as smoothly as Stella has predicted, and then they were in a small, plain departure lounge. Shortly, a dark-skinned, gray-haired woman whose family resemblance to Ky was clear came through the docking tube.

"Ready to board?" she asked. "I'm the captain and first pilot. Ginny Vatta. Second pilot's Daran Vatta."

"Yes, thank you," Rafe said. "I'm Ser Bancroft; this is my assistant, Ser Teague."

"Come on aboard, then. We're in the queue, and we might get bumped up one if that oversized hulk of a passenger liner just ahead of us doesn't get her stragglers on board by the deadline. I hear some of them went off on a bender here and are having to pay fines."

She led the way through the docking tube, ducked through the hatch into the little ship saying, "Watch your heads," and a few meters up the narrow passage turned to look at them, pushing open a door.

"Here's your cabin—you'll be hot-bunking unless one of you sleeps on the floor. Toilet and basin straight across, one for the whole ship. Sponge baths only—we're limited in water, but it's not going to be that many days and the air filters are good. There's one spare seat across from our third crewmember, just forward of the galley; the galley seats two at a time. Crew have priority. There are games on the console, if you like games. For departure, one of you sit with the engineer, one of you in the rack. You'll likely feel some acceleration in spite of the AG."

Rafe glanced at Teague. "You take the rack; I'll sit up." He followed the captain forward, past the tiny galley with its oven, sink, hotplate, and a table now latched up against the bulkhead. The engineer sat facing aft, watching a bank of displays covered with wiggly lines and symbols Rafe didn't know. The seat he was given faced forward. Beyond was the pilots' space, two well-padded couch-seats, arms studded with controls and the entire space in front of them a mass of displays except for a forward screen or window—he couldn't tell which, from his seat. He fastened the safety harness as Ginny Vatta watched, then she stepped through the opening into the cockpit.

She did not close the hatch between the two compartments, but spoke to the second pilot in a rush of slang that Rafe couldn't understand. He could see her, or part of her, and leaned out a little in the aisle to see more. Now she had a headset on and talked softly into it. He could make little sense of what he saw on the screen or through the window, until something pale slid by, speeding up as it went, and he realized that they were moving, that the large pale thing was part of the station or another ship docked there. He felt only the same faint vibration he had felt from the moment he stepped on board.

Now the forward screen showed a few lights at a distance he could not estimate, but they moved across the screen slowly. The instruments he could see flickered, displays changing; he thought back to the bridge of Ky's first ship, the old freighter he'd been on for that hair-raising trip from Lastway to . . . where had it been? But this was far more complex, and so much smaller.

Something clunked under the deck; his feet felt it.

"Engaging," the engineer said. Rafe glanced at him. The man was staring at his displays; Rafe tried to see which one he was looking at, but couldn't. "Ready, Captain."

"Hold two. Traffic." The captain's voice. Another stretch of silence, in which Rafe could hear his own heartbeat. And then: "Engage and go seventy percent."

"Seventy percent."

The push came as if someone had shoved the seat into his back. It was like taking off in an airplane, nothing he'd felt before in space. And it went on. And on.

"Eighty," said the captain.

"Eighty."

More pressure . . . was there *any* artificial gravity compensation? Rafe couldn't tell. He wasn't about to black out, he told himself, but he was definitely uncomfortable, and the longer it lasted, the more uncomfortable he felt.

The courier was as quiet inside as any other ship, just the little *whish* of air from the vents and that one *clunk*. Even as he thought he would have to say something about the pressure, it disappeared—all the gravity disappeared for a moment, then his hand flopped down onto his lap as the artificial gravity took over.

"Transition successful," the engineer said. He turned to look at Rafe. "Sorry about the blank moment. We need to get that lad Toby back on this ship to figure out why. The other courier the new system's on doesn't do that."

"We can't be in FTL already, can we? It took two days, leaving Nexus."

"That was a standard passenger ship. We do things differently, and yes, we're in FTL flight. Will be until we're in Slotter Key space."

"Right," Rafe said. He looked back into the cockpit; gray shields covered the window—if it was a window. But Slotter Key all in one jump? Just what had Toby been inventing *this* time? The captain turned to look at him.

"Orders were to get you to Slotter Key quickest. We'll come into the Slotter Key jump point in six days, barring a technical problem. If you know how to make tea, make a couple of mugs for the crew."

"Yes, Sera—Captain—" Rafe said. He could feel her gaze on his back as he took the few steps to the galley. Following the directions on the dispenser was easy; it had been preprogrammed for "Pilot, Second Pilot, Engineer." Six mugs with the Vatta logo were in the rack above. He filled two for Pilot and Second Pilot and brought them forward.

The captain took hers, sniffed, nodded. "You figured it out."

"We do have such things on Nexus," he said.

"I'm sure you do," she said, with a little emphasis on *you*. He smiled and handed the second mug to the other pilot, who nodded.

"What about you?" he asked the engineer.

"Not right now," the man said. "I've checks to run. Want to watch?"

"Yes," Rafe said. Better than sitting still with nothing to do. He followed the engineer back down the passage. Latches he had not noticed opened compartments filled with color-coded tubes or what looked like something from a chemistry lab. Over the course of the next few hours, Rafe realized that the crew did not want him alone in any space but the cramped cabin or the toilet. He could hear Teague snoring away through the door into their cabin, so he followed the engineer around, hampered by his disguise. All the way aft, past the hatch where he'd entered, the engineer lifted a ring in the deck and opened a steep ladder to a lower deck with waist-high tanks and pumps throbbing softly.

"Must I?" Rafe asked. "If you need my help, of course I'm willing, but otherwise—it looks cramped and sounds noisy and I already have a headache."

"Just for a few minutes," the man said. "I need to check on three gauges and a circuit; it won't take long. And the captain doesn't want you out from under someone's eye."

As he'd suspected. Allowing himself a dramatic sigh, Rafe took off his suit jacket, folded it and set it on the deck, and followed the engineer. He recognized some things from *Gary Tobai*. Pipes, cables, gauges mounted on the bulkheads, which curved here even more obviously than above.

The engineer left him standing by the foot of the ladder and moved first aft, where a housing covered something he didn't recognize at all—surely not the drives? But where else could they be? The man took a reading from some gauge, then came back past Rafe to look at gauges near the various tanks. He looked at Rafe and smiled. "All nominal," he said. "The data shows up on the screens in my office up there, but one never knows if someone—something—has foxed the scans. We believe in superfluous work as a preventive of problems."

"Good thinking," Rafe said.

"You've been on a ship before—not just as a passenger," the man said.

"Yes," Rafe said. "How did you know?"

"People always ask what things are. You didn't."

"I could just be counting the seconds until I can get back upstairs where it's quieter, given my headache."

"No. You looked, you recognized, and you stayed out of my way. Care to explain?"

"Not really," Rafe said. "If Sera Vatta didn't tell you, then she had a reason. It's not my place to share information she may not want you to know."

"You're saying she knows."

"Yes," Rafe said.

"Interesting. We'll go back up now. I suppose you won't be offended if I mention that the way your"—he touched his own abdomen—"moved when you came down the ladder, I know it's not real."

"Sera Vatta knows that, too," Rafe said. "But she agreed that my use of a disguised outline was necessary both before I left Cascadia and on arrival at Slotter Key."

"She didn't tell us she trusted you."

"She would have had to tell you why."

"There's something about you . . ."

"Yes. And if you ask my associate, and he is in the mood to cooperate, he will tell you that indeed, there is something about me."

"Vatta's had enough trouble," the man said. "Part of my job is seeing we don't have more."

"Good," Rafe said. "But I'm still not going to tell you all of my—or Sera Vatta's—secrets. She advised me to put a plug in it until I got to her aunt Grace." He pulled his shirttails out and began unfastening his shirt. "I will, however, take off this very uncomfortable appliance, since you've seen through it." With the shirt off, the paunch section came loose easily; Rafe pulled the two back sections free, then skinned out of the harness that had held them in place. He put the shirt back on, oversized as it now was, once more hiding the blades in their sheaths. Then he pulled the cheek shapers from his mouth and stuffed them in his trouser pocket.

The man's eyes widened as the transformation completed. "You're—"

"Ser Hilarion Bancroft. Says so on my ID. So says my DNA, at the moment."

"But really—"

"Reality: you don't want me to cause you or the ship or Vatta trouble. Reality: I don't want to cause you or the ship or any part of Vatta trouble. I hope to do Vatta a very good service, in fact, but for that I need to be on Slotter Key talking to a different Sera Vatta, whom I've yet to meet, but who knows about me in several personas."

"You don't want me to tell the captain?"

"I don't want you to tell anyone on this ship who is a blabber, and I'm hoping that you're not. I presume the captain had her suspicions or she wouldn't have had you keep me in sight. And I rather doubt, after all that's happened in the past few years, that any Vatta captain is a blabber, but I had to mention that. Would you rather *I* told the captain? Even though Stella told me not to?"

Silence. The engineer looked at him, and Rafe knew he'd arranged his own face into a mildly interested expression.

"Ginny's solid," the engineer said finally. "I'm her youngest brother, Pero. I take after my mother's side; she's a Pierce. Daran's her other brother, five years older than me. Best we all know, I'm thinking. How's your headache?"

"Pounding. I'd really like a mug of tea myself."

"Go on up, then."

Rafe gathered up his accessories, pulled open the skin covering the paunch pad, pushed the harness into it, then pressed it closed. Then he tossed the pads up through the hatch to the deck above, went up the ladder much more easily than he'd come down, and picked up the pads and his jacket off the floor while the engineer followed him up and latched the hatch back down. Rafe paused partway to put the pads in the shallow storage locker above the door to his and Teague's compartment, then went on into the galley and pulled down two mugs, selected a strong black tea for himself, and put his mug in the slot. "You?" he asked Pero.

"I'll do it." When Rafe had removed his own mug, now full of steaming tea, Pero made his own selection and pushed his mug into the slot. "If you need any meds for that headache, it's the left-hand drawer there. All the usual."

Rafe opened the drawer. Several brands of medications for headache, rhinoviruses, stomachaches, sinus congestion: he chose one he recognized, popped the blister on the card, and drank two orange-and-green tablets with his tea. "I think I'll go lie down in our compartment," he said. "If that's all right with you."

"Fine. I'll give the captain the word that you have something to tell her when you're feeling better."

Captain Ginny Vatta did not have to be told Rafe's identity when she saw him in his normal shape, with his face no longer distorted by his disguise. "You!" she said, in almost the same tone as the engineer. "You're the one who got Stella and Toby off Allray—"

"She could possibly have done that herself, but as she'd taken refuge in my place of business, without knowing it was mine, it seemed wise to come along. There were other complications."

"And you're the one Ky—Admiral Vatta—got involved with."

"Yes."

"You know she's—"

"Somewhere on Slotter Key and no one's found her yet. Yes. That's part of my mission."

"Part?"

"Part." Rafe raised an eyebrow. "Captain, you undoubtedly know many things about me. All you really need to know is that Stella—your CEO—and Ky know me and trust me. In spite of everything."

"I heard Ky ripped you a new one at a reception after the war."

"She did. And we made up afterward, which you also know, I'm sure."

"But nothing came of it."

"I wouldn't put it that way," Rafe said. Those times they'd planned to meet and something had come up. The plan Ky's trip to Slotter Key had interrupted. "We're both busy people with a great deal of responsibility; we haven't been able to get together nearly as much as we would both prefer."

"Well, then. When we arrive in Slotter Key space, you'll need to be back in disguise?"

"Ideally, yes. And conveyed to wherever Grace Lane Vatta is."

"Far be it from me to interfere with anything Gracie has in mind," the captain said. "Or with Ky's love life, if she's still alive to have one. The rules remain the same, though: don't try anything on this ship without telling me first and asking my permission. Got that?"

"Got it," Rafe said. Mental fingers tangled behind his back.

"Good," she said, and stood up. "Now about your associate . . ."

"Teague," Rafe said. "He's an associate of someone I've known for years."

"He's getting a transform, isn't he?"

How had she figured that out? He didn't answer, and she just nodded.

"We've had some done, after the big killing," she said. "Aunt Grace set it up. Trying to save more of the family, make them less obvious. Six months to a year, most of ours, and dead-tired the first quarter year. That's what I noticed. Young, a little clumsy, and he's been sleeping hard since he came aboard. You're tired, too." No actual question.

Rafe shrugged. "I've had a temporary DNA squirt to match my persona's ID, but it's mostly that Stella and I stayed up late talking. I've done the temps before; they don't bother me."

"Ah. Well, then. Anything you need to know about Slotter Key you haven't already looked up? We have a complete atlas, up to date as of our departure, in the ship's system, if you want access."

"I'd like that," Rafe said. He had not been able to find much on Slotter Key from Nexus, and hadn't had time in Cascadia. "All we had in our files was outdated political organization and current market analysis." His headache had vanished.

He spent the next several hours poring over the atlas. Date of first terraforming, continental masses and arrangement—it was old-style terraforming, and some inconvenient continents had been simply blown up in places to create islands instead. Mass extinction, introduction of extra-planet materials to affect chemical ratios, seeding with very basic biologicals to start with, later introductions hundreds, even thousands of years apart. Slotter Key had been someone's very long-term project, though none of the data suggested whose.

Rafe had never been particularly interested in terraforming processes; he'd always been grateful that someone else had turned hundreds—thousands?—of unsuitable planets into places humans could breathe the air, drink the water, and subsist on the local vegetation and animal life. He'd assumed it was all done by humans—who else would shape planets for human convenience?—but now, faced with the time scales, he wondered. How long had humans been off their original planet? He didn't know. He'd never cared.

Yet wherever humans had gone in space, they'd found both unsuitable worlds and worlds already stocked with plants and animals from their ancestral home. That now struck him as very, very unlikely.

Even more unlikely that someone had done it for later generations without ever coming back to interact with them. The humans he knew weren't like that. Altruism on that scale was out of character.

Had something happened to them? Or—a cold draft seemed to flow down his back—were they not altruistic at all and coming back at some point to demand payment for the largesse they'd created? Had anyone ever considered that?

He put that thought aside—nothing he could do about it now. The files the captain had left him had things of more immediate interest.

Slotter Key's current population was just over one billion humans, scattered in a belt of temperate-to-tropical climate around the planet's equator. Five or six major cities; Port Major was the planetary capital. A dozen or so regions—mostly clusters of islands close together—sent representatives to the planetary Parliament. Remaining continents smaller than those on Nexus, all inhabited but for Miksland, labeled in the atlas as "Terraforming Failure." What did that even mean? Toxic?

The captain appeared again, pointed to the screen he was looking at. "That's the closest land to where the shuttle was reported down. Worthless, just rock and ice. Some kind of field that blocks communication. Luckily we don't need it, so nobody bothers with it. Structural terraforming now would likely cause a catastrophe."

"Why would anyone destroy a continent anyway?" Rafe asked. "The atlas says—"

"I have no idea," the captain said, sitting down across the aisle. "All I know is we have more islands and smaller continents than most other planets. Some say it's good for climate; others that it's good for biodiversity." She shrugged. "I'd rather be in space."

"How far back was it terraformed?" Rafe asked. "Is this atlas accurate?"

"I don't know that, either. Our real history goes back only five hundred forty-three years; that's when the first colony ship arrived. We Vattas came later. I guess it looked pretty much then as it does now, except for what we've built on it."

"It's odd we have no clue who did it, even though these files claim someone understands what was done," Rafe said. "Nexus has more history than Slotter Key—our schoolbooks say it's been settled well over a thousand standards. Bigger population, too. Four continents all bigger than what you've got." He looked again. "This Miksland's likely to be cold even in summer, isn't it? And what season is it now?"

"Spring where Vatta headquarters is, Port Major. In Miksland it's winter already and going to get worse. That's why no one thinks Ky could still be alive. Part of that ocean freezes in winter; a survival raft won't stand that."

Rafe repressed a shiver. Here in FTL space, he could not pick up any ansible signal. All he could do was hope that Ky was still alive. He had given up on that hope before, and she had lived. He would hope.

CHAPTER EIGHTEEN

MIKSLAND
DAYS 33-39

When the second party arrived four days later, Ky had opened the second hut, and Betange had located another two caches of nonperishable food. Each hut had a storage closet holding sealed bundles of bedding, toilet supplies, and cleaning supplies. No one had yet found any controls for the water supply. Ky had designated a site well away from the buildings for a latrine, though the frozen ground meant it had to be built up with stones and snow. Buckets served for indoor use, as they had in the rafts. They still had to gather clean snow and ice for water, melting it on the kitchen stoves.

The arriving party had stuffed contrived packs out of the storage pockets from one of the rafts, so they had ration packs and water sacks; they'd even dragged one life raft partway and then weighted it down with rocks to be fetched later. "I thought you'd want the materials and supplies," Marek said. "Even though we couldn't manage to bring it all."

"Yes, indeed," Ky said.

"And I took down the canopies on the other raft and weighted it down, too, so if we have the time and energy, we can retrieve them. We're not going to use them come summer, are we?"

"No," Ky said. "We can't steer them and none of us have enough knowledge of the currents and weather patterns to be sure of hitting inhabited land. If there was a forest up here, we could build something with a bit of keel and a rudder, but there's nothing big enough."

"I didn't know it had *any* vegetation. And animals—we saw these four-legged things, bigger than cows—"

"So did we. If we can figure out a way to kill them—"

He gave her an odd look. "You have a firearm, don't you?" When she didn't answer at once—how had he known that when others didn't?—he went on. "I mean—I assumed an officer of your rank—and you wouldn't have left it on the shuttle."

"Yes," Ky said. "I have a pistol, but the ammunition I have is safe for shipboard and station use, not ideal for hunting an animal that size."

"I could try; I'm a pretty good shot—"

"Master Sergeant, with the sabotage, we have to consider that I may need a firearm for something other than those animals. We may have unfriendly visitors, not rescuers."

"Oh. I see."

"Right. So high on my list—though behind shelter, food, water, and clothes—is defense. We haven't explored everything here yet. This is clearly a military installation shut up for the season—or longer. The doors opened to Spaceforce ID cards and a code number from the Rector of Defense's office."

"What? Cosper didn't tell us that."

"I'm telling you and my aide. Not everyone. We still may have a traitor among us. The others think I just guessed or had another source, perhaps from the Academy. If a high government code opens these locks, then Spaceforce is involved in all this—the shuttle, the life raft supplies, and this place. We don't know why, we don't know who, but we're going to find out."

He nodded. "How much food do we have? Enough for the winter?"

"No. That's why we need to hunt. I'm hoping we find something smaller and easier to catch than those whatever-they-are, because I suspect as soon as we kill one of them, the others will vanish and not be seen again."

"Fuel?"

"Another problem. We've been running the generator nonstop to get both huts above freezing and melt snow for water, but it'll run through the fuel we found—the barrels in the generator hut—in another ten days. I'm hoping there's more underground, or another generator down there—something. If we cut the generator time, it'll give us more days, but I doubt it'll be enough. Melting the snow and ice is our only water source right now."

"But you still think we have a chance?"

"More than a chance," Ky said. "It's like I said that first day. If we keep focusing on now—what we need, what we can use—we will survive the winter and we will make it back."

"You're that sure."

"I'm sure *I'm* not giving up," Ky said.

He grinned. "You got us this far, Admiral. I believe you."

"I've considered moving all the bunks into one hut—that gives us easy room for eight, everyone sleeping in a bunk rotating in three shifts. Then we'd need heat in the other one only for melting snow and ice, and cooking."

"Good idea," Marek said. "Might also consider stacking snow up around the lower walls for insulation."

"Snow?"

"Blocks of it—there's a lot of airspace in snow. Used to make snow forts when I was a kid—our place was up on Foster Mountain. We had snow every winter. I was twelve when we moved to the city. What about that mine shaft? You think there's more good stuff down there?"

"I don't know yet, but I definitely want to find out. Anything—

food, a way to get water without melting snow, more fuel for the generator, or anything we can burn for heat."

"It's funny," Marek said, looking around. "This isn't anything like a full-scale military camp. More like you'd think a small scientific station—meteorology, maybe—only eight bunks total. They must fly in, in the warm season. But are there aircraft that could carry eight passengers and luggage—surely they bring in their clothes, more food, fresh stuff maybe—and fly back somewhere without refueling? And without guidance on the airstrip? We all heard what you did: terraforming failure, uninhabited, barren, nothing of interest."

Ky nodded. "And I keep thinking there has to be more to it. Someone's known about the place; the locks responded to current codes, but the buildings aren't new—twenty standards, or fifty—and if that's an airstrip, which it probably is, it's got stuff growing on it. How fast can stuff grow in this climate, anyway? And why didn't it ever show up on the weathersat data?"

"And why, since it responds to Spaceforce codes, haven't they sent someone down here to see if we've found it?" He shook his head. "Next things next. I'll get those bunks moved; you want power off over there?" He jerked his head toward the second hut.

"Not yet; we're going to need more water tonight."

Within an hour, four double bunks lined two of the walls of the main room of the first hut; the table and one desk now made a longer table, enough for eight at a time to sit to a meal. Everyone had had a mug of thin cracker-soup, good and hot, with Marek and Jen reminding them to go slow, and nobody had puked yet. Ky counted that a win. It would take days to bring them up to full rations—*if* they could find more food.

The first eight climbed into the bunks; lights went off in the main room. Already the room was warmer, with all of them in it, warm and stuffy. Smelly, even. Well, they'd had no chance to bathe and nothing clean to change into since they'd dressed to board the shuttle. Of course they stank. *She* stank.

She went to the kitchen and took one of the empty pots, as Betange was washing dishes. "I'll get more snow," she said. She slipped through the door and closed it; they had found the latch that left it unlocked for normal use, and she checked it as always to be sure it was in the open position.

The cold bit into her instantly. Overhead, green fire with streaks of pink danced in the sky; the snow seemed to ripple in response. She walked carefully across to the drift against the wall of the generator shack and filled the pot with snow, packed it down as hard as she could, filled and packed again, then carried it back.

Now the inside felt almost hot, but the blower wasn't on. She carried the pot into the kitchen and set it on the stove to melt.

"This is much better," Betange said. "Thank you, for insisting we come up here. I didn't believe we'd find anything but bare rock. How did you know—?"

"I didn't," Ky said. "But I knew we had to move. If we had to pile rocks with our bare hands up here to make a shelter, we had to move—there was no more food—"

"I know. I know, but—you must be a very lucky person."

"Possibly," Ky said. She hadn't thought of it that way, arguing the first group into following her up here, when they were weak from hunger and ready to give up. It had been a blind leap, spending energy without knowing if it was useless. Finding that road surface, though—from there on she had been sure *something* lay on top of the cliffs.

When the others had finished with the dishes and put them away, Ky said, "You can sleep in here for a while, if you want. Leave the light on, though. I'm going over to check on the water at the other hut."

"Don't you ever sleep?"

"Next shift," Ky said. She turned the stove down, then went out again and across to the other hut. Jen was there in the kitchen, a blanket around her shoulders, half asleep in a chair.

"Sorry, Admiral," she said. "I thought someone should make sure snow didn't boil away." Jen hadn't volunteered for chores before. "And it's . . . more private here. Couldn't we have this hut?"

"You need rest," Ky said, ignoring that question for the moment. "And I need you rested. Get another couple of blankets and lie down—I'll wake you when it's time. I may go out and gather more snow when this is melted."

Jen seemed asleep in moments. Ky turned the stove low, then went into the main room, barely warmer than outdoors. With a cautious look out the door, she went to one of the desks and felt along its side for a power cable, then followed it down to the outlet on the floor. She unfastened the top of her protective suit, then her uniform jacket, then her shirt, and ran her fingers into the neck of her personal armor. There it was, the power cable for her cranial ansible. And, in the inside pocket of her jacket, the adapter Rafe had given her.

She checked on Jen again. Still asleep. She plugged the cable into the desk's outlet; the tiny green light came on. The other end of the cable went into the jack for her implant. And the internal switch . . . *there.*

Scent flooded her olfactory neurons, and a rush of excitement caught her breath. It worked, and maybe it could bypass whatever was blocking other signals. But the scent did not change, and her attempt to send the connecting code to Rafe brought no response. Was it blocked? Or could he be—not out of range, for they had tested it at astronomical lengths—but perhaps in FTL flight? Perhaps coming to Slotter Key? How long would that take?

She would try again every night, she told herself, and went to sleep. But for the next several days, she found others awake and using the other hut every time she went in, apparently determined to make use of the second hut. Marek even suggested it should be the official watch station, so the first hut could be used for sleeping, as they'd divided the use of the rafts on the beach. It was clear he assumed they would stay in the huts all winter; he argued against trying to get through the door set into the hill.

"It doesn't respond to the same code; it could be very dangerous to force it. Set to explode or something."

"We have to do something," Ky said. "We still don't have enough food."

"We should hunt. We should at least try." He paused, then went on. "Someone may have more experience hunting with firearms than you, Admiral. I used to—"

"Not now," Ky said firmly. "We'll take a look at the other surface buildings—those hangarlike things. They might be storage. Some barrels of fuel for the generator, other supplies. But if nothing shows up, we'll have to risk trying that door."

He shook his head but did not argue further.

When she finally managed to evade the others—having chivvied them out of the second hut so she could inspect it, then turn off the power, to save fuel, it was the thirty-ninth day, by her count, since the shuttle crash. Six since they had made it to this shelter, days filled with one nagging problem after another. She thumbed the door latch so no one could come in, checked that the stove was off, turned off the lights, and then connected the cable. Her implant overrode the ansible signal momentarily with a BATTERY LOW warning, then BATTERY CHARGING, and finally the familiar smell made her wrinkle her nose. Would he be in range?

CHAPTER NINETEEN

SLOTTER KEY, PORT MAJOR
DAY 36

Vatta Transport's courier *Morningstar* appeared on scan, one of a list of arriving spacecraft. Grace noted its arrival on the morning report, remembering Stella's encrypted message and MacRobert's broad hint. "Someone you should check out," she'd said. "Claims to be one of Osman's, but I doubt it." *Morningstar* had priority routing—all Vatta ships did—and in much shorter time than any other could have done it, it was docking at Vatta's own section of the main station. A Vatta shuttle brought it down safely; Grace watched the landing with grim satisfaction. Vatta shuttles did not fail.

By 1130, the car had arrived. From the surveillance images, neither passenger looked anything like Rafe Dunbarger. A tall skinny fellow, whose skin was an unusual shade for Slotter Key—yellow-brown, with brown freckles—and a plump florid man who minced along as if his feet hurt. She called MacRobert from his own office; he arrived before they did.

She had of course seen media images of Rafe Dunbarger—and for that matter, images of his father and the entire Board of Directors of ISC, plus a few others of their senior managers. It had been her task, when she was head of Vatta's corporate security staff, to know a lot about any other corporation Vatta had dealings with, competitive or otherwise.

She looked now at the plump, prissy man mincing along the hall. He looked nothing like those images, except the dark eyes with their hard focus. A good disguise, for those who knew him only from images, but she wondered if he thought he could fool her. If he did, he had a surprise coming.

Once inside her office, however, he gave her a very different grin as he pulled a standard security cylinder from his pocket and set it on her desk. "I'm sure you know I'm really Rafe Dunbarger," he said. "And with your permission I'll take these uncomfortable appliances out of my face."

"Don't you think you should leave my office the way you came in?" Grace asked.

"Probably," Rafe said. "But in that case perhaps we could talk elsewhere? Your gravity is heavy for me, and the rest of this weighs more here than it does at home. My feet really do hurt and my face is this red because I'm sweating."

"Stella said you were absolutely convinced Ky is alive," Grace said. "She's also told me you two love each other, so why is this not hormonal wishful thinking?"

"Because it's not my hormones but technology," Rafe said. "It's also technology that was—is—both very secret and very dangerous. Development was stopped, but as I had been the test subject—for a certain consideration—I was left with the prototype. It would have been fatal to me to remove it."

"And it lets you know if your girlfriends are still alive?"

Rafe looked at her. Grace had heard about his stares, and stared back. She had her own weaponized gaze.

"She's alive," he said without looking away. "I am sure of that. I do not know how much longer."

"Can you tell anything about her condition, her whereabouts, anything—"

"No. Not without getting closer and plugging the device in."

"And you think our ansible needs tuning—how are you going to work there and here both?"

"I may be able to do some work on the ansible remotely," Rafe said. "You don't have good scan on that continent she was near when the shuttle went down."

"Miksland," Grace said. "We know something—" She looked at Mac, then at Rafe's very silent—too silent—companion. "But before I tell you that—what about Teague?"

"Technical help," Rafe said. "Electronics, on the one hand. Cold-weather specialist, on the other. He was involved in the rescue of my family."

"Are you a killer? Is he?"

"Like Ky," Rafe said. "Yes to both."

Grace felt a glow she recognized as total satisfaction. She had been right all along when she'd told Ky's mother that the girl wasn't just a softhearted busybody—that underneath she was more like Grace than any of the others. Ky's mother had recoiled in horror, insisting that her daughter was "normal." And clearly Rafe—harmless as he looked in that fat suit—was of the same sort. Maybe, just maybe, Ky would have a partner suited to her needs while still young enough to enjoy it. She hadn't been that lucky, for a long time. She glanced at Mac, who had met Rafe on Cascadia. He'd been right, too.

"How long can you stay?" she asked Rafe.

"Until we find her, and until we find out who did this," he said. "Teague's contract with me is for a year, but he might be willing to extend it."

"Gary might not," Teague said. His voice had an odd quality to it, reminiscent of a much younger man whose boy-voice was in transition to an adult timbre. She looked more closely at him. What *was* he?

"Transitioning, Sera," he said, as if he'd read her mind. "Complete biosculpt. What I did was legal, but there was blowback from the other side."

"Ah," Grace said. Had biosculpt been available in her own time of blowback, she might have done that. She lifted her left arm. "I hope it doesn't itch as much as this did."

"I heard, Sera. Wondered you didn't go for a prosthesis; it's a lot quicker to full function."

"Software," Grace said. "Software can always be compromised."

His attention sharpened. "Indeed, Sera."

"Is your trouble likely to follow you here?" Grace asked. "Do they know where you are?"

"Shouldn't, Sera, but I won't say it couldn't happen. I went straight into clinic, was declared dead, got a temp twenty-one-day on top of the biosculpt initiation, and ID to match the combo, and left Nexus with a different face, name, and bioscan data. They could track Edvard Simeon Teague to Cascadia, and maybe to here—but the name I was born to, and the body as well, are in Nexus records as dead, and the ashes scattered at sea. By the time I go back, I'll be someone else, immigrant from somewhere far away. Not traveling with him." He glanced at Rafe and then gave Grace another straight look.

"What should we be looking for, in case?" she asked.

He dug into a pocket and pulled out a data cube. "Any of these— it's the data my boss has on that group, and I'm wanting to trade it for papers from somewhere other than Slotter Key. Assuming you have the capacity—"

Grace looked at Mac, who raised an eyebrow then nodded. "We can do that," she said. Teague flicked his thumb, and the cube flew through the air. Grace caught it and handed it to MacRobert. Teague gave a brief incomplete smile and returned to his former expression.

"If I could have a quiet place and a power feed," Rafe said, "I could use my device now and better define what needs to be done."

Grace pointed. "There's an outlet over there on the wall, and we can all be silent."

"That's not what I meant. I meant alone."

"Alone. Here? No, that won't work. I know too much about you, and I'm not turning you loose unsupervised connected to our power supply. You can do that at home. Mac, can you get these gentlemen to the house for some good reason?"

"Certainly. And I'll put these"—he waved the data cube—"on the scan list."

"I'll be home by 1500," she said. "I've got that appointment at the clinic and threats from the doctors—again—if I miss it."

"Your arm?" Teague asked.

"Yes. I re-injured it a few weeks ago, which is why I wasn't on the shuttle up to meet Ky, and why I'm not either dead or wherever she is, *if* she is. I've missed a couple of appointments and they worry too much."

Grace arrived home to find MacRobert in the dining room with Teague. Rafe was not in sight.

"He's in the guest room," MacRobert said. "Doing whatever he does. They've both had lunch. You?"

"I'm not hungry," Grace said. "It's healing just fine and I think they were disappointed. All they did was poke, prod, pull, and twist, so now it's hurting but that will let up soon."

A door opened somewhere in the house, and plumbing communicated where. Teague looked tense. "You have scan here, right?"

"Yes," MacRobert said, before Grace could answer. "And we both know the house very well. Downstairs bathroom; I heard him walk from the bedroom down the passage."

Teague flushed. "I'm used to being the one linked in."

"Relax, Teague," MacRobert said. "You're not the one involved with her niece. Great-niece. Whatever she is."

Grace ignored that, watching Rafe come into the room. He had shed all his appliances and changed into casual clothes that fit perfectly. His expression did not.

"I am able to confirm that she is alive. I could not communicate directly because she does not have a power source for the device she holds."

"How do you know she's alive if you can't communicate?"

Rafe did not quite focus on her face, Grace noted, and as she watched, his face paled and he sagged; Teague caught him and moved him into a chair, then pushed Rafe's head down between his knees.

"What's wrong with him? Do you know?"

"No." Teague kept a hand on Rafe's neck. "But I know a man about to faint when I see one."

"I'm fine now," Rafe said. Teague stepped back. Rafe looked up, still resting his forearms on his thighs. "I have a splitting headache," he said. "Maybe it was that. But Ky's alive."

"Could you tell if she was ashore somewhere?"

"Not without a better map than I've seen," Rafe said. "I have direction, but not precise distance."

"He does solve a problem," Grace said to MacRobert.

"Who?" MacRobert looked at her, then at Rafe; Grace felt impatient. Mac was usually quicker than that.

"Rafe. You know that map anomaly we found, that you said would be dangerous to fix? He's not us; he's not from here; he can demand access to any ISC equipment by virtue of his title." She turned to Rafe. "I don't expect your system ansible can do close-in surveillance of Miksland, but don't you have relay satellites between the system ansibles and a planet's surface?"

"Indeed we do, and some of them are capable of fine-scale surveillance. But that's your problem—what about the map anomaly?"

"Slotter Key's own survey satellites quit recording data from Miksland several hundred years ago, and what should be the archived scans it did make are lost. We hadn't noticed, because it's uninhabited, near the south polar ocean, and nobody really cared. Terraforming failure has been the explanation for ignoring it completely."

"And you now think it wasn't ignored by everyone, just by those who wanted you to think it was."

"Yes. Possibly." Grace touched the projector controls and brought up a hologram of the planet. "We're here." She rotated the globe slowly. "This is the closest approximation to where they came down, and this outline of nothing is Miksland. This is what MacRobert found in the university library annex—deep in the archives." Another touch, and a sketch, reproduced to scale with the globe, filled in part of the poleward coast and a little of the plateau. She zoomed in on that. "We think an unofficial explorer landed on Miksland a long time ago and sketched what he saw. Why he didn't record it properly I don't know, but his map ended up in a university library archive along with other old maps, including the imaginary lands found in some fiction. And now—overlay this very old scan—"

"It's—what is that? Some kind of installation?" Rafe tilted his head back and forth, trying to make something out of the vague lines on the terrain the explorer had sketched.

"Could be a runway," Teague said. "With some structure at one end."

"A landing place for aircraft? Even shuttles?"

"We don't know," Grace said. "Because we can't get the satellites that are over Miksland regularly to take a simple ordinary scan of it."

"That we can manage," Rafe said, with a glance at Teague. "Who's your ISC rep here?"

"You don't know?"

"I'm an imperfect CEO; I'd have to call home to find out."

"We don't have one. One of the things Stavros—former Vatta CEO—had requested of ISC was an office here on the planet. We don't have a crewed ansible platform, either. Turned out to be useful, when we turned it back on. Just a matter of flipping a switch, I was told."

"And you haven't flipped the switch to see what Miksland really looks like now?"

"We turned on the main ansible; nobody knows how to operate

repeater satellites remotely. We'd have to send a ship and a technician. But if you, as ISC—"

"Teague," Rafe said. "Not me. He won't be recognized as me under any circumstances—he's a good eight centimeters taller than I am."

"Ten," Teague said. "When I don't slouch."

"Teague can be an ISC system inspector: Slotter Key did unauthorized repairs and though we aren't prosecuting systems for that anymore, we want to be sure you haven't damaged the equipment. We know there's something nonstandard. I—as myself and CEO of ISC, back on Nexus—asked Stella for the favor of a fast ride over here for Teague; Stella and I—as Bancroft—pretended I was another of Osman's bastards and she shipped me here to be vetted by you."

"But he'll still be tracked, going out there—"

"Of course. It's not clandestine. It's ISC. I can mock up the right ID; I have access. That's why he's been here, talking to you, because you're the one who authorized the repair—he's been trying to get you to describe exactly who did what. Whoever you sent—you know who, right?"

"Of course," Grace said.

"Well, Teague will spend a couple of hours talking to whoever that was, before boarding a Vatta ship to go inspect every one of our installations in this system. Including a look at our repeater satellites in low orbit, at which time he will see if they also have the lockout for Miksland. Because if they do, and no one here had tinkered with them before, then someone in ISC was involved in the original blackout of that continent. As well as someone here, probably in Spaceforce."

"That far back?" Grace said.

"Has to be," Rafe said. "And not for any good reason."

DAY 37

The next morning, Teague, now in a serious dark-gray suit and carrying a black attaché case, arrived at Slotter Key's Defense Department HQ with Grace, to be introduced to her staff as an ISC security inspector. He insisted on handing out a statement on ISC letterhead detailing ISC's revised position on independent repairs of ISC-installed ansibles.

"But we're sending and receiving with no problems," said the communications chief. "Nothing's wrong."

"Nothing you can *detect* is wrong," Teague said. "I assure you— I have been inspecting locally repaired installations since Ser Dunbarger the younger took over, on his express orders, to be certain that the equipment is fully functional, and to interview those who made the repairs, and see if they meet our standards for maintenance. If they do, then ISC will certify your system and your personnel, and you have the choice of performing all maintenance locally, or continuing to retain ISC to perform both routine and emergency maintenance for you."

Grace managed not to let her brows rise. This was not the same Teague who had lounged around her house, draping himself over the furniture as if his skeleton were only loosely strung together.

"Well . . . if the Rector agrees . . ."

Grace lifted her hands. "I tried to talk him out of it, but we are still bound by our original contract with ISC—they have the right to inspect their equipment at any time. And he says he thinks something is lagging our system somewhere—possibly something we did in the repair, or connected to the original damage."

Teague held up one hand. "In forty-seven percent of the inspections I've made, whoever first damaged the ansibles also damaged the repeater satellites, thus causing dropouts and slower transmission rates. Rector Vatta tells me that you have experienced intermittent slowdowns and at least two dropouts related to specific repeaters since your repair."

"That's true, but—"

"Then it's imperative that all those repeaters be inspected, and—if necessary—repaired *properly*. This inspection incurs no charge; it falls under paragraph seventeen, line twelve of the original contract."

"How long will it take?" And, with a glance at the slim black case, "How much equipment will you need?"

"A matter of days," Teague said. "I requested Rector Vatta to arrange for that Vatta courier to transport me, when she said your own insystem ships were substantially slower." He gave a prim smile. "ISC prefers that I not spend more time in one system than I must, as there are many yet to inspect. Use of private transportation is preferable in many situations; no insult is intended."

"The Vatta courier Ser Teague arrived on, *Morningstar,* has been refueled and is ready to take him where he needs to go," Grace said.

"And will you also transport him to his next system?" That with an edge of sarcasm.

"That is a matter that Ser Teague will discuss with Vatta's CEO, I expect," Grace said. "As far as I'm concerned, Slotter Key's obligation is satisfied by ensuring Ser Teague's work here is expedited insystem."

Teague gave her a stern look; Grace glared back. Her chief of communications would interpret that wrongly, she was sure, just as she intended.

"And I expect a report, Ser Teague, of every change you make in settings, and an explanation of why it was necessary. If you expect Slotter Key to take over its own maintenance—"

"As I said, Rector Vatta, there is a choice. ISC is prepared to resume all maintenance functions—"

"As inefficiently as you did before?" the communications chief said.

"That was an act of war," Teague replied. "For which, in our original contract, ISC is relieved of responsibility for the duration. We cannot guarantee service in such event. But in the amended contract, which I will discuss with your head of state, customers are freed to make their own repairs. Manuals are available; I have a copy with me, and will provide it when the new contract is signed. We can also provide training, at a fixed cost, should it be desired."

"Which isn't *our* concern," Grace said to her staff, in a tone that conveyed she thought it should be. "That's for the legislature and President. Though I've no doubt we'll see a copy of the manual, as ansible service is a matter of security." She turned back to Teague. "The *Morningstar* crew is ready; your transportation is waiting downstairs, Ser Teague."

He bowed slightly and left her office.

Grace looked at her desk. "Time to get to work," she said to the others. "I have plenty to do, and if you don't, I'll share." They left, murmuring excuses. Grace touched her desk, transforming the apparent empty slab of wood into a screen full of tabs. But instead of touching one, she simply stared at it. Ky was intelligent, resourceful, determined—but Grace knew well that the planet had weapons Ky had never faced. Gravity. Cold. Time. Even given Rafe's certainty that she had survived so far, how much longer could she? And what about the others, those who were her responsibility as well?

CHAPTER TWENTY

SLOTTER KEY NEARSPACE, VATTA SHIP *MORNINGSTAR*
DAY 38

"Where's your friend?" Daran Vatta asked as Teague came through *Morningstar*'s docking tube.

"With Rector Vatta," Teague said. "Or rather, in her house. I've got his instructions."

"And I've got hers," Captain Vatta said.

Teague nodded. "Captain."

"Call me Ginny, now we're on the same mission. How's your transform coming?"

"I'm in the part where I'm making up for lost awake time. It feels like my bones are moving inside the soft tissue."

The captain wiggled her shoulders. "I wouldn't like that. You want the big ansible first?"

"Yes—Rafe says we should start with that."

"Strap in, then. We're going to use the hot button."

Slotter Key had only one ansible platform, carrying both a general communications and a financial ansible. Teague had easily absorbed Rafe's information about what might need to be done—or look like it had been done—and after a series of hard-G shoves, he suited up and checked everything Rafe had told him to check. The automatic system that had reported to ISC when it was turned on had then reduced capacity by 5 percent; Teague had the code to bring it back up to 100 percent and keep it there.

Then another transit back to low orbit around the planet, moving from one repeater satellite to another. These were much smaller, though larger than Slotter Key's own weather and communications satellites, all painted bright white with the ISC logo typical of ISC installations.

When they had matched orbit with the first of five, Teague suited up, hooked in his tether, and went out the courier's air lock, monitored by Daran. He laid one of the patches Rafe had given him against the maintenance hatch of the repeater and peeled it away carefully, stowing it in the pouch Rafe had labeled EVIDENCE 1, then recorded that repeater's serial number in video. He tucked the pouch in a carry bag and opened the hatch. Rafe had said the software to make the repeater refuse to accept calls to, or incoming from, a segment of the planet's surface would have to be plugged into the repeater's control panel, not uploaded from below.

He looked the panel over carefully. This—and this—and all those—were normal, standard ISC installation. But that, plugged into a jack on the lower right, was not. He used his suitphone to call Rafe; the signal bounced to the repeater in a better position to relay the call to Grace Vatta's house.

"Found it," he said, when Rafe answered. "Take it out now?"

"Run Analytics 27a-14," Rafe said. "The big one?"

"What you thought. Slowed down, but the code worked; it's at a hundred percent now." Teague used the control panel keypad to enter the code for that Analytics string. Rafe, he knew, could now access the same data he was getting. He waited for Rafe's response.

"It's going to trigger something if you pull it or fry it," Rafe said finally. "You can't—I couldn't, unless I took the thing inside and took it apart very carefully—keep it from signaling. But you can restore function. Pull it."

"Done," Teague said, pulling out the little yellow-tipped device.

"Enter 72RZ459. That'll give us directional control of video scan from down here. How long to get them all done?"

"Captain says several hours to get from one to another if you don't want them bumped out of orbit."

"Fine. Sleep when you need to. Pull all those components, bring them back here—though they may self-destruct so ask if there's a good solid vault in the ship. Same codes for each, run the same Analytics before you pull 'em."

"I'm okay. See you when I get back."

Teague closed the maintenance hatch gently and wiped the surface with a cloth that left a slight glaze on the shiny paint. Maybe someone else would like to contribute trace data.

Back in the ship, he asked about safe storage for something that might blow up or melt or otherwise self-destruct.

"Safe? That would be throwing it into a star. How big is it?"

Teague pulled it from the carry-bag. "This."

"Oh, well. And there's more than one? They'll all fit in the ammo storage; it's supposed to withstand all the ammunition blowing at once. Never tried it, though."

He looked at her and did not ask. He had seen no signs of weapons aboard *Morningstar*. "You're cold and you're still in trans," Daran said. "Sit here and I'll fix you some tea. Strap in; Gin's going to shove us again."

Teague did as he was told; Daran fixed him tea and handed him a couple of ginger biscuits, then headed aft. Through the open cockpit door, Teague could see the captain wiggling the handset gently, easing them away from the repeater before throwing them at the next. He sipped the tea, realizing he was in fact cold and hungry, and had finished one of the biscuits when Daran came back with a thick-walled box.

"This should do it, unless they're really suicidal," Daran said. "And we can monitor what's going on inside." He pointed to a readout on one side. "Put it in there, and I'll put this back in the vault."

Teague dropped the little object in the box; Daran closed it, carried it back aft . . . Teague thought better of looking around the corner to see exactly where. He himself was neither Vatta nor ISC. And he wished his bones would quit writhing around.

Three hours later, they were hanging about three meters off another of the repeaters, and Teague suited up again, readying his carry-bag. The procedure was the same, except that he did not call Rafe this time, and he came back aboard feeling more tired than he expected, until he added up the hours since he'd slept last. "I need to rest before the next one," he told the captain. "My hands aren't steady."

"We'll go back to the station," the captain said. "Only safe place to hang out, close in like this. Bunk in Vatta's crew overnight quarters, start again in eight hours. You can catch some sleep now, if you want."

"No thanks. Knowing I'll have to get up and walk steadily when we reach the station, I'd better stay up until then."

"Hang on, then, it'll be rough."

Teague had never imagined a pilot of anything—water-boat or spacecraft—taking such delight in pushing a vehicle near its limits. Then he considered what little he knew of the Vattas, the few he'd met and those he'd heard about. Apparently they liked a kind of danger he hoped never to encounter.

By the time they reached the station, he felt nauseated as well as exhausted. Captain Vatta steered him firmly into the hands of the Vatta section's medbooth, where he got a shot of something to settle his stomach and a tab for sleep. "You'd best stay here," the medic said. She was entirely too cheerful, he thought, but he was asleep before he knew it.

* * *

Grace arrived home to the news that Teague was bunked in on the station, and Rafe had confirmed the blocking of scans over Miksland, and unblocked them.

"We can expect whoever did this to notice," he said. "That's why I didn't unblock normal communications channels, just the satellite visual scan. If Ky's people found out their comunits were working, they might give the other side too much info."

"What about your special link?"

"Nothing yet. Here—I've got the scans loaded up for you. I can block them again, from here, with the changes Teague made."

"Very resourceful," Mac said.

"My code still gives me access to all ISC equipment," Rafe said.

The scans came up on Grace's main screen. "That cloud will pass," Rafe said. "There—you can see the coast—that bay—that orange dot on the white?" He froze the image. "Zooming. It looks like some kind of fabric."

"Part of a life raft, it could be," Mac said. He glanced at Grace. "So they made it that far."

"Now heading away from the water," Rafe said, "you can see shadows on the terrain—and there are the buildings. And the runway."

"What's the tower?"

"I don't know, but it's there. Those two look like hangars, and these two look like ordinary military prefab huts. Guard post, maybe?"

"If they could get there—" Grace did not finish the sentence.

"Somebody's there." Rafe reached over and tapped out a code. The display darkened, but the two smaller buildings glowed. "Heat signature. If the bad guys can snag the scans—and they probably can—they'll know someone's there. That's why I want to turn the scans off, now that we know for sure they're there."

Grace nodded. "Do it."

Rafe tapped in another series of commands. "It's blocked. We have these to look at—some from their night, a few from their day. But I'm still sure they have an automatic warning to let them know someone's been tinkering with the satellites."

CHAPTER TWENTY-ONE

SLOTTER KEY,
UNDISCLOSED LOCATION
DAY 38

Merced Tolganna frowned as a light blinked orange on the third box, second row, of a stack positioned in the last row. No lights ever came on there; she'd been told they were old tech, kept for scavenging spare cubes and connectors, but nobody had ever touched them, at least not on her shift in her twenty years in Central Data's secure vaults. She looked up the manual she'd been issued the day she arrived, and scrolled along until she found the list. Inactive reserve units, outdated, no maintenance needed. Right. Then the curly mark that meant a footnote somewhere.

"Should a unit spontaneously activate, inform supervisor—" followed by a list of names and dates. Her current supervisor was Nils Rolander. The one time she'd called him for an anomaly, he'd chewed her out for interrupting him and threatened to dock her pay if she called for "a simple matter you could have taken care of" again. She couldn't afford to lose pay, not with Stan's cough getting worse. "Include serial number, time of activation, and type of code."

Code? The box was ancient; she had no idea what code it might have started with. She called up the schematic, looked at that serial number, then walked over to the stack where she could see the original blinking light, just as it had been mirrored on her display. On, off, on off, very simple. Orange. Serial number . . . yes, the same.

Maybe she could fix it herself and not have to call Rolander. At least she could check if some mischievous person on another shift had reconnected it to power, but the boxes fit snugly enough in the rack that she couldn't see behind it. She put her hands on either side of it and tugged. It didn't move. Been there so long it had grown onto the shelf. Probably the footpads had deteriorated into black goo. She tried to lift the front a little, break the contact. No movement.

Back at her desk, she had a thin metal strip she'd used before for unsticking recalcitrant boxes. She fetched it and worked it under the front of the box. Sure enough, she could lever the front up a little, and as she'd suspected the footpads stretched a little. They needed to be replaced. She worked the metal strip vigorously until she had the footpads separated from the short front legs of the box, then— holding the front up perhaps half a centimeter—tugged hard. Harder. The box made a sort of scrunching sound and the blinking orange light turned red.

Clearly it was malfunctioning, and the sooner she disconnected its power supply—if this wasn't due to some chemical deterioration inside—the better. Merced braced herself and yanked hard, with all her strength. She felt the back legs come loose and staggered back just as the box disintegrated in a bright light that was the last thing she ever saw.

Alarms went off, emergency lights flashed all over the building, a recorded voice announced "Evacuate! Evacuate! Evacuate!" Not until all the regular employees had left the building did anyone enter the room where Merced had worked. One man stopped at Merced's desk and called up the activity log for her shift. The mess at the far end of the stacks offered no more information than the log, but that was enough.

"Stupid woman," the man said. "Why didn't she just inform her supervisor? She'd looked up the procedure in the manual."

The second man sighed, fogging the faceplate of his protective gear. "Now we'll have to do a new background check on her. Maybe she suspected something."

"Or maybe she was just bored."

They cleaned up the mess, and by the time they'd satisfied themselves the area was safe once more, Nils Rolander had arrived. By then, another of the boxes was blinking.

"What a shame about poor Merced," he said. "I would never have suspected her of initiative."

"We'll have to do another background check—"

"Yes, of course, Ted. And I see there's another signal gone off. Someone's messing with our systems—"

"Bet it's that old woman."

"Old—?" Rolander raised his brows.

"Vatta. She must've gotten around our fellow in AirDefense finally."

"Or her niece is alive. Or both of them—"

The three men looked at one another for a long moment.

CHAPTER TWENTY-TWO

SLOTTER KEY, PORT MAJOR
DAY 39

Rafe Dunbarger jerked as if he'd been stabbed and dropped the plate of eggs he'd just picked up.

Grace looked up. "What's wrong?"

"I—I have to go—" He turned on his heel and walked unsteadily, swiftly, in the direction of the guest suite.

His face was a peculiar unhealthy shade; she wondered what he'd eaten the day before. "Does he do that often?" she asked Teague.

"Not very," Teague said. Grace glared at him, but Teague seemed impervious to her glares. "It may be his temporary biosculpt wearing off."

"I forgot about that," Grace said. She hadn't, but it was a possible explanation.

"We should let him alone," Teague said, spreading jam on toast.

"Tell me, Teague," MacRobert said as he walked in. "Do you like fruitcake?"

"Fruitcake? That thing with dried fruit where they pour brandy on it and set it afire?"

"No," Grace said, with a quelling glance at MacRobert. "That's plum pudding. Quite different. I must make you a fruitcake some-time." She looked at MacRobert. "Just a plain one, nothing fancy."

"Where's Rafe?" MacRobert said. "I have some information for him."

"He felt ill," Grace said. "He dropped that plate." She pointed with her fork.

"Um," MacRobert said. "Waste of good eggs." He scooped it up and put the mess in the trash, then wiped the floor, finishing just as Rafe came back.

"She's there," he said, looking straight at Grace. "We made contact. She's in one of those huts, as we thought."

"How?" MacRobert asked as Grace said the same thing.

Rafe lifted one shoulder: refusal to answer. "She described the buildings; they've gotten into only the two huts and a shed with a generator. There's electricity, but not for long—not enough fuel un-less they find more."

"She's alone? How did she—"

"She's not alone. She's with the others that were on the shuttle, twenty of them. Some died from sabotage of the survival suits—the Commandant, his aide, the pilots, two more. And then two after. She'll get me a list of names. I warned her about using the comunits, even if they come alive—that whoever's secret this is will be aware the scans were unblocked for most of a day. She was exhausted, I could tell—but she's alive!" He paused for breath, then went on. "They don't have enough food for the whole winter; there's some kind of entrance to a bunker or a mine, but it won't open to the same code."

Grace looked at MacRobert; his eyelid flickered. He thought he had figured something out. Teague had the totally blank expression he used when he was determined not to let anyone see anything of his reactions. Rafe—Rafe was excited, happy, ready to act.

"I need transport," Rafe said. "A plane—long-range—that runway is long enough—"

"It's more complicated than that," MacRobert said. Rafe turned to glare at Grace.

"We haven't told you everything yet," she said. "It will take awhile."

CHAPTER TWENTY-THREE

MIKSLAND
DAY 40

Ky made it back to the first hut and found Marek awake in the kitchen.

"All secured?" he asked.

"Yes. Power shut down, though I didn't lock the door," Ky said. "If we find enough fuel, we can open it up again for the extra space."

"Open bunk, left side bottom," he said.

"Thanks. Wake me at shift change if I'm not up." She lay down. She didn't feel like sleeping; finally getting a contact with the outside world had her mind racing. Rafe was here; he knew why no one had come for them; he knew about dangers she'd barely guessed. And how was she supposed to warn everyone not to use their skullphones or comunits without creating intense curiosity about how she had come up with such a wild notion? She dozed off finally.

In the morning, she woke determined to explore every possible resource in the area. So far they had found six empty barrels that had once held fuel for the generator, a half barrel more of fuel, no more full ones. No sign of a well house, or any pipe or pump for water. Ky wondered if the crew that had been here had brought water in by air. She looked down the smooth strip of snow that reminded everyone of a runway—because the land undulated, she couldn't see all of it— then over at the two big humped buildings that might be hangars. She considered climbing up onto the cabin roof, or up on the tower, for a better view, but for now other things had more priority. Those two big humped buildings that might be hangars, for instance. They could explore the runway another day.

"Over there, Admiral!" Corporal Riyahn said. Ky looked. Out from behind a rumple of land she hadn't noticed, a file of at least twenty of the gray-brown animals she'd seen earlier ambled toward the runway, then pawed at the thinner snow and lowered their heads to eat whatever grew under it. Barely a hundred meters away—if she'd had a rifle, and not her pistol, she could have dropped one eas- ily. With a pistol—she remembered her early training with firearms. She might hit one, or simply spook the herd.

She walked slowly toward them, gesturing to the others to stay back. The animals ignored her for the first ten meters, fifteen meters, twenty, then one lifted its head and stared. Others looked. Ears wag- gled: forward, back, forward, back. She stood still. One stayed alert; the others went back to eating. She took one step. No reaction. An- other. No reaction. Another. The sentinel waggled its ears and two other heads came up. She walked backward three steps and stopped. The sentinel tipped its head side-to-side, the antlers making a wider sweep. All the heads came up, but they didn't move off. Ky turned and angled back toward the others, watching from the corner of her eye. Soon all were back to eating.

"They've been hunted," Marek said.

"Yes. But not recently, and I think not often. Maybe only in sum- mer, when people come here. I'd need to be a lot closer to get a good shot with my pistol and the ammo I have."

"I could hit one at that distance," Marek said. "Maybe not a clean kill, but wound it badly enough we could catch it. If you'd allow—just two rounds, at the most."

"We don't even know what they are," Ky said. "Some kind of deer, maybe?"

"Whatever they are, they're probably good eating," he said. "I wonder if they'd get used to us, enough to let us get really close."

"I hope so," Ky said. "Because they're the best food source I see." She glanced at the sky; clouds had thickened overhead, and even as they stood there, the first flakes of snow fell. "We'll go back, see what we can find in those other buildings."

Snow fell more heavily as they walked, and by the time they were past the first hut and nearing the generator shed, they could hardly see their way. "We need more ropes," Marek said. "Someone could get lost in this."

Ky said nothing. She could think of many things they needed more of—water, food, fuel for the generator, a working communications device other than her cranial ansible. They made it safely inside and set about cooking their boring and meager supper.

"If I had my father's rifle," Sergeant McLenard said, "we'd have had fresh meat tonight. Easy shot. Admiral, did I hear Master Sergeant say you had a firearm?"

"Pistol," Ky said. "Optimized for short-range, in-ship use."

"Ah. Not as easy then. Too bad. But still, if we could get close enough—"

"When the weather settles, I'll certainly try," Ky said.

DAY 41

They woke to blinding blue-and-white beauty. Ky squinted against the glare. Right in front of the hut door, some animals had left their mark: droppings and footprints. Not the hooved and antlered creatures but something with paws, and droppings that looked like those of big . . .

"Dogs," McLenard said, squatting down to look closely. "Really big ones. You can tell dogs by the arrangement of toes."

"Can you tell how many?"

"Six at least. This sun is so bright . . . we could get snow blindness; we should go back in and make eyeshades." Inside he spoke softly to Ky. "We shouldn't go out alone at night. They might not be dogs, but wolves. There are some in the northern forests, but these tracks are of larger ones."

"Do wolves attack people?"

"Rarely, there. Deer, mostly. But here—depends how hungry they are, I imagine."

With eyeshades in place, they went back out. Ky soon spotted the herd they'd seen before, grazing along the margin of the runway.

"Someone had to bring them," Inyatta said. "Whoever terraformed the place. I never studied Origin biology, but my guess is they're from Old Earth. And if someone put grazers here, they'd have put their natural predator or some equivalent here as well."

"They'd have to be from the time people first got into space," Marek said. "Whatever was left on the home planet by then. I mean, we're told it was in bad shape, many species already gone."

Suddenly all the animals jerked up their heads and stared—not at the humans, but in a different direction. They moved, not in a panic, but in a group. Ky looked where they had looked. Something moved, just visible behind the nearest rise. "What's that?"

"I have no—"

A tall shape rose into view, turning toward them. Another followed, and another.

"*That's* not anything I ever saw in a picture of Old Earth animals," Inyatta said. "Unless they had shaggy elephants. And elephants were gone by the first colonizations. Besides not fitting on spaceships."

Ky watched as the animals trudged nearer. Much bigger than any animal she'd seen, like pictures of elephants, only covered with long coarse hair. Ears like ragged flaps of thick woolly blanket, dramatic tusks gleaming in the sun, long noses hanging down in front. Despite their size, they moved with surprising grace. The leader stopped. That long nose—trunk, she remembered, was the name for it—lifted, pointing at them.

"They're downwind of us; they're getting our scent," Inyatta said as the rest lifted their trunks.

"We'll go back now," Ky said. She wished they had real weapons. Her pistol would be no use against something that size.

In the next hour, all the animals wandered away, the deer-things in one direction and the hairy elephants in another. Ky turned her attention to the other buildings, assigning a group to examine each. The two that looked like hangars had huge sliding doors chained together, the chains locked with a simple padlock for which they had no key. "Bolt cutters would work," Sergeant Chok said. "If we had any." The doors did have small windows, one each; they brushed off the snow and looked into the dim empty space of the first building, hoping to see barrels of fuel for the generator, even aircraft. "Something in the back corners, maybe, but until we get the doors open I can't tell what it might be," Chok said. The next had some machines inside, but they couldn't tell, in the dimness, what they were.

That left the building beside the tower. Only a small part of it showed; it ran straight into the rise behind it. They had already tried the Rector's code on the door, but it didn't work. Was Marek right? Could the door be rigged to harm anyone who tried to force it open? Marek's group was still over at the more distant hangar. It was her decision. Frustrated, she asked for suggestions.

"There's a crowbar in the generator shed," Ennisay said. He jogged off and came back with it. "There's a sledgehammer, too, and an axe and other tools. I found 'em this morning when I filled the generator's fuel tank and knocked over those boards stacked at the end."

"You could have mentioned that before we went to the first hangar," Chok said. "We might've been able to break the chain."

"Never mind," Ky said. "Let's get this open. Ennisay, go back and bring all the tools you find."

In the end it took well over an hour to destroy the lock, using the crowbar, sledge, and a pick, but they finally wrenched the now-damaged door open, revealing a small square chamber. "It may never lock again," Sergeant Cosper said, with satisfaction.

An overhead light came on when Ky stepped inside. Rough concrete floor, concrete walls, large enough for all six of them. To the left was another door, closed, with a pushbar on it and a sign: AUTHORIZED PERSONNEL ONLY.

Ky walked over and pushed the bar; the door, thick and heavy, swung open silently. Beyond, lights came on in a sequence, revealing a corridor slanting down into dimness. "Sergeant McLenard, stay in the antechamber. You can close the outer door, but don't try to lock it. Chok, Ennisay, you're with me." She started down the slope; the others followed. As she went, lights turned on ahead of her. After about ten meters, the corridor turned right and continued downward. Ky checked to be sure there were no secret doors that might shut behind them. After another ten meters, the corridor turned right again.

"You have any idea how far down we've come?" asked Chok.

"No," said Ky. "The slope is not as steep as a stairway; makes it hard to figure."

"At least it's cut off the wind," said Ennisay. "Feels warmer, whether it is or not."

Ky nodded without answering. The ramp ended in a space larger than the chamber above with a wide opening to the left. Here, too, lights came on, this time along a straight, level corridor as wide as the opening, with doors on either side. All were closed. All had keypads but no card slots. Although they were labeled, the labels meant nothing to her; clearly they were codes. She tried the first door, expecting it—like the outer door—to refuse Aunt Grace's code, but to her surprise it opened. A small room, not more than three meters wide and deep, lined with metal shelving, the shelving full of boxes. Two were open and partly full: one of white paper, one of yellow.

"Admin," Chok said. "The spoor of the paper pushers."

Across the passage, the shelves of a larger room held a wide variety of electronic gear: desk comps, pocket coms, printers, cameras, surveillance gear including both wire-guided and wireless fliers, each carefully wrapped in transparent fabric and labeled, this time in familiar symbols. "Whatever this organization was—or is," Ky said, "it's certainly well supplied with equipment. I wonder if they'll know we broke the lock or turned the lights on."

She turned as a clatter of boots on the ramp neared them. Marek and his search team came into the main hall. Marek whistled.

"If they noticed, they'll come rescue us," Ennisay said.

"They'll come, at least," Marek said. His brows drew together; Ky noticed a bulge of muscle at the side of his jaw.

Ky moved on to the next rooms. Later they would have time to examine everything in each of them, but she still needed to find something they could use to survive. Fuel for the generator. A water source. Food. Clothing.

The next door on the right opened into a larger room lined with racks that held weapons familiar to all of them. An armory—and one full of Slotter Key military weapons stamped with the familiar logos. An unlocked door on the far side opened into a practice range with a shooting gallery and a line of targets on cables at the far end. Cabinets on two walls held ammunition, cleaning supplies, replacement parts, fully charged powerpaks for the weapons that needed them. Two long workbenches filled the center. On one, a standard-issue rifle lay clamped in a stand. She went to it, recognizing the biometric control panel just as Marek said, "No good; these are all palm-locked."

"If we can break the code, we can hunt with them," Cosper said.

"Later," Ky said. Her mouth watered at the thought of fresh meat. There had to be a way to unlock those weapons.

Across the passage again, and this time something immediately useful: a store of clothing, from olive-green heavy-duty cold-weather suits through indoor shipsuits to underwear, in a range of sizes, all with Slotter Key military tags inside. Clean, whole clothing—now if they could find water enough to bathe and change, what a difference that would make. Ky resisted the temptation to grab gloves off the shelf—she didn't really need them down here.

"Almost paradise," Inyatta said. "Warm, no wind, new clothes—"

"Maybe it'll have water and food as well," Gossin said. "Or a magic tunnel straight to Port Major." Nobody laughed.

Next down on that side was a door without a lock, a swing door, and inside what Ky had hoped for—a large shower room and toilet facility, much like those she'd used at the Academy. She turned one of the faucets; a trickle of water came out and stopped. A loud click came from overhead and a mechanical voice blared:

"THIS FACILITY IS NOT AVAILABLE FOR USE AND REQUIRES AUTHORIZATION FROM OFFICER TO RESTORE FUNCTIONALITY. IF OFFICER IS PRESENT, STATE NAME, RANK, NUMBER."

Marek looked at her and raised an eyebrow. Ky shrugged. It couldn't hurt to try. "Vatta, K., Admiral—" and uttered not her aunt's number, but the one she'd been given at the Academy.

After a moment, the voice spoke again: "FUNCTIONALITY RESTORED." This time the water ran from the faucets, hot from hot and cold from cold. Ky turned them back off. Was the speaker connected to an AI of some kind?

"Locate mess," she said, testing that idea. No response. Several other commands—to open doors—also produced no response.

"If it's an AI, it's a very limited one," Marek said. "Maybe they had a problem with troops leaving the water on or something."

"So we'll explore," Ky said. She led the way to the end of the passage, a T-intersection. To the left was a short passage with two doors on one side, one on the right, and a heavy door with a lock panel and wheel, like a pressure door. To the right was an open arch.

That led into a dining area: four rows of three tables, each topped with eight upside-down chairs. To the left, behind it, was a kitchen, with a serving line dividing kitchen from dining: long metal counters, cooktops, ovens, storage below for large pots, all neatly covered, implements hanging on racks, bagged to keep them dust-free. At one end an opening led into a large pantry with coolers, open empty racks for produce, and rows of canned and boxed foods. Ky's mouth watered.

Specialist Gurton opened one of the coolers: neatly wrapped packages of frozen foods, clearly labeled. "I could start cooking now," she said. She turned on a faucet; water came out. Then she touched one of the cooktop controls and a red light came on. "It's all working. We could have a real meal."

Ky almost said yes, but Marek spoke first. "Cleanup first. Everybody showers, gets into clean clothes, then we can eat." He looked at Ky. "If the admiral agrees."

"Cooks clean up first," she said. "Get a start on the meal. But not too rich a meal at first. We still need to be careful about that."

"Good point," Marek said. "Two of you—" Two hands went up: Gurton and Kamat; he nodded. "Get clean clothes from the storeroom, see if you can find hairnets and kitchen gloves, then shower." The two volunteers hurried off. To Ky he said, "Send someone back topside to bring the others down?"

"Yes. Let's see what we have for sleeping quarters next." More questions rose with every discovery, but she had to focus on the immediate needs. Water, food, warmth, someplace safe to sleep . . . but this whole place felt safe. Which could mean it wasn't.

The entrance to quarters was only a few meters back up the main corridor, a passage with no door and doorways opening off it. First on the left, a small office. "Watch station," Marek said before she commented. "Good place for it." They moved down the passage, opening all the doors. On the left, a large open bay with bunk beds. Bedding, neatly folded and sealed in clear bags, lay on the foot of each. On the right, smaller rooms with two or four beds each, also with bedding. "NCO quarters," Marek said. "That's probably officers' quarters down there." He nodded toward the end of the passage, where one door ended the passage, and another was set nearby on either side. "My guess is the end one's yours, Admiral, as ranking officer. Your aide will take one of the others."

"You'll take the last, as senior NCO?"

He shook his head. "No, Admiral. I'll take one of the NCO rooms nearer the watch office up there. Lets me keep a closer eye on things. We have plenty of room; no one will be crowded."

Ky opened the door to the end room. She found a small suite: an office with desk, chair, two side chairs, shelves along one side and cabinets below, then a door into a comfortable bedroom with another desk built into shelving and cabinets on one side. Power outlets showed at the back of the desk. On either side of the bed a small nightstand with a light; power outlets on the wall beside both nightstands. Two comfortable-looking chairs. A closet with a built-in clothes 'fresher and a lockbox with a key in the lock. She stowed the flight recorder and the IDs she'd collected in the lockbox, and took the key with her. She felt the bed and thought of lying down just for a moment.

In the distance, she heard excited voices and returned to the main corridor. Jen stood near the sanitation suite door, counting people off. She looked at Ky. "Admiral. It's too bad we didn't find this place right away."

"Agreed," Ky said. "Would have saved us those miserable days down on the beach." She didn't mention Jen's opposition to her exploration. "Still a lot of questions to answer about this place."

"Just a moment," Jen said to Droshinski and Hazarika as they started to enter. "Let the admiral go first."

"No," Ky said. "I'll wait. And I can show you where you'll be quartered, Commander."

"But I need to—"

"I don't think anyone's going to skimp on their shower," Ky said, grinning. "Come on—you'll have a real bed and some privacy."

Jen sighed but followed as Ky led the way down the passage. "You can have your pick of these two rooms," Ky said, gesturing to the doors. "I've claimed the one on the end. It's got a little office in front where I can do paperwork and we can talk in private. I haven't seen the others yet; they may be the same."

Jen opened the door to the right. She also had two rooms, both smaller than Ky's. "Very nice," she said. "Who's got the one on the other side?"

"Nobody," Ky said. "Marek refused it; he wants to be up the passage nearer the watch office."

"You offered him an *officer* suite?" Jen's brows were up.

Ky wondered what Cascadian rule she'd broken this time. "He's the senior NCO, two grades higher than any other."

"But it put him back here with us—with two women. It would have been . . . unseemly."

"It's—" Ky stopped. She had been saying *It's different here. This is Slotter Key, not Cascadia* too much. Yet it was true: in Spaceforce, men and women bunked in the same passage, even in the same bay.

"It is not appropriate," Jen said with emphasis. "I know this is an emergency situation and I said nothing in the life rafts. But now that there's room, it matters. The very fact we're so isolated and few in number . . ."

Ky managed not to say, *You remind me of Aunt Grace at her worst.* "Well, he refused," she said instead, "so it's not an issue."

"He refused very properly," Jen said. "*He* knows what is appropriate; you are lucky he is with us."

"If you're satisfied with your quarters, let's go get some clothes and start moving in," Ky said, hoping to cut off that topic. She turned to leave.

"I don't suppose there will be any proper insignia," Jen said. "It's important to maintain appropriate appearance—"

If she heard *appropriate* many more times today, Ky thought, she would say something inappropriate. On purpose. She held her tongue all the way down into the clothing stores.

There she gathered enough almost-fitting clothes to last several days and tried on several pairs of indoor soft-soled shoes until she found one that—with two pairs of socks—fit well enough to walk in without tripping. When Jen had an armload of her own, they returned to their quarters. All the others were either in the showers or already out. Ky dumped all but a utility uniform, underwear, and socks on her bed and headed for a shower.

Hot water and soft soap were sheer bliss. She felt both grime and muscle knots melting away. Now she could really see how thin she'd become in only a few tendays, ribs and hip bones prominent. Well, food and exercise would fix that. Maybe there was a gym in this place, too. And a clinic. One cut looked puffy and red. Others, too, would have unhealed injuries. And they needed a laundry: one or two 'freshers would not be enough for everyone.

Once in clean new clothes, she padded sock-footed out to the main room, ran her hands through her clean hair, and braided it snugly to the back of her head. She heard another shower running. Jen, most likely. She picked up her dirty clothes from the floor, wrinkling her nose at the smell. It was worth trying what the 'fresher could do with them, but she suspected her uniform would never be the same.

By the time she had put her survival suit and uniform into the 'fresher and set it on long cycle, she could smell something cooking. She fished in the desk drawer for a fresh cord and tied off her braid. She heard Jen next door, opening and shutting her inner door, and met Jen in the passage.

"Good to be clean again, isn't it?" Ky asked.

"Necessary," Jen said. She looked Ky up and down. "We need to find a way to put your insignia on these things." She had her own pinned to her shoulders.

"I don't think anyone's going to mistake me for anyone else," Ky said.

"That's not the point," Jen said. "If you—" She clamped her mouth tight, gave a little shake of her head, and followed Ky down the passage.

"I wanted mine to go through the 'fresher," Ky said. "They'll be shinier when it's done, probably."

"Oh. Well, then. At least you're thinking about it."

Ky could think of no answer to that. "Let's see what Gurton and

Kamat have found for supper," she said. The closer they got to the mess hall, the better the smell. When they came in, Marek signaled the others; everyone stood. A separate table had been set for her and Jen. As soon as they sat down, the cooks brought in the food.

"It's just a simple stew," Gurton said. "Not too rich, as you suggested."

"It's not basic gruel or fish," Ky said. "So it's perfect."

"We did put some oat flour in it."

"Fine."

Halfway through the bowl of stew, she felt much better. She slowed down, aware she'd been gulping it in, in spite of having advised others to eat slowly. "Talented cooks," she said to Jen.

"It's excellent," Jen said. "What about an inventory of the supplies?"

"Tomorrow," Ky said. "Unless the cooks want to stay up and do it tonight. But I imagine they'll be tired enough when they've cleaned up the kitchen. Tonight I'll talk to Marek about a work roster."

"Not much to do down here," Jen said. "It's all automatic."

"As far as we know," Ky said. "We still don't know what the power source is, how much fuel there is, what the water source is, and how to monitor the environmental conditions. We need to check every door, every room. How much more is there to this facility? I'd expect some kind of medical area, perhaps even a full clinic, and a gym that could be used in bad weather. A library? A communications center? Perhaps a local weather station giving a readout of conditions on the surface."

"Isn't this enough? Water, food, sleeping area, clothing?"

"It's great, Jen, but why is it here? There's not supposed to be anything on the whole continent. Yet here we are, with supplies for at least a hundred." She took another bite and swallowed it. "We need to know what it is, how it got here, and why it's not known."

"Secret military bases aren't unknown."

"True, but they're usually known to the military. Marek said he didn't know about this one. None of the others seemed to know it was here, though I'm going to ask every one of them, now that we're in a safer place."

"But it's a Slotter Key base, so it's not a problem, is it? If they come here seasonally, they'll find us and take us away, won't they?"

Jen, Ky reflected, must have led a very sheltered life. Of course, that's what Cascadian culture and law were for, to shelter Cascadians from unpleasantness. "Not necessarily," she said. "Secrecy suggests that our presence could be embarrassing or dangerous for someone. In which case—" Ky ran a finger across her throat, then took another spoonful of the stew.

"Surely not! That would be—wouldn't it be illegal?" Jen had put down her spoon and paled again.

"Yes. But if we're all dead, we won't be taking it to court."

"You really think—?"

"I don't know yet. But I don't want to find out the hard way. I want to get us all back to Port Major alive and well." That, after all, was her mission. Ky finished the rest of her stew. She felt pleasantly full, though she could have eaten more. She looked over at the other tables.

Gurton came over at once with two small bowls. "There's a dessert," Gurton said. "The custard didn't set, but it tastes good." A beige-colored thick liquid . . . Ky wondered what it was as they took the tray over to the others.

She dipped her spoon in it and took a cautious taste. "Sweet," she said. "And creamy. I imagine it would set up if left in a cooler overnight."

Jen tasted it. "Yes—it's good. I hope they do it again, if there's enough of the ingredients."

"Inventory tomorrow," Ky said. "Tomorrow we'll start a new schedule." She ate the rest of her near-liquid custard and took the bowl back to the serving counter. "A wonderful meal," she said to the cooks.

"She knows more about cooking," Kamat said. "I just did what she told me."

"Good assistant," Gurton said, smiling at Kamat. "Sir, if you'd like, I could do a lot of the cooking."

"Let me talk with Master Sergeant Marek. We need to rotate duties so if one gets sick there's not a gap, but good food's important."

"Yes, sir. It's just that I did have training in both cooking and kitchen management."

"That may seal your fate," Ky said, grinning. "We'll get you some help for cleanup, but count on cooking tomorrow—and we'll need an inventory of supplies and equipment."

Marek and the others stood as she approached his table. "At ease," Ky said. "Master Sergeant, Specialist Gurton has volunteered to continue as cook. She's trained, but she should have some help—an assistant, and also cleanup crew daily."

"Yes, Admiral. I'll assign them."

"Tomorrow we'll inventory the kitchen, the clothing stores, any other storage area we find. I'm sure there's more to this facility."

"Wake-up at 0600?"

"Yes. Inspection of quarters, then breakfast, then work details. You and I will need to talk about that. I rely on your judgment for balancing maintenance and exploration. Commander Bentik and I are returning to quarters for a planning session." Senior NCOs preferred to be left alone to arrange work details, she knew. "I'd like your opinion on security issues; let's meet at 2100 for a short conference."

"Yes, Admiral."

Ky collected Jen and headed back to their quarters. Her 'fresher was still running, not surprisingly. She picked up two clipboards, gave one to Jen, and settled into the chair behind the desk in her front room.

"Here are the issues I see as most urgent," she said, jotting them down as she spoke. Jen seemed comfortable enough writing away, her gaze intent, as Ky talked about securing the facility from intrusion from outside, setting up a regular rotation of door guards, cleaning, cooking, and then exploration of the rest of the facility.

"I thought you might give everyone a day or two off," Jen said when Ky ran down. "It's been so hard—"

"Yes, it has," Ky said. "That's why we need to get back to a regular routine, something that feels normal instead of chaotic and just barely survivable. They're tired now, of course, and I don't expect full efficiency for the first days—from either of us, for that matter. But now that we're in a safer place with adequate supplies, we need to recover mental and physical sharpness. If we can't find any gym equipment down here, I'm sure Sergeant Cosper will have ideas— running up and down the ramps if nothing else."

"I suppose," Jen said.

"It's just like being on the ship," Ky said. "Routine is comforting and sustaining as well as productive. Remember what it was like?"

Jen scowled. "Of course I do. I know what's right, Admiral."

"I know you do, Jen, but I know you're also tired, malnourished, and not your usual self. Give it a few days; you'll see." She waited; Jen said nothing, but the tight muscles in her face relaxed. "So let's review the priorities. Do you see anything that looks out of order to you?"

Jen looked at her notes. "Well . . . I'd put searching for medical supplies one up on this list."

Ky nodded. "I agree."

"And you don't mention enabling the weapons in the armory— what about that?"

"Once we found all the food, I was less concerned about hunting," Ky said. "If there's enough to last until next summer, we don't need to. And in this weather, I don't think anyone's going to show up on the doorstep. Which I would like to get better secured."

Jen nodded. "What about laundry—finding 'freshers for everyone's clothes? Even with a roomful of new clothes, troops will need to clean them."

"And not by hand in the kitchen sinks," Ky said.

"Of course not!"

"Put that on the list. I wish I knew how much water is available—"

"Already on the list. High priority."

The list was long enough to keep everyone busy for the first few tendays. "Jen, you're off duty tonight. Get some sleep until wake-up; after this, we'll share the night watch."

"But Master Sergeant Marek can—"

"There should always be an officer available," Ky said. "You never know what might happen."

Jen nodded. "Good night, then, Admiral. See you in the morning." She left; Ky heard her door close, then the inner door.

Ky wrote out orders for the next day, and at 2100 walked down the passage to the watch office. Marek and Betange were there. "Excuse me, Admiral," Betange said, and left the office. Marek stood up. "Have a seat, Master Sergeant," Ky said. "I've just roughed up some orders for tomorrow; this much should be doable, I believe."

He looked them over. "Perfectly doable, Admiral. I'll see to it. I have a watch rotation for tonight." He handed it over.

Ky nodded approval. "Call me if you need me. Starting tomorrow night, Commander Bentik and I will share night watch, but I wanted her to get a full night's sleep tonight."

"You could do with that yourself, I imagine," Marek said.

"I'm a light sleeper," Ky said. "I may be up and down; don't worry about it. Being down here out of the howling wind and cold is rest in itself."

"That it is, Admiral," he said.

She dozed off briefly at the desk in her office, then woke when the 'fresher beeped that it was finished. Her PPU and uniform looked somewhat better, but still had an odor. The 'fresher was cycling, its readout said. She laid the clothes over a chair in the front room, shut the door between the two, and lay down. The 'fresher beeped again when it was ready for another load, waking her again, this time from better sleep. Now it was 0345. She had her implant alarm set to wake her at 0530, well ahead of the others. Might as well put the clothes back in the 'fresher and hope it wouldn't go off until it was time to get up. As she drifted off, she remembered that she hadn't warned the others about com security. Tomorrow.

CHAPTER TWENTY-FOUR

MIKSLAND
DAYS 42–48

When the general wake-up went off, Ky had showered and dressed, and the 'fresher had finished a second round of cleaning and cycling. Her uniform looked clean but worn, the fabric scuffed where her PPU had rubbed on knees and elbows. The PPU itself showed only minor damage outside, and on the inside no longer smelled of too many days of continuous use. She put the new clothes she'd worn the day before into the 'fresher and pinned her insignia to the shoulders of the utility jumpsuit. If it made Jen Bentik feel happier, it was worth looking as if she thought the Slotter Key personnel would fail to recognize her.

Down the passage she heard the bustle of others waking up, hurrying to and from the showers, and readying their bays and rooms for inspection. She let Marek and Staff Sergeant Chok take that. Breakfast was hot cereal with a sweetener stirred in. Not that different from the gruel they'd been eating, but more of it, and it tasted better.

"Lunch will be soup," Gurton told her. She had Betange with her this morning. "And if the bread isn't out by then, it will be by supper."

"Sounds great," Ky said. "Good work."

"We'll get started on the inventory as soon as the bread's rising; Master Sergeant's sending us two more helpers."

Ky took a working party up to the surface to clean the two huts and bring down anything they might use. When they were done, she stayed behind to lock up and shut down the generator. That allowed her privacy to call Rafe on the cranial ansible and explain where they were now.

"Can you call every day?"

"I don't know. I haven't tried yet. Let's say at least every ten days, just in case I have to come back to the surface to make contact in privacy." If she did, she'd have to turn on the generator and electricity; that made secrecy difficult.

By the time she got back down, the others had opened all the doors they could, including three on the left arm of the T-intersection before the door that closed the corridor off.

"That one won't open to the same code," Yamini said. "We could pry it open, but Master Sergeant Marek said not. He thinks it might lead to something dangerous."

"We can leave it for now," Ky said. "At least until we've explored what we can open."

The first door on the left side opened into a small clinic. Ky had Lundin check it out. "Most of the meds are missing," she said. "Anything that would be considered dangerous or easy to abuse; I imagine they take those along when they leave. But there's plenty of stuff for headaches, stomachaches, wound care. Nutritional supplements, too. And an older-model medbox for serious injuries. If it's all right with you, Admiral, I'd like to check everyone's health status, get baseline weights, and so on."

"Excellent." Ky marked off "clinic" on the clipboard she now carried with her. "If you can open the clinic after lunch, I'll pass the word."

"Yes, sir," Lundin said. "Thirteen thirty? I'll have a sign-in sheet."

The laundry was the second door on the left, easily big enough to deal with clothing, PPU suits, table and bed linens. Another concern off her list; Ky jotted down a reminder to set up a schedule for laundering linens as well as clothes.

Across from the clinic, the door opened on a gym with a row of different exercise machines, mats in a stack in one corner, and other exercise equipment stowed neatly on shelves and racks. Sergeant Cosper led Ky around, showing it off. "Can I set up PT sessions?" he asked. "We really do need to start work on conditioning."

Ky nodded. "Yes, as soon as Tech Lundin has baseline weight and nutritional status for everyone. She'll tell you about any health problems she finds that may require a change in program."

By the evening meal, Ky knew they had enough supplies to last for most of a year. If the power stayed on, if the water flowed, they were safe, warm, and would lack nothing until someone could rescue them.

"It feels more like a classic hog trap than rescue," Ky said to Jen as they ate.

"Hog trap?"

"Legend. You build a fence with an opening, put grain in it every day, and wild hogs start coming in to eat. After a while, when they're used to standing in there to be fed at a certain time of day, you feed them and close the opening. Fatten and kill them. Mind you, I've never seen either a wild hog or a hog trap, but that's the story. A warning not to be seduced by unexpected good fortune."

"But who would want to trap us, and if they did, why not do it down by the shore?"

"I don't know. But why is all this"—she gestured—"here? Power on, ready for us to use?" She remembered Rafe's warning suddenly. "And if your skullphone pings, don't use it. I'll tell Marek to tell the others. If there's someone who doesn't want us here, no use advertising our location."

In a few days, Ky could tell that her crew, as she thought of them, were recovering rapidly from the earlier ordeal. They moved more briskly, following the routines she and Marek had laid out, and seemed more alert. Clean, in clean clothes, their hair trimmed, they looked and acted more like ordinary personnel, not desperate survivors.

The only thing that bothered her was hard to define, a growing sense that there was tension in the group that never came to the surface where she could analyze it. Were they hiding something from her? And if so, why? The only thing she could think of was Jen's persistent fussing about standards—something Slotter Key personnel might find irritating, but be too polite to tell Ky. But Jen didn't seem to interact much with the others except Marek, and he didn't seem bothered.

Perhaps there wasn't anything going on. Perhaps it was just the whole situation, the change from constant peril and fear of death to safety and relative ease, from constant exposure to cold, wet, and wind to the sameness of their new environment. Irritations and tensions suppressed by imminent danger now being released. Perhaps creating a competition of some sort would help. She mentioned that to Marek; his response was noncommittal. He was perfectly polite, as always, but he seemed, now that they were in a safer place, more remote than he had been, more immersed in managing the day-to-day activities. But again, there was more to do.

She shrugged mentally, making notes in her own log. Hard to believe it was more than forty days since the shuttle crash. Jen developed the annoying habit of knocking on her door several times a night to ask a question or complain about something, whether it was her turn on watch or not, so she was never sure when she could safely use her internal ansible. She had told Rafe she would try to contact him every ten days—and that was now only a couple of days away. She needed to know more—what Grace knew and surmised, what Rafe himself was doing, what her command back at Greentoo was doing. She didn't even know if Grace had contacted her flagship—if Pordre and *Vanguard II* were still in Slotter Key nearspace.

CHAPTER TWENTY-FIVE

MIKSLAND
DAY 49

Two nights before the ten days were up, Ky finished her late round shortly after midnight and lay down to catch a few hours' sleep. Tomorrow night would be Jen's watch. Sleep did not come. She could not shut off the thoughts racing through her mind. One what-if created a cascade of others, and any of them might be critical. Her internal timer reminded her of time passing, one slow quarter hour after another. She didn't want to have her implant put her to sleep. She wanted to settle her own restless thoughts.

She heard nothing from Jen's room next door, nothing from the passage. Well, then, she might as well risk calling Rafe now. First, she opened her outer door and looked down the passage. Empty. Light spilled out into the passage from the little watch office up near the main corridor, where Master Sergeant Marek was on watch tonight—a rotation he shared with the two staff sergeants. She made her way silently toward it. It was empty: the watch log neatly centered on the desk, a scriber beside it, nothing out of place. She glanced at the log—routine entries, perfectly normal. Nothing Marek might need her for.

Back in her quarters, she pulled the cable loose from around her neck, plugged it into the outlet on the desk in her bedroom, and lifted the tip that would plug into her implant's external socket. As she moved the tip closer to her head, her implant flashed a warning. DANGER! HIGH VOLTAGE!

She dropped the cable end; her implant warning disappeared, and she saw a red light on the attached transformer that she hadn't noticed before. That made no sense. They had successfully recharged the four remaining handcoms from outlets in the mess that looked just like this one. High-voltage outlets there, for some of the appliances, had clear warning labels. This was just an ordinary desk outlet; it should carry the normal voltage.

Gingerly, she unplugged the cable and padded across the room to try the outlet on the far wall. This time she watched the telltale on the transformer: red. All the outlets should have been the same, standard voltage for the standard items an officer might carry and use, including a cable to recharge implant batteries if necessary.

For an outlet to provide a dangerous over-current—enough to defeat the built-in transformer—could mean only one thing. It had been sabotaged with intent to injure or kill anyone who plugged an implant power cable into that outlet. And she was the only one who should use these outlets.

Her skin prickled; she felt the same hyperalertness as before a battle. Who had done this? When? Was she the only intended victim? How many outlets were compromised? She would have to find out without getting killed in the process. First, test other outlets that were supposed to supply normal voltage. She unplugged her cable again and made her way back up the passage. Marek still wasn't back from his rounds, but he'd probably gone up to check the outside door. No one was in the kitchen; the breakfast crew wouldn't be up for another several hours. The long steel tables and counters, the racks of utensils, the pots overturned in the drying rack gleamed under dim nightlights. The room smelled of soap and disinfectant.

She could see well enough without turning on the bright work lights, and walked to the far end, where a row of electrical outlets backed the work counter and smaller machines stood ready for the breakfast crew. Mixers, one with a dough hook and one with beaters, a bread slicer, toasters ... she unplugged a mixer and plugged her cable into the same socket. Green light. So whoever had sabotaged her outlet hadn't intended harm to everyone. Just her. She had an enemy.

She unplugged the cable, coiled it around her neck under her uniform again, and plugged the mixer back into the wall outlet. She didn't want to contact Rafe now—not in this exposed place. First she had to find out when and how the sockets in her quarters had been altered. She had recharged her pin-light battery using the outlet near the bedside table herself, only a few days before. It would have burned out, if the current had been too high. So it had been all right then. Someone must have altered it since. Easy enough, as she was out of her quarters most of the time.

"Somebody in here?" Marek's voice, a sudden flare of light as he turned the kitchen lights on full, startled her.

"I couldn't sleep," Ky said. Her heart was racing; she made an effort to keep her voice steady. "I was about to rummage around and make a cup of tea. Would you like one?" Even as she lied, she wondered why. She would have to tell him about the outlets; someone else might be hurt by plugging anything into one.

"Admiral." His voice had an edge to it. "*You're* the last person I expected to find sneaking around in a dark kitchen." In her heightened alertness, she felt his words as a threat.

"That's reassuring," she said, putting a touch of humor in her voice. "I should have turned the lights on, but I thought the dims were bright enough. Since I haven't found the tea tins, and ended up over here with the mixing machines—"

"A sergeant never forgets where the hot drinks and the kettle are," he said. His voice seemed completely relaxed now, without the edge of suspicion she'd heard at first. But why suspicion? She was duty officer that night, with a perfect right to be anywhere. He walked over to one of the cabinets, opened it, and pulled out a square tin. "Here. And I'll put the kettle on. And bring mugs."

Ky took the tin and opened it. It held single-serving packets of several different tea varieties, including tik in packets carrying the Vatta brand logo. She hadn't seen one of those for years; her gaze blurred for a moment and she almost plucked one out. Then she chose instead the green-marked packet of a competing brand. Two of those? Three? He might like his stouter than she did. She carried the open tin over to the counter beside the stove.

The kettle hissed as it heated. Marek came back with two mugs. "You don't drink your own family's tea?"

"I grew up on it," Ky said. "By the time I went to the Academy, I was sneaking cups of other kinds, just for variety."

"I can understand that," he said. He rummaged in the tin, extracting a red packet with a yellow triangle on it. "Since you're up, I can give you the latest report: nominal readings on all the gauges for power, water, ventilation. Nobody awake but you and me and Corporal Riyahn who's on the outer door. I went up and looked out—it's blowing a gale and I couldn't see two meters, so nobody's going to sneak up on us tonight. I told Riyahn he could barricade the door and move down to the first turn below, where it's warmer. I checked the rooms again on my way down to this end, then heard an unexpected noise in the kitchen—"

"And came to check, as of course you should. Finding an admiral lurking in the dimness, wishing she didn't have to fumble her way back to the main light switches to find tea."

"You may be closer to sleep than you think. Unless tea keeps you awake."

"Not me," Ky said. "I grew up next to a tik plantation. Another reason to drink another kind. Tik tea can keep me awake; nothing else does."

"And yet you couldn't sleep. Want to talk about it?"

His voice was warm, calm, the voice of someone who could be trusted. Similar in tone to that of the many good senior NCOs who had been so important in her career. Or . . . the voice of someone who could seem trustworthy, the voice of a betrayer. Ky thought about the implications of the brand of tea he'd chosen. Did he know she knew that San Kreslan was a Miznarii corporation? She certainly knew Marek had no implant, though given the scars on his head that might be a medical issue. She'd assumed from the scars that was the reason Marek didn't have one, but . . . maybe not.

"It's nothing," she said. "Just a headache. It could be the weather; I used to get headaches at home when a storm was coming in. One reason to prefer life in a spaceship." Her mind began throwing up scraps of memory, of Marek's interactions from the shuttle crash on. Was he what he had seemed? Or something else? She couldn't be sure. Precisely because he was the senior NCO, she had relied on him to act independently; he saw more of Jen Bentik than he did of her.

"You don't use your implant to regulate your sleep?"

"Only before combat," she said. "Then I set it to wake me up an hour and a half before we come out of FTL, and it makes sure I've had the sleep I need."

He shook his head. "I don't know as I'd trust something like that. All those electrics inside your head. But—you haven't had any problems with it? Or could the headache be caused by it?"

"No," Ky said. "As far as I know, implants can't cause a headache. As for sleep, I need that function rarely. Most of the time, natural sleep works well enough. I don't want to be overly dependent on it, after all."

"Wise," he said, and took another sip of his tea. "So at the Academy, it didn't bother you not to have an implant?"

"No . . . well, a bit at first, like all those who'd had them. But I'd had only a child's model. My parents wanted to upgrade mine at sixteen, but I knew by then the Academy required us to train without, so I refused. Thought it would be easier for me, and I think it was."

"You probably don't know this," he said, "but I'm Miznarii. We don't use any artificial aids."

His voice was relaxed, but Ky noticed the little muscles around his eyes tightening.

"I noticed you didn't have an implant," she said, trying for the same relaxation of voice and posture. "But some people just don't, one reason or another. A friend's father had neurological damage from trauma and couldn't use one."

"It's true Miznarii aren't the only ones without implants," Marek said. He seemed completely relaxed now. "I suppose, as much as you've traveled in space, you've met some?"

"Yes," Ky said. "Though more who are opposed to more advanced humodification techniques, as well as those who use them." She took another sip of her tea. "I'm sure you know about my departure from the Academy; I can assure you that I do not blame all Miznarii for the actions of one or a few."

"I'm glad to know that," he said. "I didn't think you would, but—it's reassuring."

So was the unease she'd felt a reflection of his concern that she might distrust him for being Miznarii? Or something else? She wasn't sure. She needed to be sure.

Ky left the kitchen ahead of Marek and went to the women's section of the toilets. He went to the men's section; she heard a flush and then his steps moving back out. She sat there, her thoughts running in circles to no useful conclusion, and then went back to her own quarters, nodding at Marek who was in the watch office entering something on the computer. She was even more awake now. It could not be—could *not* be—that a senior NCO in Slotter Key Spaceforce was a traitor. Someone in a lower grade, maybe, but Marek was so completely the good NCO, the responsible, competent senior on whom young officers and junior enlisted could depend. She could not believe he was anything else.

And yet. Facts, not belief, were needed here. She reviewed everything she knew and had observed of him from the moment she'd met him, pulling up details from her implant yet again. Nothing, no clue at all, in his demeanor when she met him first, or in the way he acted after the passenger module landed in the ocean. He hadn't objected to her taking command, though he'd questioned it briefly. He'd been competent with the hatch and the slide, with the launch of the first and second rafts. Nothing at all to show he had been involved in the sabotage of the shuttle. Nothing in those first days in the rafts . . . a few times he'd disagreed, suggested something she hadn't approved, but he'd accepted her decisions, and such single incidents weren't unusual between an officer and a trusted senior NCO. And there her memory snagged on a detail.

The puffer fish and its spines . . . yes, it had come up under the other raft, the one with Marek and Jen in it. But in all the chaos that followed, why hadn't he launched the spare raft until she yelled at him, and why had he inflated it inside the raft, where it blocked those who needed to get supplies and themselves into it before their own raft fell apart? He'd been talking to Jen—but once it was clear they were in danger, why didn't he go on and act? Why didn't he push the spare over the side before pulling the inflation ring?

The inflated spare and its canopy had cut off her view of most of the other raft; she'd heard Marek calling orders from the other side of it, but until Chok was able to drop the canopy, none of the wild throws at the spare raft accomplished anything. Surely Marek hadn't intended that. Unless he wanted them to fail in the end. And that would include him; it would be murder *and* suicide.

And the secret of this base would have been secure.

Her implant brought up that one brief view she had of the gap in the raft's floor, before the inflating spare raft blocked it. The outer layer hung down from a ragged tear that might have been the shark's attack on the puffer; the inner layer showed a long, clean cut, as if made with a very sharp knife by an experienced hand. Had Marek or someone else panicked and cut the floor to let the fish free before it took the raft down? Who had actually made that cut? Why hadn't Jen said anything?

Assume for the moment it was Marek. Why would he do that? And later—she went over the whole thing again, more slowly than before, querying her implant for details. That first narrow gash in the cliff wall, where he'd suggested they land: the rocks guarding the entrance to it had been clearly visible, the danger obvious. Granted he wasn't from a sailing family, he'd said, but—he had been competent with knots, throwing hitches as fast as she could. Particularly in the aftermath of losing a raft and some supplies to—supposedly—the puffer-fish spines, why would he suggest trying to land there? Did he want them all to die?

He had argued briefly for continuing north, but had cooperated when she'd insisted on landing in that wider bay. He had not been the one pilfering rations—the evidence was clear that Vispersen and Lanca were to blame. Though—they'd had only three ration packets with them, and ten more had been missing. Yet she could not see Marek deliberately hastening the death by starvation of others.

But he'd been opposed to her exploration inland, even though it was clear they would run out of food where they were. Yes, dividing their forces to look for something better would have been foolish if they hadn't already exhausted the resources they had. And yet . . . suppose he *had* known about the base. It would mean he was involved in some conspiracy within Spaceforce. If he'd been coerced into it, it could mean he—even his family—was at risk of retaliation if he didn't prevent its discovery by others.

And since she'd told him about using the Rector's code to get into the huts, he could have changed the code to keep them out of the main base. It could explain his stated concerns about the dangers of entering an unknown facility; it could explain his repeated suggestions that he—as an experienced hunter—should take her sidearm to go hunting one of the animals they'd seen. For that matter, how *had* he known she had one? Jen could have told him, maybe. His treatment of her aide, which had led Jen to praise him so often, could be an attempt to divide the two remaining officers.

But this was still all speculation. That he was a Miznarii didn't disturb her; her family had no real bias against them. Saphiric Cyclans, whose beliefs were considered "weak" even by Modulans, regarded other religions as cultural elements, not threats. Vatta had Miznarii employees, both on ships and planetside. She had never blamed all Miznarii for that Miznarii cadet's request or the trouble it caused her, even after learning he had been acting on orders from other Miznarii.

Every religion, she'd been taught, had some bad people in it. Even in Saphiric Cyclans, the religion of her childhood. Some distant cousin of her mother's had made a fortune selling harmless but also useless extracts of a particular fungus as a cure for a half dozen conditions, all the while performing the Cyclans' minimal rites with great devotion and precision.

But having met some violent anti-humods now, she had to admit concern about a Miznarii NCO whose behavior was more than possibly . . . odd. Troubling. Suppose this *was* a secret installation, and he was in on it. Suppose he was willing to breach it, or let others breach it, to save some of them . . . but not all. Who would be in the *not all* but the officers, especially the foreign, offworld officers, over whom he had no real influence?

Once she began thinking like this, she could not stop. Detail after detail came to her, and each one seemed as damning as the last. Particularly whatever had been done to the power sockets in her quarters . . . no one overpowered a socket unless they intended harm to a device or a person. His specialty code was E&C; he had to know the importance of delivering the right voltage to different parts of various devices. He knew electronics; he knew implants used low-power connections and probably knew that implant cables were never used in high-voltage sockets. And he might well assume that she would top up the battery for her implant once she was near a source of electricity.

Who else might have the right skill sets? She ran through the roster. Several of the others had some knowledge of communications, or some experience with electronics, but how could they get in and out of her quarters without Marek's knowledge and connivance? He, like she and Jen, could go anywhere; the others would be noticed if they were out of place.

Only Marek had the skills and the opportunity. He had set a lethal trap; her avoidance of it wouldn't stop him. And he had fooled her before; for her own sake and that of the others, she must not be fooled again. So a confrontation would come, inevitably, and best that it come when she was ready for it.

She took out her pistol and looked at it. She had cleaned it as best she could when alone in the hut up above; she had not yet, in the few days they'd been here, used the armory. Her ammunition clips still held a choice of rounds; she stared at them, thinking hard. She had no qualms about killing in general—she had killed before, in close quarters as well as at a distance, in space combat. But she had always killed those she knew were enemies, those who openly attacked her first.

Her stomach roiled as if she were standing on the edge of a precipice. Killing in the moment of danger—facing a declared enemy—that was different. Now ... she contemplated planning a killing, creating a situation in which she would have the advantage. And what if she was wrong? What if it was someone else? Even if right, how would she explain what she had done to the others? How could she expect them to accept it, with no proof at all? Yes, the outlets were delivering a high voltage, but as far as they knew, it might have been anyone, or it might have been high-voltage all along, for some special piece of equipment used by those who came seasonally.

And if she didn't take the initiative, and he killed her? What then? Command was responsibility—she could not leave the others to whatever he decided to do with them. To what his bosses chose to do.

She had to act to protect them as well as herself, to protect Slotter Key itself from whoever would intentionally crash a shuttle like that.

How would Marek analyze the threat she posed? Would he realize, from anything she'd said tonight, from her appearance in the kitchen, that she now suspected him? She must not walk into a trap; she must anticipate what he might do. The rewiring of outlets had been subtle, indirect, and if she had died, it very likely would not have been traced to him. Would his next attempt be something similar? A drug in her food or drink—or in everyone's but his? Would he turn to direct violence? She wished she had his service record.

She looked down at her ammunition clips again and considered which was best to use, most effective, safest for anyone else who happened to be near. Chemstuns, frangibles, spudders, each with advantages and disadvantages. She made her choice.

With that choice, she felt relaxed enough to sleep. She padded over to her outer door in her socks and set the lock. He could break in, of course, but she set her implant's security level to high. Any touch on either the door or the lock would wake her without revealing that to the person outside her door.

She lay down on the floor on the off side of her bed, her pistol under the pillow she took from the bed. When she woke again, two hours later, nothing had triggered her implant alarm, and she felt remarkably rested . . . and even more convinced she was right. It was nearly time for the morning buzzer. What would Marek have come up with? She fastened her uniform jacket, and—pistol comfortably nestled in its holster—opened the door. The next door, Jen's, was ajar.

Her heart thudded. Had Marek killed Jen? But he knew she herself was the more dangerous one. Why would he attack Jen? She stood still, listening. Not a sound from the passage; then the sound of the morning buzzer. Time for the next shift to get up for the watch change. Creaking of beds, thumps of feet hitting the floor. Ky stepped out, closed her door behind her, locked it. Whatever Marek was doing, soon the others would be out and about. He would probably avoid a confrontation in front of others.

She walked down the passage toward the toilets and showers. She saw McLenard and Kamat come out of the barracks, headed for the mess. They were today's kitchen helpers, she remembered. She heard Marek's voice from up the passage to the ramp upstairs and the sound of boots—someone else coming down. Everything seemed normal, but what about Jen? How was she going to tell Jen and when?

Just then Jen emerged from the bathrooms, her uniform perfect as always. "Good morning, Admiral Vatta," she said as usual. "I trust you slept well?"

"A touch of headache overnight, so I went in the kitchen and made tea," Ky said. "Better now."

"I need to speak to you privately," Jen said, in a much quieter tone. "The staff office?"

"What is it?" Ky asked, not moving. She didn't have time for another of Jen's complaints about someone out of uniform or failing in Cascadian standards of courtesy.

"It's a personnel problem. We really should be private."

The staff office would not do, nor would her own quarters. Marek had been in both and might—probably did—have surveillance running. "Let's take another look at the T," Ky said. "Nobody goes down that way."

She led the way. The T was, as nearly always, completely empty. Down at the end, the pressure door's locks and wheel looked just the same as always, and Ky was uneasily aware that they were now at the end of a perfect firing range, next to the target. She looked back down the passage and stepped into the laundry.

"Now—what's the problem?" Ky asked.

Jen pursed her lips in exactly the way Ky's mother had years ago. "The *problem* is a personnel matter. Surely you are aware of the way your over-familiarity has eroded proper military discipline."

"My over-familiarity? What are you talking about?" This was the last thing Ky had expected.

"You chat casually with enlisted personnel about non-task topics; you allow far too much free time; you even—and it pains me to have to say this to a fellow officer—you even spend idle time alone, with . . . with Master Sergeant Marek."

Ky felt a flash of anger, but her implant flushed the hormones down to normal levels. "I had a headache last night and went to the kitchen to make tea. Master Sergeant Marek was on duty, and found me there. You can ask him."

"You weren't back in your quarters for over an hour! That's more than tea!" Red patches stood out on Jen's cheeks. She looked as tense as if she were about to spring at Ky.

Ky stared back, confused. What was this about? "What do you think I was doing besides drinking tea and then going to the toilet?"

"You're always spending time with Master Sergeant Marek. What do you think I'm thinking? What everyone's thinking?"

It was so ludicrous Ky nearly burst out laughing; the last of her anger vanished. "Sex?" she asked, trying to keep the laughter out of her voice. "With *him*?"

"He's a very attractive man," Jen said in a prim tone. "He's older, mature, perhaps reminds you of your father . . ."

"*What?*"

"And that's why you're becoming too familiar—"

"Jen. Commander. Stop right there." Ky held up her hand as she took a deep breath. "Master Sergeant Marek is the ranking enlisted in this group, and the ranking member of the Slotter Key personnel. When I took command—"

"Which you had no legal right to do, I hope you realize!"

"Who do you—" No. Never ask a question to which the answer can be something you don't want to know. "I was the senior surviving officer and I do have a Slotter Key Spaceforce background."

"But—"

Ky held up her hand again; Jen looked angry, but didn't interrupt. "And I asked Master Sergeant Marek if he would have a problem if I took over. He did not."

"What could he have said, with you the returning hero? Using your prestige to overwhelm—"

"He could have cited military law—I'm sure he knows it—and so could I. Slotter Key military law allows for transfer of command to any commissioned officer in an emergency when the usual chain of command is broken. That's why Major Yamini—a Slotter Key Space-force adviser aboard Captain Argelos' ship—agreed to operate under my command at the Battle of Boxtop. I'm sorry you weren't there; it would have saved you concern about the legality of my taking command here."

"That may be true," Jen said in a tone that conveyed doubt, "but I'm talking about more than your taking command. It's your demeanor with Master Sergeant Marek—and with the others as well. You are not maintaining appropriate discipline. It's not like it was down on the shore—it's not an emergency anymore. We're in a safe place, warm, dry, with plenty of food—but you allow undue familiarity, and indeed you practice it yourself."

Clearly Jen had a load of grievances, but time was passing and Ky could not let this go on all day. How could Jen think the emergency was over? They were still unable to communicate, except by a cranial ansible she dared not use now, still isolated, still in danger the moment they went outside into the frigid winter. Ten or twenty days of comfort did not mean they were safe forever.

Jen went on. "I know about you and Marek . . . I saw him come out of your quarters at 1400 three days ago. It wasn't his shift—"

"Where were you?" Ky asked. So Jen had been spying on her—bad enough, but why?

"In my quarters. I heard voices in yours, and then—"

"You looked out your door—"

"Yes. And Master Sergeant Marek came out and when he saw me he looked . . . well . . . embarrassed. And he made a sign with his hand and shut the door behind him. He greeted me politely enough. I asked what he was doing in your quarters, and he said he'd been checking on an anomaly in the electrical circuits, which I did not believe for a moment. When he'd gone down the passage, I knocked on your door and you didn't answer. I suppose you were pulling on your clothes." That in a tone of prudish outrage.

Ky fought down her own anger, struggling for a cool, level tone. "I didn't answer because I wasn't there, Jen. At 1400 three days ago I was topside doing a weather check. Did you not think of checking the signout roster?"

"You could have had someone add your name."

Worse and worse. "You think I'd alter a roster?"

"If you were trying to hide—that."

"I'm not trying to hide anything. I spoke to Tech Lundin on the way up the passage, and Ennisay and Kamat had the top guard. Ask them, if you think I'm a liar—but if you do, then we need to have a serious talk about *your* behavior. If Marek was in my quarters and you heard voices, then someone else was in there, too. I was not."

Jen still looked angry. "And you just did it again."

"What?"

"You just call them by their names. You almost never use proper address. It's *Medtech* Lundin and *Private* Ennisay and *Specialist* Kamat—"

Ky's patience snapped. "I've told you before: this is Slotter Key. We have our own usage. Last names without rank or grade are the way we say it when it's clear who's meant. What's not acceptable is you—my aide."

"It's my duty—"

"No. It's not. Apparently you decided some time back that I was wrong in taking command here and instead of asking me about the legalities—which I would have explained, and so could Master Sergeant Marek—you went on from there to imagine that I was guilty of other inappropriate behavior, including having sex with an enlisted man, without ever checking to see what I was actually doing."

"But—"

"And that is *no* part of an aide's duties, or any military officer's duties. You owed me the basic courtesy of coming to me as soon as you had such concerns, and of ascertaining that you had the facts right before making such accusations."

"I did come to you—about spending so much time with Master Sergeant Marek—and I know it bothered him—"

Ky registered the change in Jen's tone. The meaning came a moment later. "You know—how?"

"He said—I could tell he was distressed—I asked if I could help—he said he was worried about you. Being so young and so inexperienced."

This could not go on, not here, not now, and not after what Ky had discovered the night before. She let her voice harden. "Commander, we have spent enough time here; we will continue this discussion in a more suitable place. Come with me."

Jen had gone from flushed to pale. "What do you mean—?"

"What I said." Ky pushed away from the wall and headed back to the main corridor. "Come along." As she walked, she thought about Jen's story of seeing Marek come out of her room. That certainly fit with her suspicions, but why another person in the room? Surely he hadn't used her room for an assignation with one of the female enlisted. One of the storerooms would have been safer. And who had it been? If Jen hadn't been so convinced it was Ky, she might have found out who the other saboteur was.

She could not afford anger right now: now was the time for very clear thinking. Most of the things she might have done in other circumstances would not work here and now. She could not have Marek arrested: they had no security force equivalent. She could not call for a trial: she had no legal jurisdiction and she knew that the rest of the Slotter Key survivors would not go along with that even if none of the others were co-conspirators. Just killing Marek without warning would break the bond between her and the others, and they all needed to cooperate to survive. Even with the supplies and shelter they'd found, only a coherent group would make it through the time until thaw. If in fact it thawed here.

And what then? Every indication was that this station was in use regularly. At some point, those who had built it, maintained it, used it—and kept it secret—would come back. They would not be pleased to find survivors in their facility. Most likely they'd kill the others. She had to prevent that, and that meant keeping the entire group together, healthy, fit, prepared for whatever might happen.

Which also meant dealing with Jen, and Marek, and whoever else Marek had been working with, because all of those were undermining her, dividing the group into opposing segments. Jen first—Jen had no attachment to the Slotter Key survivors, except perhaps to Marek, and could not take over if Ky fell.

"What about breakfast?" Jen said, pausing at the juncture that led to the mess hall.

"We're not done," Ky said. "We can eat later. This way." Jen scowled but followed her up the main corridor.

Where could they go and be alone, unheard, and yet not too vulnerable if Marek had spooked and thought of killing the two officers at once? She dismissed the restrooms, the storage rooms. The armory—that could work. And she could change the ammunition in her magazines to what she preferred for an indoor firefight.

Where was Marek? Voices from the mess suggested that most of the others were eating breakfast. She had to hope he was there, too.

CHAPTER TWENTY-SIX

MIKSLAND
DAY 49

Marek watched the others eat their breakfast; his own bowl of porridge was untouched. He wasn't hungry; his stomach was tight with anxiety. Why had Admiral Vatta been fumbling around in the darkened kitchen? Her story about a headache might be true, but he hadn't found her in the clinic with a packet of pills—and she hadn't been near the cooktop or the sink. What if she suspected something? What if she'd realized—but how?—that the power supply in her quarters had been sabotaged? If she had plugged in, she should be dead. He felt sweat gathering on him, a reaction he could not control.

"What's the matter, Master Sergeant? Are you sick?" McLenard sounded genuinely concerned.

Marek shook his head. "No, just thinking. Don't worry; I'm not going to waste food." He had to eat. Others were watching him now. He had to act normal, as if nothing at all bothered him. Everything was fine. His stomach still felt tight, but he forced down a spoonful of porridge, then another. Surely he could finish a bowl of porridge. Each spoonful seemed to swell in his mouth, harder to swallow than the one before. He kept on, with no more interruptions, until his bowl was almost empty. When he looked up, the others were snatching hot sweet rolls off a tray; he got up quickly, took his bowl to the hatch for dirty dishes, and swiped out the remainder of his porridge with a rag, shaking it into the trash.

"You all right?" Kamat, one of the kitchen scrubs that day, peered through the hatch at him.

"Fine," Marek said. "But I thought of something I need to do." He made it to the closed stalls in sanitation and threw up tidily, then flushed it away, washed his face, and looked at himself in the mirror. He looked as he felt, hollow-eyed, off color, sweating. No wonder they'd asked him if he was sick. Would a shower help? Would anything? He had hoped Admiral Vatta would plug in that abomination in her head and die instantly, painlessly, to be found the next day. She didn't deserve to die, really; he admired her as much as any officer he'd served. She was smart, brave, and a good commander. She'd saved his life. Maybe he should have let go of that rescue ring, died that first day.

But his employers might have killed his family even though he was dead, because he had not kept strangers from the secret base. It was his fault they had made it to land, his fault they had left the beach, all of it his fault, they would say. So she had to die, but he'd hoped it would be quick and he wouldn't have to see it.

All because she knew this place existed. Had been inside it. And would not keep its secret. Commander Bentik had seen her one night in the second hut, a power cable plugged into that abomination in her head, talking softly. She had already told someone where she was. Sometime in the next months she would open that next door—he wasn't sure why she hadn't already done it, except they'd been busy and he'd argued that it might be dangerous. She would find proof that this base was clandestine—she already suspected that. She would find the commander's office, explore the desk, find the empty gun case . . . and all too easily figure out who might have taken it.

When warm weather came, when his employers came back with the seasonal crew, she would confront them—he knew that—and then they would kill everyone. The only way to save the others from his employers—the only way to keep them alive—to save his own family—was to ensure that they all agreed to keep the secret of this place's existence, and limit the secrets they knew about. He swallowed hard against another rise of burning liquid. Perhaps she hadn't found out about the power . . . but his gut was sure she had.

He had seen her talking to Commander Bentik on his way to the mess hall; neither of them looked happy. And he had not seen either when he hurried out, nauseated, after he ate. Bentik was on his side, he knew. She had accepted his comments about the admiral's immaturity almost eagerly; she was someone of his generation and that meant . . . he was not sure what, with a Cascadian. But she had already been cold toward the admiral, critical of her command style, and she had warmed to his attention. Had she told Admiral Vatta about their conversations? That, he knew, would not go over well, if she had.

He washed his face again, took deep breaths. His color was coming back to normal, but he still looked far too troubled and grim, and his attempt at a smile looked clownish. He heard other toilets flushing, flushed his again, another handwash, and then out into the main room, where five people were brushing their teeth at the row of sinks. Without speaking to them he went to his own quarters and retrieved the pistol he'd taken from the armory and concealed under his mattress. Riyahn had known how to disable the palm lock, and he had a full clip in it. Now to find out where the admiral and her aide were.

The armory door was closed, as it should be. Ky tapped the code onto the pad. Jen stopped an arm's length away as the door opened.

"What are you doing? Why do you want me in there?"

"Because it's quiet and out of the way and the door locks from the inside as well as outside," Ky said. "Come on."

"You—you're going to shoot me!"

Ky let contempt edge her voice. "No. Don't be ridiculous. We have nowhere else in this complex as secure, and when officers have a disagreement they do not argue in front of enlisted. I know Cascadia has that rule as well."

Jen reddened but came into the armory quickly. "It was rude to call me ridiculous."

"Yes, it was." Ky locked the door. "And it was rude for you to claim I was sleeping with Master Sergeant Marek. Tit for tat. I remind you again that you are on Slotter Key, not Cascadia Station." Ky put an acoustic tab on the inside of the lock. If anyone tried to key in, she'd hear it. Jen, she saw, had moved to the other side of the room, back against the wall near the ammunition cabinets. Ky glanced around at the weapons racked behind transparent covers, organized by type. No gaps in the displays—but was that really all? Some weapons racks stored more than were apparent.

She pulled out her personal security set and scanned the room. Sure enough, there were pickups in three places; she reset the controls and hoped her set's output was accurate in reporting that they had been scrambled.

Then she opened the nearest ammunition cabinet, shut and locked it, and opened the next. Jen stiffened and gasped. "Are you going to shoot—?"

"If I wanted to shoot you, I'd have done so already," Ky said. "I have plenty of rounds for that. I'm checking inventory."

"But nobody can use any of these—"

"So we were told. If I find a brick missing I'll be fairly sure someone else is armed."

Jen stared at her. "You think someone stole a weapon?"

"It's possible. Did you?"

"Me? Why would I—I don't even know how to use one."

Ky shrugged. "When I first saw these open, there were thirteen bricks—cartons—of 10mm rounds in *this* cabinet. Seven cartons of solid slugs, three of flechettes, three with chemstun rounds. Now there are none. 10mm wasn't a standard Slotter Key military caliber when I was in training here, and none of the weapons in these racks use that caliber ammunition. But I have a pistol that takes 10mm rounds, and Marek knows that. Someone took—or hid—the ammunition that fits my weapon. I need to know if I can trust you—so answer the question: did you take any ammunition out of any of these cabinets?"

"No! Of course not! Why would you doubt my—"

"Because of what you've said. It's clear you are being influenced by Marek; you and he have discussed me behind my back; you or he or both assumed a sexual relationship. That is disloyal, and not something I expected from any Cascadian. So I do doubt you, and on good grounds. Your behavior would warrant disciplinary action in a Slotter Key unit. Explain to me how you convinced yourself that your actions have been appropriate."

Jen blinked. "You think *I* was disloyal? What about you?"

"Right now, we're talking about you. What part of military courtesy includes gossiping about your commander with an enlisted man?" Ky kept her voice level.

"I didn't—it wasn't like that."

"Explain it to me. What was it like?"

"You don't have to be so harsh—you're scaring me." Jen's voice rose.

"Commander Bentik," Ky said, "answer the question."

"It wasn't gossip. It was—I was concerned. He was concerned. We were discussing legitimate concerns—"

"Secretly," Ky pointed out. "Even if they were legitimate concerns, you were conspiring against a commanding officer—"

"No!" After a moment, Jen went on. "We weren't—but he was concerned. He came to me as an officer—he said you were . . ." She reddened again. ". . . too casual with him. With everyone, really, but especially him, and he didn't know how to handle it. That you were too young to have such high rank, and clearly you were a genius with space combat, but he'd seen brilliant young women officers before and they mostly had this weakness when it came to relationships with men. They . . . they didn't know how . . . he hoped I would be able to help you, he said, because I was more mature, more stable . . ." Her voice trailed away; her gaze shifted from Ky.

"And you believed him," Ky said, making it almost an accusation.

"Well . . . yes. You said yourself he was a good senior NCO; I could see that you liked him, trusted him. He was always respectful, serious, concerned about everyone. Very conscientious."

"And flattering to you," Ky said.

"He never said anything like that!"

"He flattered your age and experience. I can imagine it felt natural. Deserved."

"Well . . . yes. I *am* older. In *my* military, *I* would be the commander. I come from a good family, with a good reputation. I do have more experience—"

"In some things, certainly. In others perhaps not." Ky struggled to find words Jen could understand and then accept. Her anger had cooled; she felt a twinge of pity for this woman, so upright, so convinced of her own virtue. Marek would have noticed by now they weren't at breakfast. Would he panic and come after them? Did he have a weapon? "My problem now—as the senior officer, as the officer presently in charge of this unit, irregular as that may be—is that you, who should be my second in command, have no experience in either our present tactical situation or commanding non-administrative troops. Worse, you do not respect my experience in those areas."

"I—I do respect you—"

"Really? Because what you've said this morning—and your behavior with Master Sergeant Marek—certainly doesn't sound like it to me. It sounds much more like someone who has completely lost respect for her commander, both as a competent officer and as a person of character."

Jen said nothing, looking as if she was about to cry. Did she finally grasp how far out of line she had been? For the sake of them all, Ky could not afford to pity her, not now. "We are still in a dangerous situation," Ky said. "Not merely being marooned far from any aid during the worst of winter, dependent on this facility and what it holds—which at least seems to be sufficient, with care, to last until spring. But also the fact that we are occupying a facility that is not supposed to exist. Has it not occurred to you that those who have such secrets want them kept? That a change in seasons may bring us not rescue but those intent on protecting their investment here and killing us?"

"Of course they wouldn't—even Slotter Key is civilized—Marek said—"

"What?"

"He said whoever used that landing strip would not mind that we used this in an emergency—they would be glad we'd survived; they'd take us back to the capital."

"Marek said." Ky shook her head. "Marek is not in *your* chain of command. Neither Cascadian nor SDF. You have no reason to trust what he says except that you prefer him to me."

"That's—that's paranoia—"

"Master Sergeant Marek," Ky said, biting off each word, "tried to kill me. He changed the voltage in the outlets in my quarters—he was probably doing that when you heard those noises you were so sure were a sexual escapade."

Jen's mouth fell open. Ky went on, not pausing.

"That is not the first thing he has done. He argued against landing in the bay, and then against exploring inland, even though it was obvious we could not survive at the shore without more supplies. After we found this base, he thought we should stay in the huts topside—you must have heard that—when it was clear the food stores there were not enough to last out the winter. Several times he tried to talk me out of my sidearm, claiming he was a better shot and might bring down one of those animals."

"But he cares for the troops—"

"Yes, I believe he does. But not as much as he wanted all this"—Ky waved at the room—"to remain a secret. I suspect he thinks he can convince his allies—the ones who built the place—not to kill them all. I think he's wrong about that. Someone who's kept a secret like this as long as it's been kept—while using regular military to work in it—will have killed before without a qualm."

Ky opened a third cabinet, and then a fourth, rummaging through to check every container of ammunition. "Ahhh . . ."

"What?"

"Simple misdirection. Here are the 10mm rounds." She set the boxes on one of the worktables, took out her spare clip, and changed out the chemstun rounds in it for more flechettes. "I can't use chemstun rounds here until we locate some gas filters. Haven't seen any yet. Slightly suspicious. They're standard emergency stock for all Slotter Key military installations. Or were. It has been a few years."

"You think someone took them—like they hid the ammunition?"

"Could be. Could be they weren't supplied here for some reason." Ky slid the last round home in that clip and considered the one in her pistol. All spudders now, the solid rounds that could punch through vital equipment in a spaceship or station. Did she want a mix with flechettes? She decided against it, not wanting her weapon unloaded for even an instant. She pocketed the remaining rounds, put her five chemstun rounds in the box that had held flechettes. She moved all the boxes to the first cabinet she'd opened, checking this one more carefully, and found five of the boxes of 10mm spudders behind the front stacks.

She wished she knew what weapon he had and what his proficiency really was. Though he had tried an indirect, clandestine method first, she was certain he had a firearm by now and would use it if nothing else worked to quietly remove her. Was it something that used 10mm ammunition? She did not want to face chemical rounds without protection.

The alarm she'd put on the door pinged. She looked at Jen, motioned to her to get down, out of sight from the door behind one of the worktables. She had her own weapon out, and eased over to the near wall. The door opened. Corporal Inyatta's voice: "Admiral? Are you in here? Master Sergeant Marek is looking for you or Commander Bentik . . . we all are." Inyatta's hand was on the doorframe; her head poked in, but she was looking across the room, toward the door to the firing range.

"What made you look here?" Ky asked. Inyatta startled, then looked along the wall at her, wide-eyed.

"Admiral? Uh—Master Sergeant said—" Inyatta's focus shifted to the firearm pointed at her. "You aren't—please—"

"Just answer my questions," Ky said. "Where is the master sergeant?"

"Uh—behind me—and he's—" Inyatta staggered forward, obviously pushed hard by someone behind her. Marek lunged through the door, swung around and fired at Ky but missed, his first shots ricocheting off the reinforced walls while her first shot took him square in the chest and the second in the head as he slumped. His pistol fell, skittering on the floor still firing until the magazine emptied. One of the ricochets thumped into her back; she felt a flare of heat from her armor. Even as shouts and screams broke out in the passage, it was over.

She was alive, with no more than a bruise; Marek lay in a pool of blood, spattered blood and brain from the head shot beyond; Inyatta was down on the floor a few feet from Marek, also bleeding. The now-familiar surge of triumph faded this time into regret. She had liked Marek. She had wished—even after being sure of his treachery—that she would find some way to spare him that would also save the rest.

Ky glanced aside and did not see Jen. "Jen! Are you all right?" No answer. "Corporal Inyatta?"

"I'm hit," Inyatta said. "I don't know—"

Corporal Riyahn burst into the room, wild-eyed and screaming. "You murderer! You killed him!" He scarcely looked at Ky as he stooped over Marek's body, reaching for Marek's firearm.

Someone from outside yelled "Stop! *No!* Don't!"

"Stand back, or I'll shoot," Ky said. Riyahn looked at her; his eyes widened as he took in her weapon pointed at him. His hand pulled back from Marek's pistol as if he'd had an electric shock.

"No—don't shoot me!"

Ky walked forward, next to the wall, keeping her weapon trained on him. "Hands on your head. Now!" He stood up, raised his hands. "Walk to the opposite wall. Stay there until I tell you differently. If you do not, I will shoot." He moved jerkily, slipped on the blood, recovered, kept moving toward the wall.

The voices outside had quieted to soft murmurs Ky could not quite distinguish. They sounded scared, which they would be. All that blood. The smell of blood and death. Familiar to her, by now, but most of them, she knew, had never seen combat.

"Staff Sergeant!" Surely one of the staff sergeants would be with that group, but which? Kurin, she hoped. Kurin knew her best. Silence outside now, a long moment.

"Staff Sergeant Gossin, Admiral, now senior NCO." Gossin's voice expressed distrust and resistance.

Gossin had been in the lifeboat with Marek. What stories had he spun for her? "We have at least one injured person, Staff. Find Tech Lundin and send her in."

"Here, sir. I'm coming in—" Lundin, sounding more composed than Ky expected. But as a medic, perhaps she'd seen accident victims, even murder victims, before.

"Wait! She's still armed; it's not safe." Gossin's voice.

"Staff, stand down. I'm not going to shoot a medtech. Corporal Inyatta needs her."

"She's not going to shoot me," Lundin said, still calm. "Let go of me."

"She better not," Gossin said. "Admiral, I wish to express my disapproval of your illegal behavior."

Lundin came in and went immediately to Inyatta. She had brought her kit with her.

"We can discuss that later, Staff. Right now, I need two people to take Corporal Riyahn into custody and keep him there until we can sort this out. He attempted to grab Marek's firearm when he first came in. It's evidence."

"Evidence?"

"Yes. No one should touch it, or mine, until they've been recorded for any future court."

"You're . . . you would submit to a court?"

"Of course," Ky said, as if she had never in her life evaded a court procedure. "Now—I suggest Sergeant Cosper, if he's handy, and anyone else you choose."

Gossin gave the orders, and Cosper and Barash came in. Ky lowered her weapon; Cosper and Barash took Riyahn out. Ky heard Gossin say, "Take him to the senior NCO quarters; you'll find restraints in the watch office."

Ky laid her pistol on the nearer worktable and walked to the door where she could be seen, and see the others. It was possible Marek had armed someone else; she doubted it, but it was a risk she had to take. The greater risk was spooking already-frightened people into attacking her. A ring of frightened faces stared at her, Gossin slightly to the fore. Gossin looked first for the gun that wasn't there, then at Ky's face.

"You all have questions," Ky said, her voice steady. "But right now we have things to do. Staff, I'd like you to come in and witness the scene. Have you ever been part of an investigation before?"

"No, Admiral." Gossin's tone was less hostile.

"You will need a recorder, as well. There were some in that room up the passage—"

"I'll get one," Betange said, and set off without further orders.

"Where's your weapon?" Gossin said. "Do you have a second one—?"

"My pistol's on one of the worktables; no one should touch it until it's been examined." Ky looked past Gossin at the others. "Anyone else have experience with an investigation?"

A soft chorus of *no*s and head shakes. Betange returned with a recorder. "I know this model, sir."

"Then he's your recorder, Staff. Come on in and let's get started."

Ky could feel Gossin's reluctance, but Gossin followed her into the armory and looked around, her face stiff. "Who shot first?" she asked.

"Master Sergeant Marek. Staff, I'm going to move to where I was standing when Marek came in, so you can get an idea what happened. Were you with the group when he came in?" Ky walked back and turned around to face Gossin and Betange.

"No . . ."

"Sir! There are holes in your jacket!" Betange pointed.

"Probably from ricochets. I was facing this way and felt something hit me in the back."

"But—you're wounded."

"No, I'm wearing personal armor," Ky said. "I always do. And you, Betange, need to record the position of every person and item in the room, as well as what the staff sergeant and I say. It's very important." He nodded and pointed the vid attachment at Marek's body, then his weapon, then at Inyatta and Lundin kneeling beside her, and finally at Ky. He had paled, but his hands were steady on the vid.

Gossin looked around again, this time with a more thoughtful expression. "I heard the first shots as I was maybe ten meters down the passage, coming this way," she said. "There were six or seven people nearer; I couldn't see exactly what he did. And he had just come in the door when he fired?"

"He had Inyatta look in first, probably because she'd show which part of the room I was in. Then he pushed her in, came through the door, and pivoted. I was not sure he had a firearm until I saw it; I made sure he was a lethal threat before I fired."

"And he missed you?"

"Yes. Probably his arm was still moving when he pulled the trigger. He had it locked on full auto; he dropped it after I shot him and it went on firing from the floor, recoil moving it. That's why it's as far from him as it is."

"Why did you shoot Inyatta?"

"I didn't." Ky kept her voice level, informational. "I fired two shots at Marek; both hit, chest and head. Inyatta was hit by a round from Marek's dropped weapon."

"Can you prove that?"

"When Betange records the details of my weapon, yes: the clip was full, and two rounds will be missing from the clip. And you can see that Marek has entrance wounds in chest and head."

Gossin glanced back at Marek's body. From her expression, she might never have seen a violent death before. "I . . . see." She swallowed. "And Commander Bentik?"

"I don't know. She was hiding behind that table. I haven't looked yet, but she could also have been hit, either by a ricochet or one of the stray rounds after Marek dropped his weapon."

"Sir, I want to get Inyatta down to the medbox in the clinic—I'll need helpers." Lundin sounded as calm as ever.

"Of course, Lundin," Ky said. "Just make sure they don't touch Marek's body or anything else in the room. We want to give Staff Sergeant Gossin and Betange time to record everything in here."

"Yes, sir." Lundin went to the door, carefully not stepping in any of the blood, and sent someone to bring a litter from the clinic.

"I could walk," Inyatta said from the floor. "Just a little help."

"No," Lundin said. "Just wait."

"Admiral," Betange said. He nodded toward the far table. "It's the commander. I think she's hurt. There's blood under her head."

"I'll check," Lundin said, moving that way. "And you should come, too, as witnesses." Gossin and Ky followed her.

Jen was clearly dead; at least one round had taken her in the head as she hid, and Ky felt a stab of guilt at this death she had not intended but for which she was surely responsible. She had brought Jen to this planet; she had not recognized in time what Marek had done, and she had brought Jen to this room. Why hadn't she told Jen to hide in the interior firing range instead of this room?

"When you've got Inyatta settled," she said to Lundin, "send someone to Stores, see if they can find something to wrap Marek and the commander in." She looked at Gossin. "Can we agree they both died of gunshot wounds?"

"Yes," Gossin and Lundin said together.

"Then we need to move the bodies, and get this space cleaned when you, Staff, are through with your examination."

"Yes, sir," Lundin said, and stood up just as the two she'd sent for a litter returned with one.

Gossin gave Ky a look mixing doubt and curiosity. "Admiral, you—I know you have killed before, in the war. But that was blowing up ships. This is different, isn't it?"

"Very," Ky said. She closed her eyes a moment, then looked directly at Gossin. "I have been in close fights before, Staff. Remember, my whole family was attacked wherever they were; I was on a Vatta ship." The incidents raced through her mind, like a fast slideshow on a travel site, one image for each fight. "Shot at, poisoned, shot at again . . ."

"And that's why you're so calm?"

"I suppose." Ky stood up. "Betange, have you recorded the commander's body? Then it's time to record the weapons, close-ups as well as locations."

"How did you know I didn't have a firearm, too?" Gossin asked. "You—when you came to the door unarmed—that surprised me."

"I didn't know. But I didn't want to scare you more."

"It was risky."

"Yes." She nodded at the change in Gossin's expression. "And it was necessary. Would you have trusted me enough to come in here and examine the scene with me if I'd had a pistol in my hand? Or even in a holster?"

"No, Admiral," Gossin said. "I'd have—I don't know what I'd have done exactly, but I wouldn't have trusted you." After a moment she said, "You trusted me not to shoot you even if Marek had armed me."

"It was a risk I had to take. You've been solid before now; I thought you would be. Still—this would shock anyone. Everyone. Scare some of you, and with reason. I'll tell everyone what I know, once we've finished with this room. It's time to look at the weapons."

Marek's, now that she looked at it closely, was not the same model Gordon 421 9mm she had used in target practice as a cadet at the Academy, but the 421-R model with doubled magazine and full automatic, usually an officer's weapon. It lacked the familiar Space-force logo stamped into the metal. Marek could not have concealed that on the shuttle or in the raft. Where had he found it here? The butt had the usual palm-lock plate, but the blood and brain tissue it had skittered through, still firing after Marek dropped it, obscured it. Ky cleaned the blood off and put her hand there. Nothing. So it was palm-locked to him. Owned by him, or assigned to him . . . could have been either. He had to have been here, at this base, before.

Betange approached. "Ready for another recording?"

"Yes. You'll notice that this weapon has no Spaceforce markings, but it's a model Spaceforce uses."

"Palm-locked?"

"Yes. Would've been ideal to get a palm print off it, but he had it on double-auto, and it had . . . organics all over it." In a serious lab, it might've been recoverable, but not here and now. "If you scan this, right here, you can see the rate-of-fire setting."

Betange scanned the weapon, the workbench, the rags she'd used to clean it. "Done, Admiral."

"You'll need to scan my weapon as well." Ky nodded toward her pistol. "Personal, purchased at a weapons shop on Lastway years ago." She released the clip, then removed the last round from the chamber.

"As you can see, the clip was full, and I fired two rounds, both of which struck Master Sergeant Marek."

"I'm not a firearms expert, Admiral—"

"I think my recorded testimony that this is my weapon and I did shoot the master sergeant should suffice, but if not the court can have the weapon tested once we're back in Port Major. Meanwhile, I'm going to clean it. You should watch, so you can record that I'm not boring out the barrel or doing anything else that will alter the evidence. Be sure to collect the two cartridges." In a few minutes she had the pistol clean, and turned to Gossin. "Do you want to keep this as evidence, Staff, or shall I keep it?"

Gossin hesitated, then nodded. "It's yours; you keep it. I trust you're not planning to kill anyone else."

"I'm not. Now I need to check on Riyahn and see how involved he's been in all this. When you've got the bodies wrapped up, we'll take them up to the surface where it's cold. I'd like to take Marek's weapon with me; it may help Riyahn keep his facts straight. But it's your call; you're in charge of this investigation."

Doubt returned to Gossin's expression. "It's a mess, and it's—"

"Ugly, dirty, smelly . . . and, most important, unloaded. Psychological effect only."

"Go ahead, then."

"Let me know when the bodies are ready for transport. See if there are enough spare boards or litters in the clinic; it'll be easier to carry them that way."

"Just leave them outside?"

"No, in one of the huts where they'll be safe from animals and just as cold. Then all this mess needs to be cleaned up; Lundin will probably want it disinfected as well. She'll tell you how."

"Yes, sir."

Sergeant Cosper had Riyahn tied to a chair in the little office at the end of the barracks passage. "He's not talking, Admiral Vatta."

She hadn't told him to interrogate Riyahn. She hadn't told him to pick the least suitable place—a room they would still need to use, a room full of things a dangerous person might use dangerously. Yes, the restraints were stored here, but he was supposed to have put Riyahn across the passage, in NCO quarters.

Riyahn did not look dangerous now, but he had tried to grab Marek's weapon. She laid the pistol, gory as it was, on the desk; Riyahn stared at it and said nothing.

"Sergeant, wait outside. I will speak with Corporal Riyahn myself."

"Admiral—"

"Thank you, Sergeant." Cosper gave a minute shrug and edged past her to the door.

"He's your size, Admiral. I wouldn't untie him if I were you."

"No fear." With Cosper out of the room, it seemed larger: the man had a talent for looming, seeming to take up more space than he actually did. She looked at Riyahn; he looked down.

"Y-you killed him and now you're going to kill me." Riyahn's voice trembled. "And Sergeant Cosper hurt me and yelled at me. My hands hurt."

"Did he hit you?" Ky pulled a pad of paper off the shelf, a stylus off the desk, and scribbled *Riyahn* and *Cosper* on it.

"N-no. He grabbed my arm too tight and twisted it behind me, and then he tied me too tight. My nose itches and I can't scratch it."

"You threatened an officer," Ky said. "What did you think would happen?"

"I thought you were going to kill everybody. I was going to protect—"

"By snatching up an empty weapon and trying to kill me?"

"No—I mean—it was there, I thought I could—"

"Kill me with it." Ky shook her head. "Marek tried to kill me and only managed to kill Commander Bentik."

"No! He didn't want to kill her; he wanted to kill—" Riyahn's mouth fell open and stayed open a moment. "I mean—"

"You knew Marek wanted to kill me?" Ky nodded and noted that on paper. "And you did not report it?" She underlined what she'd written.

"Well . . . no . . . I couldn't. He said you were a traitor to Slotter Key, and you had seen classified things and had to be stopped—"

"Killed, you mean."

"I suppose. I didn't want to—I tried to talk him out of it—What are you doing?" That last in a squeak, as Ky picked up Marek's weapon.

"It's evidence," she said, tapping the barrel against her other hand. "I think you knew he had it, and possibly where he hid it. I'm going to lock it away safely—you will not know where—and then lock you up."

"You're not going to kill me?"

"Not . . . now." She drew that out, watching him. "If I don't find a reason to kill you, you will be remanded to Spaceforce Security to stand trial for attempted murder of a senior officer and conspiracy to commit murder of Spaceforce personnel. If I remember correctly—" The relevant passages from the Spaceforce Code came to mind, even though she had a different implant now. "—Section five, paragraphs 3.14 through 3.23 list the punishments for those and several other crimes I suspect you committed, and I imagine you will spend most, if not all, the rest of your life in a Spaceforce prison. I hope to see to it that you do."

He said nothing, staring at her with the same terrified expression he'd had on the raft that first day and several times since.

"Now. Until a relief force arrives"—a relief force she suspected might be intent not on rescue but on cover-up—"you will be confined away from the others; you will obey the orders of those I assign to guard you, and if you disobey you will be killed. We do not have the resources to waste on you if you are not cooperative. So: will you be cooperative, or should we end this now?" She nudged Marek's weapon. Would he realize that she could not use it, that he himself could not have used it?

"No—please! Don't . . . I'll do anything."

"Excellent." Ky reached back and opened the door. "Sergeant Cosper?"

"Admiral."

"You will find a small room suitable for a cell and see that it's cleared out, provided with a couple of blankets and whatever else a prisoner should have. When it's ready, take this man to the head, give him a bottle of water, and lock him up."

"His clothes, Admiral?"

"We don't have any prison uniforms here that I know of, Sergeant. Make him secure, whatever that is, within human decency."

"Right."

"And I'm sure you realize we'll need to have a guard on the door at all times."

"Yes, sir—uh, Admiral. Right away."

"I'll be meeting with the others. Call if you need me. You will bring Riyahn to the general meeting later this evening."

Ky detoured by her quarters to get her outdoor gear. When she got back to the armory, she found Staff Sergeant Gossin directing the cleanup. Marek's and Jen's bodies were already in bags, and two long backboards, bright red with EMERGENCY USE ONLY stenciled on them, stood by the wall.

"Found the bags on a bottom shelf in the back of Stores," Gossin said. "We'd inventoried only the food and water supplies. Lundin gave us the boards."

"Right. Glad you found them. Let's get them up to the surface."

It was already dark topside. Eerie blue-green light danced in the sky, and vague shapes moved beyond the huts. The deerlike things, she decided after a few moments, not predators. They lugged the bodies over to the nearer of the two huts, and Ky unlocked the door. Inside, it was as cold as outside, cold as any freezer.

"Where do we put them?"

"On the floor there. We'll lock them in; the animals can't get at them and they'll keep."

Once the bodies were down, Ky stooped to touch each one and let herself remember them as people she had known, then named them aloud. "Jenaaris Bentik. Ildan Marek. May you have rest."

"Even though—" began Droshinski.

"Punishing the dead brings me no joy, whatever they did," Ky said. Poor Marek, a decent man caught in someone else's machinations. Poor Jen, dropped into a situation for which she was unqualified. "Yes, he tried to kill me; he conspired against me and possibly against us all, but—I cannot find it in me to hate him."

Outside once more, the hut locked, they stood a few moments in the bitter cold, watching the play of light over the snow and the buildings. "Well," Ky said finally. "The day's not over yet. Let's get back down and call everyone together."

By the time she was back down the ramps, Sergeant Cosper had transferred Riyahn to a locked room. "I took out everything in it but blankets and a pillow for him, and he's wearing only pajamas and socks. He's been to the head; he's got a bottle of water and a bar of concentrate. What about feeding him long-term?"

"We're not going to starve him. He'll get rations same as the rest. Right now we need him in the mess hall. Do you have a guard on his door?"

"It's locked and I'm away just to report to you."

"And he may be desperate. We can't risk his escaping. Put a telltale on the door, with the alarm set to loud, when you take him back after this meeting."

Gathered around one of the big tables in the mess hall, they seemed a much smaller group than the day before. Two dead. One injured, now in the medbox, one under guard. They looked tense, worried, and no wonder, Ky thought. They had much to worry about.

"You've had a shock," Ky began. "I'm sure you're wondering what happened, why Commander Bentik and I were in the armory, why Master Sergeant Marek had a firearm, and what exactly led up to what happened. Here's what I know." Ky outlined it all, everything she knew for certain. Everyone looked at Riyahn for a moment; he didn't look up. "Some of you," she said, "were told by Marek that I was a traitor, or unfit to command because of my age. Some of you probably believed him. He was an experienced senior NCO, and you didn't know me. You may still wonder about me, distrust me. If enough of you believe I'm a danger to all of you, you can manage to overwhelm and kill me—I have to sleep and eat and use the facilities sometime, after all. But I'm convinced that your best chance of survival—of getting home—is if we all band together and I continue as your commander."

"I'm with you, sir," Kurin said, glancing at Gossin.

"I am, too," Cosper said.

"With you," McLenard said.

"Thank you," Ky said. All those who'd been in the life raft with her were nodding, leaning forward. Some of those who'd been in the other raft looked frightened still.

"The admiral's right," Gossin said with a slap on the table. "I'm with her. I didn't understand before, but when I put it all together, from the shuttle crash to here, she's made good decisions and we're alive now because of them."

"And," Ky said, "there will be a legal investigation after we get back to Port Major. Staff Sergeant Gossin and Tech Betange have a record of the investigation they performed in the armory, and my testimony. So, questions?"

"You didn't notice anything wrong before?" Droshinski asked.

"I noticed some things that troubled me," Ky said. "But I attributed them to the stress of the crash and the difficulties we faced. No one is perfect; the struggle to survive exposes everyone. Looking back, I can certainly see things I might—in another context—have identified more clearly."

"You never let Master Sergeant Marek borrow your pistol to go hunting," Kurin said. "Was that one of them?"

"Yes. It seemed off that he kept asking. But even more, from my own experience, I'm not likely to hand over my only weapon to anyone." She looked around the group. "I'll be re-interviewing each of you individually. From the evidence, Master Sergeant Marek was part of a larger conspiracy, the kind of thing someone could be caught up in without knowing it, and the kind that might threaten the life of everyone here." Should she drop the final bombshell? Yes. "We must prepare for the arrival of troops that may *not* be intent on rescue but on protecting a secret."

"You really think that—?"

"It's possible; I think it's likely. I know this base was kept secret; people who keep secrets generally want them kept, and it would have taken a lot of power and money to keep this one." When no one said anything or raised a hand, she went on. "It will be necessary to change duty assignments and rotations since we have fewer personnel. Staff Sergeant Gossin will prepare preliminary profiles for me that highlight combat and communications skills. We may be able to circumvent the communications lockout that we've experienced—" A hand went up. She nodded at Tech Hazarika.

"Admiral, won't that just bring down the—whoever they are—on us faster?"

"Not if we can link directly to Rector Vatta without it being detected," Ky said. "If I can contact Rector Vatta, so she knows we're alive and where we are, I believe she will mount a rescue as soon as the weather allows. But the others might get here first. We need to be ready."

The faces ranged from blank to worried again. That wasn't good. She replayed her last words in her mind. She knew better: just facts weren't what they needed now. She made herself relax. Smile.

"I'm convinced we can survive anything," she said. "That's what we are—survivors." She paused. Two of the blank faces relaxed into an expression—not of confidence, not yet, but no longer frozen. "We've proved it, since the shuttle ditched. If we'd been easy to kill, if we'd been weak or stupid, we'd be dead." A few grins now.

"When Simon and Lazy stole rations and ate the puffer fish and died—" Corporal Barash scowled.

"They were stupid. You lot—you were smart and tough when it was hard, when you were seasick, cold, hungry, scared." She waited, letting them remember it. "And we're still here. In spite of everything, you all—every one of you—did the right thing time after time. You never gave up. Minute by minute, hour by hour, day by day. And I know you will keep at it, one task at a time, one day at a time, until we're home."

"But if they—the ones coming—"

"Whatever *they* do, whoever *they* are, *we* will make it," Ky said. "We have time. We're not going to sit here and make it easy for them. So: what I'm asking you all, right now, is this." She saw them stiffen again, bracing for something near-impossible. "Who's hungry? I missed breakfast; we all missed lunch. I could use a snack, and I'm sure you could, too. Who're today's cooks?"

Droshinski raised her hand. "Inyatta was with me, but she's—"

"She's going to be fine, Tech Lundin says. A few days in the medbox. Spec Gurton, I know it was your day off, but you're our senior cook. Can you fix us something quickly?"

"Right away, Admiral," Gurton said. She got up and headed for the kitchen. "Ennisay, get the oven going."

Ky could feel the relaxation, the rising level of confidence, as Ennisay, Droshinski, and Gurton headed for the kitchen. "We'll spend the rest of the day reorganizing schedules, seeing what mix of expertise we have now, doing routine maintenance, and then after dinner we'll have another meeting to exchange ideas. The memorial service for Commander Bentik and Master Sergeant Marek will be tomorrow morning at 1000, here in the mess. That should allow time for you all to make sure you have a suitable uniform—"

"You're giving Marek a *memorial* service? After he tried to kill you?" Barash again.

Ky felt her brows rising. "Certainly. I have praise for him; he worked hard to make things work for you." She turned to Sergeant Cosper. "You may return Riyahn to confinement now, Sergeant."

"Does he get what they're making?"

"No," Ky said. "He hasn't earned it; the rest of you have. Basic rations only." Riyahn looked ready to cry.

CHAPTER TWENTY-SEVEN

MIKSLAND
DAYS 50-56

Over the next few days, Ky noticed a healthy change. Staff Sergeant Gossin came to her after the memorial service to thank her for recognizing Marek's years of service. "You know I served with him once—thought I knew him. This—it was a shock. I wish I'd recognized something was wrong before, Admiral, but I didn't. He didn't exactly criticize you, not directly, so it didn't strike me as disloyalty. He was sympathetic—said you were so young and it must be hard for you. But looking back—it made you seem less capable—and that was wrong."

The group outliers, Betange with his concern about his younger siblings, Kamat with her extraordinary beauty, interacted more with the others. Inyatta, after three days in the medbox, came out cheerful and ready to take hold again. Hazarika didn't rush to support Droshinski's drama, and Droshinski herself seemed steadier, less inclined to outbursts, though she was still more exuberant than most of the others. It became obvious which of them Marek had been grooming as conspirators, as attitudes shifted and tension eased. Several came to Ky individually to apologize. And it was also obvious that her aide had been thoroughly involved in Marek's activities. Those who had never been swayed by Marek's opinions had a far more negative opinion of Jen than Ky had realized.

"He was flattering her and she was falling for it," Droshinski said. Ky, just outside the mess, stopped to listen. Inyatta was on mess duty for the first time since she'd left the clinic. "That was obvious."

"I just couldn't believe he was doing anything really bad," Inyatta said. "I mean—a master sergeant. They're—"

"Human," Droshinski said. "Just because he was married, you think he didn't want some?"

"Anya! They're both dead—"

"And so what I say can't hurt them. I'm not saying he was all bad, or she was all bad. I'm saying they were just ordinary people, man and woman, trapped in a survival situation—both vulnerable— isolated from their families—" Droshinski's voice took on the tone of a vid-thriller ad again.

"He was planning to kill the admiral. He tried to kill the admiral. You don't think that's bad?" Inyatta sounded both amused and annoyed.

"Of course I do. But you wouldn't catch the admiral falling for a bit of flattery, now, would you? Her aide did. Of course her aide was older, getting to that age—"

"She was the same age as Marek."

Droshinski shrugged; the shrug carried into her voice. "That's different. She was single; remember when she said so? All prim and stiff, the way she was, as if however she lived was the one right way to live."

Inyatta laughed. "You didn't like her because she came down on you for unprofessional conduct, you and Haz."

"She came down on me because she was a stuffed prune from Cascadia," Droshinski said. "I wasn't doing anything with Haz but letting him worship my aura. She'd have known that if she'd had any sense.

But you notice she didn't bother once she was getting sweet words from Marek. And then once he'd gotten her on his side, she started poking around, seeing what we said about the admiral, undermining her, trying to get us to agree she wasn't any good. There's unprofessional conduct, if you like!"

Ky, overhearing this from outside the mess, agreed with Droshinski's final statement, but enough was enough. She stepped through the doorway, and that broke up the conversation. Droshinski and Inyatta stood up. Ky greeted them. "And now for the usual daily inspection, which I'm sure you've prepared for."

"Yes, sir," they both said. "Kitchen's all squared away."

"Come on, then." They followed Ky into the kitchen, where the counters, sinks, and cooktops gleamed, stools were pushed neatly under the main workspace, all equipment was off, cords coiled, all pots and dishes clean and put away. Ky had expected that; this pair worked well together. She found nothing amiss; when she'd finished gave them a nod and "Well done." The day's menu was posted on the cabinet nearest the cooktop. "So we're having—what is this?"

Inyatta spoke up. "So far we've just had steamed rice or steamed barley to put stew over. I found enough farlo meal in the pantry for maybe ten meals, so I wanted to use it. We use it at home a lot. Ishbani is a stew served over it; I'm going to use one of the dehydrated packets for that, and steam the farlo. It'll be spicy—" She gave Ky a questioning look.

"Nice change," Ky said. "We had something similar at home but called it mother-in-law; my parents always laughed when they said it. It took all morning; my mother had everything made from scratch."

Droshinski laughed. "Mother-in-law stew? Whose mother-in-law?"

"I have no idea," Ky said. "Apparently someone back in the families."

Ping.

"Did you hear that?" Inyatta put a hand to her head and looked back and forth from Ky to Droshinski.

Ky nodded. "I did indeed."

"So did I . . . It's my skullphone but it can't be."

"Mine's greenlined now," Inyatta said, grinning. "I can call—home, I guess—" She looked at Ky.

"Wait," Ky said. "Didn't Marek tell you—?" Her mind whirled. Of course he hadn't passed on her order. Nor Jen. "Listen—don't use your phones, any com device. I know—I'll explain later—that the com block was intentional and someone lifted it, hoping to find out who's here. We have to tell the others—nobody call home, or anywhere else."

"You're worried about the people who kept this a secret? Staff Sergeant Marek's friends?" Droshinski frowned.

"Employers, I suspect, but yes."

"But if we can call our friends, they can help us. Stop them—" Inyatta looked from one to the other.

"Our friends don't know who the bad people are any more than we do." Droshinski raised her brows at Ky. "You want us to wait? What if the others are already calling home?"

"They may be," Ky said. "Need to find out." She headed out into the main passage. Anyone with an implant had probably heard the ping and very shortly figured out what it meant. Her next thought was that she wouldn't have to find a safe outlet and secure time alone to contact Rafe. Much safer for them both if she could use ordinary communications, even though the ansible-implant connection was the most secure. Her implant gave her an analysis of the available connections, public and private, carried by the repeater satellite now in range.

"Admiral!" That was Gossin, in the duty office as usual this time of morning. "There's a signal in my implant—"

"I know—it just pinged me, too," Ky said. "And Droshinski and Inyatta, so it's a general one. I've asked them not to call anyone yet—we need to locate everyone and find out if someone's been hasty."

"Showing initiative," Gossin said, grinning.

"That's right," Ky said. "But I'm hoping for some impulse control, and a chance to contact the Rector first. We do have enemies."

"I'll go find them—or I could just call—" She looked at Ky.

"Better not. Anyone tracking might listen in. Know how many we are."

"Right." Gossin hurried out the door calling for an assembly. Ky checked the barracks—no one there, this time of day. No one in any of the smaller rooms, or in the showers; Gossin, she saw, had brought people out of Stores and Maintenance. And here came Ennisay down from the upper entrance. "We've got a signal!" he yelled, before seeing Gossin and the group in the passage. "What's wrong?"

"Nothing yet," Ky said. "Assembly in the mess, right now." She turned to Gossin. "Riyahn—we don't want him calling, either."

Gossin nodded. "Understood, Admiral. He doesn't have an implant, so no skullphone, and we made sure he had no pocket com on him when we locked him in. There's nothing in that closet he could make one from, either."

"Good," Ky said. "But bring him along."

When they were gathered, she laid out the situation as she saw it. "We don't know why the communications shutdown was cleared at this time, or who did it. We do know the shuttle was sabotaged and Master Sergeant Marek was associated with whoever runs this secret establishment. We know they're not friendly to anyone being here."

"Wish we had an aircraft or something."

"So do I," Ky said. "But we don't. So I don't want anyone calling home until I've seen if there's a way to make contact with the Rector—"

"Are you sure she's not involved?"

"If Aunt Grace wanted me dead, she'd make me eat a whole fruitcake," Ky said. A few chuckles, probably from those who didn't like fruitcake. "But seriously—if she wanted all of us dead, including the Commandant, she'd have had the shuttle blow up above atmosphere. Failproof, simple, complete."

A few nods, this time.

"So: some of you have probably heard that I'm acquainted with Ser

Dunbarger, the current CEO of ISC—" Nods. "Before he took over that organization, he was a passenger on a ship I captained—my cousin Stella brought him aboard and he was going under an assumed name—"

"I heard he was a criminal," Ennisay said. "Is that true?"

"All I know is that he helped two of my cousins escape from assassins during the widespread attack on Vatta family members," Ky said. "He was helpful as well while aboard my ship. And what is useful now is that he taught me a way to shield a skullphone-to-ansible connection from interference or a data-suck." She had promised Rafe not to reveal the internal ansible, but this—she hoped—was a suitably disguised description of what she wanted to do.

"You can do that?"

"I hope so," Ky said. "I'll need to input more power into my skullphone; I'll be using a powerjack. Shouldn't take more than a few minutes."

"You'll want privacy," Gossin said. "We can clear out—"

"No—just wait here, please. I'll use Commander Bentik's quarters."

She opened the door to Jen's room; she had checked it only briefly after Jen's death, looking for names she would need to contact later, to explain. The room had the faint stale odor of disuse; Jen's few personal belongings were neatly laid out on the desk, including her comunit. Ky sat in the desk chair, unwound the cable from her neck, and plugged it into the wall socket, then stared at the connection in her hand, the baleful red light glowing there. But surely Marek would not have killed an ally.

She pulled the plug from the socket and sat a moment, thoughts swirling. Marek *would* have killed Jen. He would have killed Jen intentionally, in the same way he had tried to kill her, if Jen had used her own external power cord. Once she was dead, Jen would have been next. And how many others?

She sat until she was certain she had her face back under control, and then returned to the group now assembled in the mess. "Commander Bentik's room outlets were also compromised. Staff Sergeant Gossin, we need a check of all outlets here, even those that seem to be functioning normally with kitchen equipment and the like."

"Yes, sir; immediately. There's a set of tools in Maintenance—" She looked around the table. "Hazarika, you're with me." She stood and turned to leave.

"I could help," Riyahn said. "I could undo what Marek told me to do—"

"Nobody would trust you," Cosper said.

"Sergeant," Ky said. He subsided, glaring at her. Riyahn looked near tears again. "Corporal, you do realize that you are under suspicion. Why didn't you volunteer to help us earlier?"

"Yes, sir—Admiral—I'm sorry, I just—I was scared—"

"Rabbit," muttered Cosper. Ky gave him a look that stopped whatever else he was about to say. "Sorry, Admiral."

"You could have been responsible for multiple deaths," Ky said to Riyahn. "No credit to you that you weren't. I can think of a half dozen charges that should be filed against you once we're back in contact with Spaceforce. If you think undoing the sabotage will make all that go away, I can tell you it will not." Riyahn stared, eyes brimming. "But," she said, holding up a finger, "if you are willing to work with Staff Sergeant Gossin, identify *all* the sockets you sabotaged, and repair them—and if she reports that you worked well—I will include that in my report on your performance since the shuttle crash. Sergeant Cosper"—she gave him a brief glance—"will accompany the work party, and should you be tempted to do anyone mischief—" That phrase taken directly from the Military Code, archaic as it was. "He will deal with you summarily. Is that clear?"

"Y-yes, Admiral. I want to help, really I do."

"Well, then." Ky stood. "The rest of you, wait here—I'll only be a few moments, and I have several ideas to put forward."

Out in the passage, she pulled Cosper aside. "Corporal Riyahn will be very useful to both me and Spaceforce if he switches his allegiance all the way. He's not particularly brave—"

"That's obvious," Cosper said, with a sidelong glare at Riyahn, standing close to Gossin like a chick cowering near a mother hen.

"So you don't need to try to scare him; he's already scared. I want— and Spaceforce will want—his cooperation to uncover more about whatever group uses this place. We cannot trust him, certainly, but if he is treated fairly, he may attach to us. Do you understand?"

"Yes." Grudging, that was.

"I know you'd like to pound him into mush, Sergeant, but that's not going to get me or Spaceforce what's needed. Lay off unless he actually does something wrong. That's an order."

"Yes, sir." He turned toward the others, then back to her. "Do you really think he knows anything useful?"

"He might. My guess is there's a seventy percent chance he does."

"Yes, sir. I understand."

"Go on, then."

Ky turned back to the mess as the little work party started down the passage. "Well, now. I don't know how many outlets Riyahn and Marek sabotaged, but I'm glad no one found out the hard way. I'm especially glad the mess hall appliances all work." That brought a chuckle. "For now, we're fairly secure, or think we are. We're warm enough, we have water and food and power. But we also know we have enemies. Until I found out about the sabotage, I thought it was reasonable to stay here, on this level, as Master Sergeant Marek had advised. But knowing he was part of whatever conspiracy's going on here, we need to know what's behind those doors we haven't opened yet. Yes, it might be a dangerous defense . . . but it might equally be something that explains what's going on, something that gives us an edge over whoever shows up to kill us."

A hand went up, Staff Sergeant Kurin. Ky nodded to her. "Admiral, are you *sure* they would kill us?"

"After what Marek did, yes. Someone spent a lot of money over a lot of years setting up this scam, and I'm certain they do not want it discovered now. You've seen the animals on the surface. We don't even have a name for those huge hairy things, but they're here, along with the ones we do have names for, which means they're Old Earth–based life-forms."

"Or from somewhere else that's where Old Earth got its biota," said Droshinski. "What if—"

"For now, we're sticking to the what-ifs of the present," Ky said before Droshinski had a chance to make a dramatic story out of her idea. "I'm willing to entertain ideas aimed at increasing our chances of surviving past the arrival of either the conspirators or a rescue party. You can come to me privately, or bring something up in one of our open meetings. To start with, how many of you are curious about what's behind those locked doors?"

All the hands went up.

"Good. We'll start with the door Marek showed the most concern about. We're not all going at once, just in case, though I frankly think Marek was lying about the danger. Staff Sergeant Kurin, Spec Gurton, Spec Kamat, you're with me on this one. I'm hoping we find a control room for the power system, maybe a communications center, and information about the technical specifications that will give us a clue who's responsible."

Out in the passage, they met the first working party coming back; Staff Sergeant Gossin had a grim expression, and Riyahn looked even more scared than before.

"What is it, Staff?" Ky asked.

"Compromised outlets anywhere you or Commander Bentik might have gone to plug something in privately," Gossin said. "Riyahn told us about them—they're all marked now, and some are fixed. I thought we should come tell you before fixing the rest, as there are three in the women's bathing area and one in the watch office."

"I didn't know," Riyahn said. "He said it was to make them not work with any communications devices—"

"Really? And since no one's coms or skullphones worked anyway, why did he think that was necessary?"

"He said this was all very secret and we'd all get in a lot of trouble if anything leaked out about it and all it would do was fry the device—"

"Like someone's skullphone? And you didn't think what that could do to the person?"

"I didn't—I asked him—he said—he said it had to be done. And—and he was a master sergeant. He said it was an order—"

"You knew perfectly well it would kill," Sergeant Cosper said. The threat in his tone was clear. "You knew that; don't lie anymore!"

"Corporal Riyahn," Ky said, in a quieter voice. "You are in hot water up to your nose. This is not the time for excuses. Did you or did you not know that the higher current could kill someone?"

"If—if the—that skullphone—didn't have a safety on the switch—it—it could. But I hoped—I thought everyone would have that."

"Did Master Sergeant Marek think that?"

Riyahn looked down, shoulders hunched. "No, Admiral."

"Did Marek ask you to do anything besides change voltage in the electrical sockets?"

"Um . . . yes."

"What?"

"He was having trouble changing the lock settings. I showed him how to bypass the passcode and change to a new one—"

"Did he have you reset the doors I hadn't opened yet to the same code?"

"Yes."

"Do you know what the new one is?"

"Uh—I think so."

"Well, then, tell me what you think it is."

Riyahn stared at the floor. "I'm not sure I remember it exactly—"

"Life has a price," Ky said. "I suggest you remember it exactly."

"Um . . . 48311965 . . . uh . . . 5753. I think."

"We will test it shortly. If it happens to be a code that blows a security device, I'm sure Staff Sergeant Gossin and Sergeant Cosper will know what to do with you." She looked at Gossin. "Have him restore the sockets, all of them, while I see if his code will open this door. If it does, I'm going to be exploring down the left branch from the T."

Riyahn's code worked on the door, and nothing blew up at them. Ky led the way into the passage beyond; lights came up just as they had on first entering the facility. Windows onto the passage revealed two large control rooms, one to the left and one to the right. On the left, Ky recognized a communications center, full of familiar screens, consoles, control boards, with headsets and keypads laid neatly beside each console.

"What do you think, Kamat?" Ky asked.

"Communications, definitely. Satellite uplinks, ansible-capable sets, local nets . . . do you think it would be safe to activate the local net, if we disabled the satellite uplinks? It would make it easier to communicate when we're spread out down here."

"If you can do it so it won't be detectable topside, yes."

"I see short-range comunits racked on that wall." Kamat pointed. "And the squawker's easy enough; that's this unit here. That would allow general announcements."

"Good. You can do that after we've taken a look at the other room."

Across the passage, the other room held readouts for all the environmental controls—air, water, heat, light, power supply to the local grid. It felt warmer than the passage outside. Lights glowed on all the consoles, a steady green that should mean normal operation. Ky looked at the other readouts but didn't understand most of them. The far side of the room was also glassed in, with a large lighted area beyond, extending beyond the room's window. When she walked closer, she felt dizzy for a moment. Far below, three rows of round shapes extended into the distance. The floor beneath her feet vibrated slightly.

"Those are turbines," Gurton said. "At least as big as the ones at Cavanaugh Dam, and more of them."

"Cavanaugh Dam?" Ky asked. All that could be seen were the round, slightly mounded shapes; they might have been breakfast buns. But the floor's vibration and the steady hum proved Gurton right.

"Across the continent from Port Major, Admiral. Power generation at Cavanaugh Dam supplied a wide area. We had a field trip there when I was fifteen. I wonder where the power's going here. One of those turbines would provide much more power than this installation—at least, what we've seen of it—needs."

"What about fuel?" Ky asked. "It can't be hydro, can it?"

"Nuclear . . . geothermal . . . I don't know if I can tell; it's really not my field." She moved away, glancing at one console after another. "I think it's geothermal," she said finally. "Here's the datastream on the source, but I don't know what the numbers mean, except it's deep boreholes. The labels on the controls aren't original—I'll see if I can unstick one—" A long pause; Ky walked over beside her. Gurton had peeled back a label in the familiar writing and underneath were symbols Ky had never seen before. "I don't know what that is," Gurton said.

"I don't, either." Ky queried her implant and came up blank. "It's no language I know." Ky shifted her weight back and forth. Was the hum of the turbines getting louder? Or was she just reacting to the mystery? "Does anyone know if we should be changing controls or something?"

"No, sir." Staff Sergeant Kurin had come into the room. "If it's like most geothermal installations, it could run on its own for the down season, because we're not using much power compared to its maximum."

"Good. We'll close the door on this and let it do what it's doing."

Farther down the passage, other door insets showed. Ky went on. A conference room, complete with table and padded chairs. Offices, some furnished with gray metal desks and chairs, others more luxurious, with large wooden desks, comfortable chairs, a sideboard. She opened the door of the largest and found facilities for making hot drinks, a wine cooler with bottles of wine and a few of beer, a shelf of liqueurs. Behind the desk hung a Slotter Key Spaceforce plaque,

enameled in bright colors. And on the desk, a nameplate: COLONEL
B. R. GREYHAUS, COMMANDER.

The name meant nothing to her; she rummaged in the desk and
found a small green-covered book. A paper book, like the precious
volumes that had gone up in flames when her childhood home was
bombed. This one, when she opened it, was handwritten in a conventional script and resembled the Slotter Key logs in the Commandant's
personal library. It was not, however, a ship's log, she saw within the
first few pages. It was full of information about this very facility. She
flipped over to the last page.

"As per orders this facility on seasonal shutdown 15 days early to
accommodate elimination of threats to mission security. All research
personnel withdrawn 10 days prior; Pingat Islands base advised via
usual channels no further need for SAR readiness due to local operations. Anticipate return to normal operations at usual date in new
year." She flipped back; the "usual date" was defined by day length:
thirty days after the equinox.

Two days later, the last entry. "Base secure. All communications
blocked until return. Mission report forwarded to command.
(signed) B. R. Greyhaus." The date was ten days before she had arrived in Slotter Key space, seven days before the shuttle flight. Here
was proof the shuttle flight had been sabotaged, that someone in
Spaceforce knew about it—had arranged it. And that suggested the
Commandant's presence on the shuttle was the primary reason it was
sabotaged. It would have been easy for them all to die—if the pilots
had not managed to achieve separation in time, if the weather had
been worse, if they had not been able to deploy the life rafts, then
reach land, then reach this sanctuary—they would all have died, and
no one would have known what happened. All the deaths would have
been attributed to the shuttle failure.

No one knew what had happened even now but those here, the
survivors, and now Rafe. It hit her, all at once, that this could have
been a strike at her family as well. Not only her, but her aunt Grace,
the new Rector of Defense.

"Anything useful?" Kurin said from the doorway.

"Very," Ky said. "This place closed earlier than usual because of us—whoever made the plans knew that there would be a shuttle flight with the Commandant on it, and ordered this place closed seven days ahead of time. Told the Pingat Base nobody was here and to cease SAR activity early."

"Ensuring they wouldn't search for survivors . . ."

"I read it that way. The Rector may have pushed them to do a flight or two, but if they were part of it—do you know anything about the Pingat Base?"

"No, sir. I was never stationed there. There's one northern base that closes down in winter, but two that stay open to provide SAR for polar flights just in case."

"I also know when this Colonel Greyhaus expects to be returning. Which gives us that long to figure out how to deal with whatever comes with him." She held out the book; Gurton looked at it.

"Seems like plenty of time . . ."

"But it will go fast," Ky said. "We have much to learn, and much to do to prepare." She opened the bottom drawer; deeper than the others, it held a polished wood case the right size for the weapon Marek had used. She pulled it out and opened it; the molded lining held the outline of that model, and a small gray plastic tab. "And there's a palm-lock code key."

"Marek knew it was here," Kurin said. "So that's how he got hold of a weapon."

CHAPTER TWENTY-EIGHT

PORT MAJOR
DAY 57

"Why doesn't she answer?" Rafe paced back and forth.

"She will have a reason," Grace said. "And it will be a good one."

"Unless she's hurt. Unless the fuel ran out and they have no electricity—and no heat."

"If it were that, she'd have let you know," Grace said. "Sit down; you're going to knock something over."

Rafe sat with a thump on the nearest chair.

"I have great-nephews steadier than you," Grace said.

"They aren't—they don't know Ky."

"True, but that's not the point. Tell me, have you figured out yet who it was that reconfigured the satellites in the first place?"

"No," Rafe said. "And not because I haven't tried. I've been through all the records I could reach, and those you unblocked for me. One of the founding families, I'm fairly certain."

"Any idea why?"

"Found something they wanted to hide," he said with a shrug.

"Other than the land itself?"

"I think so. From orbit, the scans show void spaces under and near that landing site. It can't be a mine—any conventional kind of mine—because there'd have to be more surface evidence, even if the extraction was done underground. There are old topographic signs of something . . . a very long time ago . . ." As he talked on about what his analysis of the scans taken by *Vanguard II* had shown, he seemed calmer, but Grace recognized the tension under all that. She felt tense herself. MacRobert had reported some unusual communications traffic that he couldn't completely categorize. "Who owns that place, anyway?"

"Excuse me?" Grace pulled her mind away from its own tracks, replayed what he'd said. "*Owns* it? You mean Miksland?"

"At least that part of it. We know someone's been there—do they own it, or are they trespassing? Didn't anyone ever lay claim to it?"

"I don't think so," Grace said.

"So there's no record at all of a claim—you said there was a record of someone visiting it—"

"Yes, but he was considered eccentric at best and crazy at worst. His family finally put him away."

"He was letting out a secret they knew about, and wanted kept. Who was he? Who are his living relations?"

"Nobody, I think." Grace cocked an eyebrow at him; he ignored her. "Mac said they died out over a hundred years ago."

Rafe leaned back in his chair. "If I were a conspiracist, I would be looking for someone—two families, or two branches of one family—who somehow managed to convince everyone that place was barren, toxic, and useless. And then perhaps quarreled. One killed off the other, leaving the survivor in possession of a whole continent nobody else would bother with. All its resources available to one family. What would you Vattas have done with a continent all your own?"

"Probably moved away. It's in a very harsh climate zone."

"Yes, but you've seen the images now. It's not just bare rock or frozen tundra. It becomes more and more biologically complex on a gradient from south to north; by the north coast, there's even some temperate forest at lower altitudes. I realize Slotter Key doesn't have as large a population as Nexus, and you're not stretched for resources, but people could live there, if they knew how. I can't imagine that some of them wouldn't want to. It's odd. And I still want to know who else knows about it. Someone must." He glanced at her. "You Vattas were founders here, weren't you? Surely you know something."

"Founders? No. We're latecomers, not even early colonists. Third wave, if that, since we didn't exactly come in a wave. Nemordh Vatta arrived 173 years ago, roughly, with his family on a ship that—to be blunt about it—he stole from his former employer, somewhere the other side of Nexus, after being cheated by his employer of half his earnings, and cheated on by his wife with his employer. We would prefer you not publicize that, by the way."

"Your dynasty was started by a *thief*? Stella didn't tell me that—"

"I wouldn't call it a dynasty, but yes. And Stella didn't know. According to his personal journal, he had been an honest man for all of his life until—in a fury with his employer and his wife—he took off in the stolen spaceship with the rest of his family. Then he—" She stopped as Rafe jumped up and ran out of the room.

"It's Ky," she heard as his footsteps receded down the hall.

MIKSLAND
DAY 57

Rafe answered her call quickly and began a spate of questions before Ky could even say hello. Ky waited them out, and when he slowed down said, "I'm fine, there was a bit of trouble because someone had hot-wired a number of sockets to be high-voltage. It took awhile to clear them—"

"You could've been killed!"

"But I wasn't. I found the base commander's logbook—we opened up another section of this place. Start Aunt Grace looking for a Colonel B. R. Greyhaus." She spelled the name for him. "Someone knew ahead of time something was going to happen that might mean outsiders finding this place; he was ordered to close it early. Doesn't give any names—"

"Who tried to kill you?"

"Not just me. My aide, as well."

"*Who?*"

"Master Sergeant Marek and Corporal Riyahn."

"And?"

Ky sighed. "I killed Marek; a stray shot of his killed my aide. Corporal Riyahn is cooperating with the authorities in hopes of not being executed. Things are better now. Is my flagship still in the system?"

"Yes, though it's been ordered back to SDF headquarters. Apparently Admiral Pettygrew has usurped your place."

"Not usurped. I chose him; I set up the emergency protocol. After thirty days without contact and it's been—what, almost sixty?—the governments involved probably leaned hard on him. They probably pressured him to order Pordre back, too; Dan wouldn't do that on his own unless there was a situation. *Is* there a situation? Is SDF in action?"

"Not that I know of. Nothing in the news. Pordre's told your aunt he intends to stay, no matter what. But really—you couldn't have found even *one* safe outlet earlier than this?"

"Not in a private place, no. You still want me to keep your secret—"

"Dammit." She could hear him take a long breath. "All right. I want you out of there. But nobody authorizes flights in for another hundred and something days. Are you sure you're safe down there?"

"All systems working. We're fine. I wouldn't worry until it's closer to spring. Is there any way to push a lot of data through this link fast?"

"Not really. Oh—I'm sure you noticed regular skullphones and other devices are now able to get a signal. Wasn't us—the other side. I doubt any of that's secure."

"That's why we're not using them. I'll be calling more often, but don't worry if you don't hear for a short time."

"Ha." A strong smell followed. End of call.

PORT MAJOR

Grace settled herself to wait for Rafe's report and had just closed her eyes for a restful nap when MacRobert came in looking grim.

"Something's moving and I can't get the details."

Grace sat up and blinked. "Any clue at all?"

"Minimal. Pingat Islands Base requested some replacement parts for their Air-Sea Rescue craft. Those craft should've been inspected and any parts ordered last fall, before the weather closed in. A major I know in Requisitions told me it's a huge order, big enough to require flying one of the big troop carriers down there. He questioned it; his boss questioned it; someone upstream told them to shut up and fill it, that if Pingats wanted all their supplies at the start of the flying season it would save fuel and time to send them on down instead of a flight every ten days."

"Who upstairs?" Grace asked.

"No clear answer. I'll keep digging. I tugged the list off the line," MacRobert said. "And brought it to you without printing it because I'm not trusting very many people these days." He handed the stick to her.

"What else?" Grace tucked the stick into her left pocket.

"Little things. Three deaths, one unreported for a long time on the grounds the body couldn't be identified, all over on Fulland in one of the big server farms. That death occurred as the result of an explosion and fire in one of the smaller units, and the investigation was handled internally because no customer service was interrupted. It would have come at about the time Rafe's pal unblocked the scan satellites passing over Miksland. The other two were the partner and adult son of the first victim. Neither of those deaths aroused suspicion, but they had been insisting to friends that something was wrong about the report of the first death."

"What else?"

"They were all Miznarii. Low-level jobs; the one killed in the explosion was just a nightshift clerk monitoring normal equipment performance. Supposed to call a higher-up if any indicators twitched."

MIKSLAND
DAY 57

"Contact made," Ky said to the others. "The Rector knows we're alive and where we are, but she's also found evidence that our worries are not misplaced. This base is affiliated with a segment of the military that may be about to commit treason. For now we're safe; for now we'll look for every possible asset that can help us escape and survive when the time comes. On average of weather, we have 160 to 180 days to prepare."

Gossin raised a hand and Ky nodded. "For which? Attack or rescue?"

"Don't know yet. I'll be in contact with the Rector off and on. Everyone else, stay off com. Anything else?"

"I found something odd in that closet in the control room," Hazarika said. "A dozen or so of these little cylinders." He pulled one from his pocket. "I thought they might be security gear, but they're not. Could be data storage, if we found a reader it fit."

"Maybe magic wands," Droshinski said. Everyone laughed.

CHAPTER TWENTY-NINE

MIKSLAND
DAY 93

Ky couldn't relax. In subsequent contacts, Rafe had kept her up to date with what he'd learned, including the unusual supply requisitions for Pingats—surely meant for here. Somewhere somebody was planning how to kill them all, and she could think of dozens of ways they might do it. Explosives, bioweapons, chemical weapons . . . delivered from a distance on the planet, or sent in from space, or landed on the continent with troops. And here they were, with TARGET painted on top for anyone who knew of their existence. *We will get you out,* Rafe had said, but that meant waiting where they were. Where the *enemy* knew they were. Where the enemy or the enemy's weapons might arrive first.

She should be moving them somewhere, but she was supposed to stay here. She leaned into the exercise machine, pushing, driving for more speed, more kilometers, more . . . and finally, completely out of breath, shaky, she stopped. The machine stopped. She'd redlined again, and the automatics cut the power.

She had to find something they could do to get out of the trap they were in. She had done the right things so far: gotten the crew to a shore, away from that deadly beach, out of the inadequate little huts, and into warm shelter with plenty of food and water. Her people were healthy and fit now, but without weapons, mobility, and a better grasp of what their enemies planned, they were still doomed. They had no mobility other than their own feet—too slow, too risky, and very much too traceable.

She looked around the gym. Gossin, Kurin, and Chok were on machines like hers. Sergeant Cosper flapped a pair of heavy cables as if they were ribbons; he stopped when she climbed off the machine and watched her walk toward the door. He had that look again; he was going to say something—

"You really should do some stretches, Admiral—"

The whooshing sound of the other machines stopped. Ky didn't look at them, but at Cosper. "When did you start thinking I don't do stretches, Sergeant?"

"I never see you—"

"You never see me shower, either. If you doubt my fitness, would you like a round of hand-to-hand?" She hoped he'd agree; she wanted someone to throw at a wall, big enough, like Cosper, that he wouldn't break, but would make a satisfying noise. And learn humility.

"But you're—but officers and enlisted—"

"It's an unusual situation here, Sergeant."

"I'm a lot bigger than you are," he said. "And probably fitter."

That did it. He thought she was too small? Maybe she'd throw him extra hard. "There's one way to find out," Ky said. She tipped her head a little. "Mats over there. Spotters handy." She waved a hand behind her to indicate the others. "I'm not in your formal chain of command, so no dings on your record if you break something." As if he could. She'd killed Osman Vatta one-on-one, and he'd been bigger than Cosper. She looked him up and down. "I don't suppose you're worried about being hurt—?" Her tone made it a question, just one shade shy of insult.

"Of course not," he said. His jaw muscle twitched. "As you wish, Admiral."

"Excellent. I need a swallow of water, then I'm ready." She had been ready for a long time. The anger she had not let herself face, anger for many things, rose to awareness. Shooting Marek had not eased it, but increased it, for she still thought Marek had been fundamentally decent, a man corrupted by forces he did not understand or control. In a different service, he would have remained the prototypical good senior NCO, loyal to his service and mentor to the troops he led. Someone had taken advantage of him, of his not having an implant, of his being Miznarii, of his having a family, just as they had of the cadet who had caused her trouble and then committed suicide. Just as they had of the rigger on Moray who'd helped an enemy get command of new-built ships.

Cosper was different. Cosper was just another arrogant bully who needed a solid taking down, and she was going to enjoy giving him one. And she would work off some of anger's dangerous energy as she did it. Without killing him. She didn't want to kill him; she needed every survivor if they were all to survive. But if she could tarnish Cosper's shiny impervious ego just enough to protect others from his bullying, all the better.

The bout began slowly, because Cosper was merely arrogant, not stupid, and she saw in his gaze that he was realizing this was a very bad idea. Ky tired of that by the second time circling the mat. She moved in, her awareness as always both crystalline and a little distant, and he grabbed her arm in a move she remembered from her Academy training. He would do this, and then that, and supposedly she would fly up in the air and come down flat on her back. But she'd been many places and in deadlier danger, so the flying part was her idea, and her other arm found its target, as did her knees, and when they both hit the ground he was facedown and she was on top of him. She stood up. He lay there a moment, then pushed himself up.

"How did you—?"

"Leverage. Physics. The advantage of being shorter. If I'd been your height it wouldn't have worked as well. Let's go again."

She decided, on the third throw, not to launch him into the wall, satisfying as that might be, because the bruises on his back were already coming up and she didn't want to risk damage that would slow him down if she needed him for something useful. So she dumped him back on the mat, headlocked him before he could move, and said in his ear "I expect you will quit bullying the others, Sergeant. Is that clear?"

"Yes . . . sir. Admiral."

"Good. If you want to learn any of the throws I used, I'll be glad to teach you. Later."

She released him and got up. She felt much better, and definitely ready for her shower.

Cosper, when he clambered up, looked at her with something more than admiration. "I didn't know—"

"Well, now you do. We've both done enough now. We have a busy day ahead." Ky walked off, daring him to mention stretches, and signaled the other three with a flick of her fingers.

Still, as the shower beating down revealed that she, too, had incipient bruises, she had not figured out what to do next, how to anticipate what the enemy was up to. She was going to have to contact Rafe again and make clear *what* she needed to know and that she needed data *now,* not five minutes ahead of the attack.

When she assembled her little troop, she was struck once more with how amazing it was they were all still alive. Not only alive, but fitter than they had been right after the crash. She had to admit that much as she disliked Cosper's methods, he had hassled and bullied the others into better condition. "Where are we with communications?" she asked.

"We can pick up satellite broadcasts, which suggests they can pick up anything we send that way," Gossin said. "We don't have a way to test tight-beam security, not that I'm familiar with. Lakhani found a crosslink between our transmissions and a landline."

"A landline to where?" Ky looked from Gossin to Lakhani.

"I don't know and don't know how to tell," Lakhani said. "It could be a buried cable to somewhere else on Miksland, or it could connect to one of the marine cables."

"To . . . what's the likeliest?"

"I'm not sure, sir. Finding which way a buried cable goes means getting up on the surface and trying to work through the snow and ice. It might go any direction. There might be a marine cable between Partin Reefs and the Pingat Islands Base, but it would run well north of Miksland. But those cables are all old, you know. The marine cables were put in early, when the planet was first declared open for colonization. After the first wave, when trade picked up, then more satellites went in and ISC installed an ansible."

"But cables are supposed to be more secure than satellite, right?"

"Yes, sir, even with encryption. You have to have a ship and a way to find and then actually touch the cable to pick up anything. But the codes used back then aren't the ones we use now. I don't know them."

"Someone will," Ky said. "And as long as we don't know that code, and don't know who's on the other end, we can't use our main com because someone might be listening."

Nods around the table.

"Are you picking up anything at all on the broadcasts?"

"Nothing about the shuttle, if that's what you mean. Sports scores from the Southern Association srithanball tournament. Market reports on commodity prices and investment tips. Provinces are about to inaugurate new legislators: we can watch that tomorrow, if anyone's interested. *Impossible Dreams* is in its sixteenth season—"

Ky laughed. "I watched that when I was in secondary. Not at the Academy, of course. Has Bryony married Zaldur yet?"

"Oh, yes," Droshinksi said. She ran her fingers through her hair and tossed it. "It was magnificent, that wedding, and they had twins, but then Max DeLonga kidnapped the twins and Bryony, and drugged her and—"

"And now she's hiding out because she escaped with one of the twins and thinks she's being hunted, the other twin was kidnapped again by Max's accomplice who was going to blackmail Max, Zaldur killed the accomplice and didn't know the baby in the house was his own child so he left a note for social services—"

Ky had not suspected Gossin of being an *Impossible Dreams* fan; she seemed entirely too practical for that.

"*Now,*" Ky said with emphasis, "we have other concerns. It's still just an hour program, right? Put it on a stick and anyone who wants can watch it in their off time."

They settled again, with a chorus of "Yes, Admiral."

"I've finished reading Colonel Greyhaus' diary," Ky said. "And I'm now sure of the date this base usually opens for the summer season. I expect someone will be coming before that, with intent to kill us. They'll be looking for the earliest break in the weather, the very first time they can get transports in. But we don't know which way they'll be coming from or how many they'll have. I'm going to try another skullphone call to the Rector today and see what she's managed to find out."

"Do you want us to continue looking for more hidden spaces?" Staff Sergeant Gossin asked.

"Yes. Given the complexity of what we've seen, I'm certain there is more to this facility. We don't have the right keys yet, is all. Staff Sergeant Kurin, any progress on decoding the weapons in the armory?"

"Not yet, Admiral. But we can dismantle them completely, bypassing the palm locks. It will take an estimated hour per weapon to take them apart and put them back together, and each one will have to be recalibrated."

"Will that damage them?"

"Yes—they lose autolock-on-target and auto-zoom on the 'scope. Anything electronic goes when you tinker with the palm-ID lock.

They'll still fire, though, and the autoloader is mechanical, not electronic."

"Go ahead. As many as you can. We'll start training with them on the range as soon as you have enough for six."

"Yes, sir. I'll need Hazarika and Drosh."

"Fine. Off you go."

She made the rest of the day's assignments, then went to her quarters to call Rafe, with Kamat standing guard outside the door.

In seconds after she sent the contact code, Rafe answered. "Well?"

"All's well so far. What's your situation?"

"Extreme frustration." His report was organized, compact, dense with data. She let her implant take it, knowing she could replay later, and listened to the nuances of tone. He wasn't just frustrated, he was seriously worried. So was she.

When he finished talking, Ky reported what she'd read in Greyhaus' diary. "What about those marine cables? And how can I cut them off the satellite hookup? We need a broadband connection."

"I know that. Cables—that's hard connection, right? Optical or metal?"

"I don't know. We haven't tampered in case they can detect it."

"Leave it alone. Too risky. Here's a code you can use on handhelds, probably better from the surface. It's direct to a satellite we've moved to hold position in range of your location. It'll shunt any signal with this code to a new segment."

"Got it," Ky said, as the code came up on her implant data screen.

"Clear." The signal vanished, with a last whiff of stink. Ky unplugged her power cable and replaced it around her neck. Dumping Cosper had eased some of her tension, and Kurin's success in circumventing the palm locks on the weapons did even more, but that and general fitness was all they'd accomplished in the last forty-five days or so. Judging by the average day Greyhaus had recorded for return—and she knew that might be long or short this year—they had 135 to 140 days left to prepare. Weapons would help; she could start figuring out how to defend the place; but what they really needed was a way to leave that didn't depend on walking and dragging ammunition boxes through the snow.

There had to be more to this place. They had to find it.

PORT MAJOR, RECTOR OF DEFENSE OFFICE
DAY 95

"Rector?"

Grace looked up. Olwen looked unsettled, not like her usual cheerful, competent self. "What is it, Olwen? Is everything all right with the family?"

"Yes, Rector, but—I'm so sorry, but I need to resign. Next week. You know I mentioned my husband was looking for a new job, and of course we thought in Port Major, but he's been offered a wonderful opportunity somewhere else. It's too far for me to commute, with the children in school and all."

It was more than inconvenient; Olwen had proven herself far beyond any background checks. But there was no way she could stop the woman leaving. "I'm sorry to lose you, Olwen," Grace said, folding her hands in front of her. "Remember that you will have to sign out properly—it usually takes two days to do all the paperwork, so let Arnold down in Personnel know right away—or have you?"

"I—I wouldn't until I'd spoken to you, Rector. I hope you aren't angry—"

"No, I'm not angry." Or not at Olwen. At her husband, maybe, for not wanting his wife to work and figuring out a way to make it impossible. But not at Olwen. "Go on and call Personnel and Security—get the process started." And she'd have to find a new assistant right in the middle of this mess with Ky. She forced a smile, and Olwen made a little sort of dip and withdrew. And now she'd have to break in a new one. She sighed and considered whom to contact first. Too bad she couldn't have Rafe or Teague. She called Mac.

"I don't like it. Her replacement should be checked out for more than a week."

"I know, Mac, but what's the best way to go? I can try to snag someone out of Vatta Enterprises—"

"They won't have the security clearance required. I'll get you a short list today and start in on them."

"Thanks."

"You do realize this could be a move by the other side—"

"Yes, of course. But I need someone in that position. I can shift some of the calls I make to my skullphone."

"Good. Later."

Two days before Olwen left, Grace and Mac had finally chosen her replacement from the short list and he appeared in her office for the first time. Grace resented having to change assistants, and knew that colored her view of the presentable young man—young to her, though he was thirty-six—who came in the following morning. She did her best to be cordial when Olwen showed him in and announced him.

"Rector, this is Derek Connabi, my replacement." Olwen sounded sad.

"Ser Connabi, welcome to my staff. I'm glad you were able to change your position at such short notice." Automatically Grace assessed his physique—neither weedy nor muscular—in terms of conflict. He stood well, upright but not stiff. He was a shade less handsome than his résumé image, of medium build, dark with gray eyes. "Olwen has scheduled the morning to show you where everything is and get you started. Tomorrow is her last day."

"Thank you, Rector. I'm honored to have been chosen for this, and hope you find my work satisfactory."

"So do I," Grace said, to find out how he would react.

"Then, Rector, I had best let Olwen start bringing me up to speed."

Grace nodded and watched him give a slight bow, then depart. She really did not want Olwen to leave, but Olwen was leaving, and this was the best replacement they'd found.

* * *

"What do you think of your new assistant?" Mac asked the next evening, after Olwen's farewell party had ended.

"He hasn't done anything wrong yet," Grace said. "But then he's hardly had time."

"Any feelings about him?"

Grace shrugged. "I'm a cranky old woman who hates change and I liked Olwen. That's my *feelings*. Rationally, he passed your security check—"

"Shorter than I like—"

"And you'll have time to dig deeper now that he's here. We agreed on the algorithm—not choosing the most obvious candidate. We didn't have time to make a deep list. He's the best guess, and we'll just have to see." She looked at him. "Do you have reservations now?"

"No . . . it's just having to make the change so quickly." He shook his head, as if warding off a fly. "Never mind. I'll keep looking, you keep being careful."

Over the next ten days, Grace decided that Derek would do; he was quiet, professionally correct without being stiff, organized and efficient, and showed no inclination to pry into her own affairs. She had set the usual number of subtle traps, things that had caught others up to mischief, but he didn't trip any of them. MacRobert hadn't found anything suspicious, not so much as a single late bill payment—in itself suspicious, but not that suspicious. She wasn't entirely comfortable with him, but she knew she was slow to adjust to new personnel. And she had a great deal to do. She could not spend all her time hovering over his every move.

CHAPTER THIRTY

MIKSLAND
DAY 134

Ky watched the lowest-qualifying group line up in their places on the range. Even they now handled their weapons with confidence and, just as important, absolute adherence to correct procedures. The best group was excellent—not surprisingly, all those had grown up in rural areas and hunted for the table. But the others were catching up fast. These—the worst six—might be reliable at shorter ranges by the time they'd have to use their skills. She was sure they'd need them. Her late-night calls to Rafe, and what he told her about Grace's investigations, made it clear that her guess had been right.

She still hoped to find a way out of the complex. In less than a hundred days, the enemy might come storming down the ramps—or chase them across the snow-covered landscape topside. Neither option appealed. Yet so far, though they were all sure there were void spaces that should open into this complex, they had not found any entrances. They'd tapped the walls, pushed and tugged at anything that protruded anywhere, attempted to lift the floor covering, without success. Rafe had used a variety of satellite scans that suggested underground passages kilometers long that led away to the west, north, and south, multiple chambers, vertical shafts . . . but none of these were any use if they couldn't get in.

When that day's firing session was done, she let Staff Sergeant Gossin supervise this group's cleaning and stowage of their weapons, hung her earmuffs on their peg, and left the armory.

When she opened the armory door, Kamat said, "Sir, Ennisay and Inyatta have found something they're excited about. Past the power control room, they said, left-hand side. It's open now."

"Good." She hoped it was good. "I'll go now. Come with me; let's see what they've got."

"Inyatta thinks she's found what might be a back door," Kamat said. "When you weren't available, she told me."

A back door would be helpful, but not enough; surely the enemy already knew about it. They'd put someone there to watch it, see what came out. But it was an option. If they could get out first, if they had someplace to go, a way to survive on the surface without being immediately detected . . . could they ambush those who came to ambush them . . . her thoughts raced on, not so much making plans as marking possible plans to be made.

When they came to the opening, she saw that it was not a door, but a section of wall that slid aside, revealing a much thicker panel than she had suspected. No wonder tapping hadn't found it. Ennisay had been posted there, waiting for her. He was grinning from ear to ear. "We found it, Admiral," he said. "You were right—it was here all the time."

Of course it had been there all the time. "How did you find it? How did you get it to open?"

"Corporal Inyatta thought it might respond to one of those bar things we found in the power center, Admiral. We took two of them. I had one side of the passage and she had the other. She insisted we try every centimeter of the walls, top to bottom, both sides, punching every control on the bar. And it worked. It actually worked."

"Good for you," Ky said. She ran her hand down the near side of the opening. "What's this little dimple?"

"Corporal Inyatta felt that, too." Ennisay sounded surprised. "She thought it might be a switch or something. I didn't notice it."

That was no surprise. "Can you feel it now?"

"Yes, sir. She made me. She said maybe it had been painted over."

"Or maybe people who needed it would know where it was. Good work anyway. Where is Corporal Inyatta?"

"Exploring. She even got lights on. She went left."

The temptation to head right, just to see another branch, did not quite overwhelm the need to catch up with Inyatta, in case of trouble. "We're heading left, too," she told Ennisay. "Stay here, let anyone else know where we're going."

Inside the gap, the space was large enough for eight to ten people abreast, with ramps leading down to the left and right to a passage visible below. Ky and Kamat went left. At the foot of the ramp, the passage led straight on for another hundred meters. Inyatta had found other entrances—openings gaped on either side—but left a bright arrow of marker on the wall to indicate she had gone on. Ky glanced into each room briefly. Several were empty of anything but a table or two; some looked vaguely like laboratories, though she didn't recognize any of the equipment. At the end of the straight stretch, the passage curved to the left, straightened again, and she saw Inyatta coming back toward them.

"Admiral! Glad you're here; I've something to show you." She turned back the way she'd come, waving for them to follow.

When they caught up, Inyatta had stopped before a blank wall, in a space wider than the passage. "It's a lookout. See?" The wall blurred, then an image formed on the screen. They were looking out, as if the wall did not exist, over the shore where they had once camped. A tattered remnant of a life raft showed above the snow; the bay was still frozen solid under a leaden sky. "We can zoom," Inyatta said. She ran her hand along the lower edge of the image and the image jumped toward them, now showing the bay's opening to the ocean beyond. Something moved, yellowish against the pure blue-shadowed white of ice.

"An animal," Ky said. "What is it?"

"I don't know for sure, but I think some kind of bear," Inyatta said. "Look how it walks. And look—I can use infrared." Now the bear was a moving flame in shades of orange and purple against a near-black background. "Or lots of other settings—any wavelength, polarization . . ."

"I've never seen a bear of any kind," Ky said. "Except in the zoo, and it was black with a white mark on its chest. What can it possibly find to eat out there? What if it falls through? Have you recorded it?"

"I've got some images, yes. It can't be native, can it? It has to be part of the terraforming, doesn't it?"

"How big is it?" Ky asked. Bears, she vaguely remembered, were omnivores. At least that's what the label on the bear exhibit in that zoo had said.

Inyatta zoomed the image again, reverting to visual wavelengths. They had nothing to reference the bear's size, if it was a bear. Big, yellow-white fur, long black claws, black eyes, black nose.

"What do you think of those rooms we passed?" Ky ran her own hand over the control panel to see what other controls she could find. The image split between the zoomed one of the animal lying motionless on the ice and the wider view from the top of the cliff overlooking the bay. She had a choice of filters, wavelengths, optical effects.

"I can't be sure, but I think two are labs of some kind. I did go into one of them—jugs of chemicals, though I don't know what the labels mean. I had only basic chem in school. And I think there's a lot more to find. These control rods don't open anything unless you press them onto the right spot, and you have to feel for the spots. Takes time."

Time they didn't have. "We need to find as much as we can as fast as we can. Either more ways to defend ourselves in here, or a way to survive and hide outside. Now that we know more exists, I can assign more people to it. How many control rods were in the power room?"

Inyatta gave her a startled look, didn't ask questions. "A cabinetful, plus three lying out on consoles. Enough to give one to each of us."

"Good. Come back with me; mark an X back at the main corridor so no one else wastes time on this. We may need to station someone here—wait—are you sure there's no exit?"

"Yes, sir. Not on the walls, anyway. I haven't explored the floor or ceiling."

"We'll leave that for later. The vid feed's coming in from somewhere on the cliff; an exit's not likely to be much use." And would give pursuers high ground. She never wanted to see that beach again, except looking down on it from the air as they flew away.

As they walked back to the entrance to this new set of passages, Ky explained to Inyatta and Kamat what she knew of the coming threat. "So you understand what we need—we'll take all day today looking for resources—a few hundred ground-to-air missiles and manuals for them wouldn't come amiss, for instance, or some kind of tracked vehicle that would take us with all our supplies for three or four tendays far enough away to give us a chance of escape—anything of that sort. Empty labs we don't understand, just a look, mark 'em as seen, and go on. Though if any of the techs recognize something, I want to know it."

"Yes, sir."

"I'll have the mess crew today pack lunches. I'm going back to get things started. Kamat, everyone needs one of the control rods. Bring a dozen of them to the entrance. Ennisay can hand them out as people come in."

Back in the familiar area, Ky told everyone she encountered to go help explore the discovery. In the kitchen, the cooks were eager to join in and quickly made sandwiches, piling them in a roasting pan and carrying that down to the new opening. Ky went to her quarters for her logbook and stylus, considered contacting Rafe, but decided to wait until she had more information. She met Betange in the main passage.

"Sir—you have to see this!" Betange looked more excited and even happy than she'd ever seen him. "It's amazing!"

"What?"

"We found this big room—huge, like a really big hangar—and it's full of machines. I think they're vehicles. And Sergeant Chok found a big cold room full of glass tubes with things in them. Animals and other things."

That sounded more interesting than the empty rooms they'd found, but not immediately useful. "Let's see the machines first." Ky picked up one of the control rods from Ennisay and followed Betange into the right-hand passage, past several branches. It was a long way; she lost track of the turns, but knew her implant had recorded them. She was sure they were outside the footprint of the spaces above where they had been living all this time.

Finally, the passage opened into a vast space, lit by panels far overhead. Arrayed in neat lines on the floor were machines, clearly mobile, some with wheels and some with cleated tracks. About a third were painted pale cream and light gray in a camouflage pattern that would, Ky realized, be hard to see in snow. They looked like other machines she'd seen on Slotter Key and elsewhere, and she climbed up on one to look inside.

"That's weird, isn't it?" Betange said. "No seats. None of them have seats."

"Driven standing up, I suppose," Ky said, squinting to see if she could spot brackets for installing seats. No. The floor of the cab was plain, smooth, painted gray. Moreover, the front below the windshield was also plain, smooth, painted gray. No instruments. No control surfaces: wheel, joystick, anything.

"So far we haven't gotten one to move. I'm not sure how."

"Does any part of it open up?"

"There's a hatch in the back we can get open, and the side door on the off side opens. There's nothing in the back, but it would hold about half of us. Not that it does any good if we can't get it outside."

Ky walked around to other vehicles, examining the floor and the vehicles both. "They're all parked on a marked area, did you notice?"

"Yes. Very military, I thought."

"Hmmm." Ky leaned down and ran her hand along the incised strip. At the off front corner she found a slight dimple. "Feel this, Betange."

"It's . . . just a little sort of dip."

"Like the one beside the door that Inyatta found."

"There was one beside the door to this."

"So this will do something if I push the command rod into it, don't you think?"

"You don't know what it will do." Now Betange looked worried.

"We need a way to get these things working, and then get them outside. This might open another door, or start an engine or whatever the motive power is. And if I do it, it can't be anyone else's fault, can it?" He still looked worried. "Go tell the others to get over by that back wall," Ky said. "I have an idea."

Betange moved off with suspicious quickness. When the others were clustered with him, Ky crouched outside the marked space and pushed the rod into the dimple. Without sound or warning, the outlined rectangle rose up, and far above icy air, snow, and light poured in as the overhead opened. Ky got a pile of snow on her head, shook it off, and saw the ceiling close around the rectangle below the vehicle. Which was now up there, wherever "there" was, being snowed on. Where it had been, a rectangular hole half a meter deep, edges sharp as if cut with a knife, gaped before her. Its floor was smooth, glossy black with a faint pattern of grid lines on it.

"That may not have been the smartest thing I ever did." Ky shivered; the whole space felt cold and now her hair was wet, snow melting on her head.

"What did you *think* would happen?" Chok asked. "What if you'd been standing closer to it?"

Ky laughed. "Sorry, Sergeant, but you sound like my father used to when I tried something stupid. I thought maybe the power would come on and maybe if I got in the cab there'd be another dimple and some controls would appear. I did not expect that." She gestured at the snow, now melting.

"Do you think that thing, whatever it is, is outside?"

"Yes. And I have no idea how to get it back. But it does mean we can move these outside without having to push them or start them and drive them along passages we don't even know about yet."

"But we can't get them to move."

"Yet," Ky said. "I'll bet we can get them to move in time. We have very smart people here, including you, and strong motivation to become mobile—an enemy intending to kill us all if we don't evade them. Or kill them."

"How many, do you think?"

"Enemies? The data my aunt's been able to collect says transport's being requisitioned for supplies for combat troops to Pingats. At least a hundred. She's not sure which troops yet."

"That many? And no idea who's doing it?"

"She's trying to find out without alerting whoever it is. And at the same time assemble a relief force ready to jump as soon as the weather allows."

"So that's why you're so eager to get moving." Chok nodded. "A hundred to eighteen isn't good odds."

"Exactly." Ky checked her implant's time stamp. "It's almost time for a meal. Take a break, then finish cataloging the vehicles, check for this-level exits from the place, and work on getting some control of these things. Be back at the barracks by 2200; we're all going to be working long days. I'm going to see if I can spot the escaped whatever-it-is outside."

"Might be best to wait for daylight."

Ky shook her head. "You are definitely acting like my father, Sergeant. Which means sensibly, so yes, I will wait until tomorrow."

CHAPTER THIRTY-ONE

PORT MAJOR
DAY 168

"More oddities," MacRobert said. "Personnel assignments mostly in the planetary units. Enlisted Miznarii, early career, in Enforcement, assigned in small groups—no more than three at a time, over the past half year—to something called Training Group Foxtrot."

"Someone doesn't like Miznarii?" Grace looked up from her work.

"Someone wants Miznarii for something clandestine," MacRobert said. "Some of our best operatives have been Miznarii. They have no implants, so their implants can't be salvaged and queried."

"Of course—so they're to be used and—blamed and discarded?"

"Plausible deniability. Suicide implants, even." MacRobert took a sip of his drink and went on. "Interestingly, Training Group Foxtrot, its personnel and weaponry, would fit comfortably on the craft that's been assigned to carry spare parts down to Pingat Islands Base."

"They're after Ky—"

"Because she's seen their secret base. They'll kill everyone there and try to remove all traces. They know we have surveillance capability now; that's why they blew up that bank of equipment and the unfortunate night clerk. They may be wondering who exactly fixed the scan satellites—"

"Someone would know a Vatta ship was up there—"

"Very likely. And a tech from ISC. Put those together, and they will assume you know something. I'm doubling your security."

"Damn it—" Grace glared at him.

"No. We cannot afford to lose the Rector of Defense in the aftermath of losing the Commandant. I want to talk to Rafe and ensure he keeps Ky informed of what she's facing."

"We can't let them get to her. I can rescind the orders, send *loyal* troops—"

"Assuming we have any. And we can't move troops or matériel any faster than the other side—it's still deep winter down there. We have the advantage that they don't know what we know—or all of what we know. I want to talk to Rafe and get his assessment of what's up there in Ky's flagship."

"You could call—"

"I could. But until I'm more sure the communications link is really secure, I don't want to."

Rafe came back in with a sheaf of hardcopy. "I did a little analysis on this, Mac; hope you don't mind."

Mac shook his head. "Just tell me."

"One thing I learned from ISC's military errors is that items of equal mass may be substituted in a list, giving a correct standard weight, but being something else entirely. One of ISC's sector commanders was actually smuggling large amounts of high-value contraband in packets weighing the same as small-arms ammunition or in insulated containers weighing the same as food for the crew. Which is why we had a fleet that wasn't even paper, but mostly hot air and thought bubbles."

"And you're saying we've got that?"

"No. But I took your standard average weight for a fully equipped military police soldier—and found that it was exactly the same as this item here: SKSF-4381B-1596572, Rotor, Replacement, et cetera and so forth. They requisitioned one hundred ten of those. And the boxes of 'Fasteners, screw, hex, count 24' just happen to weigh the same as a box of ammunition, count 20, for the standard small-arms weapon you use. Quite a lot of fasteners. And though I don't know anything about Slotter Key riot control and air-to-surface and surface-to-air missiles, I can't help but wonder about those things whose labels are all in code, or that I don't recognize. Canisters always suggest some kind of gas weapon to me." Rafe raised an eyebrow. "I really don't think your whatsit islands base commander is trying to be fuel-efficient with repair supplies."

"Training Group Foxtrot," Grace said.

"Indeed," Rafe said. He handed the hardcopy to MacRobert. "You'll know better than I what all of those are. Trouble for Ky, I would think. We need to get down there."

"We can't yet. Weather's too bad. And if they know we're coming, they might just bomb everything to slag."

"Not if they have enough invested in using it," Rafe said. "They wouldn't keep a secret that long if it didn't have value for them—same as with ISC and ansible technology."

"Speaking of ansibles." MacRobert leaned back. "I need to have a talk with you, Rafe, about communications security. I've been wanting to talk to Ky's flagship, but I don't know if it's a secure link. The guys I know and still trust aren't sure, because it's not our system. You say you've got an absolutely secure method, but I understand it's proprietary ISC tech."

"I'm going to the kitchen," Grace said. "I feel an overwhelming urge to start making fruitcakes again. And yes, Mac, my arm is up to it."

"You know," Mac said, when the kitchen door had swung shut. "Just because the Rector is out of the room—"

"Doesn't mean she's not listening." Rafe nodded and pulled a privacy cylinder from his pocket and thumbed it on. "And she may even be listening past this, since you're up to date in your surveillance equipment."

"Are we?"

"Oh, yes. If I didn't know better, I might think you'd imported some particular instruments from the mercs—from Mackensee. Little bird told me you and their Master Sergeant Pitt got friendly back at Cascadia."

"Competent woman, Master Sergeant Pitt," Mac said. "But that relates to what I want to ask you. We're not that far away from a likely window to make a flight down to Miksland. Neither the Rector nor I—both too well known and too high up—can move troops around and gather a team larger than maybe a dozen, two at the most. And we both think the opposition might be mustering as many as a hundred."

"Or more. I'd think they might use their own, as well—civilian corporate security."

"I'm wondering what resources are up there, in that flagship, but I don't want to risk asking her captain. Yes, we have tight-beam, but any group that can mask a continent from surveillance for over a century—"

"Might break a tight-beam's security. It actually can be done; ISC figured it out but hid the tech. So you would like me to secretly contact Ky's flag captain and see what fighting resources they have?"

"Yes. As soon as possible."

"Unfortunately, my special tech does not mesh with her flagship's, but I do know ways to overprotect tight-beams. I'll get busy on that." He stood up. Mac held up his hand.

"Just a moment. I had considered asking if the flagship could communicate with Mackensee, get us some contracted troops—"

"You'd bring *mercs* onto your own planet?"

"How do we know *they* haven't?" At Rafe's startled look, Mac nodded. "How do we know that tinkering with the surveillance satellites wasn't done by an outsider? Even a renegade ISC employee on the take? Mackensee won't take both sides in a conflict, so the quickest way to find out if the opfor hired them is to see if they can be hired here for someone else—us. If they can, they'll also know if any other company is already here, and tell us."

Rafe cocked his head. "I believe, Master Sergeant, I did not fully appreciate your talents before now."

Mac chuckled. "You young fellas rarely do until a pinch comes. Specially the smart ones, like you."

"So first thing is to give the tight-beam from here some extra protection and then—?"

"I want to talk to that captain. I don't know him, but I'm sure the admiral briefed him on what she knew of the situation here, whom she trusted."

Rafe nodded. "I'll get to it now, if that's all."

"All for now."

Mac watched him go. For all that he wasn't Ky Vatta's blood relative, he felt a familial connection through Grace, and he had not been at all sure that young man was a fit partner for the woman Ky had become. He was older, skilled in ways Mac hoped Ky hadn't picked up, as smooth a liar as Mac had ever met, and he'd met plenty. A killer, too. Admitted it . . . but then, Ky wasn't the naïve young cadet he'd known. Blood on her hands, too, some of it up close and personal.

"You've got that look," Grace said. She stood in the kitchen door, apron on and a large wooden spoon in one hand. He could smell molasses and spices. She looked exactly like someone's grandmother or great-aunt, traditional and harmless. Except for the eyes, and the bulge of something hard in the apron pocket.

"What look?"

"That *If he harms her I'll pull out his guts one centimeter at a time* look. You're not still feeling protective about Ky, are you?"

He shrugged. "It wouldn't do any good if I were."

"They're well matched, those two," Grace said. "Like us, though we're older and more sedate—"

Mac snorted. "You? Me?"

"Well, you have that correct military demeanor. Expressionless face, when you want it; no overt emotional cues."

"I used to. Being around you has roughed up the edges a little. But if that's all it takes for sedateness, your sweet-old-lady act is overkill."

Grace shrugged, both shoulders rising the same amount now, he noticed. "So what can you tell me, you and Rafe?"

"Some things we can't."

"Of course. Those at the top are the last to know and the first to die."

"Not always the first," Mac said. He took her hand. "There may be consequences. You may not be happy about it."

"There are always consequences," Grace said. "And if something exciting happens and saves me from terminal boredom in a job you pushed me into—"

"It could happen," Mac said, watching her closely. "It could end badly, or it could end with the need for a sudden departure."

"I'd like to get the Vatta situation nailed down before that."

"Um. How long after we retrieve Ky do you think that will take?"

"That bad, eh? Fine, then I'll put the family on alert, get Stella back onplanet—"

"Will she be safe? Never mind, sweet old lady dear, I know you can handle that."

"I wonder if we should contract some outside muscle," Grace said, looking away from him into a distance greater than the other side of the room. "Didn't you say you'd met a nice senior NCO in some merc outfit that Ky knew?"

There was no outflanking Grace Lane Vatta; he knew that by now. "It's something to think about," he said mildly, patting her hand.

She yanked it away. "Mac—"

"Without bothering your pretty little head," he said, ducking ahead of her swipe with the spoon. He was out of his chair before she made it out of hers, but the end of the spoon got him anyway. She was that fast. "Plausible deniability," he said from a distance he knew was not safe if she wanted to hurt him. "You're still in the government. Needed."

"True." She sat back down, tapped the spoon handle on the table. "So don't tell me what you think would get me in trouble, but I'm glad to see that our crooked minds still wander in the same directions."

"You have corrupted me," Mac said, with a little bow, not taking his eyes off that spoon. "You are the elder—"

"Oh, stop it. We have other games to play now."

"Which you like. Yes. Rafe's working on making our tight-beam more secure. I'll be talking to Ky's flag captain when he's ready."

"Good. Tell me, is there any way to get a few kilos of edibles down to Pingat Base?"

"Now?"

"Not quite now. A few tendays."

"Why?"

"It occurs to me that the base commander there had reason to be angry with me. Perhaps a special treat would . . . soften his attitude."

"Fruitcakes?" Mac said. "You forget, I've heard about your fruit-cakes."

"There are fruitcakes and fruitcakes," Grace said. "Some you want to last a very long time and some you want to be eaten rather sooner." She grinned at him. "No diamonds in these; it would not do for a Rector of Defense to bribe a base commander so openly."

"Let me taste one."

"They need to soak in brandy," Grace said. "And none of this batch is for you. Not one bite. I'll make you something else."

Something in the seriousness of her tone rang a tiny bell. "Grace?"

"Don't worry, dear Mac." Now she patted his hand, knowing he hated that as much as she did. "All will be well."

"In the end," he said. His stomach clenched for a moment. Surely . . . best not even think of what she might do. Or had done. Joining a Vatta, as she had explained several years ago, was a perilous choice.

Rafe reappeared from the hall. "Link's ready," he said. "I do have a pick on it, so I can monitor from another set to detect any interference, but it should hold and I will be studiously ignoring the conversation."

"Of course you will," Grace said. She patted his shoulder as she went back to the kitchen. Rafe looked startled, then lifted an eyebrow to Mac.

"She's making fruitcake," Mac said, as if that explained everything. Maybe it did. "We are warned not to steal the smallest nibble; she will make something for us later."

"Who's she poisoning?" Rafe asked, going straight for the obvious.

"I hope I'm wrong in my surmises," Mac said. "It may be a simple gesture of friendship. Come, let us go persuade that no-doubt-very-upright flagship captain to do doubtful deeds."

"You've both been reading real literature," Rafe said. "Stop it."

Vanguard II's captain, initially chilly and formal, warmed up as Mac explained why communications previously had been so limited. "I've got an ISC tech monitoring this line to be sure it's clean and stays so. If I break off suddenly, someone tried to put a ferret down the hole."

"What's the word on the admiral? All I know is that you told me you're sure she's alive. Surely not still in a life raft?"

"She is alive; she's on that continent that you can see bare-eyed near our south pole but that we haven't been able to get a scan of until recently."

"We noticed that. What happened?"

"We think the same people who sabotaged the shuttle have a secret installation there. The admiral is inside it, with the survivors from the life rafts. For the moment, they're safe: they have supplies, they're underground, and she thinks the power source is geothermal. They can't go anywhere else; the weather's too severe. We can't go there for the same reason."

He went on to tell the captain what Ky had told Rafe—what she had found out, and what she suspected. "So," he finished, "when the weather moderates, come the austral spring, we expect the bad guys to show up to kill them all and try to keep the place secret."

"But you can mount a mission as well, can't you? And why doesn't she contact us?"

"We're afraid any communications from there might be compromised. She has a . . . a device she can use for secure contact to the ISC tech, but it's nonstandard and doesn't interface with anything else. At least, that's what he told us. The installation has com equipment, she said, but she suspects it's all being monitored by the enemy. So what we've come up with—"

"We who? You and the admiral?" Suspicion colored Pordre's voice again.

"The Rector of Defense and I. We're trying to keep communications with the admiral to a minimum, on her suggestion."

"Did she say to call me?"

"Yes, if we were sure the tight-beam wasn't compromised. She also said she appreciated your steadfast support, and if worse came to worst, and her death was confirmed, she knew you would take care of everything properly. Commander Bentik was killed in a firefight with a traitor among the survivors. Sorry, sir, I should have reported that earlier."

"A firefight . . . was the admiral wounded?"

"No, sir." Mac stopped there. Would the captain ask for details? A longish pause suggested the captain was considering doing just that, but he did not. Well, then, now came the ticklish bit. "Captain, there's a . . . an unusual request. It's not directly from the admiral, because— since she hasn't contacted us for several days, not an unusual gap— she is unaware of some of the Rector's staff's discoveries about the probable saboteurs."

"So—this is from the Rector? You're in her residence, aren't you? Why doesn't she talk to me herself?"

A very reasonable question. He wished he knew more about this

Captain Anton Pordre. But surely Ky would have picked someone with political acumen for this particular trip. "Plausible deniability, Captain. She would like this to be known as your initiative."

"*Would* she?" Another long pause. "Well, then, tell me."

"She suspects that her office's communications with subordinate commands may not be secure—and thus gathering a ground combat force large enough to handle the force being assembled by the saboteurs without alerting them is not likely. And starting a civil war is . . . unhealthy."

"We don't have ground troops aboard." Pordre sounded both annoyed and stubborn now. "We have only ship security; they're not infantry."

"That's not what the Rector was going to ask," Mac said, keeping his own voice calm.

"Well?"

"You might consider hopping out of the system—out of range of local eavesdropping, if there is any—and contacting Mackensee to see if they would take a contract here. Short-term, and very soon."

"You—the Rector wants me to bring mercs onto her own planet?"

"I can't say what the Rector wants. Personally, however, given what we don't have and what we're facing, I think some good mercs to put down an insurrection would be a fine idea."

"Do you happen to have any contact data? A particular individual?"

"I believe, Captain, that going through their main portal and mentioning the admiral's name should get a quick response, but if you want someone who knows me—your local contact—there's a Master Sergeant Pitt. We had some productive conversations back on Cascadia after the Battle of Nexus Two."

"Thank you, Master Sergeant MacRobert."

From the tone of the captain's voice, he was making, or had just made, a decision. Mac crossed mental fingers and said nothing, waiting what seemed like far too long before the captain spoke again.

"I believe that we need to take *Vanguard* out of local contact for a few days," he said. "I will be contacting you on the usual schedule, in the hope that any ticks infesting us do in fact overhear the conversation. I will express concerns about the due diligence of Slotter Key's Defense Department and also concerns about security, and admit that I'm under pressure from SDF and must consult them. That I expect to return. I find, having just looked it up, that the admiral did indeed leave information on Mackensee in my emergency file. Will that do?"

"Thank you, Captain; that will do very well."

"Your estimate of the opposition's task force?"

"One to two hundred combat troops; we haven't been able to define it more tightly. Some of the equipment is worrisome, including chemical."

"Funds—"

"Will be available via the Rector's discretionary fund."

"Expect a call in about ... two standard hours. Time enough, if someone knows of this call, but not its contents, for me to lose my temper and start readying the ship for emergency departure. And you to inform the Rector of whatever you need to."

"Thank you, Captain."

"I want her back as much as you do," Pordre said, and cut the connection before Mac could reply.

CHAPTER THIRTY-TWO

PORT MAJOR

DAY 175

"I wish we knew more about Ky's flag captain," Grace said. She had come back from her office late, and she looked even tighter-strung than usual. "Are you sure he's trustworthy?"

Rafe, a spoonful of consommé halfway to his mouth, raised his brows. "You expect me to know?"

"I thought Ky might have consulted you, with all your contacts—"

"I believe she consulted other contacts. But I have met him, and had no bad feelings about him. Ky doesn't tolerate incompetence, and she has her own antennae about trustworthiness."

"She wasn't happy about using a Spaceforce shuttle."

"I'm sure Pordre wasn't, either. As it happened, they were both right. But Pordre . . . I don't think he's one of the worshippers who think she's beyond fault and a genius at everything—"

MacRobert choked and covered it with a cough. Teague grinned, watching them all. Rafe ignored them and went on. "It's healthier to be a little—not skeptical, I don't think, but conservative—in his understanding of her."

"There's no chance he wants her dead so he can take over?"

"Pordre? No. He's too junior. She's been quite frank in discussing succession of command if anything should happen to her. The relevant governments, and the senior staff of the SDF, all made suggestions. She did consult me about that, because prior to Turek's pirate consortium, the biggest fleet in this end of the galaxy had been ISC's. She thought its organization was pretty good, despite the obvious problems; she didn't want to invent a bad wheel to replace a broken one."

"And?"

"I don't know who she picked. I do know she laid out what she thought the various systems should do—how to allocate patrol sectors and so on—and how the overall command structure should be set up. Her staff back at SDF headquarters would know the details. She might have told me if we'd ever gotten that vacation."

"I think he's solid," MacRobert said. He wiped his mouth and put his napkin down. "Like you, Rafe, I had no bad impressions of him." He looked over at Grace. "What happened today? You're strung tight."

"Troop reassignments and a dead body," Grace said. "We assumed all along that the opposition was using Spaceforce personnel."

"Yes, they're on the lists—"

"Well, they're not now. All the personnel originally assigned to the research facility have been reassigned to joint maneuvers with the Twenty-Third Recon as part of Vermillion Cloud, the annual training exercise at Boole, up north."

"But who—"

"And the dead body is their erstwhile commander, Greyhaus."

"The same Greyhaus—"

"That Ky reported about, yes. Collapsed suddenly during a briefing, attempt at resuscitation unsuccessful. His exec, Major Gallinos, took over, pending official change of command. And that's all I know."

"You think—?" Teague spoke before anyone else got it out.

"I think treachery through and through," Grace said. "I can't determine who switched Greyhaus' unit's orders. Mac, that's your assignment tomorrow. Who is going to be on those planes heading for Miksland? Nobody seems to know that, either. Are they civilians? Criminals? A private army?"

"How many?" Rafe asked.

"Two hundred," Grace said. "I rousted out Personnel, who first insisted they were the same unit number and somebody'd made a mistake, and then said they were a recruit unit on the usual three-week field exercise. But they couldn't tell me which recruit unit, where from. You don't like me upsetting troops, Mac, so you figure it out."

"We only have three enlisted recruit training bases," Mac said. "It should be easy—but why would they send recruits to dig out the survivors? Unless they don't expect any resistance."

"It's Ky," Rafe said. "They'll expect it."

"It's not recruits," Mac said, frowning. "Recruits chatter; they don't keep secrets reliably."

"How qualified were those they replaced? How experienced?" Rafe asked.

"Well trained, but as I said before we haven't had a serious problem in many decades—since I was young, in fact—and so they've never actually been in combat."

"They'll want combat-experienced troops because they know Admiral Vatta has that experience," Teague said. He leaned forward. "Where would they get combat-experienced troops?"

"Mercs," Rafe and Mac said simultaneously.

"Or pirates," Teague said. "Didn't Turek have some ground-pounders? And we know not all the pirates were killed in the war. Enough ships escaped—"

Mac looked at Teague, brows raised. "But why would anyone hire pirates? Especially pirates who'd lost a war?"

"Because they've worked with them before," Grace said. Her fist came down on the table. "I am a blind idiot not to have seen it. We never did find out who was behind the original attack here, on Slotter Key. That the President was complicit, yes, but not where the weapons came from, who planted the bombs under the old headquarters, or who pushed the button on that drone."

"You thought it was Osman, didn't you?"

"Osman," Grace said, "had sons. And allies."

CHAPTER THIRTY-THREE

SLOTTER KEY, MIKSLAND
DAY 204

"Sir, someone's tickled the communications."

"What?" Ky looked up from her own logbook.

"Pulled data from meteorology. I didn't interfere, but I have a capture on what they got. There's a weather break in eighteen days, plus or minus four."

"We knew that was coming," Ky said. "Tell Gossin and Kurin, we're now on high alert. They'll move as soon as it opens. So will the Rector, no doubt. We'll move sooner. Start packing." The miserable brain-dead machines still would not move. So they would have to walk. Because she was not going to let her people die in a hopeless trap. How far could they get in eighteen days? Farther than if they sat here wishing for miracles.

CASCADIA STATION
DAY 213

Stella Vatta stared at the screen and hoped her thoughts were not in a balloon over her head. She was not a ball to be tossed back and forth on long, tiring voyages. She was Vatta's CEO; she had a business—no, several—to run and she needed to be in *one* place, with her *own* staff and clean lines of communication to Vatta's many locations and enterprises. This had better be the last trip request for a standard year.

Yet she knew she would go, and even as she snarled inside, she pressed the signal for her personal assistant to come in. While imagining shaking her great-aunt Grace upside down to see what came out, she gave quiet, precise orders for what needed to be done while she was gone. One of Vatta's two fast couriers was actually onstation, but the crew were resting. Stella wished for the luxury of an actual passenger ship, with a cabin bigger than a cell and some amenities to enjoy during the voyage—exercise space, a real bath, a massage service, meals in a proper dining space—but Grace's message, transmitted via Ky's flagship, had been specific: come at once, fastest means possible.

Nothing about Ky. Had her body been found? What was going on? She had agreed to a blackout on the topic, just in case Ky had survived and there was a chance enemies were still on her trail, but not-knowing gnawed at Stella. She and Ky had finally resolved all their adolescent difficulties; they had a good working relationship, and now . . . she missed her more volatile cousin.

She spent the next two standard hours working through the usual midweek tasks that rose to the CEO's attention. Her PA reminded her that she had been scheduled to speak at the opening ceremonies of the new Vatta plant on Cascadia itself; she recorded the speech, which took another hour, and wrote personal notes to the new plant's manager and the town arbiter regretting that she had been called away on business resulting from her cousin's untimely disappearance or death—they supposed the latter, given the circumstances. Polite responses came within the next half hour.

The crew should wake by 1500 local time. How long to prep the ship? Ginny Vatta, the pilot, usually kept her courier hot, refueling before she left it. So it was time to go to her own apartment, take that last luxurious bath, and be ready to leave when the crew was ready. Given the message Grace had told her to leave in Gin's queue, that would be very fast.

She was inhaling perfumed steam, up to her neck in hot water, when the alarm sounded, followed by a crackle from the speaker in the bathroom and the sound of a gasp. Seconds later, a crash as the locked door to her personal suite was breached. She was already out of the tub, feet shoved into nonskid hard-toed slippers, weapon retrieved, grabbing for her emergency armor, when she heard them in the next room. She had one arm through the vest; she shot into the bathroom door, the round opening a gap. Two steps aside, other arm through the vest, slapping the fastening in back, *don't breathe in case they use gas.* Her mask was on the shelf behind her; she felt back with her left hand as two rounds came in, shattering on the tub wall. *Don't breathe.* She felt the edge of a temporary mask sticking out of the box, snatched it, pressed it over her mouth and nose. One cautious breath . . . good, but not enough. The better mask was under the counter . . . why had she put it there? Without taking her eyes off the door, she crouched a little and fished around. There.

A faint hissing from the door, and the door handle slid out, smoking slightly, to clang on the floor. Stella caught a glimpse of a weapon through the opening and fired through it—a spudder and a frangible. Curse words out there. She grabbed a fresh magazine from the stack on the counter, switched out the partially used one, fired a quick four shots—spudders and frangibles—then hauled the full-spec mask over her head and fastened it. Her skin was itching now—that other *had* been gas all right, and some might get to her bloodstream through her bare, still-wet skin.

Silence from the outer room. She climbed up onto the counter, pushing the station emergency button as she did so. Then up the apparently decorative lattice that served as an escape ladder if she needed it.

The door burst in before she could push up the ceiling panel and climb through. Two figures in full protective gear paused for a fatal instant. Two quick shots and they were both down. She really wanted to pause long enough to get more clothes on. She could see at least one body on the floor of her bedroom, and hear voices—but now familiar voices that identified themselves.

And here she was, crouched on a ledge near the ceiling, and bare as an egg but for the vest and the gas mask. And her clothes on the far side of two dead bodies sprawled on the bathroom floor.

"Sera Vatta! Are you here?"

It was the security guard for this sector. Stella knew her voice. "I'm in the bathroom," she said, loud enough to be heard. "I was in the tub. Be careful, there's gas residue."

Though, with the door open, not as much. She might as well climb down. She did so, carefully, as the security personnel moved into her bedroom.

"Do you need assistance, Sera?" came the sector guard's familiar voice.

"If you could bring a robe from my closet," Stella said, in as calm a voice as she could manage, "I would be most grateful. I would have to step on the bodies and possibly contaminate the scene to get to my clothes in here."

"Of course, Sera." A few soft sounds, then the woman put an arm through the door opening, one of Stella's robes draped over it.

Stella took it, set the gun convenient to her hand on a higher ledge, and shrugged into the robe, running her hand down the seal. Then she picked up the gun again, took the last step down, carefully not touching the tangle of legs on the floor—ignoring the churning in her stomach—and walked into the bedroom. Two more bodies lay there, one with a mangled hand as well as the fatal wound.

"This is the weapon I used," she said holding it out. "It is loaded and still has a round in the chamber. I presume you will confiscate it."

The guard lifted her helmet shield. "No, Sera. No need. You were attacked in a most discourteous way. They entered your private rooms uninvited, even into the bath suite. That would call for an execution if you had not already killed them."

Stella blinked. She was still not used to Cascadia's cultural settings. She had not imagined that they would treat her killing four people so lightly, just because the men had been discourteous.

"I am sorry, however, that they intruded at all. It is my fault that I allowed myself to be stunned—"

"Are you all right?" Stella asked.

"Yes, Sera. My relief was due; he found me and revived me, but they had already broken into your apartment. And you yourself are unhurt?"

"Yes," Stella said. "Though I'm afraid there's much to be repaired."

"Please accept my sincere apologies for what happened," the guard said.

"Of course," Stella said. She hoped that was the right thing to say. "I am sorry you were impaired, even momentarily, and I hold you blameless. The responsibility is theirs—" She glanced at the bodies.

"My team will record the evidence, then remove the debris," the guard said. "I am not certain that, this late in the day, we can arrange repairs—"

"Do not trouble yourself," Stella said. "My office can make arrangements while I'm gone."

"You were leaving?"

"Yes. I've been called back to Slotter Key urgently. My cousin, as you know, has been missing—"

"Admiral Vatta!" The guard's face took on an expression of avid admiration. "Is there news?"

"All I know is that I am to return to Slotter Key as quickly and quietly as possible." She looked around the room. "I have failed in the second requirement, that of discreet, quiet departure."

"I'm sure the most important thing is that you find out about Admiral Vatta," the guard said.

Stella repressed a sigh; it might be considered rude. But really—Ky was a hero, to be sure, but she herself had started businesses that brought in substantial benefits to Cascadia. And yet her value to them sometimes seemed to come primarily from being Ky's cousin.

"I cannot hold out much hope she is still alive," she said, pitching her voice low. "Crashing into an icy sea, and no word all this time. Everyone says there's no way she could have survived on a life raft, even if she survived the crash. And yet—I cannot give up completely."

"Of course not." The guard shook her head. "Perhaps there is news they do not wish to spread abroad. Perhaps she is alive but impaired. No word has come from her flagship, either."

"Will it be a problem if I finish packing?" Stella said.

"No, Sera. If you would like a little time to dress and pack, we can stand right outside the door."

"Fifteen minutes," Stella said. She wanted out of the sights and smells and mess of it all, and she wanted to call her office and her crew—they should be awake by now—and get an escort to the docks.

"A half hour would not be too long," the guard said, bowed politely, and left.

Stella dressed, including her everyday body armor, picked up the always-packed duffel, and added lounge clothes for the trip itself, her makeup case, the gas mask, the gun, and IDs. She notified the office that her assistant would need to come, assess the damage, and arrange repairs. She learned that the crew was already aboard the courier, readying for the flight, and would contact her in the next few minutes. She checked what she had against the list in her implant, then stepped carefully back into the bathroom to pick up the box of quick-masks and the rest of the ammunition, including the half-spent magazine. As she walked toward the bedroom door, she checked herself in the mirror. Her face showed nothing of what had happened; nothing marred her appearance, her clothes, her small luggage. Aunt Grace would approve.

CHAPTER THIRTY-FOUR

MIKSLAND
DAY 215

"When are you going to tell them this place wasn't made by humans?" Staff Sergeant Kurin had piles of supplies stacked along the walls, supplies that—it was now obvious—could not be carried by the eighteen survivors. Eight days until they expected the enemy to arrive: eight days of water, eight days of food, plus weapons, ammunition for the weapons, and communications gear—they were fit, but not that fit.

"When we're not trying to evade an invasion force," Ky said. She felt like kicking the nonexistent tires of the vehicles they were working on. Trying to work on. "Besides, it was modified by humans, right here on the planet, or it wouldn't have been full of clothes for us to wear, food we can eat, and beds to sleep in. And for all we know, the terraformers are human."

"This is not a human-designed machine."

"Unless the humans who designed it wanted to frustrate all who came after."

"It's got to be driverless," Inyatta said, sticking her head out from under one of the vehicles. "Some planets use them. One of my cousins tried to modify his father's field unit so he could nap while plowing."

"How did that work?" Betange asked.

"Not very well. He didn't think about having it slow down before turning at the end of a row. But the thing is, they exist. We've all seen them in vids from the older worlds."

"There's got to be some way of turning them on and programming them, then," Ky said. "I don't see any standard input slot."

"If they were made by another culture," Inyatta said. Before anyone else could speak she put out a hand. "Wait—hear me out. As the Admiral's said, we've seen things we don't recognize at all. Not the new stuff—the old stuff, like those marks on the controls under the labels we *can* read. So if this was made earlier—by some culture that came before the colonists we know about, and then moved on—"

"Why would they leave?"

"I don't know," Inyatta said. She pushed herself the rest of the way out from under the vehicle. "But that's not the point. The point is, if this—all the parts of this we don't understand—was made by another culture, we have to recognize it could be very, very different."

Ky nodded. "That's true . . . but if we're not the same, can we use any of it, or is this a waste of time?"

"I'm thinking of what I know about driverless things. Inventory robots. Delivery units. Some use a sort of electronic map in the vehicle; others use a guideline."

Ky remembered something she hadn't seen in years, her first visit to Vatta's semi-automated warehouse at Port Major. "So we need to know how to give these things a destination—but we have no idea what destinations are possible. There's got to be a map and some kind of control surface *somewhere*."

"I'd say tear one down and look, but if it's a completely different culture their software might be so different it'd take years to figure out."

"Humans figured out the controls for power and communications—"

"I think the communications we see were built into gap space by the people who occupied this place," Betange said. "And they may not have done anything to the power supply, just retrofitted standard Slotter Key stuff so they could use it easily. Did you notice that the light fixtures are much newer than the openings for them?"

"No," Ky said. It had never occurred to her to wonder if the age of the fixtures matched the age of the building. Tech thinking—and, in the circumstances, she was glad she had techs to notice what she ignored. "So . . . what in this space looks new? Is it possible that the humans using the facility never made it this far? And if so . . . maybe that could be useful to us?"

"We could hide out here? Bring food and water and some mattresses—"

"It's ventilated—the air's not stuffy—so I'd worry about gas."

"We've been so focused on the vehicles," Gossin said, "that we haven't searched for more things these rods will open. Or where on vehicles such dimples might be."

"One day," Ky said. "Today, look for any hidden doors, controls, anything on the vehicles or in the rooms. Anything you find, or any other ideas you have, let someone else know, and pass it up to me. Betange, come with me and let's see if the newcomers modified anything in the power control room other than putting stickers over the original labels."

By suppertime, they had discovered that no sign of modern— "newcomer"—change existed beyond the door Inyatta had found. Access hatches had been cut to intercept power cables, and there were what looked like master switches—though not common usage ones—behind some of the hatches. Next to those were clearly newer control boxes using the types of switches and labels common on Slotter Key. Betange explained all this to Ky.

"It would've taken an experienced electrician—probably a team of them, and plenty of money—to convert the output to something our appliances could use. What do we call whoever did the original installation, oldtimers?"

"Good enough," Ky said.

"I wish I had a crew and time to really study it." Betange—completely focused and interested—was a different man from the anxious, depressed one she'd seen for so long. "I don't quite get it—the complexity of it, the reasoning—but it would be great to know. Were they even human?"

Ky blinked. "Do you really think they weren't?"

"Admiral!" That call came from somewhere back down the passage. "We got one running."

Ky hurried back that way; Betange followed.

The vehicle was a twin to the one Ky had launched through the roof exit. Instead of up, it went forward and back, and wove an accurate path through the other parked vehicles as Droshinski tapped the control cylinder.

"How did you do that?"

"*Cautious* experimentation," Chok said, grinning. "Turns out there's a dimple inside this back end we've been calling the cargo area and one inside the cab. If you push a rod into one of those, the rod extrudes little textured buttons—show her, Droshinski."

Droshinski held out the rod. Ky could see the buttons. "This one at the bottom is *stop*. The others are *away*, to *me*, and *turn*." Ky nodded, repressing a desire to grab the rod and start pushing buttons. "It won't hit another vehicle," Droshinski said. "It won't hit a wall. It turns whichever way there's more room."

"We think we've found guide paths, though," Hazarika put in. "When it goes between parked vehicles, it always stays on the same path, and the path is not equidistant from adjoining vehicles. And one guide path leads straight to that wall—" He pointed. "It'll go close, but then back up and turn around."

"I think that wall's not a wall," Droshinski said. "I think it's a big door."

"There's a dimple over here," Lakhani said. "But we didn't try it yet."

The same control that opened the other doors did not open this one—if it was a door and not a wall—but it did generate a sound, a rising and falling tone.

"A warning," Sergeant Cosper said. "Like a siren, but not so loud."

"Droshinski, try driving that vehicle toward it; let's see what happens."

A startled look from Droshinski and Cosper both. Then the vehicle rolled forward, turned, and straightened out as it approached the wall. A wide section of wall—wide enough for any of the vehicles—slid sideways, opening onto a gently sloping passage where lights blinked on, one after another. The vehicle rolled through.

"Stop it," Ky said. "Back it up—we don't want that door to close again with it on the other side." Droshinski stopped the vehicle and backed it until it was in the new entrance.

"I could ride it through, and then bring it back," Droshinski said.

"I hope you can, but I'd like to find out without your getting stuck on the other side. We do need to know what's down that corridor." If it came out somewhere useful—if it could be blocked from intrusion by the enemy—if there were multiple entrances by which the enemy could penetrate—if, if, if.

"Now she's got it open, I can head down that way on foot," Cosper said. "Get some idea of what's there."

"Try it," Ky said. "But not past any doors—and not farther than a kilometer, if it goes that far."

Without any ifs at all, the passage, plus a working vehicle, gave them mobility. Just one vehicle could carry more than all her people combined. "Get another working. As many as you can," Ky said.

"Wherever we go is better than staying here, and now we have supply carriers."

By the end of the day, they knew all the vehicles would respond to commands, and Cosper had made a second foray down the tunnel, leaving his pack as a marker at ten kilometers, the farthest distance Ky would let him go.

CHAPTER THIRTY-FIVE

MIKSLAND
DAY 216

The next morning, their meeting had a different tone. "We have supplies. We have small-arms weapons, enough for everyone," Ky said. "And now we have transportation. Time to leave."

"But we don't know where that goes! What if we're trapped?" Corporal Barash's voice rose.

"Admiral's led us well so far. Why not trust her?" Yamini glared at Barash.

"Easy for you to say!" Barash glared back.

"What d'you mean by that?"

Ky thumped the table. "No personalities. Thinking. Barash, what do you think will happen if we just stay here?"

"You say there's a force coming that will kill us."

"I asked what *you* thought."

"I—I don't know. They might be on our side, the ones who land first. Rescuers. You said you'd been in contact . . . why wouldn't they come? Or we could hide until they do. We could—we could hide in that part the others never found."

"That we *think* the others never found. We can't be sure. If they do know, or if they have some kind of detection that can find more voids, this is a nice big open trap. Clearly this secret—the whole continent, this base, whatever else they're keeping down here—is important to whoever it is—a family, a corporation, even a foreign government. They might even be willing to drop a bomb that would blow the top off this to get us."

"But they couldn't hide that."

"They've been able to hide everything up to now. I think they're desperate to keep their hold on this continent and its contents—this base and whatever else. Our side can't be certain of getting here first; they don't know how much opposition they'll face. They're trying to move fast, and secretly, but they know the opposition is aware of them."

"Your aunt is the Rector; surely she can have whatever she wants. Troops, transport, weapons—" Gossin, this time.

"Apparently not." Ky looked around. Faces now were sober; some were once more scared. "You remember when Vatta was attacked?" Most nodded. "There's still opposition to her, as a Vatta, within Spaceforce and the Defense Department; she had a row with Air-Sea Rescue when the shuttle went down. She's not sure she can trust all the senior commanders."

Ky paused, but no one said anything. She went on. "There are troops on our side, but they're not in position yet. Another few days, but we may not have another few days. What we can do here—improvise blockages, create killzones—is not enough. We can't protect against heavy weapons, and we don't have enough of us—or weapons or ammunition—to fight a prolonged battle. Sure, I would prefer to know where every branch of that tunnel goes, how deep it is, what's on the surface, but we don't have the time. We're leaving as soon as we've loaded the vehicles."

"We should take all the control rods we can find," Inyatta said.

"That will keep them from opening the secret doors or operating any vehicles we leave behind if they blow them open."

"Good thought," Ky said. "Now—since we have vehicles and aren't limited to what we can carry—"

"Food," Gurton said. "How much should we take?"

"Everything we can get into a vehicle," Ky said. "Concentrates first, but if we can take every scrap, all the better. Then they'll have to use their own supplies, and that will delay them, at least a little. Staff Sergeant Gossin, you're in charge of assigning work parties to strip this place of everything we need or they might use against us. Staff Sergeant Kurin, you're in charge of getting the vehicles loaded, making sure they can move with what you pack inside them, with room for personnel as well. Pick your four; you'll get more help when all the supplies have arrived here."

Gossin began assigning work parties for the rest of it. Ky went back to Greyhaus' office and dug through his desk for anything of possible use to Grace. She had to use a chisel and hammer to break the lock on one drawer, but what she found was worth the delay. A list of contact numbers, some with names—officers in various military units, all the way up to very high ranks—and some with initials only and code numbers after. Journals, like Greyhaus', from previous commanders of this facility, dating back . . . over two hundred years. And more.

She had brought a duffel from Supply, and loaded all that, along with the flight recorder from the shuttle, into it, then carried it down to the hangar. Here Kurin was already ticking off incoming supplies, while Kamat, Betange, and Barash were arranging them in vehicles by weight and bulk, and Hazarika was stacking ammunition.

"We've got all the weapons down here; I found more ammunition in Stores, heavy locked crates. Do you want it?"

"Yes," Ky said. "If they make it into the tunnels, I want them to think we will shoot back. It should slow them down a little, anticipating ambushes."

"Right," Hazarika said.

Packing proceeded well as the hours rolled by. All the control rods they'd found, all the food—surely more than they would need—medical supplies, water, the most useful sizes of pots and pans, tools, firearms and ammunition, clothes including extra protective suits, powerpaks to recharge batteries, all the outdoor survival gear they'd found in Stores (two tents, four small portable stoves, four water purifiers, ten sleeping bags, folding seats and one folding table, two fishing rods and a tackle box of lures, extra line, and hooks).

"Clearly somebody was out wandering the countryside," Sergeant McLenard said.

"Probably the officers," muttered Lakhani. "Hunting and fishing."

"Very good," Ky said. "We're almost ready to leave; do a final check of the rooms and see if you find anything left behind, and be ready to guide the others back down."

"We could eat here tonight, couldn't we? Even sleep here? They can't get here before late tomorrow at the earliest—" Gurton said.

"*If* we're right about their plans and the weather where they're starting from. We can't be sure of that. It's too close. We need to be farther away when they arrive."

The little caravan moved almost silently through the hangar door into the tunnel. When the last had passed, they all stopped on signal, and Ky walked back to shut the door using the control rod and the dimple on the tunnel side. She hoped that meant it would stay closed even if the enemy found the hangar and figured out which wall might be a door.

The first few kilometers of their journey counted, to Ky, as known territory; Sergeant Cosper had walked ten kilometers out and back, noting every marking he saw, every light fixture, even (using a level they'd found with the tools) the slope of the passage floor. The tunnel tended downward so gently that the view behind was obscured only when they went around turns. The first two of those were at right angles, but the next was a gentle arc. Ahead of them, lights in the overhead came on—not the familiar lights of any Slotter Key office building, but sections of the overhead that had looked the same plain gray as everything else flicking on to a greenish-white glow. Behind them, the lights went off again.

Droshinski had discovered that the vehicles would not move faster than fifteen kilometers an hour in the tunnel. So it wasn't long before they saw the pack Cosper had left to mark his most distant point. Ahead the tunnel seemed straight and level, vanishing in darkness. Another hour passed, and another. Ky, in the lead vehicle, heard a loud shout from behind. She signaled a halt and when all had halted, walked back to see that a wall had cut off the tunnel behind them, ten meters from the back of the rearmost vehicle.

"It just slid out—no warning, nothing!" Sergeant Chok, tasked with being rear guard, looked as upset as he sounded.

"Have you tried opening it with a control rod?" Ky asked.

"No, Admiral. I didn't know if you wanted—what it might mean—"

"Try it."

Chok walked over to the new wall and felt around the margins for a dimple. "It's not here."

"Try the middle of the space," Ky said.

"Aha. Here—" He touched the rod to it and fingered the sequence that had opened other doors. Nothing happened.

"Are we trapped?" That was Droshinski, who should have stayed with the vehicle she was controlling. "What if there's another—?"

"Put this one in reverse, Droshinski. See if the door opens when traffic approaches." It would make sense, Ky thought, to have safety doors at intervals that protected others from . . . whatever those who'd built this place feared.

With the usual dramatic toss of her head, Droshinski climbed into the back of that vehicle while Chok and Ky moved to the side of the tunnel. As it reversed, the door slid aside.

"Forward now," Ky said.

And as the vehicle once more cleared ten meters between itself and the door, the door slid shut again.

"Whoever they were, we share some ways of thinking," Ky said as

Droshinski climbed out of the vehicle. She looked forward to see clusters of her team outside their vehicles. As she walked back to the front of the line, she said the same thing to each cluster: "Not a problem; the door reacts to vehicles just like the one in the hangar. We're going on."

In another hour, the tunnel opened out into another room, not quite as large as the hangar but large enough to park the vehicles side by side and walk around outside them. Six doors on one side and two on the other. "Try them all," Ky said. Inside one was a room with obvious water fixtures, though they did not look like standard Slotter Key versions.

"Rest stop," said Ennisay. "Like it's an ordinary road trip."

The fixtures worked; water came out of faucets, flushed through toilets, and even (Ennisay got wet trying this out) rained down in abundance in what was afterward obvious as a shower. "I thought it was just part of the floor," he said, dripping. "And I found the dimple and wondered what it did so I pushed—"

"You didn't see the grille in the overhead?" Cosper asked.

"I didn't look up."

"Bet you will next time," Cosper said. Ennisay just grinned.

Ky looked into the space behind the next door—four tables, each with six stools around it, all the same gray as the walls and overhead. What might be a serving line of some sort along one side. Or something else entirely. Gurton said, "Since we're experimenting—" and sat down on one of the stools, only to jump up when the table opened a seam at her place and extruded a bowl with some dry gray-green substance in it. "That can't be food . . ." She picked up the bowl and sniffed at it. "Somebody didn't wash the dishes?"

"Or freeze-dried food that only needs water?" Betange said.

"I'm hungry," Ennisay said. "It's been four hours—couldn't we have a meal?"

"A snack," Ky said. "And not food that we find down here. Food we know is safe for us."

"I could just try wetting it," Gurton said. "Just to see what happens."

"Food from our own stores," Ky said. "A snack. We're not going to stay here long."

Others came and sat down; when all the stools at one table were full, the table extruded a central cluster of . . . something that might be containers. One looked like salt. The rest were unfamiliar.

"Condiments," Betange said. "The aliens have condiments and they sit around during meals. More and more like us."

"They might *be* us," Yamini said. "Ancestors."

"Or not," Ky said. She bit into one of the chewy snack bars Gurton had packed, feeling the day's strain weighing on her. The others looked tired, too, but they hadn't gone far enough to risk stopping here for the rest of the night. She finished eating, drank some water, and used the facility while the others finished their snacks. Then she looked into the other spaces. Two had shelves jutting from the walls that looked rather like spaceship bunks, twelve in each of the rooms. She felt the surface of the lowest. Though it looked all of a piece with the walls and floor, it felt soft, like a thin mattress.

Across the passage, one room was full of opaque canisters almost waist-high, stacked three wide on either side, with an aisle between them. They were labeled, but not in a script she knew. On the walls above hung the same kinds of cleaning equipment familiar to humans everywhere. Brushes, mops, a shelf of something that looked like small balls of moss but felt like something to scrub pots with.

The other room looked, at first glance, like a laboratory or laboratory supply room. Tall transparent containers of different-colored liquid and a faintly tangy odor. Ky moved closer; the room's light brightened. Inside the jars she could now see shapes—translucent, taking the color of the liquid. A long string of little bags, each with a dark dot in it. A sinuous line of . . . bones? segments of one thing? . . . with feathery fronds extending to either side. Each jar bore a yellow label with a single symbol on it—again, she could not understand it, but when she reached out to trace the symbol, it flashed a bright blue light at her.

That had to mean *Don't touch.* She looked around once more, forced herself to ignore what wasn't going to solve their problems, and went out, closing that door.

Kurin came out to join her in closing all the doors, and the others climbed aboard the vehicles. They left the area as they'd found it, all doors closed.

"I think they're a lot like us," Kurin said. She was in the first vehicle with Ky.

"They eat, they drink, they excrete, they must lie down on those shelf things because what else would you use a soft-halfway-down shelf for? And cleaning supplies."

And whatever that was in the last room. Nobody'd mentioned that, and Ky wasn't going to.

After another three hours of travel, they passed another portal that closed behind them. Ky signaled to keep going. If they found another rest stop, they might as well stop for the night. An hour later, there it was: the same as the last except somewhat larger.

"We need to loosen up," Ky said before Cosper could start in on fitness training; he looked pleased that she'd mentioned it. "Ten minutes," Ky said. "Then we set up for the night."

Nobody complained about the vigorous calisthenics and stretches. Afterward, when they discovered four rooms, not just two, with beds, they each claimed a bed, clustering in two of the rooms, leaving the rest for Ky to choose from.

Gurton investigated the kitchen/dining room, discovering a cooking surface behind the plain counter, and set to work on a hot meal. Some were dozing by the time she served, and immediately after Ky sent them all to bed.

The room she chose for herself had two electrical outlets on the wall without bunks. What would the mystery people have used for voltage? She checked with her implant cable; the green light came on.

How likely was it that a different race or culture, or humans from before electricity was used on Old Earth, would choose a compatible voltage to . . . whichever side of Old Earth it was that used 110 instead of 220?

But safe. Except—she didn't need to call Rafe now. They were out of the old base, doors locked behind them, and he wouldn't be expecting to hear from her tonight anyway. It would be smarter to wait a few days, until they were farther away—maybe even had found another route to the outside—and she could tell him where she was, a long way from any enemy. She put away her special cable and went peacefully to sleep.

DAY 217

Despite her confidence in the obscurity of the hidden doors, and the fact that they had all the power rods they'd been able to find, Ky woke early and chivvied the others into action. "We can do twelve hours," she said. "Fifteen minutes at the rest stops; half an hour for lunch. Twelve hours will get us 180 more kilometers." If everything worked as well and no better than the day before. If the enemy hadn't figured out where the entrance to the rest of the facility was, and how to get their own vehicles into the tunnel. Because their vehicles would not be self-driving and would go much faster, she was sure.

The day ground on, hour after hour of rolling almost silently along in a traveling bubble of light, doors opening in front of them, closing behind them. She was stiff every time she got out of the vehicle, less and less glad to be climbing back aboard. Finally they came to the opening where Ky had planned to stop for the night, and everyone climbed down, groaning and muttering.

"Exercise period?" Cosper asked.

"Definitely," Ky said, over the groans. "Including you, Gurton— I'm sure you're stiff, too."

An hour later, she agreed when Droshinski said, "At least we can shower and change clothes—but I wish we had a 'fresher cabinet for the dirty ones."

While the others continued to clean up, Ky wandered through the other rooms, similar to those she'd seen before. What were those shapes in jars? And what were they for? How old?

"Sir? Gurton's serving supper."

"Coming." Ky closed the door as she left the mystery behind and set her mind firmly on the present and future. Everyone bedded down early, making up for the night before. Again, Ky thought of contacting Rafe, but decided that they hadn't traveled far enough yet and she had nothing really to say.

DAYS 218-219

In the next two days they covered 360 kilometers of gray tunnel, most of it straight, with interruptions at the same regular intervals. Although the tunnel never seemed stuffy, and the lights and water continued to work, Ky felt certain that no one had been down this way for centuries. The silence was oppressive, once they stopped for a meal or a night's rest. Conversation lagged. They went through the exercises Cosper insisted on without enthusiasm; Ky, focused on what might be happening outside, didn't try to rouse them to any.

On the second night, she contacted Rafe. He sounded exhausted and distracted when he answered.

"Where are you?"

"Out of the main complex. Our vehicles can only go fifteen kilometers an hour, but we run them twelve hours a day."

"So you're well away, that's good. Supplies?"

"Ample food and water for two or three tendays, if we can use the vehicles the whole way; if we have to go on foot, it'll be tighter."

"And where exactly are you now?"

"There's a passage—the only one that we found—leading from the main complex. You should be able to do a void-scan and see it. It started out heading north, but we've had some curves and I'm not sure now."

"That's good—sorry, Ky, I've got to go. Teague's calling me."

Ky shook her head, shrugged, and lay down wondering if he'd actually heard everything she'd said. Where were their enemies? And their friends?

CHAPTER THIRTY-SIX

SLOTTER KEY, PORT MAJOR
DAY 218

Rafe and Teague, working together with Rafe's own tool kit and another set of special devices MacRobert procured from somewhere, were tracing the power supplies to the facility they thought was the site of the unusual fatalities. Grace, home from the office, reading files she'd hunted down, looked up from time to time. What they said was cryptic, techtalk she didn't know, but both the intensity of their concentration and the rising tension kept her checking in on them every little while. The file she'd pulled and was now marking offered hints at something deeper, less amenable to immediate action, than the flow of electrons to and from that facility.

Finally Teague said "Ahhh" in a tone that could only mean success, and Rafe said "Gotcha." She looked up again. Rafe turned away from the table and grinned at her.

"Good news?" she asked.

"We found it and we've identified all its input gates. Moreover,

Teague—and I bow before your genius, Teague—has coerced the power input main controller into accepting us—that is, Teague—as its new lord and master."

"And what have *you* done?" Grace asked. "You're looking far too smug to be a mere sidekick."

"Indeed," Rafe said. He puffed out his lips and raised an eyebrow. Grace laughed. "You wound me, Rector Vatta, indeed you do. To the core. However, because I am a sweet and generous soul . . ." Here Teague looked startled and Rafe glared at him. "When have I been less than sweet and gracious to you, Teague? What I was about to say . . . with Teague holding the controller at bay, I was able to induce a small power surge into one of the subsequent switches, and get into one—only one so far—of the server arrays. Those files are even now being sucked by the financial ansible, and apparently—but only apparently—being sent outsystem to a bleached recipient. Which would be me, if I were on Nexus, but I'm not and it isn't. Moreover, though usually a large send would trip an alarm, it won't now."

"I suppose you've already read all of them?"

"No, only a few headers. Enough to know we will want to read them in detail later. Right now I'm just sucking them away before doing whatever you want done to the installation. It's going to take awhile, even at max bandwidth, because the owners of this facility—not being utter fools—not only had quite competent security measures in place for intrusion, but anticipated that a slow outward bandwidth might be useful in preventing a faster loss." He smiled at her, a smile of such limpid, innocent joy that she knew it was faked. "What would you like done with this facility later?"

"Blow it up," Grace said. "In fact, why wait?"

"You don't anticipate needing any of the data stored there?"

Grace considered. "It might be useful. But it might be more useful to have the opposition's attention focused on their own problems, and not on Ky and the others."

"They're apt to react hastily and violently," MacRobert put in.

"I know. I know, and it's dangerous, but it's dangerous either way.

Throwing some confusion into their day—night—seems preferable to me. Though, since Rafe and Teague are not Slotter Key military personnel, I cannot order them to do so."

"A couple of foreign hoodlums?" MacRobert considered. "Mischief makers? Foreign agents? I don't think they'll go for that. They know perfectly well Ky's your niece and the military's your responsibility; they know about your past as Vatta's corporate spymaster. Even if they don't have any hooks into your office at all, they'll anticipate your involvement. It's going to rebound onto Vatta no matter what."

"It might. It probably will. When would be the ideal time to disrupt them?"

"Just as their mission starts," MacRobert said. "Especially if that's their communications link to their mission commander."

"Would they communicate early?" Rafe asked. "I was thinking they'd have it all worked out to a certain point, and might not report until they'd arrived."

"Depends how much fine control they want of their mercs. Would they trust them to run the op silently, or would they want to check up on them?"

"Remote surveillance," Grace said. "They won't transmit unless something goes badly wrong, but they will listen in."

"Via that facility," Teague said. "And the satellite they use."

"Which we control," Rafe said. He was watching his screen.

"There's not a way to increase the bandwidth?" Grace asked.

"Not without their knowing it right away. Separate alarm on that little item; if I could get to the hardware I could do it, but I can't do it from here, not with more than a sixty percent probability of success. And that's not enough."

"Right you are," Grace said. "Mac, where are the transports? Still dark on base?"

"Yes. No lights around them, no sign they're going to sneak out tonight. Of course there might not be, but yesterday sundown the vehicles were still parked nearby. No heat signatures of ground vehicles around them at all."

"Let your suck run, Rafe, and see if you can get into another array. In the long run, you're right—we want their data, enough to figure out who's behind this."

"When's Stella due?" MacRobert asked. Grace looked over at the table. He was frowning at something on his own pad.

"Why?"

"There's a news note from Cascadia. Four dead in mysterious and extremely discourteous assault in a respectable housing sector. A reminder to citizens to secure their quarters and report anything suspicious to the proctors. A reminder that discourtesy will not be tolerated and decorum must be maintained in all circumstances. Nothing from Vatta Enterprises, nothing from Stella."

"You think that was Stella? Did you look at the arrival/departure screen?"

"Looking now . . . merging with news. The dateline for the assault story is three—no, four—days back. Vatta courier departed in regular service, whatever that means, the same day as the assault . . ."

Grace leaned forward. "Stella's people would have informed us of her death or serious injury, I'm sure. Four dead and a courier departure suggests to me that she dealt with four discourteous persons and is on her way here."

"I thought Stella was the gentle one," Mac said, brows raised.

"Stella is quite capable." Grace shook a finger at him. "She doesn't like violence, or killing, but she also doesn't like being hurt and wants to stay alive. I'm certain the deaths were necessary in this case. Evidently the Cascadians agree, though I swear I do not understand their obsession with manners." She put her stack of files down. "I'm going to bed. I have an early meeting at the ministry tomorrow morning. Which of you lads is taking the watch?"

"I'll take first," Rafe said. "I want to see if I can niggle my way into another array and start sucking it dry. Teague, do you want to get some sleep now?"

"Sure." Teague pushed himself up.

Next morning, when Grace appeared, a red-eyed Rafe reported that he had sucked three of the eight arrays dry. "I can't do the others; I'm too fogged. Ky called and I gave her what we know up to now. They've left the main base; they got some vehicles moving. Not very fast, and she doesn't know where the passage leads. Finally." He yawned, shook his head. "Sorry. I've got to get some sleep. Teague will be here all day. I'll wake him now. If you want to download the files I shipped up to safe storage, he can pull them for you."

"Breakfast first?"

"No. I just need sleep." He headed for the bedroom. Grace and Mac ate their breakfast in peace; Teague appeared as they were leaving for the workday.

"Shall I redirect files to your office?" he asked.

"No," she said. "Send me a summary, if you find something juicy. I won't be back until evening, unless there's an emergency."

She said goodbye to Mac at the door to her building and he headed off on whatever he had in mind for the day. Sometimes he explained his plans and sometimes he reappeared at lunch, or in the evening, bringing home new packets of useful information about this or that. "It's less restful, but more fun, than running the security office at the Academy," he said. "And I'm on my own. If I take a four-hour break in one of Port Major's exotic brothels, nobody knows about it."

"You're sure of that?"

"Oh, yes. I'm the one who bugged the place; I know how to fox the bugs."

They had laughed, both aware that he was teasing her in her persona of Rector, not partner. She was used to his going about his duties—vaguely defined as they were—without consulting her on every plan or change thereto. "Lunch?" she asked. "Today's fish stew."

"Maybe. I'll let you know." He waved; she waved; she entered her office to find not only the quarterly meeting, but a string of appointments, waiting.

* * *

The quarterly budget meeting went on too long, as it always did. Grace paid close attention to which departments wanted more resources, and what for, and refused to commit to approving the whole thing until she had time to "make more inquiries." Nobody left satisfied, including her. She managed to keep her temper in check. Mostly.

Her assistant Derek's com light blinked. "Rector, Master Sergeant MacRobert requests that you receive a skullphone call from another party."

Grace blinked. That was not the way they usually communicated, and *what* other party? "I will speak with Master Sergeant MacRobert," she said. "Is he here? Send him in."

"He is not here, Rector. He was calling from . . . um . . . Joint Services Regional Command Three. That's—"

"Ordnay, I know," Grace said. Half a continent away, hours away by the fastest transport, and he hadn't told her he was going that far. Why?

"He disconnected after making his request, Rector."

Grace's skullphone gave its usual annoying internal buzz that made her back teeth itch. "Thank you, Derek," she said and punched the intercom off. The skullphone buzzed again. Why was Mac being this roundabout, setting up a call from another person through her assistant, instead of calling her himself? It had to be both important and secret, but why? He knew she preferred directness, especially with allies. What could possibly—*bzzzzt*—be his motive? Or . . . someone else's motive. That thought sent a cold chill down her back. She tongued the skullphone's alarm, turning it off.

"She's not answering." Arne Savance looked up from the console. "Nothing." He glanced at his boss, then at the older man strapped to a gurney, his unconscious face slack with the drug. He knew who the man was: retired master sergeant MacRobert, rumored to be the

Rector's lover and certain to be her agent. "Maybe should have kept him awake, Ser?"

"No." His boss had never shared a name. "He wasn't cooperative, and he's got a block it'll take longer to break. The assistant believed us, but perhaps the Rector had her alarm turned off. Perhaps she doesn't take skullphone calls in work hours. We'll keep trying."

"Call the assistant back, ask again?" Arne thought it just as likely the Rector had smelled a rat, but he had learned early in this organization not to offer suggestions.

"No. Static on the line won't fool the assistant again. We'll move MacRobert to another location; you stay here and monitor—if she answers, play the tape, and of course record anything she says. Full band."

"Yes, Ser."

The boss gestured to the two other men in the room, both burly and wearing what looked like hospital uniforms. They wheeled the gurney away, and the boss left with them. "Don't doze off, Arne. No breaks. Your relief will be in later."

Warnings, demands . . . he did not glare resentfully at the door when it closed, because he was sure the room had surveillance. He had thought—and Len as well—that this job would be both easy and stable, something they could rely on while the children were young, so Len could stay home with them and also work on his sculpture. So even though he had known, vaguely, that Malines & Company was bent as a corkscrew, he had believed that there was a straighter side, hiring ordinary techs and clericals, where he could draw a good salary and keep well away from the harsher activities that gave Malines its reputation.

It hadn't worked that way. But as long as he kept his head down and said *yes, Ser, no, Ser,* and *right away, Ser,* the money came in regularly, sometimes even a bonus. He and Len had a pleasant apartment in the Malines & Company neighborhood, the children were thriving in school, and Len could afford studio space and materials for his work.

He felt vaguely sorry for the old man on the gurney—but that wasn't his problem. His problem was monitoring all the Rector's communications, and especially her skullphone calls. And, long-term, doing exactly what he was told, when he was told, so that Len and the children were safe. He had been shown images of what could happen to the children of those who attempted to leave Malines & Company.

Over the next two hours, his mind wandered occasionally to the Rector, the little he knew about her, and the old man on the gurney. She was a Vatta, she was old, she had a bud-grown arm from having the original shot off. That cost a lot, and it had happened before she became Rector. How had she paid for it? What did it look like? He'd never seen her, except on a newsvid, and she was dark, like most of the Vattas, wrinkly, old. That's all he could remember. This old retired sergeant—was he a friend? Why would a Vatta like her be friends with someone like him? Surely they weren't really lovers.

Finally, his diligence was rewarded by a light on the console: the Rector was making an outbound skullphone call. Not, unfortunately, where the boss wanted her to make it. He captured the code; his console ran the code against the pre-loaded list. Her home com. He logged the call, and its duration, but was not able to record content. Skullphones had tighter security than ordinary phones, and the boss had told him not to tinker with any of the Rector's modalities. "Just record, or send the tape if she replies to the call."

Teague answered Grace's call on the house phone, and listened as she reported what had happened and what she had learned so far.

"He's not at Joint Services Regional Command. Wasn't expected, hadn't arrived, no one had seen him. My assistant says the call supposedly from him was full of static, and that he apologized for it. He thinks it was MacRobert's voice but he's not sure now that questions are being asked. All my incoming calls are recorded; I've listened to it and I don't think it's Mac, but it's close—it might be a composite recording or they might have an actor capable of sounding like him. I doubt the call came from that far away; it might even have originated from Port Major, but I can't tell. Would you be able to trace it?"

"Not from here," Teague said. "I'd need to get into your office system to have a chance. It'll have to be accessed there, I'm almost certain. You want Rafe; he's better at that."

She'd kept Rafe away from her workplace since that first day. She could hardly bring him in now and turn him loose on the communications system without risking his being discovered. So far—she thought and he thought—the cover story of his being an ISC technician sent to work on the system ansibles had held up.

"Problem?" Rafe asked. He sounded less sleepy than she expected.

"Yes," Grace said. She explained again, adding, "I think someone's snatched MacRobert. That would take very experienced operatives. I don't know if it's our main opposition or something else. He was close to the former Commandant; it could be that other elements have other agendas."

"Priorities," Rafe said. "Is it more important to find out where that call came from, or find and retrieve Mac?"

"Can you do one without the other?"

"How much time between when you two parted and the call?"

"Several hours; the meeting started ten minutes after I got there and lasted about two and a half. The call came in shortly after that."

"My take is he's here, in Port Major. I'll put Teague on that. Can you get me a hard-line link to your assistant's desk com?"

Grace paused. What he wanted was technically illegal. Dangerous, to let someone with Rafe's skills delve into the headquarters phone system. And yet—what choice did she have? Leaving aside her feelings for Mac, he was a longtime Spaceforce operative with secrets no one outside Spaceforce should know. His implant had an interrogation protocol, but if he'd been drugged, would it work? "Use your disguise. Call for an appointment with me concerning . . . let me think . . . your contract to fix the ansibles and my agreement that your work is satisfactory so far. I'll tell my assistant you called me, that he should squeeze you in."

"Two hours," Rafe said. "It takes that long to put all the pads in and be able to clear the scanners. I'll brief Teague and get him on his way—"

"Not to get caught, I hope."

"He's slippery," Rafe said. "Later."

Grace explained the need to squeeze Ser Bancroft in for an appointment in two hours—"ISC business, apparently. Something to do with the ansible work he and his associate have done." She dealt with the other appointments, all of them things people could have figured out for themselves if they'd been thinking. Then Rafe arrived, and came in still talking over his shoulder to her assistant, in a voice that was his, and yet not him.

"And that's the choice I've been authorized to give the Rector— a full-service contract, or onsite training for— Oh, good afternoon, Rector. I was just saying—"

"Do come in, Ser Bancroft. I'm afraid I don't have that long, but I understand you've a message from ISC headquarters?"

She shut the door behind him and let him take her seat at her desk. His briefcase, full of an array of instruments, opened at a touch.

"Yes, Rector," he went on. He picked up her desk com, tipped it upside down, and loosened screws as he talked. "There's a new policy on maintenance, as I suspected there might be, and it saved a trip back here to wait and see . . . as you know, your local repair of your system ansible was sufficient for it to work, but not at 100 percent speed and efficiency, because your local technicians did not understand the finer points of its construction." He went on talking what sounded like a typical sales presentation as he took the outer case off, disemboweled the innards, and spread them on the desktop. Tiny pincers attached here and there to various bits, with leads back into his case.

Without a change in his voice—in the same prissy Cascadian accent—Rafe went on even as he glanced up and winked, his hands moving confidently among the instruments. "My assistant, Ser Teague, has been looking for a suitable site, and suppliers, in anticipation that your government may choose the onsite education option. You may not know that he is a certified technical instructor for ISC, as am I, and either one of us might be assigned here for the instructional period—" He nodded to her, pointed a finger. *Your turn.*

Grace took up the conversation smoothly. "Ser Bancroft, you surely know that as Rector of Defense I cannot speak for the entire government—" She winked.

He took over again, another spate of glib verbiage, and they continued to exchange speaker and listener roles until he mentioned "system security" and that provided an excuse for her to turn her privacy cylinder to full.

They grinned at each other.

"I'm reading your system and your system's call record," Rafe said, in his normal voice. "Thank you for getting that call-time for me before I arrived. Your assistant said there was static—that can be artificially induced, of course. Ah. That call did not match any satellite record, so if it was at a distance, it was through local wireless or landline. There's a local wireless call—"

"You're sucking all the phone records?"

"Luckily for me, Slotter Key's communications are ninety-nine percent government-owned. A hundred percent here in Port Major. I'm into your system; I'm into everything. Let's see. Comparison . . . two matches. Wireless; transfer nexus number 84—that's Bolt and Fifty-Seventh. The other is a landline, both to this office within a few seconds of each other. Landline . . . 15 Bolt Street, commercial account, Malines Shipping and Handling."

"I was only told of one."

"Right. The landline call came in first."

"Where's Teague?"

"Somewhere in the warehouse district. Do you know that area?"

"Malines is organized crime," Grace said. "They own several blocks, and control an area larger than that."

"I'll contact Teague. Just let me reconstruct this; won't take long." Rafe's fingers seemed to flicker in Grace's gaze as he pulled connections, replaced components, reassembled her desk com. "Thing is, your assistant's bent. How long have you had him?"

"Quarter year, a little more. Olwen's husband got a job at Dalmouth—it's only about seventy kilometers, but she has children in school and didn't want the long commute."

"Around the time of Ky's arrival?"

"No, about—let me think—ninety days or so after the crash. You think there's a connection?"

"No reason you should. Who did her husband get a job with, and does Malines have enough influence to sway an employer without her husband knowing?"

"Probably. He's not street-smart, nor was Olwen. But Derek—he's done a good job until now."

"A good job keeping an eye on you. All right. The topic is a possible maintenance contract. Kill the privacy."

Grace reached for the cylinder, starting to talk before she turned it off. "That's my opinion, Ser Bancroft [click] but I can't promise that the Council or the President will have the same." Slick as wet seals, she thought, as she and Rafe finished up what would seem like the same conversation, eventually passing the question of which imaginary maintenance scheme to choose off to another branch of government, and finishing with polite social comments.

CHAPTER THIRTY-SEVEN

PORT MAJOR,
HARBOR SECTOR
DAY 219

Teague eased his way along the crowded streets of the shopping district, eastward toward the port area. The shopping district extended a tongue of attractive gentility all the way to the waterfront, providing reasonable access for a tourist while taking him within a short distance of warehouses, transport depots, and eventually the working docks. Occasional whiffs of fish and spoilage eddied along the pretty sidewalks with their cafés and shops. He had been here before; he was certain some of the people would recognize him. His transformation had matured; he felt comfortable now with the different length of leg and arm, with the color of his skin, the texture of his hair, how he looked in the mirror, and how he felt moving around.

Lines had formed at street vendor carts; he opted for the quick-serve window of a café tucked into the side of a street so narrow it might have been an alley. "Whitefish wrap," he said, just like the man ahead of him, and he had the correct change ready for the hand that reached for it. His wrap, fish and vegetables in a spicy sauce wrapped in a flatbread, matched half the food pedestrians were carrying. Instead of turning back to the street he'd left, he moved on, not hurrying but not loitering, either.

He'd been told, two tendays ago, that down here was "Malines' place," a rough quarter to stay away from if he didn't want trouble. He'd walked down that other street once, straight to the end, briskly, as if he had business at the docks at the end. He had in fact gone into a wholesale hardware dealer, inquiring about a possible job. Now he headed in a different direction, one block over, his electronic kit active, feeding data into his implant, and in his hand a black business folder with an ISC logo on the front. Inside were instructions from a "Region IV Maintenance Education Upgrade Center" directing him to find potential locations for training local technicians to ansible work at ISC's standards, including the requirements by square meters, electrical service, environmental quality, and so on.

On his own, on the basis of prior trips into the city, he had decided that somewhere in the neighborhood of Malines & Company was the nearest place MacRobert could have been taken for interrogation. But which of the blocks, and which building on that block?

MacRobert, inert and apparently unconscious, listened to the voices discussing what would be done with him. He did not approve, but he did not show—by a flicker of eyelid or a change in heart rate, breathing, or blood pressure—that he was no longer fully under the drug they had used. He'd had just enough time to trigger his implant's safety mode.

"Dead to the world," said one of the voices. "The monitors say he's still deep in."

"He's old," said the other. "Takes longer. Let him be another hour, maybe two. Then the antidote'll wake him up quick. Now, his heart might give out."

The sound of feet moved away; a door opened and closed. MacRobert lay still. He assumed the room had surveillance, and he was probably still hooked up to whatever life signs monitor they used. He might not have the two hours—they might return in ten minutes to make sure—but for the moment, he was better off playing dead, or nearly.

Why had they grabbed him today? He assumed whoever had done it was in league with those who'd sabotaged the shuttle, but who, and why? Had someone detected Teague's and Rafe's intrusion into their data center? Or his own poking around in Spaceforce assignments? Or was it a general attack on the Rector and those known to be on her staff?

All would be clear later, he reminded himself; he had more to do to make his implant secure in case they probed it. He triggered the next phase of his implant's safety mode. Certain information disappeared from his access; the top level—the first a probe would find, and what he now believed to be the implant itself—proclaimed itself a replacement module, with a date of placement a year and two tendays before. Its data tree included "Medical History: Current Treatment Plan" and informed him that he was entering Stage 2b Age-Related Dementia with memory loss, speech disinhibition with confabulation, fine motor tremor (stage one), and gross motor discoordination not affecting locomotion; that he also had early-stage cardiac insufficiency, moderate hypertension, and an enlarged prostate, being treated with a variety of medications administered once daily under supervision.

When he queried for more, he found a set of simple instructions: a morning alarm meant get up, then shower, clean his teeth, depilate his face, use deodorant, put on specified clothes in the specified order, check that all fastenings were fastened, to the kitchen, eat breakfast, take the medications he was offered, go to the car, and get in. He could access graphics that walked him to and from approved nearby stores and guided him to appropriate selections inside, then to checkout. In case he wandered, he had access to graphics that would guide him back to Grace's city residence or automatically call for medical aid if he fell.

The door opened. He lay still. "No change. I told you—it'll be another couple of hours."

"Have you made the call?"

"Not yet. She's in a meeting: no messages."

So they were going to use him as a hostage against Grace? Good luck with that. He wanted to chuckle at the thought, but knew better. He was old, sick, senile, and helpless under the drug's control. He felt a sting on the side of his neck, but did not react. A dull scraping, as the probe tried for the emergency implant port, the one that would let them download without damaging his brain.

A flood of curse words, some he'd never heard before but knew by the tone were curses.

"What?"

"It's a replacement. He must've failed a psych eval at his annual physical last year. They pulled his implant and put in a medical message: diagnosis, treatment plan, medications. Next layer's all the kind of thing these people need. Step by step through the day, help getting to a store, finding what to buy, and so on."

"How can he be that bad? Why's he not in care?"

"Rector, probably. She likes him. Maybe she doesn't mind sleeping with a half-wit; she's old herself."

They laughed. MacRobert thought of killing each one slowly, but did not allow himself to move.

"So he's no use to us? Interrogation won't work on him?"

"It might. Or he might remember his childhood, his mummy kissing him good night, and nothing since he was five. And he's of use to us because the Rector cares about him, has kept him with her for a year since he failed the psych eval. That's our lever. We keep him alive and healthy—well, healthy enough—and see if she'll cooperate. If not—the ocean is deep."

"The ocean is deep, and the fish are hungry," said the other, as if it was a ritual. It probably was. Footsteps moved away; the door opened and closed again.

Two hours to wait. Maybe. Maybe longer. Maybe they'd decide to dose him again, or maybe they'd let him wake up and try questioning him, seeing if he was really impaired. He felt impaired, with the main data banks of his implant closed to him. He put so much in there, and—like anyone used to an implant—didn't bother remembering what wasn't needed short-term. That was a daunting thought. He couldn't now remember the name of the continent Ky was on—he remembered Ky on her last day as a cadet, and something—something important she'd done—but the rest was hazy. He knew, in a vague way, where Spaceforce Academy was, but he couldn't remember his access code or the phone number. Maybe the Miznarii had a point about implants being a form of humodification.

He did remember how to bring his implant out of safety mode. That would unlock the data banks. But it might be dangerous. He lifted his eyelids just a little. He didn't know what he was looking for. He should know. He should know if the scary people were there, or had left something to watch him, but—it was too tempting. He performed the mental trick that took his implant out of safety and back into performance.

    access main data? y/n

Yes. He could spell yes. Data poured back into his awareness. Now the blur of a distant wall made sense: gray, lined with acoustic baffling material. If he screamed in here, no one would hear it. The door had the same coating. Surveillance? Most surveillance cameras had a blinking light; he saw none through his lashes. He opened his eyes a little more. No cameras. How odd. His implant informed him he had been completely unconscious for two hours, unresponsive for another forty-three minutes, and the visit by his captors had been seven minutes twenty-eight seconds before. Grace's meeting would be ending soon, he expected.

Sound baffling had the added effect that he could not hear his captors returning. Not good. He expected they would be back after calling her, to show he was alive, to threaten . . . and he needed at least a few seconds to put his implant back in safe mode and make it seem the replacement implant of an old man sliding into senility. He didn't want to do that. Even the short time he'd endured that loss bothered him much more than he'd expected.

His implant informed him that five minutes had passed. Then six. By then he had wiggled his feet, his hands, realizing that he was restrained, though not painfully, where he lay. If he couldn't even get up, he couldn't do much about escape—yet. He took several minutes subvocalizing more instructions to his implant. He did not have a drug analysis application, and attempting a skullphone call could probably be detected. He wished he knew what drug he'd been given, and how long it was supposed to act, because surely they'd dose him again if Grace didn't return their call. Unless they wanted him awake, to see if he really was confused.

And it was troubling that even now, with his implant's full function connected again, he could not quite remember what he'd been doing when he was taken, how that had happened. He added a few more things to his fixit list, then put his implant back into safety mode and restored covert status.

It felt like being stuck in the aftermath of concussion. Everything he had just been thinking about, had done, disappeared into a fog. Where was he? What had happened? He wasn't comfortable; he didn't recognize anything; he did not know the two men who came in to him some interminable time later.

"She's not going to call." Teague, ambling along the street with his briefcase and his list of criteria for instructional space, heard that from the hidden spike-mic. Aha. The range of a spike-mic varied with the material of the walls it read through. All the walls around him were brick. He knew the speakers were just inside the brick wall on the same side of the street. A warehouse-looking building, Ma-lines & Company. Ahead of him, a couple of burly men lounged at the entrance. Without breaking stride, he used his skullphone to ping Rafe and walked up to them.

"If it is possible to speak to the building manager?" he said. His accent wasn't quite Cascadian, but it certainly was not local.

"What are you doin' around here? Where you from? What's those papers?"

Teague blinked, squinting a little at them. "It is my job. It is my assignment. To find space to start instructional program for techni-cians to do advanced maintenance on system ansibles and their boosters."

One of the men snatched the papers from his hand.

"Excuse me, that is not correct," Teague said. "Those are my pa-pers."

"They were. Let's see—" The man looked at them. "Wait—ISC? You work for ISC?"

"Yes, yes." Teague nodded several times. "It is my assignment to find space to start instructional program—"

"We heard that already." The man who held his papers looked at the other one, the one who had moved slightly to block Teague if he tried to grab the papers back. "Cole, this might interest Dugmund. Give him a call." To Teague he said, "Why are you in this part of town? Didn't anyone tell you the dock district is dangerous for strang-ers?"

"It is the daytime," Teague said, as if nothing could be dangerous by day. "And docks have warehouses and warehouses have empty spaces sometimes. On my world temporary rental of warehouse space costs less than the same in office buildings. It is not . . . not in-tending any insult, but it is not as comfortable or fancy as the office space, but for instructional space it can be made useful cheaply as it is not for long-term use. Eventually local educational institutions take over the job of training new technicians, but initially, and to ensure compatibility with all aspects of ISC equipment, only ISC can train."

"I suppose that makes sense," Cole said. "Our boss would like to speak with you. Our warehouse is usually full, but merchandise does move in and out. An opening might arise at some time; he wouldn't want to miss out on a deal." He nodded to the other man without saying his name. "Give him back his papers; he can show the boss."

Teague considered the advantages of dispatching both of them, but other pedestrians were in view. Instead he went inside when Cole beckoned, into a wide passage with doors open to offices on either side. "All the way back," Cole said from behind him. Teague's instruments reported that the offices were fake-fronts, empty, open at the back to the larger space, and that Cole was coming closer behind him. Handy.

Still holding the papers, he let the pick slide into his hand from his sleeve and slowed, closing the distance, turning to his left. "Say— maybe you should give these to your boss yourself—" He held out his hand, offering them.

Cole, startled, stopped off balance, grabbed for the papers, and Teague thrust the pick through Cole's hand. Its thin sheath shattered; the powerful paralytic drug took hold even as Teague moved in, his right arm around Cole's shoulder, pushing the pick, now protruding from Cole's hand, into his chest. He squeezed the handle, injecting more of the drug. Cole shuddered; eyes wide. He could not breathe; he could not speak; he could not do anything but die as the drug reached his heart and then his brain.

Teague swung the now-sagging, inert body over to the nearest fake office door, opened it, and let Cole fall inside. One down. He glanced back. The other man was still outside, had not come to the door to watch. He activated another of the instruments, giving him a view in his implant of the building's plan. On the ground floor, behind the fake offices, there were ten enclosures, seven of them full of dense material. Merchandise, most likely. Two of the other enclosures were small, only a few meters wide and long. One was larger.

MacRobert, he was sure, would be in one of the smaller ones. But which? He changed the adjustment, added in the spike-mic tuned to human voices.

"We should probably give him another dose. If she doesn't call soon, he'll be wide awake." Voice one, no ID.

"We could just let him stew. It might loosen him up. Nobody can hear him, anyway." Voice two, no ID.

"You saw the implant scan. Heart condition, brain deteriorating. Probably anything he tells us will be useless."

"It might influence her when she does call."

"What if she's got people looking for him? What if she's contacted— what was that base you said?—and knows he was never there."

"She'll think he was taken there, or en route. Or, if in the city, by someone Spaceforce-related."

Teague knew where the speakers were now, just outside one of the small rooms. A sound-baffled room. Two voices outside. He changed settings again and wriggled the stunner in his sleeve down to his hand, concealed by the papers. On this level, only two more figures moved around, at the back of the building, isolated by a solid wall up to the next level. Above were a dozen at least, arrayed in rows—the real offices, he suspected.

The passage he was in ended at a door with a window. He went to it, tapped very lightly, then opened it and went in. Nothing, as he suspected; instead of a back wall, a gap to either side and a shoulder-high blank wall beyond it. He hesitated, aware of the camera above this space, and looked back and forth as if confused.

"Hello?"

No answer. He moved to the right, beyond the line of fake offices on the side of the passage he'd come from, into another, its right wall outlining the larger empty room. Ahead of him, two men standing in the passage turned to look at him then moved toward him quickly.

"Who the hell are you? How did you get in here?"

Teague flapped the papers he held. "Ser . . . Cole? One of the men by the door . . . he called somebody . . . you? He said I should meet the boss? He said this way and he was behind me, but then he wasn't?"

"He must've called Dugmund," the taller man said. "He should have taken him upstairs all the way." The men exchanged looks. "I'll go. Won't be long. You—what's your name?"

"Edvard Teague," Teague said. "You can see on my papers—" He offered them, taking a step closer. "It is about seeking rental space for a training facility for—"

"Let's see, then." The man reached out. He was in balance, and clearly very fit. The second man, alert and equally dangerous looking, made his earlier kill move too risky. Teague shifted his grip on the briefcase, touching a button on the handle with the inside of his ring finger. As the taller man took the papers, Teague thumbed the stunner control; the second stunner, extruded from the side of the brief-case, caught the second man. Both went down, twitching. Teague stunned them again. The door to the sound-baffled room opened easily; the man on the narrow cot, bound to it, stared at him wide-eyed, frightened. It was MacRobert, but he did not seem to recognize Teague. That must be the drugs they'd used.

He pulled the other two into the room, blocked the door open with a wastebasket so his spike-mic could pick up sounds outside, and sliced through MacRobert's restraints. Under the blanket, MacRobert was naked, and Teague saw none of his clothes in the room. What he did see was a rolling cart with medications and injec-tors ready. He injected both men, a full vial each—it might kill them and would certainly keep them quiet. He stripped the one closer to MacRobert's size, finding an interesting collection of objects he stuffed quickly into his pockets, and turned back to the cot.

MacRobert was sitting up, clear-eyed now. "Teague," he said. His voice was weak, a little hoarse.

"Yes. Here. Get dressed."

MacRobert reached for the shirt and shoved an arm into it. "Where are we?" His voice sounded more like him.

"Malines' warehouse, one of them."

"Are they dead?" MacRobert had both arms in the shirt and a leg in the trousers.

"Not yet," Teague said. "Do we need what's in their heads?"

"Possibly, but we need out of here more, and we need them not to be able to say how."

"Fine." Teague loaded the injector again and gave them each two more vials. "That should do it."

Mac, dressed but barefoot, pulled shoes off the smaller man. He shook his head at the man's socks, one with a hole in the toe and the other in the heel. "Sweaty, too," he said, pulling the socks on with a grimace. "And the shoes don't really fit." He pulled the closure over as far as it would go. "I may make more noise than usual."

"Can you run in them?"

"I will run in them." Grim confidence in that.

"There's a guard at the front door, that I know of, and the back two-thirds of the building is isolated from this area. Building's at the corner of Horn and Bleeker Alley." He was on the skullphone, pinging Rafe with the location as well as telling MacRobert. The phone came live.

"Situation?"

"Three down, subject alive, expect trouble on exit."

"Can hold ten?"

"No more than six, I'd say. Outside, inside?"

"Get close to the exit. Expect distractions."

He turned to MacRobert. "Ready?"

"Very." For a man supposedly suffering the conditions Teague knew had been loaded into his implant, and the aftermath of abduction and drugging, MacRobert looked remarkably alert.

Teague led him back the way he himself had come. When they arrived at the back side of the fake office at the end of the outer passage, he could see through the door the tall door guard coming toward them, talking into a handcom.

"Lovely," Teague murmured. "Here—take this—" He handed MacRobert a blackjack. "I'll open the door, and he's yours. First, anyway."

The tall man didn't give Teague a chance to open the door; he yanked it open himself, saying, "I said I'll find him!" and MacRobert whapped him neatly with the blackjack. Teague caught the handcom before it hit the floor and thumbed it off.

"Have anything less basic?" MacRobert asked, pocketing the blackjack.

"Have a stunner," Teague offered, handing over his.

"And you?"

"Another stunner in the briefcase, a couple of good knives."

They headed down the outer passage. Teague glanced at MacRobert just as the older man whipped around and fired the stunner back toward the interior. "Just one," MacRobert said. "Keep going."

Noise outside then, and sirens approaching. Then a crash, the sound of bricks or stones clattering down, glass breaking. Teague could feel the impact through his feet. Dust shimmered down from the ceiling.

"Good," MacRobert said. He was grinning now, eyes bright and face no longer pale. "The party's started."

"Party?" Teague asked. "Oh—and I have a pistol in my right jacket pocket, if you want it. Belonged to one of those guys I dragged in."

"I do." MacRobert took it, popped the clip. "Spudders. Perfect." He snapped the clip back in and chambered a round. "You have one for yourself?" He put the pistol in his pocket.

"Yes. I'd rather not display it. It makes me a target."

"And it's noisy. Reliable, not stealthy. This stunner's down to thirty percent."

They were almost to the outer door. Teague motioned MacRobert to stay back, pulled a 'scope from his right sleeve and bent the end of the fiber to make a corner, then slid it to the edge of the doorframe.

The image appeared in his implant. A ramshackle truck had rammed into the corner of the building, doing major damage to the truck and significant damage to the building, scattering bricks and broken glass over the pavement. A man hung halfway out the driver's side of the cab, bleeding down the truck door. City Patrol cars blocked the street beyond. Patrol officers in riot gear faced an unruly crowd, some of them now turning away as more sirens neared.

The image blanked. Teague's skullphone pinged. Rafe's voice: "The moment of exodus is upon us. To the right, slow, stay with me; we want some of this crowd."

Teague waved his hand; MacRobert and he stepped out, heads down, and joined those already moving to the right. Rafe, in his fat suit but dressed in dirty laborer's clothes, walked past, giving Teague and MacRobert a good look at his face.

"Got him?" Teague asked MacRobert.

"Friend of a friend," MacRobert said.

Teague nodded. They had just reached the next street when the crowd behind them roared, other pedestrians broke into a run, and Teague heard the characteristic sounds of riot gas canisters popping. MacRobert started running, a little awkwardly; Teague dropped back to shield him from contact. Rafe turned left at the corner, dropped to a walk, and strode briskly along the uneven sidewalk, staying close to the building. Teague and MacRobert followed, Teague on the outside. They passed an alley with men moving purposefully toward the street, on to the end of that block, and then another. Behind them, a siren burped, whined, burped again. Rafe glanced back but did not slow. The siren came no nearer.

Three blocks, and they were approaching the first office buildings. Another left turn onto a wider street. A vehicle parked on their side of the street blinked lights. "There," Rafe said. He went to the front door, pointing to the back. Teague opened it for MacRobert, then slid in beside him. Rafe, up front, was talking to the driver as if he knew him.

The car was already in motion, pulling smoothly away, into traffic that seemed completely normal for the time of day, just after midafternoon. Rafe turned. "Teague, MacRobert, this is Inyo Vatta. We are going to Vatta Transport's hangars at the airport."

"I've met Inyo," MacRobert said. "Thank you. Who's that hanging out the truck door, Rafe?"

"The right man," Rafe said. "There's another in the back. Both deaders. I was engaged with the second one when you pinged me, Teague." He sounded relaxed and happy. Teague, remembering Gary's briefing on Rafe's past, which had been extensive, understood. Rafe felt the way he did. Action had that effect on some people. "Mac, you should call Grace. Use my handcom; that number will go through."

"Skullphone won't?"

"Not until she knows you're safe, and then only from yours." He passed it over the back of the front seat while Inyo drove on, neither hurrying nor lagging.

Teague watched MacRobert, then turned away. In addition to the lift he always got in an operation, this was the first time he'd used his new body in a real situation. He was happy with how it functioned, the integration he'd achieved with it. He was, he thought, just as good an operative now as he had ever been, and he knew he'd been one of Gary's best. MacRobert was talking very softly into the handcom, just a couple of phrases, then he handed the com back to Rafe.

Within a few turns, they were out of the port area completely, passing tall office blocks and then a long gray wall that Teague had learned enclosed the Spaceforce Academy. That arched entrance they passed must have been where Ky Vatta walked out to meet a car very like this after resigning. He wondered why any sane person would lock themselves into the military with all its pomp and ceremony. And now she was an admiral—she must be crazy.

When they reached the airport, they passed the entrance to the main terminal, turning in to General Aviation, and then to a gate marked with Vatta's insignia. There Inyo stopped and exchanged passwords with a guard in Vatta blue. Teague relaxed as they rolled on toward a group of buildings, all marked VATTA TRANSPORT.

Inyo drove into one of the hangars where several aircraft were parked. One was a smaller, twin-engine craft that—from the number of windows—might hold eight or ten passengers and crew. Its boarding hatch was open, steps placed leading into it. The other was much larger, with no windows, suggesting a cargo craft. Crew in Vatta blue were moving luggage to a ramp-belt into it: obvious suitcases and crates that might contain anything.

"What's going on?" MacRobert asked. "I need to talk to the Rector, tell her what happened."

"Other things have happened," Rafe said. "When we're really secure, I'll tell you, but for now—*Vanguard*'s back insystem, and so is a Mackensee troopship. They came in fast and hard, but they're still two days out on insystem; shuttles can't reach the surface until they're orbital. Spaceforce is not happy about them. So far the merc ship isn't public, because the Rector put a lock on all space-based communications, to the point of demoting a Spaceforce security commander."

Teague blinked and held his tongue. His thoughts bristled with questions he obviously shouldn't ask. MacRobert, however, asked the most salient. "War?"

"Not yet. Not at all, if our side's fast and clever. I will say, in spite of being around her for almost half a local year, I still didn't anticipate the depth and complexity of the Rector's thinking."

MacRobert laughed aloud. "Boyo, you still don't know the half of that woman. I don't. To be perfectly frank—and Inyo, I know you'll tell her everything we say—"

Inyo snorted. "Me, Ser? I wouldn't dare not."

"She could run anything, including Ky's fleet and two planets, if she wanted to. Luckily for the rest of humanity, her desire for power is mostly confined to one planet and she only micromanages when she has to. Do we exit now?"

"Not yet, Sers. We're waiting for word from the Rector."

"Do you know where we're going?"

"No, Ser, and if I did I couldn't tell you."

"All right." MacRobert turned to Rafe. "You want to be careful with your Ky when you have her back. She's got a lot of her aunt Grace in her. You may think she's not as strategic a thinker, but neither was Grace at that age, she tells me. And it's no insult to you to say you're going to have to stretch to match her."

"I'm aware of Ky's abilities," Rafe said. "And respect them. We are not competitive. Well, except in marksmanship, unarmed combat, things like that."

"Good. Who really does shoot better?"

"Equal within five percent. Sometimes she takes it, sometimes I do."

"Better."

"And she's wicked fast in hand-to-hand."

"She always was," MacRobert said. "Her Academy instructors had to match her against upper-class cadets by the second term her first year. She was best against taller cadets who thought that gave them an advantage."

He stretched and sighed with relief. Teague thought some muscle kink had just let go. "She's really not—well, she was only a cadet when I saw her most—but the one thing that worried me was that although she stuck to the regs, did everything correctly, I got the feeling that her real talent was, like the Rector's, well outside any box, and the military is all about staying inside boxes until the shit starts flying. It has to be. Military personnel let loose always get into trouble; you've got to keep them focused, constrained, until combat situations, then hope they've got an outside-the-box ability. Huge problem with training young officers in peacetime. Easiest ones to train and evaluate are the in-the-box thinkers. They do what they're told with great energy and diligence and precision. Can't fault that in a cadet."

Rafe shook his head. "She surprised me when I first met her. I was thinking young, inexperienced, priggish—got part of that from Stella—and figured I could play her. Wrong."

"Sers, you may exit the car now. I've had word, and here comes your escort."

Teague tensed up, but the two men and one woman coming through a side door were in Vatta uniforms. He read them as allies. Inyo had already opened MacRobert's door; Teague got out as Rafe did. Some signal passed. "Sera Vatta has already cleared your paperwork," the woman said. "Sers, you may board now, or freshen up in the crew quarters. Sera Vatta thought you might wish that. Fresh clothes have been provided for all of you."

"I would enjoy that," MacRobert said. "If it doesn't inconvenience anyone."

"Follow us, please."

Teague was surprised at the accommodations, but glad to have a shower to himself and his own clothes from the Rector's house to put on afterward. A buffet was ready for them when he came out.

"We have a scheduled cargo flight in one hour fifteen minutes," the woman said as they filled their plates. "You will need to board twenty minutes before."

"What about the other flight?"

"Decoy. It will go to Corleigh, with three passengers as well as pilot and copilot. You will be on that manifest."

"Risky for the passengers," Teague said.

"Riskier for attackers," she said, smiling. "It only looks like a Vatta family passenger plane." She did not explain further. "Master Sergeant, if you will come into the office, there's a secure connection to the Rector's office. She's waiting for your call."

CHAPTER THIRTY-EIGHT

SLOTTER KEY NEARSPACE, SDF *VANGUARD II*
DAY 219

Master Sergeant Pitt, once more serving as liaison between the Mackensee Military Assistance Corporation and what she kept thinking of as "Ky Vatta's Fleet," had been much less concerned than Ky's flag captain when they first contacted Slotter Key's Rector of Defense and learned that Master Sergeant MacRobert had been abducted. She'd met the man and had no doubt he could take care of himself, never mind he was one or more decades older than she was. Her concern was more for Ky Vatta, alive on a remote frozen continent with local enemies ready to pounce as soon as they got a weather window that allowed it. She'd seen Ky survive bad situations before, but eventually luck always ran out. It was only a question of which time.

"I can't believe they don't have some well-trained ground troops," Captain Pordre said. Pitt had him pegged as smart, a good ship-handler, loyal to his admiral, and tenacious in pursuit of any goal. All to the good. But also of limited foreign experience, which wasn't.

"No war for a long time, is what I heard, Captain," she said when he looked at her as if expecting more. "No immediate need, people get sloppy."

That was what kept mercenary companies solvent: planets, corporations, anyone who needed troops for some reason and hadn't bothered to fund proper training for their own. Pitt, as a senior NCO and trusted liaison in many a situation, had learned to conceal contempt for the unpreparedness of their clients and display a tough sympathy she didn't actually feel. Or not very often. In a universe full of cantankerous humans—some of them lazy or ignorant and others vicious and strong—Mackensee found ample opportunity for work that did not impinge on their founder's notions of right and wrong. Few mercs lacked employment, even the worst. Mackensee, Pitt knew for certain, was the best she'd ever seen.

"Why didn't they hire you?" Pordre asked.

"No data, Captain. Could have been cost—Mackensee doesn't come cheap. Or knowing we'd been part of Admiral Vatta's forces at the Battle of Nexus. It was fairly clear in the celebrations afterward that the admiral and I were acquainted, and that she'd been involved with Mackensee more than once. An employer might have had doubts about us in that instance. Or maybe they asked and our senior staff refused, for the same reason."

"But you know this outfit they did hire? The ... uh ... Black Torch?"

"Suspected of being pirate-connected, Captain. Bad rep in terms of discipline and higher military science, but tough dirty fighters. Hard to control, for their employers." They'd had almost this conversation when she first came aboard, but if he chose to fill the necessary hours on insystem drive with things he'd already asked and she'd already answered, it was not her problem. Lavin and Cotter, over on the Mackensee troopship, were taking care of the mission planning. She would transfer back when they went into Slotter Key Local, and Ofulo, whose leg was still not 100 percent, would come here in her place. There'd been some commentary about the irregu-

larity of changing liaisons right before action, but her history with Ky
Vatta had prevailed. She knew she'd never get Ky into Mackensee, as
she'd once hoped, but she felt a connection to the young woman and
hoped to meet her again. As well, her own daughter was in the hero-
worshipping phase and had begged for an autograph.

"Ah—" Captain Pordre tapped his earbug. "Good news. Master
Sergeant MacRobert, the Rector's personal assistant, has been extri-
cated."

"I can't say I'm surprised, sir," Pitt said. "But pleased, of course. In
good health, I hope?"

"Apparently, yes. You met him, I believe?"

"Yes, on Cascadia, after the destruction of the pirate fleet. Very
capable person."

He looked away again for a moment, then turned to her. "Master
Sergeant, your CO wants to speak with you. I will inform Communications that you have permission to use a unit in the shack."

"Thank you, Captain." Pitt saluted and left the bridge, wondering
what the colonel wanted this time. She wasn't due to transfer for another day and a half, and she already knew MacRobert had been
found alive and well. She had transmitted her post-downjump report
the day before; perhaps he had some comments on it.

"It's encrypted," the com chief said. "You have the key?"

"Yes, Chief." She always had the key. It would have been a breach
of security to have the key anywhere but on her person at all times
when away from Mackensee. She slid it into the holder, and the
holder into the port, wondering once again why, when every ordinary computer she'd ever seen used the same two dataports, every
shipboard communicator manufacturer had its own proprietary encryption slot. She nodded to the com chief, closed the privacy screen,
and in a few seconds the document appeared.

CONTENTS:

1) SITREP received K. Vatta at 1320 Ship Standard this day
   via Office of Rector of Defense G. Vatta.

2) SITREP received Office of Rector of Defense G. Vatta 1320
   Ship Standard this day.

   SECURITY LEVEL DAGON

   ACTION REQUIRED: Analysis & Recommendations for Assault Group Meeting by 2200 Ship Standard this day. Ac-
   knowledge receipt.

She entered the correct code. The message went on its way and she
started reading, then stopped, blanked the viewer, and opened the
privacy curtain.

"Chief?"

"Yes, Master Sergeant?"

"This message is big and I need to be here awhile, and then I'll
need a wipe. And I have an equally big encrypted reply I have to send
by 2200 this evening. How inconvenient is that going to be?"

"Not bad. Better now than tomorrow morning. I can have someone bring you a sandwich later—"

"I'll need to lock this terminal if I leave."

"Fine. I'll tell Lieutenant Garth when she returns."

Pitt sealed the curtain again and started reading. Admiral Vatta's sitrep was concise, clear, laying out the conditions of the survivors, the
resources they had found, and her plan to keep them alive under attack.

Pitt ran a hand through her hair. Given the small number of survivors, what they expected to face, and the resources they'd been told
the opposition had, it was probably the only possible thing to do, but
it was risky. She pulled up the enclosed satellite scans of the continent. She'd been imagining "barren terraforming failure" as a simple
chunk of rock, pretty much the same from end to end, but it wasn't.
The poleward side was bleak—probably a glacier had scraped over it
at some point—with cliffs to the ocean below, but the other side had
actual mountains with forests on them.

She read through the rest as fast as she could.

* * *

The passenger compartment of Vatta Transport's night flight to Portmentor was a roomy area with seating for fourteen that converted into bunks, a conference area with a table, a good-sized galley, and even a shower as well as two toilets. The only difference from luxury passenger travel was the lack of windows. Forward, the door to the flight deck was open; a crew compartment offered two bunks for the crew, with one already curtained off. The reserve pilot had gone straight to bed. Pilots were already aboard, running through checklists and rechecking the flight plan.

MacRobert, who had been invited forward, saw a squat little tractor approaching. "Our tug?"

"Yeah. Though we're waiting for a last arrival. It's almost to the gate."

The tug moved into the hangar; its driver hopped down and hooked the towbar to the nose wheel of the small plane below them. "That still seems like a risky flight to me."

"Shouldn't be. There's additional cover, but I'm not supposed to talk about it."

"Never mind," Mac said. He saw a big dark car come around the curve of the drive, stop at the checkpoint, and approach. It certainly looked official—long, black, mirrored windows. It eased in between their plane and the small one. The view darkened as a screen unrolled from the hangar opening.

"Doors take too long," the pilot said. "And we can still see out."

Mac looked out the side window. Two men got out, one shorter and plumper than the other, then two women—one of them Grace, in one of the dresses she wore to work, and the other in a very similar dress, who looked to be about the same height, same skin color, and white hair cut short and tousled, like Grace's. All but Grace got into the smaller plane; the door closed; within thirty seconds the tug's warning lights came on, the curtain at the hangar opening lifted, and the tug pulled the smaller plane out onto the apron in front of the hangar. Mac watched the little gust of exhaust out the back of each engine as it started, as the first prop began to turn, sped up, then the second. The hangar attendant, now with signal cones in hand, ran to unhook the tug, backed up, and waved signals at the plane's pilot.

"Vatta EX-1's signaled Tower," the pilot said. "Tower's asking for passenger manifest; Lunnell said 'As forwarded.'"

The small plane taxied away, moving toward the secondary runway. The tug, already moving, came toward them.

"Best be seated," the pilot said. "We're next; she's aboard."

Mac walked back to the passenger compartment just as Grace came through the door from the back. She carried two cases he suspected contained special equipment, and she had a pistol holstered on her hip. She gave him a brisk nod. "Good to have you back."

"I agree," he said. He looked around. Rafe was visibly tense; Teague expressed a determined lack of tension. "Is this all of us?"

"For now. This flight has scheduled deliveries to make; we're picking up Stella at Portmentor; I didn't want her coming into Port Major this trip." Grace sat down in one of the empty seats. "Rafe, Teague, good to see you. My thanks for your work. Let's get busy."

"What else has happened?" Rafe asked.

"Your suggestion that we might want the data our opposition had before we blew their data center was good. I know a few more things of long-term importance—some names and commercial connections going back several hundred years—and some more immediately affecting our situation."

She paused, head cocked. Mac had noticed the regular *bump-bump* of the plane's gear rolling over seams in the taxiway; that had stopped. They were all silent for a time. Mac looked through the open cockpit door and saw the copilot reach out to touch some control. He could hear the Tower communications now, even as the engines' whine ramped up and the plane shuddered.

"Vatta Transport Flight W-5A, cleared for takeoff. You're four minutes behind, Duncan . . . family vacation takes precedence?"

"They own the whole damn line," the copilot said. "If they want off first, they get the slot. We'll make it up—good winds aloft, Weather said. Oh—Keith and I have a three-day layover out west—anything we should pick up for you?"

"You're going salmon fishing again, aren't you? You can bring me back some smoked salmon from that place you got it three years ago. Julie was crazy about it."

"Don't tell the boss," the copilot said.

"Have I ever?" The sound cut off.

The plane was moving, faster and faster. Mac leaned back in his seat, let the acceleration press him firmly into soft cushions.

"He did, you know," Grace said. Mac looked at her. "Tell the boss. It's helpful to have friends in high places—like air traffic control towers."

He was not surprised by that at all. He was surprised to find himself here, safe, with Grace and the others, on this airplane. And to be so very tired.

When he woke, he was lying almost flat under a warm blanket. For a moment he was frightened and almost dumped his implant again, but he'd already looked around. Grace, Teague, and Rafe were all asleep on their own beds. Teague snored lightly. In one corner of the space, the cabin attendant slept as well, curled in a seat that wasn't flattened out. Mac pulled off the blanket, levered himself up—someone had removed his shoes—and padded sock-footed to the toilet. He'd slept hours—four or five. When he was through, he glanced back into the passenger area; the attendant was awake, pushing back rumpled hair, and pulling the blanket from her legs.

"Ser—can I get you anything? The others ate dinner; I could heat something up."

"Nothing fancy," Mac said. "I don't want to wake them. Tea? A roll or cookies?"

She nodded and moved forward past him, into the little galley. A light came on over the cockpit door. "The pilots want a hot drink . . . here's tea for you." Mac stepped back, taking a sip of hot tea, as she poured two more mugs, setting them on a tray and then pulling wrapped sandwiches from a warming oven. She took the tray and went forward. Mac opened the warming oven and found a warm roll. "If you want sugar for that, or jam for the roll—"

"Yes, please."

"I'll bring a tray." *Go back to your seat,* that meant. He took the hint but chose to sit at the table. There was plenty of light to eat by; the attendant brought him a full pot of tea, cream, sugar, another roll, two flaky pastries, a small pot each of jam and honey, and silverware—it felt like actual silverware—wrapped in a warm napkin.

"Thank you," he said. "This will be ample." He finished the first mug of tea, and the roll with a generous spoonful of berry jam, feeling better, more solid to himself, with every bite. He poured another mug and had just taken a large bite of a flaky pastry filled with nuts, honey, and cinnamon when his skullphone buzzed. His hand jerked; he hit the teapot, dropped the pastry, and nearly choked trying to get the pastry safely out of his way. "Ughnh?"

"Master Sergeant MacRobert, this is Master Sergeant Pitt."

His mind came fully awake. It was her voice. "What can I do for you, Master Sergeant?"

"I need to get a message directly to Admiral Vatta; can you alert her that I'm insystem and that I need to speak with her? I've read the sitrep she sent Rector Vatta."

"I'm not sure," MacRobert said. "I am not current on her situation right now; I was—detained, drugged, and was sleeping off the drug until a few minutes ago."

"I see. Is there someone at your location who can? It's fairly urgent."

"I'm not certain how secure this line is," MacRobert said. "I'm not behind the same firewalls. I'll call you back."

"I'm on *Vanguard,*" Pitt said. "Transferring to one of my unit's ships in three hours. I'll be out of contact for several hours then."

"Sooner than that," Mac said.

Grace was stirring; soft as he'd spoken, she'd roused. "Mac?"

"A call from Ky's old friend in the merc fleet," he said. "They got here fast, or I was out longer than I thought."

"What's she want?"

"To contact Ky directly. Now, if possible."

Grace flung back her blanket and sat up. "Rafe: we need you."

Rafe and Teague both jerked awake, rolled off their beds, and reached for weapons.

"Not that way," Grace said. "Rafe, a mercenary rep—someone Ky knows—needs to contact Ky directly, now. Can she use a skullphone, since that thing you two have doesn't interface with anything else?"

"Another skullphone?"

"The person's on a ship, somewhere in the system—it'd have to be ansible-boosted. And Ky needs to know a call's coming."

"I'll call her. It's—oh, it's probably after noon where she is—or something dayside, anyway. Grace, tell whoever it is to wait a half hour, in case it takes me that long to get Ky to hook in."

Grace raised an eyebrow at Mac; he called Pitt and told her that Ky could take a skullphone call but not for a half hour, because it would take that long to locate her and set it up.

"Good," Pitt said. "That's still in the safety margin." A pause then, "How are the other guys?"

"Mostly dead," Mac said.

She chuckled, then her voice firmed. "It's not clear from the data we have whether a cruiser could land on that strip—do you know?"

He felt his brows rising. "You're thinking of taking your *ship* down—the whole thing?"

"It can do a planet landing. It's apt to make a bit of a mess."

"I don't know anything about the strip except what we've been able to see the last fifty days—under a blanket of snow, mostly. No data on construction, no data on foundations. Nobody knew it was there— well, nobody but those who were keeping the secret."

A longer silence. "I'll tell my captain. It's shuttle-length, though?"

"It's used to supply a base there. Heavy aircraft use it twice a year;

I'd land a shuttle on it if I had one. I don't know what defenses might be in place."

"I don't think that will be a problem," Pitt said. MacRobert could hear the grin in her tone.

"You have the admiral's skullphone code?"

"Oh, yes. She gave it to me back on Cascadia. We've chatted a few times." Another pause. "I don't suppose you have any interest in that young fellow who transferred to us . . ."

"Ky's classmate at the Academy? Hal?"

"That one, yes."

"Frankly," Mac said, "I don't. Nor, I expect, does the Admiral."

"I wouldn't mention him to *her*," Pitt said. "But as a point of information, he is not involved in this operation you hired us for, and will never be part of any contract we hold with Slotter Key or the Vatta family."

That had not even occurred to him. Now he felt a chill satisfaction. Hal would never see home or family again. "Thank you for telling me," he said. "I had not made any connection yet."

"Not surprising."

"And while we're waiting . . . the mercs your enemy's hired are on the low end of tactical skill, but very definitely dangerous. They picked up a lot of Turek's bunch who survived the war, as well as some of Turek's supplies. Street says this contract was prime and they spent a lot at one of the dealers. No data on what they bought; it would take us longer than we had to find out. We don't know for certain the ones sent were all Turek's, but the word is they're a meaner bunch now than before."

Grace, now fully awake, was gesturing. "Just a moment," Mac said. "The Rector's signaling."

"Rafe's told her a call's coming," Grace said. "And your call's gone on long enough. Just in case."

"Contact's made," Mac said. "You're free to call. I have to go."

"Thanks," Pitt said.

CHAPTER THIRTY-NINE

MIKSLAND
DAY 220

That night, in one of the smaller openings, Ky woke repeatedly to hear nothing, see nothing amiss. But every instinct told her that danger was much closer than it had been. In the morning, she was tired, and instead of eating lunch she lay down in that day's rest stop and told Gossin to wake her when it was time to leave. She had just dozed off when the familiar stench woke her instead. She fumbled the cable from around her neck, and felt along the wall for the outlet. Green light. She plugged it into her implant.

"Ky, check your skullphone signal."

"Rafe, how nice of you to call. Yes, I have a live skullphone connection. Why I have it when I haven't had it for days now—"

"You're about to get a call from someone you know, on a ship you know."

"My, how mysterious."

"Ky—it's important. Are you awake? It should be day where you are."

"I'm quite awake."

She was certainly awake now.

"Don't unplug your ansible cable. Leave that connection on, and answer your skullphone when it pings." The ping of her skullphone followed.

"Hello again, Admiral. This is Master Sergeant Pitt."

"Well met," Ky said, still wondering what Rafe had done to the phone signal.

"We'll be landing a fully equipped force in about two days; we received the sitrep you sent the Rector. Can you hold for two days?"

"Yes," Ky said, her mental fingers crossed.

"Good. See you after we land."

After that, sleep was almost impossible. She wanted to call Rafe back on the implant ansible and demand to know how he'd punched a skullphone signal through, but that would take more time than she had before Gossin came in to wake her.

She needed to stay alert and focused for whatever they actually found, and that meant—if she could stay awake this afternoon—using her implant to ensure better sleep than last night. They finished the day with another 180 kilometers covered, all boring.

NEARING PORTMENTOR
DAY 220

Rafe woke with a jerk when the pilot announced they were two hours from landing. "All's clear so far. We'll be on the ground unloading the scheduled freight; relief crew will take her on."

The cabin attendant was up; Rafe smelled coffee and what was probably breakfast. MacRobert was asleep; the Rector was awake, sitting at the table. She had changed clothes; Rafe wondered how long she'd been up. Teague turned over abruptly, opened his eyes, yawned. Rafe made his way to the toilet and back to the table.

"If you want to wait, you can shower in the Vatta offices after we land," the Rector said.

"Then I'll wait. What's next?"

"I thought you wanted to destroy their data center."

"I do. Easier and safer on the ground. If I do it from here, they could trace the source. Because we're moving."

A shuttle with the Vatta Transport logo stood on the apron nearby, pallets moving down a conveyor onto a flatbed attached to a tug. Rafe looked out the cockpit windows. Early-morning sun lit the taller buildings of Portmentor, the sea beyond showed varying shades of blue. To the right a headland jutted out, thickly forested almost to the water. Rafe could not see the mountains, looking west, but knew they were a tall mass to the east.

"And here she is, right on time—" Grace interrupted his observations.

A skinny ship Rafe recognized from his own trip in it had just landed at the far end of the long runway. "Is that the same Vatta courier—?"

"Yes. We should go out the back way. Come on." The cabin attendant handed them each gray coveralls with the Vatta logo on the back; Grace pulled hers on as if she'd done that many times before. She led the way to the back of the plane, past cargo racks full of boxes and bags. At the rear, the attendant opened the passenger exit ramp, and as they started down it, other hatches opened on the plane's sides. Ground crew pushed over conveyors and soon cargo was moving out of the plane onto more flatbed carts.

A flight crew waited at the foot of the steps; when Teague, last in line, had cleared the ramp, the flight crew headed up. Grace led the way into the Vatta offices and then up into the second level, where they had an almost-unobstructed view of the action below and what was outside the hangar. By this time the Vatta courier was almost to the hangar. Rafe gave it a glance and then looked around.

"Communications center here?"

"Through that door," Grace said. "Have fun."

Rafe glanced at Teague. "You want to do this?"

"You need me?"

"No. Just offering."

"Then no thanks. It's your game."

Rafe set to work. He already had the linkages he needed, and he uploaded the probes to power sources, carefully routing them variously, with lockouts to protect this location. One by one he opened the gates, directing more and more reserves toward the data center. Though it was just dawn here, it would be several hours before dawn there. He brought up the satellite surveillance for that sector, zoomed in on it. The sky there was partly cloudy, but he could see, in the infrared band, the heat signature of every cooling vent.

All he had to do now was open the last few circuits, the ones he'd primed from Grace's house. This . . . this . . . and finally . . . with the surge protectors all disconnected, the overload went through the entire center. He imagined the arcs from machine to machine, to everything electrical, all the circuitry from HVAC to lighting, from doors to . . . and there, the scale alongside the infrared scan shot up—much hotter inside. The first visible light, at one end of a building, brighter than the security lights on the perimeter. They would have explosive charges to protect vital data—and yes, there went the first. The second. Every office building everywhere had something flammable in it, if the temperature was high enough. There would be flames soon, with those temperatures.

Red flashing lights appeared at the entrance end of the facility—alarms would be going off. Rafe grinned at the images on the screen. Tiny dots of light were moving around, but increasingly hard to see against the glare of explosions, fire, and the steadily climbing temperature. Smoke obscured the visual bands now, but the infrared showed long blocks of white, one building after another. The only thing missing was sound, but he could imagine that. Right about now, the pipeline should—and there it was. He could see the shock wave; the communications masts went down, not onto the burning buildings but into the parking lot and entrance gates. He glanced back at the outer room, to see if anyone else was watching. Stella was there now, talking to the Rector. He turned back to the screens, now with his headset on, listening across the bands for any chatter about it.

About an hour later, what he heard made him yank loose his ansible cable and plug it in.

"What?"

The Rector, damn her, was right beside him; of course she noticed his sudden movement. "They're moving. They're moving *now*. I didn't delay them; I kicked them loose. I have to get to Ky—"

"Do it, then."

DAY 221

Again Ky woke to the familiar stench. She had gone to sleep easily that night, aware that the enemy might already have landed, but also that they had hundreds of kilometers of lead on them, with a lot of very thick doors in between. Yawning, she hooked up the cable.

"Ky! Get out now; they're almost there!"

"Calm down—"

"No, seriously—they left early. I thought frying their data center would slow them down, but it didn't."

"You fried their—how?"

"Never *mind* how—you've got to get out. We thought there were just over a hundred; there's two hundred, on four aircraft. They've already taken off from the Pingat Base and they'll be there in just a few hours."

"I told you we'd left days ago."

"But you're moving slowly—you can't be more than a hundred kilometers ahead of them."

"I knew you didn't get all I said. We're much farther away than that; more like six to seven hundred kilometers. With doors they probably can't open between us and them, assuming they even realize there are doors."

"But they were in the base every year for . . . years. They have to know every inch—"

"No. Didn't you tell me it's not the same troops? It's those other mercs. They won't know anything."

"Do you know where you're going?"

"Away from where they're landing. I told you—" She stopped. "Maybe north. How's the relief force coming?"

"Slower than I'd like. Stella just landed—uh—we're in Portmentor; we'll be flying again in a few hours, getting closer to you."

"Not too close. Let the professionals handle it."

"And what about you? Are you—oh. You're a professional, too. Dammit, Ky, be careful."

"I will be as careful as I can. And that means getting some sleep now, while I can."

"Ah. Sorry; I should have realized—"

"Get some rest, Rafe. I'm going to." She pulled the jack free and realized she was grinning. She'd surprised him again. She liked surprising him. Rafe was alive and well, the enemy had lost a data center, and somewhere in space Master Sergeant Pitt and a Mackensee landing force were on the way. Two days, Pitt had said. Even three wouldn't kill them, she was sure. With any luck she had enough lead on the enemy that she'd merely have to deal with the boredom of riding a slow vehicle in a gray tunnel for several more days.

She let her implant put her to sleep.

CHAPTER FORTY

SLOTTER KEY, MIKSLAND
DAY 222

As one of the two designated liaisons for Mackensee's landing force, Master Sergeant Pitt rode down to the surface of Slotter Key in the second shuttle. She felt some satisfaction in noting that, as usual, no plans had survived the first shots fired—neither side's.

Ky had not expected any of this, from the shuttle crash on, and certainly not to be hunted by mercenaries. The Black Torch had been inserted as a covert force; they had no reserves in orbit and—as near as could be determined—only small units of local military on their side. They had not expected the arrival of a merc troopship—probably still didn't know about it—or what was about to land right on top of them.

"Aircraft on the deck" came a voice in her headset. "Three big ones, one medium. Slotter Key military numbers. Are we sure those are Black Torch mercs?"

"Check their preferred band."

"It's them, all right. Same codes as last time we scalped 'em. And they have live scan. And auto-defense is hot."

"Master Sergeant Pitt, inform our employer that we need the go button."

Pitt switched to the channel the Rector had given her.

"Post Delta," came a male voice.

"Requesting authorization code direct."

"A moment."

Then a woman's voice. "This is the Rector. Operation is go."

"Thank you," Pitt said. She signaled to the com operator at the next desk. "You requested an open channel during action; will this suit?"

"Very well. Is this the Master Sergeant Ky knew?"

"Yes," Pitt said.

"You've met MacRobert; he'll take over if something flaps here. What's it look like?"

"Active anti-air defense set up on the ground. Not a problem; we just launched at it and I don't expect it to survive the next five minutes. We're seven from landing. They very kindly cleared the snow off the runway for us."

"Any sign of our side?"

"No, but we didn't expect any. You'd told us they'd fled deep underground."

"As best we know. They aren't talking to us."

"We're dropping fast now," Pitt said. Her helmet gave her a view out the front of her shuttle; the exhaust glow of the first dropped below her vision to a field now lit by fires on the ground.

"Tag One" came from the other com desk.

The shuttle tipped forward. Through her helmet display, Pitt saw a white bay streaked with dark water, watched the ground rise, red rock splatched with white. Level-out, and then the runway in front, the squawk of tires, the brief slither then hard deceleration.

"We're down," she said to the Rector. Ahead, the first shuttle took out both the small barracks on the surface, then its surface shimmered as it powered up the forward shield arc. Its rear ramp was down, troops in bulky winter gear moving down to cover the emergence of their heavier weaponry and vehicles. The first three drones, the small ones, went up fast into a pale-blue sky.

"Jumpers active," the com officer said to the crew. "Somebody better do something soon or this is one expensive training exercise—"

"For which we're being paid, Pete."

Flurries of code went past Pitt's eyes in the display. Drones were not her responsibility; someone else would get those readouts.

"Jumper one down," came another voice. "Guess they want to play laser tag. And we tagged 'em. Pop up Spanker."

A slightly larger drone lifted from behind the first shuttle. When it was a meter above the surface it went chameleon, and though it would be visible to some detectors, human eyes wouldn't see anything but a vague blur as it moved along.

"Tag Two, take up position." Pitt felt the shuttle quiver, and then the view changed as it zigzagged its way backward to the specified support point. Her view now was of the rise to the north of the runway. She heard the back ramp release, and knew the troops and equipment there would be unloading. An explosion bloomed from behind the nearest rise.

"Spanker One took out the battery," someone said.

Pitt passed that information on to the Rector.

"What about the transports?" the Rector asked.

"Nobody's fired on us from them," Pitt said. "If they do—we'll have to blow them."

"Of course," the Rector said. "Do it now, if you want."

She did not sound like an old woman, Pitt thought. She did sound like a relative of Ky Vatta's.

A standard hour later, they were ready to consider the door into the underground facility. How heavily was it defended? And what would they destroy that might be valuable later? A burst of small arms roused no response. The door itself sported a new lock but showed signs of having been damaged before by someone with a crowbar and axe. With the equipment they had, it was easy to drill out the lock and open the door.

Inside, they faced a small entry space and a ramp leading downward. Though daylight pouring in the door revealed light fixtures on the overhead, they were dark, and nothing recognizable as a switch was on any surface. Pitt, mindful that underground might not allow ready communication with the outside, told one of the communications teams to lay a cable. Two puppybots set off down the ramp, com-whisker tails wagging. They didn't look much like real dogs, having various sensor gadgets stuck all over them, but the name was traditional; they even had individual names, real dog names: Fly and Peg.

Pitt stayed behind the first two teams, who themselves followed the puppybots, their dark-vision goggles on. Nothing, all the way down. When they reached a level that matched what Ky had told the Rector, the bulkheads and overhead were pocked with small-arms fire. Since there were no bodies, evidently the Torch had come in shooting but found no resistance. All the doors had their locks shot out. Pitt didn't bother to inventory any of the rooms; she noticed in passing that the Torch had left the mess hall filthy, dirty pots piled on counters and dirty dishes left on the tables. Had their commander rushed them through a meal? Down the corridor to the left, there was an obvious communications center and an equally obvious powerplant control center. Beyond, a wall had been blown open, revealing other corridors and more ramps. So far the puppybots had found no trace of personnel except the mess they'd made.

The next section of blown-open wall led into a huge space, rather like a shuttle bay or aircraft hangar. It was empty, but footmarks showed on the gray floor, and at one end another wall had been blown open, revealing an empty passage leading off into the dark.

Pitt paused there, testing her ability to communicate topside. That still worked.

"Set up a communications board here. We'll test at intervals as we go—" That was the major. Then he held up his hand. "Wait—new data—relayed from that ISC fellow. Our friends report they're still ahead of pursuit but they can hear it."

CHAPTER FORTY-ONE

MIKSLAND, UNDERGROUND
DAY 222

The next day began just like the one before. Ky woke the others. They ate a quick breakfast, mounted up, and rode along at fifteen kilometers per hour for another four hours, before coming to what looked like just another open space. But the passage ahead stopped at a blank wall that did not move when a vehicle was aimed at it; the vehicle stopped instead. A search for dimples on the wall found nothing.

"Maybe there's an elevator," Betange said. "We should check all the walls."

"And the floor," Ky said. "Remember that first one."

"Which we couldn't get back down," Droshinski pointed out. "Maybe this is the end."

"A dead end, it looks like," Yamini said.

"We'll stop here for the day," Ky said. "We'll look in every chamber, feel every wall and the floor. If the enemy hasn't found a way into the old part of the facility, then we're safe enough, and even if they have, they have to figure out how to get through the various shut doors."

"Unless they just blow holes in everything," Cosper said.

She wished he hadn't said that. From the expressions on others' faces, they wished the same thing. She had finally fallen asleep when an insistent warbling noise and flashing lights woke her; everyone was waking up as well. The formerly blue-white ceiling lights now flashed yellow.

"What is it?"

"Something—not good."

"The bad guys," Ky said. "They did something that triggered a warning system. Maybe blew a hole in a wall. Load up. We'll try again to get that door open; maybe it will work in an emergency."

When Ky pressed a command rod to the first vehicle in the line, the flashing lights and warbling siren stopped. "That's a relief. Now maybe it will tell us what to do next."

"Sir—" Barash's voice sounded shaky. "There's something showing up on that door."

Dimly at first, then brightening, rows of symbols in red appeared on the door. They did not look like any writing Ky had ever seen; she had no idea what they meant. The symbols pulsed, demanding attention.

"I don't understand," Ky said. She was sure now that whoever had made the place, it could not have been anyone from their culture. She walked up to the door; the symbols pulsed faster. How could she communicate with an automated system—it must be an automated system—that didn't speak her language? Or could it have learned, in the time humans had occupied part of this facility? She repeated what she'd said slowly: "I do not understand what to do."

The symbols all disappeared. A single short vertical mark appeared, this time in blue. "One," Ky said. Two lines. "Two." A circle. "One circle." A hexagon. "One hexagon." One side glowed brighter, and then the glow moved around, pausing. Ky counted them out. "Six sides." An arrow sign. "Arrow." A line drawing of a vehicle. "Truck,"

Ky said. She patted the nearest vehicle for emphasis—surely it was observing, whatever it was.

Those symbols disappeared, replaced by red ones: a flashing red circle, then stick figures moving into the vehicle symbol. Outline of a rod touching a vehicle. A moving arrow, with a line of vehicles after it. That was clear enough.

"Mount up," Ky said, climbing into the lead vehicle. A screen rose from the front, showing red arrows on the floor leading away; when Ky put the vehicle in motion, it followed them, and the door in front of them opened. It was, she saw, at least three times as thick as the others they had passed through, and it opened much more slowly.

Beyond, the passage looked very different. Narrower, round in cross section, with a floor that appeared to be a series of grooved metal plates rather than a single smooth surface. Instead of the bright overhead lights, dimmer lights were spaced at intervals. The vehicles bumped up onto these plates; when all were on, Ky heard a series of metallic *clunk*s and felt something below make a hard connection with the bottom of the vehicle. Ahead, on the screen, a line of red arrows stretched into the distance. Onto the screen came other instructions: stick figures sitting still, then one trying to step off and disintegrating. The pulsing red circle again. Stick figures' arms out, then disappearing. Pulsing red circle. Clear as the signs in tram systems: SIT DOWN, DO NOT EXIT WHILE MOVING. KEEP ARMS INSIDE VEHICLE. DANGER.

She yelled instructions back to the others, heard them passed on. The door behind them slid shut more slowly than the others. Then, with a solid jerk, they were moving, the grooved plates sliding faster and faster. Dim lights flashed past, finally forming a pale stream along both sides. She had no idea how fast they were going, or where, but they were moving much faster than they had in the trucks. Away from danger, she hoped.

The moving plates made much more noise than their previous near-silent progress. A steady low roar reverberated from the tunnel walls. When it changed pitch, Ky looked quickly at the screen. Instead of tunnel walls she could just make out a black void stretching to either side. Then the walls closed in again, the familiar noise returned. Ky yawned. According to her implant, they'd been moving 2.4 standard hours.

DAY 222

At 5.2 hours, the moving track stopped. Sharp sounds of metal adjusting to a new normal echoed off the walls, as did voices when they spoke. Ahead a dark opening led into darkness.

"That door didn't close behind us," Gossin said. She'd been in the last vehicle that time.

"And this one didn't open for us—it's just open."

Ky turned on her helmet light and walked toward the opening. Another passage like the ones they'd driven through before and shadows that might be doors not too far ahead. The air smelled stale.

"Lights," she said. She didn't expect lights to come on, and they did not. She tipped her head back. Her helmet light revealed the same kind of light fixtures. "Bring the vehicles forward," she said to the others. "Slowly. We need to take a rest anyway, if this place has water."

The others had their headlamps on by then, a small constellation in the darkness, and one by one the vehicles moved into the space where Ky stood, avoiding her and parking to one side as usual. The rooms were in the same relative position as before, but no lights came on when they entered the mess and the washroom, and no water came from the faucets. Nothing worked in the kitchen—no burners heated.

"Electricity's out," Corporal Lakhani said. He had found an outlet and inserted a tester. "Completely."

"If the emergency signal was from the bad guys breaching the facility . . . if they figured out we had to be somewhere below and started blowing walls . . . they might have damaged the whole system."

"Then why lights along the moving plate things?"

"I don't know. Different source? And if that, then why not here? I don't know that, either."

"Are we safe from them?" Gossin asked. "Will that track move for them?"

"Again—I don't know. Get your packs; we'll have to go on foot. As much food and water as you can carry, your weapons, ammunition." As she talked, Ky found the duffel in which she'd stowed all the evidence left from the shuttle, and shoved its contents into various pockets. "Let's get going."

She felt a sudden change in air pressure, then stillness again. "They *are* blowing the doors," Betange said. A dull deep sound vibrated underfoot.

"Keep going," Ky said. But shortly after that, they found the entire tunnel blocked by a mass of dark rock, and nothing that responded to the control rods on the floor, overhead, or on the side walls.

"We missed a turn," Ky said. "Backtrack." Straight into the enemy, but maybe the enemy had other problems. Surely Mackensee had landed by now; the hunters would have hunters on their tails. Would they realize it, turn and fight? Or try harder to overrun their prey?

Kurin found a panel a hundred meters back; it opened into a side passage, too narrow for the vehicles. "And we wouldn't have found this if we'd been riding," Kurin said. They shut the panel behind them, hoping a turn of the wheel on the far side meant it was locked, and walked up a smooth ramp until it turned sharply, steepened, then turned again. Just beyond that turn they found another door, closed but not locked, thick as a spaceship pressure door. Gossin spun the wheel on its far side.

"Two doors between us," Ky said, looking around the group with her headlamp. Even Sergeant Cosper was tired. "We can risk one hour rest," she said. "Set your implant alarms for noise, as well." They all slumped down, falling asleep almost at once. Ky closed her eyes, heard nothing but their breathing, and woke when her implant woke her. The others were already stirring.

Now she could hear a vague, disturbing sound through the door. Were the enemy troops already into the side passage? Or just banging on the walls? "Hurry!" Ky said. They moved as fast as they could up the ramp, arriving at another identical pressure door that operated the same way. Beyond was an even narrower passage of raw rock hacked into a semblance of a stairway. Ky hoped that meant it was near the surface.

Ky led the way. The stair turned, turned again; uneven steps and the bright patches and black shadows cast by their helmet lights made it hard to see their footing clearly. Ky's breath burned in her chest; her legs hurt. Soon they were all panting; Ky knew the others must feel as bad.

"Five minutes," she said. She leaned on the rough wall, catching her breath. Then started again. Up, up, turn and twist, duck beneath a rock that hung down. How close were their pursuers? Would they go to the end and then backtrack or just find the panel right away?

"We'll hear if they blow the panel," someone said, just as a muffled *whoomp* reached them. Ky tried to speed up.

Finally the stair ended on a cramped rock landing not big enough for all of them at once. They could see daylight beyond, at the end of a widening passage. They had traveled through another night. Ky squinted against the brightness. This passage smelled—stank, in fact—of something alive. Some animal. She closed her eyes for a long moment, then opened them, looking down and away from the entrance. It might be wolves, or that tall heavy-legged hairy thing with tusks and a nose like a fire hose—but that wouldn't fit in here. She saw an uneven lumpy heap. Wolves? Giant wolves?

"Quietly," she said to Lakhani. "Hand me a stronger light. There's something in here."

It looked like a pile of fur. Even with the light she couldn't be sure of the shape, except that it was big, much bigger than any of them. She tried to move the light along the margins of the pile, looking for clues to its identity. Something moved—squeaked—wiggled—

a small subdivision of the pile or rather two such, with bright eyes, black noses, very red mouths with very white sharp teeth.

Not wolves; they had rounded ears, a round head like a cartoon animal. Paws with long claws. Some memory stirred in Ky's mind; her implant finally offered a picture of a smaller but similar shape: the bear cubs she'd seen in the Port Major zoo. Black, with white chevrons on their chests. The adult bear in the zoo hadn't been as tall as a human when it stood on its hind legs. This adult bear was huge. The cubs squeaked again and wriggled back into the fur pile. She could hear them suckling, slurping.

So it was a mother bear, a huge mother bear, with her cubs. Ky backed up cautiously, trying not to make a sound. The bear's nose quivered, its lips lifted over fangs as long as Ky's hand, and then it yawned. Deep in folds of fur tiny eyes opened, then closed again. It lifted one massive paw and scratched at its chest; the claws were as long as her fingers, stout enough to shred a human torso. She turned the light off and backed up again.

"What is it?" the others asked, when she'd retreated to the narrow passage. "Can we go out now?"

"There's a huge bear," Ky said very softly. "With cubs. The cubs are awake; the bear was asleep but is waking up, I think. If it wakes while we're trying to get past it, we're dead."

"We could stun it."

"If we knew we had enough charge. We might be able to kill it, with the rifles, but I'd rather use ammunition on our enemies." The enemies who had certainly found the passage entrance and were following.

"We have to do *something*—"

"For now, we'll wait. Maybe it'll go back to sleep and we can sneak past." Did bears snore? Some dogs snored. As they sat quietly waiting, she heard other, smaller sounds in the cave. Little high-pitched squeaks, the skittering of small paws. So the bear wasn't alone in the cave . . . mice, that would be, or something similar. No sound from the bear. She crept forward, dared another look at the bear. Eyes closed, mouth closed. From here she could hear the cubs still suckling. She aimed the light around the cave floor, side-to-side, and surprised several smaller animals: they looked like mice, but with furry tails. One of them scurried across to the bear and burrowed into the fur under that massive paw. The bear didn't move.

So ... if they made no more noise than some mice, maybe it wouldn't notice them. She edged back to the others, and very quietly explained what they needed to do. Boots off. Sock feet only. Single file. If the bear moved, freeze: hold still.

Ky set off in the lead, not hurrying. Underfoot, the rock's cold penetrated her socks almost at once. She couldn't hear the ones behind her, only the beat of her own pulse. As she came even with the bear, she could see it a little better in the dim light. It wasn't black but brown; the hairs backlit by the cave entrance seemed frost-tipped. The bear stirred; Ky froze. She dared not turn her head to look. It grunted, sighed, and settled down once more. Another meter. Another. By the time she reached the mouth of the cave, her feet felt like blocks of ice, but the bear hadn't roused. She stopped and glanced back.

Her little troop was moving as carefully as she could have hoped, faces taut with fear, but coming on steadily. She looked outside. The cave opened onto a ledge, with a steep drop-off; she could not tell how far down without exposing herself to anyone on the opposite slope. That slope rose higher than the cave, taking up most of her field of view, great blocks of gray rock streaked with snow glittering in the sunlight. She could not see the sky, for the overhang of the cave entrance, but she could tell that their own slope was shadowed. She could hope that anyone watching from there would be blinded by the sun in their eyes, unable to see into the cave mouth. She could see no movement.

When the others came up behind her, tapping her shoulder to indicate they had all made it past the sleeping bear, she spoke softly. "I don't see any movement, but we can't be sure. I'm going out to look—"

Sergeant Chok held up one finger.

"Yes?"

"I've had both scout and mountain training. Let me."

Ky nodded. "Fine. We need a hiding place—without a bear in it."

He grinned at her, put his boots on, and eased past her, dropping to hands and knees. The rest leaned against the cave wall as close as they could get to the cave entrance. Time crawled past. Ky put her boots back on; the others did the same. The bear made no noise behind them. Finally Chok returned, upright this time, and signaled. Ky led the others out into sharp-smelling cold air. The ledge continued, slanting down and angling slightly to the right. The overhang disappeared; far above the sky showed clear blue with a few streaks of cloud. Beside them layers of rock plunged toward the ledge. Erosion had made these into steps of various heights, mostly inconvenient. All around was the musical tinkle of melting ice and water dripping and trickling away over rock.

They came to the hiding place Chok had found—a narrow cleft between rock layers, barely big enough for all of them. They edged into it one by one. It was cold, dark, dripping, and claustrophobic. Worst, from Ky's point of view, was the lack of an alternate exit. And the obviousness. They were still too close to the exit, in the most obvious hiding place.

The forest below them gave better cover if they could get to it. Forest on their slope and the one across from them, with a snow-covered spoon-shaped space between. "We need to get down there," Ky said. Heads nodded. Once more they came out into daylight and started downslope.

They had descended almost to the trees when they heard noise from behind and above: gunfire, a roar, screams. Everyone flattened against the wall. Ky could not see the cave entrance itself, but could see the wider ledge in front of it, then a small shape, flying through the air. One of the cubs, Ky realized, as it squealed frantically, pawing the air before it hit the ground and bounced, tumbled, and finally the squalling ceased. Then the bear—so huge, even at that distance, her growling roar echoing off the opposite slope, her forelegs sweeping one human form after another out into the air, the rag-doll corpses trailing blood, the weapons they'd held falling separately, still firing. The bear dragged herself forward as more gunfire ripped into her, as smoke and light and louder noise burst from the cave. Someone had fired a rocket grenade at her.

"They didn't—" Cosper said. He covered his ears as did the others. A spray of blood, and the bear overbalanced, falling end-over-end. Rocks skittered down the slope. A stream of smoke wavered across the gap to the opposing slope and ended in an explosion that echoed back and forth. Ky looked back up at the cave. A group of humans— tiny and hard to see—rushed from the cave. Cosper said, "That was stupid—that rock could—" when a loud crack, like a close strike of lightning, silenced him.

Above the ledge, the overhanging slab leaned slowly away from the mountain. With ponderous grace it rotated until it came down on the ledge with a shock they could feel, breaking loose the front of the ledge. Overhang and ledge both tumbled down the slope, followed by an avalanche of smaller boulders.

"Move!" Ky said. "Now!"

They hurried as best they could, as the noise grew behind them: rocks falling, sliding. Were they far enough away? Ky risked another glance back and saw a growing scar above what had been the cave. Finally the noise lessened, but they kept on to the shelter of the first trees. A cloud of dust hung above the avalanche scar.

"That bear—she'd have killed us all," Betange said in a hushed voice.

"She saved us all," Ky said.

They had just made it into the first sparse line of trees when Ky heard the unmistakable whine of aircraft. She didn't have to tell anyone to get down; they were all flattened into the snow before the craft came in sight. From their position, she could now see along the mountainside. A standard tensquad VTOL pod with Slotter Key

AirDefense markings flew over their hiding spot, settling vertically into the clearing.

"Our ride home?" Gossin asked.

"Wait," Ky said. The canopy popped on one side and three figures climbed out. She thumbed the viewer controls and zoomed in. They wore unfamiliar uniforms; the Black Torch logo showed clearly. They looked at the body they'd landed near, then up the slope at the scar and the cloud of dust still visible. Another rock broke loose, rattling down the slope. Ky couldn't see, but could imagine, what they saw from their position. A dead bear, dead men, a rockfall. Would they fly away or investigate more? If they chose to investigate . . .

"It would be really handy to have that flier," Ky said softly to Chok. "We have a good position."

"Are they all out?"

"No, but I'm betting they will be."

Sure enough, another clambered out, and then another, until ten of them stood in a pattern that minimized the view of someone from above, in the cave. Then they started up the narrow cleft, directly toward Ky and the others.

"If we're really lucky, they won't get a single shot off," Kurin said.

"Wait." They had numerical advantage, eighteen to ten, height advantage, and the mercs were acting as if they were out for a walk in the park. But they carried heavier weapons. Ky passed the word down her line. When the mercs reached the scraggly conifer she'd chosen, Ky's group fired as one. Six of them dropped at once, clean kills; the others dove for the snow. Ky's troop won the brief firefight.

"Let's go get our ride out," Ky said. Surely someone in her group could fly it.

They were almost to the flier when she heard another coming, fast and low. "Into the trees!" Without hesitation, her people scrambled into cover.

Two fliers, not just one, painted in bold splashes of dark green and white with a big gold logo and their name—MACKENSEE MILITARY

ASSISTANCE CORPORATION—on the side. They hovered briefly, then landed. A team emerged from each, cautious. Ky recognized the lean, rangy form of Master Sergeant Pitt. She let out a breath she hadn't realized she was holding. The entire group, after a cursory look around, stared up the slope at the fresh scar of the rockslide and the scatter of bodies.

Ky signaled her people to stay down and eased her own way toward Pitt, close enough to hear Pitt's exasperated, "She has to be around here somewhere! That didn't happen by itself."

"Good afternoon, Master Sergeant," Ky said. Pitt whipped around and Ky found herself staring into the muzzles of many weapons.

"Why didn't you fly yourself out and save us the trouble?" Pitt asked, nodding at the first flier. She signaled to the others, and they relaxed.

"I don't have a license for this craft," Ky said. "Can you give us a lift?"

"Yes," Pitt said, "at a price. I want to know how you got past that monster." She pointed at the bear.

"Carefully," Ky said.

"You'll have to do better than that, Admiral Vatta," Pitt said. "Call in your wolf pack and let's get you back to your formidable great-aunt."

CHAPTER FORTY-TWO

CORLEIGH
DAYS 246-251

Ky hadn't wanted to come to Corleigh, but the Vatta tik plantation was one place the media could not easily invade, and for the sake of a little privacy she had accepted Helen's invitation to use the new vacation home on the other side of the cove from the house she had grown up in. It looked different, for which she was grateful: an airy beach house up on stilts with a wide veranda all the way around. She and Rafe dropped their small luggage in the largest of three bedrooms, changed, then walked down to the shore. It was the middle of winter here, but a winter milder than Miksland's summer, and as the sun set and all the colors of a tropical evening shifted in water and sky, she tried to pretend everything was the same as before she left that first time.

"We're on a tropical island at last," Rafe said. "Two of your moons are up."

She had not noticed, deep in her thoughts. She stared at the night sky and felt nothing thematically related to moonlight on a tropical beach. "It's the tropical island where my parents and brothers died." She turned, facing the paler blur that was his face. "How comfortable were *you*, back in the house where you had to kill that man?"

"Not," he said. "Not at all. We sold it—or rather, I hear from Penny that she did, for a good amount, shortly after I left. It was . . . eerie, when I went back there. I didn't fit at all."

"And you had a house," Ky said. "I have the bare place where it was and the memory of it." The memory of her mother's dead face in the ash-covered pool, so vivid in her father's implant, had faded when those memories were removed from her implant. She knew she had seen it; she just couldn't retrieve it now.

She couldn't see Rafe's face, but she heard the change in his voice, the deliberate calm. "So . . . we should go back to the beach house. At least that's not in your memories." She could almost hear the unspoken *We could make our own.*

Ky nodded; they returned to the house in silence, and during supper talked only of inconsequential things. That set the pattern for the next five days. Avoiding the past, not discussing the future, and in that empty present feeling out whether they still had a future together without talking about it. They walked the beach from one cove to the other, swam several times a day, ate meals from the well-stocked freezer without paying much attention to them. Hours on the wide veranda that encircled the house, conversations that died away in a few minutes, leaving Ky still uncertain. The nights . . . the nights were good, comfort and ease and a reminder how well she and Rafe suited each other. But she woke while he slept, her mind still replaying scenes from the crash, from the lifeboats, from Miksland. Why had she done this, and not that? What else could she have done that would have had a better outcome?

She and Rafe had both brought their comunits, and they had both locked down their skullphones. The local hub at the Vatta office nearby could transmit wirelessly to the house, but Ky didn't pick up her comunit from the table where she'd dropped it until the fourth day. If Rafe used his, he didn't tell her about it.

Nothing from Stella or Helen or Grace: they knew she and Rafe wanted to be left alone. A query from a journalist wanting an interview. And a longer communication, via Captain Pordre in *Vanguard*, from Dan Pettygrew back on Greentoo. She'd known something like this might be coming, but—

"How's the admiral business coming?" Rafe had been stirring eggs for breakfast. His expression now was wary.

Ky let out a huff of air. "It's not. Official notice—" She calculated the date from Cascadian to Slotter Key calendar. "Three or four days ago, Cascadian."

Rafe looked stunned, then furious. "They canned you? They canned *you*? It's your fleet; you created it; you saved them—everybody—"

Ky shook her head. "They had reasons. The other governments might have let me come back, but Moscoe Confederation blames me for Commander Bentik's death. Her family's prominent in Cascadian politics. Dan Pettygrew sent a long apologetic letter about it. He argued but says here it was hopeless. He thought I'd want him to stay in command, so he went along. He did insist on having my back pay and severance pay deposited to my account at Crown & Spears in Cascadia and suggests I transfer it immediately to Slotter Key. They might block transfer, he said."

"That's disgusting!" Rafe turned back to the cooktop. "Damn. These eggs are—"

"Fine," Ky said. "Or trash—it doesn't matter."

"You should—"

"I shouldn't, whatever you're thinking. Serve those eggs or toss them out and I'll do the next batch." She stood up and stretched. "I was never a very good desk admiral, you know."

"You were. You just don't realize your own—"

"Talents. Yes, I do. Rafe, you know—I told you—I didn't like that part of it. I was bored; I had even thought of resigning—"

"You didn't tell me *that*!"

"No." She nudged him away from the stove, where the pan of eggs looked like nothing she wanted to eat. She opened the recycler hatch with her foot and slid the mess out of the pan, cracked four more eggs and started again. "Get that funny-looking cheese out of the cooler."

"I don't know what it is."

"I do. You'll like the result. And some chives, and a slice of last night's ham."

Rafe leaned on the counter while Ky put together an omelet. "Our cooks would never let any of us do anything in the kitchen."

"We had a cook sometimes, but my parents agreed that everyone should know how to cook." Ky cut the omelet in the pan and slid half onto each plate. "The thing is, Rafe, after the first shock I feel free. I am not going to spend my life bitter about this. And I'm not broke— that much back pay and what Pettygrew told me was the severance, what was already in my account there—and what Stella owes me now that I've turned over my shares to her—it's not pebbles. I can do anything I want, with time to think about what that is."

Rafe had started on his portion of omelet; his eyebrows had gone up. "In light of that, then," he said, "the Board at ISC prefers Penny to me, especially because of my attachment to you. They still have ridiculous notions about Vattas. So we're both out of a job. Same as you, I turned over my inheritance and she's paying fair for it and says she'll keep me on the books with a regular remittance, as before. I was getting tired of that corner office anyway." After a moment, he went on. "So what will it be?"

"What I'd really like—" Ky paused to eat. And think. What did she really want? Not a beach house on Corleigh. Not on a planet at all. Space, then, but in what sense? When had she felt most alive? "I want excitement," she said. "Interesting things to do, puzzles to solve, new places. I don't care about the rank and all the attention, and I don't want to be stuck in an office day after day, signing papers, solving squabbles."

"Puzzles? What kind of puzzles?"

"The one I found in Miksland. That whole base the bad guys were using, that we stayed in over the winter? Spaceforce didn't build it. It was there already when the colonists arrived, with all kinds of tech that's sort of human and sort of not. Labs full of what I think are templates for different kinds of animals and plants. Our history doesn't go that far back. They came, they messed with the planet, moved things around, left and came back time and again to add to the life-forms, or maybe other things. And then left. They'd have had to start long before we think humans left Old Earth. Unless Old Earth was one of their other projects, not the original at all."

"And you want to chase that down? You don't want to figure out who was behind the trouble here? It's your home world, and it affects your family."

"No." She could hear the tension in her voice. "I don't want to stay here one day longer than I have to; I want to get off this planet and never come back. It's their problem; let them deal with it."

Rafe sighed. "Ky, I know you've had a shock—more than one—on this planet and about this planet, but this does not sound like you. You don't run away from problems—"

"This is different—"

"Hear me out. It's not like you. It may be you need more time, or better therapy than a rakehell lover can give . . . have you ever checked into your implant to see if that medical team at Moray left you any guidance?"

"No."

"Would you look at the indices and see if they did?"

"Why? I didn't want to come in the first place, and I want to leave—" She heard the rising tone in her voice, and stopped there.

Rafe said nothing for a long moment. "Then—if that's what you really want, I have a business proposition."

"A business proposition." She had her voice under control, but her neck hurt and she had to unclench her hands finger by finger.

"Yes. You have money in the bank. I have money in the bank—same as you. Let's buy a ship and go."

"Just like that?" She could not believe he'd given in so quickly; the argument she'd feared wasn't going to happen. Self-doubt vanished; she felt light as a balloon.

"Yes. Well, after we've lolled on the tropical sands another week or so maybe."

"*Now*," Ky said. She pushed back her chair. "Can you think of a better time?"

"I could," Rafe said, finishing his omelet. "But there's always another day. Frankly I think starting tomorrow is better than starting at lunchtime. Or the day after?"

"Tomorrow," Ky said. "I am capable of compromise."

Rafe laughed. "Fine, then. You cooked; I'll do the heavy labor of putting stuff in the cleaner."

A last walk on the beach, a last swim. Clothes in the 'fresher, bags open—everything was ready to go before they slept. Ky woke early, padded out to the main room, and called over to the local office to be sure the plane was ready for them.

"It's not here, Admiral," a pleasant female voice said. "It was called back to Port Major overnight." No strain in that voice; the reason had not been anything dire.

There were other planes on Corleigh, charter craft in town. She had money. "What's the current charter service's contact?"

"Admiral—" What might have been a gulp; the voice now sounded strained. "Um—you don't want to leave. The others are coming; they'll be here by noon. You could fly back then." A pause, then, "The plane can be serviced and ready to take off again in a half hour."

She did want to leave. If wishes grew wings . . . "Who exactly is coming?"

"Your aunt and your cousin, Admiral. I thought they would have notified you."

"All they told me was that I could have the house for a while and would not be disturbed." She could hear the edge in her own voice and softened it deliberately. "Perhaps they will call before they arrive. I hope nothing has happened."

"Nothing on the news summary," the voice said.

"Thank you," Ky said. When she turned, Rafe was watching her from the doorway. "Best-laid plans," she said. "We're stranded, and the next arrival is Stella, Helen, and the twins."

"That's an odd definition of *you won't be disturbed*."

"My thought exactly. We could call town for transportation and charter a flight out, but I expect they'll call here and panic if we don't answer."

She and Rafe had just time to eat breakfast before the house phone rang again.

Five hours later, the little electric podcar rolled up to the back of the house. Stella and Helen climbed out, and then the twins erupted, shrill voices sending every bird in the trees rocketing away as they ran toward the house.

"Were you like that?" Rafe murmured in Ky's ear.

"Probably," Ky said. "But there was only one of me. We'd better help."

"Not much in this load," Helen said. "The rest will come later." She looked around, her expression tense. "Where are the—Oh." The twins appeared around the corner of the house, one chasing the other, both shrieking, and disappeared again around the next corner.

"We need to tire them out," Stella said, pulling a couple of insulated cases from the podcar. "Here—this one's food, Ky. Rafe, the other is your black bag from Aunt Grace's."

Once everything was out of the podcar, Stella reset its instructions and it trundled back toward the airstrip. Ky, Rafe, and Stella moved everything inside.

"What's going on?" Ky asked. Her duffel and Rafe's were still by the door.

"Problems," Helen said. "You know that flight recorder you brought back?"

"Yes. What about it?"

"It's gone missing. And someone broke into our house yesterday when Stella and I had taken the children for their yearly checkups. Nothing was taken, but the alarm didn't go off and nobody noticed anything wrong until we got back and the side door had been kicked right off the hinges. I'm sorry we interrupted you, but—"

"You didn't, really," Ky said. "We were going to leave this morning. New plans, Rafe and I. If you hadn't arrived, we'd have been in Port Major by now—"

"What plans?" Stella asked, stacking fruit from the cooler onto a platter.

"Well—we're both at loose ends, so we're going to buy a ship and go—do things. Explore. Learn new things. Have smaller adventures." She didn't want to explain what she'd thought of. This morning it sounded less rational than it had the day before.

"Just how do you plan to finance this?"

Ky grinned. "Space Defense is giving me severance pay and back pay; you owe me for my shares in Vatta, and Rafe's got money coming from the same kind of sources, since his sister's taking over as CEO. We realized we could buy a reasonably sized ship, and decided to grab it while we could."

"Well, you can't," Stella said. She glanced sideways at Helen. "Moscoe Confederation has slapped a lien on your Cascadian accounts, pending a court hearing on damages due the family of your aide. I had a call from the local branch of Crown & Spears. Since you're still a Slotter Key citizen, they won't allow a foreign government to seize the funds you have here, but they can't guarantee it's safe to transfer them to other branches in other jurisdictions. More than that, because I transferred my permanent residence to Cascadia, if your account there isn't enough to cover whatever a court decides, I'll have to pay it out of Vatta funds there. My accounts aren't frozen, but I've been served notice of intent to collect on your behalf."

"That's—ridiculous."

"It's their laws. You've been there; you know what they're like. And Slotter Key's Budget Director has declined to pay Mackensee's fee for their contract here—claiming Grace had no right to make such a contract without prior approval, and she can just pony up the money on her own. Which means, of course, Vatta has to pay it, and that means—I'm sorry to say—that I don't have the money I owe you for your shares. Because I don't want to go to jail and don't want Grace to go to jail and don't want Helen to lose her house."

"You're not serious."

"I'm very serious. There's a fight in the legislature right now whether to try to assign us damages for the people who died on Miksland, because you didn't get them all out alive and well. Besides the money problem, which Rafe perhaps could solve, the government won't let you leave until they've satisfied all their legal wrangling." She wiped out the cooler, set it back on the floor, and turned back to Ky.

"But I want to get away from Slotter Key!" And never come back, not ever.

Rafe stepped to her side, put an arm around her. "If you're broke, I can't buy us a spaceship. I could buy us tickets offplanet, but if you can't leave, I'm staying, too. And if we're stuck here, we might as well amuse ourselves."

"It's not funny!"

"No, but it's interesting."

"I'm not interested—"

"I am. I am because it affects you, and because I am a shameless meddler who can't pass up a good mystery. Tell you what. Why don't we take the children for a swim, let Stella and Helen cook us all a good supper—" He stopped, swung her around, looked at her. "You aren't buying this."

"No." She felt petulant. She felt the way she had as a child, unfairly manipulated by adults who refused to understand how important something was, and how right she was—she felt the corner of her mouth twitch before she recognized the change of mood. "It's not funny," she said again, daring him to argue. "It may be funny later; it may be interesting later, but right now—"

"You want to hit somebody. I understand. We'll take the children swimming. Maybe you can hit a shark."

When they came back inside, the children far less worn out than any of the adults had hoped, Ky had in fact thumped a small shark for swimming too close. She came back up through the gritty broken shells fringing the high-tide line, brushing the sand off her feet on the way up the steps to the veranda. The smells from the house were meat and spices and something sweet in the oven.

After supper the twins were handed books and papers to work on at the table; the adults left them complaining about homework and adjourned to the seaward side of the veranda with a plate of cookies.

"Our investigations while you were missing didn't get as far as we'd hoped—as we were closing in, we realized someone had called in mercs, and they were going to land on Miksland earlier," Stella said.

"Right," Rafe said. "And we thought blowing the server farm—"

"You blew a server farm?" Ky turned to him.

"Yes. Thought it would slow them down, disrupt the attack, but it didn't. We hadn't been able to penetrate far enough. Mackensee was due to arrive any day, but we didn't know if they'd get here in time, which is why I sounded so frantic that time."

"And right now," Stella said, "the important thing is that evidence has disappeared—in the hands of Spaceforce and civilian law enforcement both—so we know both are involved. All Vatta facilities are buttoned up as tight as possible and still carry on the business—though we hope the enemies are all here on Slotter Key."

"Do you think it connects with the earlier attack?" Ky looked from Rafe to Stella and back.

Rafe tipped his hand from side to side. "Maybe. It's tempting to think so, but there's been no sign so far of any action off this planet."

"Aunt Grace and MacRobert are holed up in her office at the Defense Department. Grace is positive that no one mined Vatta's headquarters this time, so my department heads are staying in the building. Teague's guarding Grace's house." Stella reached for a cookie.

"How long will you stay here?" Ky asked Stella. Despite herself, she felt curiosity and determination both rising. She and Rafe could stay in Helen's house, guarding that property, and be close enough to work with Grace.

"I'm heading back tomorrow morning, now that I'm sure you're safe. That's why I brought Rafe's other kit; you and he can safely work from here—"

"No!"

"Ky, be reasonable. You can't leave the planet."

"I am not going to stay here, lolling around at a beach house, with nothing much to do but stare at a screen. I'm coming back with you. Rafe and I can stay in Grace's house or Helen's."

"But that leaves Helen and the twins—"

"I'm *not* a babysitter." One swim with the twins had convinced her of that.

"Fine, then." Stella gave her the familiar *I'm the grown-up cousin* look. "You can come with me in the morning. Someone in the office here can help Helen with the twins until I can locate reliable staff. Can they use your house, Helen?"

"Of course. Though it's already been broken into—"

"It won't be once I upgrade the security," Rafe said. "So—that's settled." He turned to Ky. "I told you another day would be better timing for going back to the mainland."

"For buying a spaceship," Ky said. She glared at him, no longer angry, but hoping to seem ferocious.

Rafe laughed. "For catching bad guys. Perfect timing for that."

Ky grinned at him; she couldn't help it. "Bad guys it is, then. But later, there'd better be a spaceship."

ACKNOWLEDGMENTS

Once again, many people helped with specific points of this book, and I will undoubtedly miss mentioning a few whose contributions, in casual conversations, slipped my memory days later. Myke Cole, writer and officer in the USCG reserve, saved me from a massive mistake and pointed me at a couple of websites that helped prevent more. Laurence Gonzales' book *Deep Survival*, along with other books specifically on cold-weather/cold-water survival, including two on Shackleton's incredible journey, kept me oriented to the various tasks, attitudes, and decisions that make for success. David Watson and others provided advice on the feasibility of hunting certain largish creatures (trying to avoid spoilers here) with a pistol and limited ammunition. Ellen McLean, David Watson, Karen Shull, and Richard Moon tackled (variously) alpha-reader and nitpicker duties on chunks of it. PBS kindly broadcast two shows that came at exactly the right moment for me, one of them about the re-creation of Shackleton's voyage. Manufacturers of life rafts and useful equipment (including hand-pumped desalinators) put not only ads, but videos, up online—I did not have to travel to find them. A scientist I follow on Twitter posted a link to a video of a particular point of "freeze-up" that provided visual and audio of that phenomenon and answered my warm-climate questions about cold-climate issues.

Where you find mistakes, they are mine; the good stuff was poured into my head (and out through my fingers) by the many (known and unknown) whose words, images, and videos tried to fill the vast caverns of ignorance.

ABOUT THE TYPE

This book was set in Minion, a 1990 Adobe Originals typeface by Robert Slimbach (b. 1956). Minion is inspired by classical, old-style typefaces of the late Renaissance, a period of elegant, beautiful, and highly readable type designs. Created primarily for text setting, Minion combines the aesthetic and functional qualities that make text type highly readable with the versatility of digital technology.

extras

www.orbitbooks.net

about the author

Former Marine **Elizabeth Moon** is the author of many novels, including *Echoes of Betrayal*, *Kings of the North*, *Oath of Fealty*, the Deed of Paksenarrion trilogy, *Victory Conditions*, *Command Decision*, *Engaging the Enemy*, *Marque and Reprisal*, *Trading in Danger*, the Nebula Award-winner *The Speed of Dark*, and *Remnant Population*, a Hugo Award finalist. After earning a degree in history from Rice University, Moon went on to earn a degree in biology from the University of Texas–Austin. She lives in Florence, Texas.

Find out more about Elizabeth Moon and other Orbit authors by registering online for the free monthly newsletter at www.orbitbooks.net.

if you enjoyed
COLD WELCOME

look out for

FORSAKEN SKIES
Book One of the Silence

by

D. Nolan Clarke

FEAR THE SILENCE.

After centuries of devastating interplanetary civil war, mankind has found a time of relative peace.

That peace is shattered when an unknown armada emerges from the depths of space, targeting an isolated colony planet. As the colonists plead for help, the politicians and bureaucrats look away.

But battle-scarred Commander Aleister Lanoe will not abandon thousands of innocents to their fate.

Flying down a wormhole was like throwing yourself into the center of a tornado, one where if you brushed the walls you would be obliterated down to subatomic particles before you even knew it happened.

Racing through a wormhole at this speed was suicide. But the kid wouldn't slow down.

Lanoe thumbed a control pad and painted the yacht's backside with a communications laser. A green pearl appeared in the corner of his vision, with data on signal strength rolling across its surface. "Thom," he called. "Thom, you've got to stop this. I know you're scared, I know—"

"I killed him! I can't go back now!"

Lanoe muted the connection and focused for a second on not getting himself killed. The wormhole twisted and bent up ahead, warped where it passed under some massive gravity source, probably a star. Side passages opened in every direction, split by the curvature of spacetime. Lanoe had lost track of where, in real-space terms, they were—they'd started back at Xibalba but they could be a hundred light-years away by now. Wormspace didn't operate by Newtonian rules. They could be anywhere. They could theoretically be on the wrong end of the universe.

The yacht up ahead was still accelerating. It was a sleek spindle of darkness against the unreal light of the tunnel walls, all black carbon fiber broken only by a set of airfoils like flat wings spaced around its thruster. At his school Thom had a reputation as some kind of hot-shot racer—he was slated to compete in next year's Earth Cup—and Lanoe had seen how good a pilot the kid was as he chased him down. He was still surprised when Thom twisted around on his axis of flight and kicked in his maneuvering jets, nearly reversing his course and sending the yacht careening down one of the side tunnels.

Maybe he'd thought he could escape that way.

For all the kid's talent, though, Lanoe was Navy trained. He knew a couple of tricks they never taught to civilians. He switched off the compensators that protected his engine and pulled a right-hand turn tighter than a poly's purse. He squeezed his eyes shut as his inertial sink shoved him hard back into his seat but when he looked again he was right back on the yacht's tail. He thumbed for the comms laser again and when the green pearl popped up he said, "Thom, you can't outfly me. We need to talk about this. Your dad is dead, yes. We need to think about what comes next. Maybe you could tell me why you did it—"

But the green pearl was gone. Thom had burned for another course change and surged ahead. He'd pulled out of the maze of wormspace and back into the real universe, up ahead at another dip in the spacetime curve.

Lanoe goosed his engine and followed. He burst out of the wormhole throat and into searing red light that burned his eyes.

━◆━

Centrocor freight hauler 4519 approaching on vector 7, 4, −32.

    Wilscon dismantler ship Angie B, you are deviating from course by .02. Advise.

    Traffic control, this is Angie B, we copy. Burning to correct.

The whispering voices of the autonomic port monitors passed across Valk's consciousness without making much of an impression.

Orbital traffic control wasn't an exacting job. It didn't pay well, either. Valk didn't mind so much. There were fringe benefits. For one, he had a cramped little workstation all to himself. He valued his privacy. Moreover, at the vertex between two limbs of the Hexus there was no gravity. It helped with the pain, a little.

Valk had been in severe pain for the last seventeen years, ever since he'd suffered what he always called his "accident." Even though there'd been nothing accidental about it. He had suffered severe burns over his entire body and even now, so many years later, the slightest weight on his flesh was too much.

His arms floated before him, his fingers twitching at keyboards that weren't really there. Lasers tracked his fingertip movements and converted them to data. Screens all around him pushed information in through his eyes, endless columns of numbers and tiny graphical displays he could largely ignore.

The Hexus sat at the bottom of a deep gravity well, a place where dozens of wormhole tunnels came together, connecting all twenty-three worlds of the local sector. A thousand vessels came through the Hexus every day, to offload cargo, to undertake repairs, just so the crews could stretch their legs for a minute on the way to their destinations. Keeping all those ships from colliding with each other, making sure they landed at the right docking berths, was the kind of job computers were built for, and the Hexus's autonomics were very, very good at it. Valk's job was to simply be there in case something happened that needed a human decision. If a freighter demanded priority mooring, for instance, because it was hauling hazardous cargo. Or if somebody important wanted the kid glove treatment. It didn't happen all that often.

Traffic, this is Angie B. We're on our way to Jehannum. Thanks for your help.

Civilian drone entering protected space. Redirecting.

Centrocor freight hauler 4519 at two thousand km, approaching Vairside docks.

Vairside docks report full. Redirect incoming traffic until 18:22.

Baffin Island docks report can take six more. Accepting until 18:49.

Unidentified vehicle exiting wormhole throat. No response to ping.

Unidentified vehicle exiting wormhole throat. No response to ping.

Maybe it was the repetition that made Valk swivel around in his workspace. He called up a new display with imaging of the wormhole throat, thirty million kilometers away. The throat itself looked like a sphere of perfect glass, distorting the stars behind it. Monitoring buoys with banks of floodlights and sensors swarmed around it, keeping well clear of the opening to wormspace. The newcomers were so small it took a second for Valk to even see them.

But there—the one in front was a dark blip, barely visible except when it occluded a light. A civilian craft, built for speed by the look of it. Expensive as hell. And right behind it—there—

"Huh," Valk said, a little grunt of surprise. It was an FA.2 fighter, cataphract class. A cigar-shaped body, one end covered in segmented carbonglas viewports, the other housing a massive thruster. A double row of airfoils on its flanks.

Valk had been a fighter pilot himself, back before his accident. He knew the silhouette of every cataphract, carrier scout, and recon boat that had ever flown. There had been a time when you would have seen FA.2s everywhere, when they were the Navy's favorite theater fighter. But that had been more than a century ago. Who was flying such an antique?

Valk tapped for a closer view—and only then did he see the red lights flashing all over his primary display. The two newcomers were moving *fast,* a considerable chunk of the speed of light.

And they were headed straight toward the Hexus.

He called up a communications panel and started desperately pinging them.

Light and heat burst into Lanoe's cockpit. Sweat burst out all over his skin. His suit automatically wicked it away but it couldn't catch all the beads of sweat popping out on his forehead. He swiped a virtual panel near his elbow and his viewports polarized, switching down to near-opaque blackness. It still wasn't enough.

There was a very good reason you didn't shoot out of a wormhole throat at this kind of speed. Wormhole throats tended to be very close to very big stars.

He could barely see—afterimages flickered in his vision, blocking out all the displays on his boards. He had a sense of a massive planet dead ahead but he couldn't make out any details. He tapped at display after display, trying to get some telemetry data, desperate for any information about where he was.

Then he saw the Hexus floating right in front of him. Fifty kilometers across, a vast hexagonal structure of concrete and foamsteel, like a colossal dirty benzene ring. Geryon, he thought. The Hexus orbited the planet Geryon, a bloated gas giant that circled a red giant star. That explained all the light and heat, at least.

He tried to raise Thom again with his comms laser but the green pearl wouldn't show up in his peripheral vision. Little flashes of green came from his other eye and he realized he was being pinged by the Hexus. He thumbed a panel to send them his identifying codes but didn't waste any time talking to them directly.

The Hexus was getting bigger, growing at an alarming rate. "Thom," he called, whether the kid could hear him or not, "you need to break off. You can't fly through that thing. Thom! Don't do it!"

His vision had cleared enough that he could just see the yacht, a dark spot visible against the brighter skin of the station. Thom was going to fly straight through the Hexus. At first glance it looked like there was plenty of room—the hexagon was wide open in its middle—but that space was full of freighters and liners and countless drones, a bewilderingly complex interchange of ships jockeying for position, heading to or away from docking facilities, ships being refueled by tenders, drones checking heat shields or scraping carbon out of thruster cones. If Thom went through there it would be like firing a pistol into a crowd.

Lanoe cursed under his breath and brought up his weapon controls.

❯❯❮❮

Centrocor freight hauler 4519 requesting berth at Vairside docks.
Vairside docks report full. Redirect incoming traffic until 18:22.

Valk ignored the whispering voices. He had a much bigger problem.

In twenty-nine seconds the two unidentified craft were going to streak right through the center of the Hexus, moving fast enough to obliterate anything in their way. If there was a collision the resulting debris would have enough energy to tear the entire station apart. Hundreds of thousands of people would die.

Valk worked fast, moving from one virtual panel to the next, dismissing displays and opening new ones. His biggest display showed the trajectory of the two newcomers, superimposed on a diagram of every moving thing inside the Hexus. Tags on each object showed relative velocities, mass and inertia quantities, collision probabilities.

Those last showed up in burning red. Valk had to find a way to get each of them to turn amber or green before the newcomers blazed right through the Hexus. That meant moving every ship, every tiny drone, one by one—computing a new flight path for each craft that wouldn't intersect with any of the others.

The autonomic systems just weren't smart enough to do it themselves. This was exactly why they still had a human being working Valk's job.

If he moved this liner here—redirected this drone swarm to the far side of the Hexus—if he ordered this freighter to make a correction burn of fourteen milliseconds—if he swung this dismantler ship around on its long axis—

One of the newcomers finally responded to his identification requests, but he didn't have time to look. He swiped that display away even while he used his other hand to order a freighter to fire its positioning jets.

Civilian drone entering protected space. Redirecting.

Centrocor freight hauler 4519 requesting berth at Vairside docks.

The synthetic voices were like flies buzzing around inside Valk's skull. That freight hauler was a serious pain in the ass—it was by far the largest object still inside the ring of the Hexus, the craft most likely to get in the way of the incoming yacht.

Valk would gladly have sent the thing burning hard for a distant parking orbit. It was a purely autonomic vessel, without even a pilot onboard, basically a giant drone. Who cared if a little cargo didn't make it to its destination in time? But for some reason its onboard computers refused to obey his commands. It kept demanding to be routed to a set of docks that weren't even classified for freight craft.

He pulled open a new control pad and started sending override codes.

The freighter responded instantly.

Instructed course will result in distress to passengers. Advise?

Wait. Passengers?

—◂———

Up ahead the traffic inside the ring of the Hexus scattered like pigeons from a cat, but still there were just too many ships and drones in there, too many chances for a collision. Thom hadn't deviated even a fraction of a degree from his course. In a second or two it would be too late for him to break off—at this speed he wouldn't be able to burn hard enough to get away.

On Lanoe's weapons screen a firing solution popped up. He could hit the yacht with a disruptor. One hit and the yacht would be reduced to tiny debris, too small to do much damage when it rained down on the Hexus. His thumb hovered over the firing key—but even as he steeled himself to do it, a second firing solution popped up.

A ponderous freighter hung there, right in the middle of the ring. Right in the middle of Thom's course.

It was an ugly ship, just a bunch of cargo containers clamped to a central boom like grapes on a vine. It had thruster packages on either end but nothing even resembling a crew capsule.

Lanoe had enough weaponry to take that thing to pieces.

He opened a new communications panel and pinged the Hexus. "Traffic control, you need to move that freighter right now."

The reply came back instantly. At least somebody was talking to him. "FA.2, this is Hexus Control. Can't be done. Are you in contact with the unidentified yacht? Tell that idiot to change his trajectory."

"He's not listening," Lanoe called back. Damn it. Thom was maybe five seconds from splattering himself all over that ugly ship. "Control, move that freighter—or I'll move it for you."

"Negative! Negative, FA.2—there are people on that thing!"

What? That made no sense. A freight hauler like that would be controlled purely by autonomics. It wasn't classified for human occupation—it wouldn't even have rudimentary life support onboard.

There couldn't possibly be people on that thing. Yet he had no reason to think that traffic control would lie about that. And then—

In Lanoe's head the moral calculus was already working itself out. People, control had said—meaning more than one person.

If he killed Thom, who he knew was a murderer, it would save multiple innocent lives.

He reached again for the firing key.

There had to be an answer. There had to be.

Instructed course would result in distress to passengers. Advise?

Valk could see six different ways to move the freighter. Every single one of them meant firing its main thrusters for a hard burn. Accelerating it at multiple g's.

If he did that, anybody inside the freighter would be reduced to red jelly. Unlike passenger ships, the cargo ship didn't carry an inertial sink. The people in it would have no protection from the sudden acceleration.

Centrocor freight hauler 4519 requesting berth at Vairside docks.

The ship was too stupid to know it was about to be smashed to pieces. Not for the first time he wished he could switch off the synthetic voices that reeled off pointless information all around him. He opened a new screen and studied the freighter's schematics. There were maneuvering thrusters here, and positioning jets near the nose, but they wouldn't be able to move the ship fast enough, there were emergency retros in six different locations, and explosive bolts on the cargo containers—

Yes! He had it. "FA.2," he called, even as he opened a new control pad. "FA.2, do not fire!" He tapped away at the pad, his fingers aching as he moved them so quickly.

Instructed action may cause damage to Centrocor property. Advise?

"I advise you to shut up and do what I say," Valk told the freighter. That wasn't what it was looking for, though. He looked down, saw a green virtual key hovering in front of him, and stabbed at it.

Out in the middle of the ring, the freight hauler triggered the explosive bolts on all of its port side cargo containers at once. The long boxes went tumbling away with aching slowness, blue and yellow and red oblongs dancing outward on their own trajectories. Some smashed into passing drones, creating whole new clouds of debris. Some bounced off the arms of the Hexus, obliterating against its concrete, the goods inside thrown free in multicolored sprays.

On Valk's screens a visual display popped up showing him the chaos. The yacht was a tiny dark needle lost in the welter of colorful boxes and smashed goods, moving so fast Valk could barely track it. But this was going to work, a gap was opening where the yacht could pass through safely, this was going to—

There was no sound but Valk could almost feel the crunch as one of the cargo containers just clipped one of the yacht's airfoils. The cargo container tore open, its steel skin splitting like it was a piece of overripe fruit. Barrels spilled out in a broad cloud of wild trajectories. The yacht was thrown into a violent spin as it shot through the Hexus and out the other side.

A split second later the FA.2 jinked around a flying barrel and burned hard to follow the yacht on its new course, straight down toward Geryon.

Chapter Two

Lanoe had to lean over hard into a tight bank to avoid the swirl of cargo in the Hexus but he almost laughed as he worked his controls, throwing his stick to the left and then the right. Whoever was running traffic control back there was a genius.

He sobered up again almost instantly when he saw where he was headed next. Thom had been thrown for a loop by a grazing collision and now he was falling out of the sky. Up ahead lay the broad disk of Geryon, a boiling hell cauldron of a planet. Out of control and spinning, Thom couldn't fight the pull of its gravity. He was going to fall right into that mess.

Geryon was a gas giant, a world with no surface, just a near-endless atmosphere. From a distance it looked like it was tearing itself apart from the inside out. It was banded with dark storms, nearly black, that hid an inner layer of incandescent neon. The buzzing red light streaked outward through every crack and gap in the cloud layer, rays of baleful effulgence spearing outward at the void.

Lanoe barely had time to get a look at the planet before the yacht pitched nose first into its atmosphere. He burned after it, down into the topmost clouds. He tried to paint the kid again with the communications laser, not expecting a result. He didn't get one.

As he tore through the dark haze of the clouds he lost track of

Thom altogether. Then suddenly the fighter burst through the bottom of a wisp of cirrus and Lanoe wasn't in space anymore.

On every side, tortured clouds piled up around him in enormous thunderheads, whole towers and fortresses of cloud with ramparts and battlements that melted away into mist every time he tried to make out details. Rivers of dark blue methane coiled and bent around waves of atmospheric pressure.

The sheer scale of it was lost on him until he saw the yacht, a tiny dot well ahead of him. It shot through a streamer of mist that arched high overhead, but the streamer was just one tiny arm of a vast storm as big as an ocean on Earth. And that was just what Lanoe could see from inside the fighter, a tiny fragment of a colossal world of clouds.

The yacht was out of place in that vast cloudspace. A mote of dust on the storm. It was still tumbling, end over end—the kid hadn't regained control. Tiny shards of debris were still pouring off its shattered airfoil, like thin smoke that traced out the yacht's spinning, tumbling path. Damn it.

At least atmospheric resistance had slowed them right down—maybe Lanoe could actually catch the kid now.

The green pearl in Lanoe's vision blinked back into existence, surprising him. The comms laser had reestablished contact.

"Thom," Lanoe called. "Thom, are you there? Are you okay?"

The kid sounded terrified when he replied. Breathing hard, his voice pitched too high. "I'm...I'm still alive."

"Damn it, Thom," Lanoe said. "What were you thinking back there? There were people on that freighter. You could have killed them."

It took a long while for Thom to reply. Maybe he was just struggling to pull out of his spin. Lanoe could see his attitude thrusters firing, jets of vapor that were lost instantly in the dark cloudscape.

When Thom did come back on the line he sounded calmer, but chastened. "I didn't know that."

Lanoe couldn't help but feel for Thom. When the kid had made a break for it, when he'd stolen the yacht and run for the nearest wormhole, Lanoe had followed because he thought maybe, somehow, he could help. To the kid it must have looked like there was a hellhound on his tail. "Get control of your ship," Lanoe told him. Though honestly it looked like Thom had already done just that. The yacht had stabilized its flight, even with one damaged airfoil. The kid had skill, Lanoe thought. He had the makings of a great pilot. If he didn't die right here. "You all right?"

"I'm fine."

"Then let's think about how to keep you that way. Slow down and let's talk about this. Okay? First things first, we need to get out of this atmosphere. Let's head back to the Hexus. I can't promise people there will be happy to see you, but—"

"I'm not going back," Thom replied. "I'm never going back."

It should have been over by now.

It should have been quick and painless. He should have hit that freighter dead-on and that would have been that.

Thom realized his eyes were closed. That was stupid. You never closed your eyes when you were flying—you needed to be constantly aware of everything around you. He opened his eyes and laughed.

There was nothing to see out there. Black mist writhed across his viewports. His displays were all turning red, but who cared? That was kind of the point, wasn't it?

Just fade to black.

If only Lanoe would shut up and let him get on with it.

"There's no way forward here, Thom. If I have to shoot you to stop this idiotic chase, I will. Turn back now."

"Why would I do that?" Thom asked.

"Because right now I'm the only friend you have."

"You were my father's puppet. I know you'll take me back there if I give you the chance."

"You're wrong, Thom. I just want to help."

Thom leaned back in his crash seat and tried to just breathe.

He was surrounded by expensive wooden fittings. His seat was upholstered in real leather. He couldn't help thinking the yacht would make a luxurious coffin.

Thom was—had been—the son of the planetary governor of Xibalba. He was used to a certain degree of luxury. He understood now how much of that he'd taken for granted. Nothing had ever been denied to him his whole life.

No one had ever bullied him in school—his father's bodyguards had seen to that. No one had ever said no to him as long as he could remember. But now Lanoe wouldn't just give up. Wouldn't just let him go.

It was infuriating.

Thom wondered why he didn't just switch off his comms panel. Block Lanoe's transmission. Maybe, he thought, he just wanted to hear another human voice before he ended this.

Even if he didn't want to hear what Lanoe had to say.

"I was just your father's escort pilot, Thom. I'm not here to avenge him. The Navy assigned me to work for him, but it was just a job. I never even liked him."

"I hated him," Thom replied, unable to resist. Maybe he wanted to justify what he'd done. "I always hated him."

"Well, that's in the past now," Lanoe said. "As is my job—I don't owe him anything now that he's dead. I came after you because believe it or not, I do like *you*. That's all. Please believe me."

"I can't," Thom said. "Lanoe, I'm sorry, but I can't trust anyone right now."

Over the line he could hear Lanoe sigh in frustration. "Why'd you even do it?" Lanoe asked. "Why kill him? In a year you would have been away at university. Away from him."

"You think so?" Thom said. "You don't know anything, Lanoe."

"So enlighten me."

Thom smiled at the black mist that surrounded him. He couldn't think of a good reason to lie, not now. "I wasn't going to

Uni. I wasn't going anywhere. He was sick. All that stress of his high-powered job just ate away at his heart. You know what they do, when your body gives out like that? They give you a new one."

"So he would have lived a little longer—"

"You still don't understand, do you? I wasn't born to be his heir."

When you were rich and powerful, you didn't have to worry about getting sick. You didn't have to make do with an artificial pump ticking away in your chest, or taking immunosuppressive drugs for the rest of your life. You didn't even have to worry about getting old.

No, not if you had a little forethought. Not if you could afford to have children. Kids whose neurology was a perfect match for your own.

The old man could have arranged for Thom to have an accident that left him brain dead. Then he could have his own consciousness transferred into Thom's young, healthy body. It happened all the time in the halls of power. The legality was questionable but a lot of rules didn't apply to planetary governors.

"I was designed," Thom said. "Built to be his next body."

There was a long pause on the line. "I didn't know," Lanoe said.

"He had to die," Thom said. In his mind's eye he saw it all over again. Saw himself pick up the ancient dueling pistol. Felt it jump in his hand. The old man hadn't even had a chance to look surprised. "Do you understand now? I'm only twenty years old, and he was going to steal my body and throw my mind away. Kill me. So I had to kill him if I wanted to live. And now I have to keep moving. For another thirty-six hours."

"Thirty-six hours?"

"His doctors will have stabilized his brain, even if the rest of him is dead. They can keep his consciousness viable that long. If they catch me before his brain really dies, they can still go ahead with the switch."

"Let me help, then," Lanoe said.

Thom closed his eyes again. Nobody could help him now.

He leaned forward on his stick. Brought the yacht's nose down until it was pointed right at the core of the planet. Opened his throttle all the way.

The yacht dove into a dark cloud bank, a wall of smoke thick enough to block Lanoe's transmission.

This would be over soon.